IN OTHER LANDS

IN OTHER LANDS

A NOVEL

SARAH
REES
BRENNAN

Big Mouth House
Easthampton, Mass.

This is a work of fiction. All characters and events portrayed in this book are either fictitious or used fictitiously.

sarahreesbrennan.com

Big Mouth House
150 Pleasant Street #306
Easthampton, MA 01027
info@smallbeerpress.com
smallbeerpress.com
weightlessbooks.com

Distributed to the trade by Consortium.

First Big Mouth House Printing: August 2017
Second printing: October 2017

Library of Congress Cataloging-in-Publication Data

Names: Brennan, Sarah Rees, author.
Title: In other lands : a novel / Sarah Rees Brennan.
Description: Easthampton, Mass. : Big Mouth House : Distributed to the trade by Consortium, [2017]
Identifiers: LCCN 2016059543 (print) | LCCN 2017026057 (ebook) | ISBN 9781618731357 (ebook) | ISBN 9781618731203 (alk. paper)
Subjects: | CYAC: Coming of age--Fiction. | Friendship--Fiction. | Bisexuality--Fiction. | Fantasy.
Classification: LCC PZ7.B751645 (ebook) | LCC PZ7.B751645 In 2017 (print) | DDC [Fic]--dc23
LC record available at https://lccn.loc.gov/2016059543

Text set in Minion.

Printed on 50# 30% PCR recycled Natures Natural paper by the Maple Press in York, PA.

For Holly Black, who knows many things, yet seems sometimes not to know she is both kind and clear-eyed, sharply hilarious and bone-deep sweet, and a bona fide genius.
I know.

I

ELLIOT, AGE THIRTEEN

So far magic school was total rubbish.

Elliot sat on the fence bisecting two fields and brooded tragically over his wrongs.

He had been plucked from geography class, one of his most interesting classes, to take some kind of scholarship test out in the wild. Elliot and three other kids from his class had been packed into a van by their harassed-looking French teacher and driven outside the city. Elliot objected because after an hour in a moving vehicle he would be violently sick. The other kids objected because after an hour in a moving vehicle they would be violently sick of Elliot.

Elliot ignored the other kids and hung his head out of the window. In a disdainful way.

Then they arrived at their destination, which could only be described as a classic example of a "random field in Devon, England." Much like any other random field in England.

"Why are we in a random field?" Elliot demanded.

"I will thump you," promised Desmond Dobbs. "Zip it."

"I will not be silenced," said Elliot.

He would not be silenced, but he was feeling unwell and being thumped usually made him feel worse, so he stood a little way off from the others and observed their surroundings.

The random field boasted a stone wall so high Elliot could not see over the top, and a woman wearing extremely odd clothing who appeared to be waiting for them. She and their French teacher had a quiet conference, and as Elliot watched them he saw money change hands.

"Excuse me, did anyone else see that?" Elliot asked. "I don't wish to alarm anyone, but get alarmed, because I think our French teacher just sold us!"

"They haven't sold us," said Ashley Sinclair. "Nobody would want to buy *you.*"

That did silence Elliot. It seemed so indisputably true.

The woman in odd clothing "tested" him by asking him if he could see a wall standing in the middle of a field. When he told her, "Obviously, because it's a wall. Walls tend to be obvious," she had pointed out the other kids blithely walking through the wall as if it was not there, and told him that he was one of the chosen few with the sight.

"Are you telling me that I have magical powers?" Elliot had asked, excited for a moment, and then added: "Because I *can't* walk through walls? That doesn't seem right."

The woman had told him she was prepared for questions, but she did not seem prepared for that one. She blinked and told him to come away with her to a magical land.

"By a magical land," she told him, "I mean a place that not everybody can see, a place with—"

"With mermaids?" Elliot asked. "I don't need you to explain to me the concept of a magical land filled with fantastic creatures that only certain special children can enter. I am acquainted with the last several centuries of popular culture. There are books. And cartoons, for the illiterate."

"Look," said the woman, "are you prepared to come away with me, or not?"

Normally, Elliot refused weird propositions from potentially demented strangers. But there was the wall, and the undeniable fact that other people could not see or touch it, and this really was like something out of a book. Elliot did not think he would be able to live with the curiosity if he did not go.

"Okay," Elliot had said finally, brandishing his phone in the woman's face. "But I have the number of the police, and I will have my finger on the call button at all times, in case you are a child predator."

She rolled her eyes, but she let him keep the phone with no objections.

Nobody else had any objections when it was explained that the strange woman would be driving Elliot back to school later. Nobody pointed out there was no sign of the strange woman's car. Desmond Dobbs said "Hurray!"

"Do you have family who will miss you?" asked the woman while everyone else piled in the van.

"Ha!" said Elliot. "That is a serial-killer question, and I refuse to answer it."

"Any family you have will be told you were offered a last-minute scholarship to a prestigious military school," said the woman. "If you choose to stay. Will anyone be worried about you?"

The van set off down the road. It seemed to get smaller very fast, heading toward the distant gray horizon of the city. Everything Elliot knew seemed terribly small, and terribly gray, and terribly far away.

Elliot hesitated. "No."

Once the van had disappeared around a bend in the road, the strange woman led Elliot up a narrow stone stairway built into the wall. They climbed and climbed, and when they had gone so high that they were surrounded by clouds, they walked through a shining hole in the wall and onto soft grass.

Actually, the magical land seemed to be mostly grass.

There were fields, more fields, several more fields, a couple of rough, round stone towers which men with weapons were exiting and entering. Elliot had cheered up when he saw a man walk by, books under his arm, who had long hair and pointed ears—there were *elves*—and dwarves—like from fairy tales, men and women alike with beards and carrying elaborately carved hammers.

He looked around for other marvels.

Mostly there were other kids. Some of them were quite big, and some of them looked no more than Elliot's age—he was thirteen, though everybody thought he was younger because they made cruel assumptions based on height. All the kids had lined up at different tables to be signed in, and now the kids Elliot's age were all standing together in a cluster waiting to be told what to do.

Elliot turned to the woman who had led him here. Her clothing did not look so strange here where a lot of people were wearing breeches and buckles all over. He had only known her for five minutes, which made her five minutes more familiar than anyone else. Under cornrows that ended in a black coronet of twisted hair, her face was impatient but not unkind.

"Is this the part where I get told that only I can save the magical land?"

"This is the part where you get trained," said the woman. "Or not. You choose."

"Trained for what?" Elliot demanded, but the woman had already strode off to be cryptic elsewhere and left him with the group of kids his age.

He was slightly alarmed. The wall on the other side had been low, but carved with graffiti so he suspected there were vandals about, his phone was sizzling, and now this.

It was so unfair. Elliot had not expected a magical land to be all fields—some of the fields had cows in them, and he was pretty sure they weren't magic cows—and other kids.

Elliot especially did not like the "other kids" aspect of magic land. Elliot had "does not interact well with peers" on all his report cards.

If the teachers had been more precise, what they would have said was "does not shut up well around stupid people," but that was teachers for you. And there were always kids who were stunned when crossed, as if they had expected that life would go their way forever.

Elliot had already spotted the two kids who looked as if they thought life was a song. Practically all of the relatively few girls were staring at them.

One of the boringly human pair of boys, the obvious leader, was tall and broad-shouldered, with golden hair, as if Nature had said, "No worries, buddy, I gotcha, no nasty tiring thinking will ever be necessary, also have a crown." The other had a bright vacant smile that someone, finding it empty, had filled with light.

The blond guy was wandering around from kid to kid, talking kindly to them and taking hold of them by one shoulder with the patronizing air of a kid who thought he was as good and wise as a teacher. He knelt and spoke to one much smaller girl in a My Little Pony T-shirt, then rose to his feet and turned away, leaving her staring after him with shining eyes as he obviously forgot all about her:

as if he were a king dispensing largesse to the peasants. The other boy was following the blond guy around, nodding at everything he said. Both of them looked entirely self-assured about the whole situation. Elliot knew their type. The blond boy looked like he would throw the first punch and the smiling boy like he would throw the second and the third, in eager imitation.

Elliot mentally christened them Blondie and Surfer Dude.

He peered around to the woods, where perhaps there were more elves, and to the skies, where he was almost sure he'd seen something that was winged but too big to be a bird.

A cough distracted Elliot from his perusal of the skies. He looked down into blue eyes and saw that it was apparently Elliot's turn on the condescension rounds.

"You should stop sitting on that fence," Blondie instructed.

"Oh, I see," Elliot muttered darkly. "Even this is to be taken from me."

Nobody Elliot was aware of had made Blondie the boss of the fence, but being tipped over backward into the mud was not Elliot's idea of a good time. He slipped off the fence and looked resentfully up at Blondie and, of course, his sunny shadow. He found tall people tiresome.

Elliot scowled. Blondie frowned. Surfer Dude kept smiling.

"Don't worry, little guy. I know this must all be very confusing for people from the other side of the Border," said Blondie.

Elliot stared for a long moment. The moment grew uncomfortable. Elliot was glad.

"This is all terribly confusing," Elliot agreed. Blondie smiled, relieved, and Elliot held up a hand to stop him saying anything. "I was *so hoping*," Elliot continued soulfully, "that somebody would come explain all this to me. Preferably someone who would do it in small words. And you two look like the small-words type."

"Sure, what do you need explained?" asked Surfer Dude.

Elliot rolled his eyes and saw that Blondie's sweet blue eyes had narrowed. He tilted his head and grinned.

"First off, this," said Elliot, and produced his phone from his pocket. It looked a little bit melty and was sending off sparks. Surfer Dude took a step back.

"You'd better give me that," said Blondie. "You could hurt yourself."

He stepped forward. Elliot took a step to the side, and the group as a whole moved away from Elliot. Everyone else had discarded their technology when it malfunctioned, because they were quitters.

"Nope," said Elliot. "It's mine."

"I think it's about to go on fire."

"It's my thing that's about to go on fire, and not yours," Elliot said firmly. "Now, why have all our methods of communication just literally gone up in smoke? Are we kidnapped? Are we going to be ritual sacrifices? Is there some sort of magical spell that destroys our ability to call for help?"

A distressed murmuring spread across the group. Blondie looked around in dismay.

"No," he said. "Everything's fine. Your little gadgets from across the Border just don't work here, that's all. They never have. You don't need them here."

"Of course not," Elliot murmured. "The Industrial Revolution was a silly business anyway."

Everybody looked confused now, not just Surfer Dude.

Elliot raised his voice. "Are you telling me none of us are going to be able to play video games?"

Blondie looked like he had his doubts about answering, but he did anyway. "I'm not sure what a video game is . . . but I'm pretty sure you can't play them here."

One of the other boys, who, judging by his clothes, was from what Blondie called "the other side of the Border" and Elliot called "the real world where stuff made sense and phones did not explode," burst into tears. Blondie's head whipped around.

"Oh no," Elliot exclaimed sadly. "Look what you did."

"I didn't—!"

"He seems awfully upset," Elliot continued. "You must feel really bad."

Blondie did not look as if he felt bad at all. He looked, in fact, as if he was going to punch Elliot in the face.

He took a deep breath and did not, which was a pleasant surprise and made Elliot feel quite cheerful.

"Go on then," Elliot said brightly, and made an encouraging yet dismissive gesture. "See to the children!"

Blondie turned and moved toward the crying boy, but he glanced back over his shoulder at Elliot, eyes still narrowed.

"Not everyone who can see the Border belongs on the right side," he observed. "Being trained to protect the Border is a sacred duty. And my father says that some people are too weak and too concerned with their own comfort to fight the good fight."

"That's fascinating. Run along."

"You can choose to go or stay," said Blondie. "So I don't think I'll be seeing you again."

"Yes, oh my God, I already understood the implication that I wasn't man enough to tough it out beyond the Border. Your attempt at an insult was extremely clear," Elliot informed him. "You're just making the whole thing laboured and awkward now."

He waved Blondie away again, and on Blondie's retreat Elliot squinted suspiciously up at Surfer Dude.

"When he said all that stuff about duty and protection . . .," he said. "Is this a military operation?"

Surfer Dude looked pleased to be asked. "Yes. They train you up, those who can pass through the Border on either side, to be guards and keep the peace between the peoples in this land and those who may come through from the other. You learn how to handle all sorts of weapons, how to form a unit, all this cool stuff."

"Oh my God," Elliot said in a hollow voice. "We're child soldiers?" He considered this and then said: "I need to sit down. I'm going back to the fence."

"You're not supposed to—" Surfer Dude said, echoing his master, but Elliot was already walking away.

He did take Surfer Dude's point, and he did not want to be pushed off the fence, so he meandered along it a little, moving farther away from the group, and as he did so he came in sight of someone else who was standing slightly removed from the crowd.

She turned as Elliot approached.

She was tall, slim, and strong-looking as a young birch tree, and as she turned her long dark hair spun out in the steadily blowing wind. It formed a trail of darkness, touched by autumn leaves twined around her tresses: her pale face stood out in sharp relief, and so did the pearl-pale curling points of her ears.

This was an elf maiden.

This was, bar none, the coolest person Elliot had ever seen.

Elliot only had to look at her solemn face for one long moment, robbed of breath by both the wind and her beauty, and he knew. This was love: not the passing fancy he'd felt for Miss Tolliver his music teacher (in which he'd become confused by having a good relationship with an authority figure), or Simon Bae (confused by admiration for his skill in their shared art project) or Clare Winters (the guidance counselor had approved and hadn't said Elliot was confused, but Clare had turned out to only understand a quarter of Elliot's jokes, so she'd been confused all the time).

Elliot wasn't confused now, looking into those clear eyes, at once dark and bright like pools in a deep forest.

He tried to collect himself. Now was no time to stare like a hypnotized sheep.

Now was the time to woo.

He had not seen any other elven girls in the whole camp. So clearly she was defying conservative elven customs by coming here, brave and alone and the victim of cruel oppression. Elliot's heart went out to her. She was probably feeling scared and shy.

"Hello," said the beautiful elven maid. "I was just thinking, and I mean no offence, but—how can any fighting force crowded with the softer sex hope to prevail in battle?"

"Huh?" said Elliot brilliantly. "The softer what?"

"I refer to men," said the elf girl. "Naturally I was aware the Border guard admitted men, and I support men in their endeavor to prove they are equal to women, but their natures are not warlike, are they?"

Elliot offered, after a long pause: "I don't enjoy fighting."

She favored him with a slow smile, like dawn light spreading on water. "Very natural."

"In fact," Elliot confessed, encouraged, "I never fight."

"You should not have to," she said. "There should always be a woman ready to protect a man in need. I take it that you are bound for the council course then?"

"I don't understand," said Elliot, and then he shamelessly looked up at her (taller, why was everybody taller?) through his eyelashes and confessed: "I'm from the other side of the Border, and this is all a little overwhelming"—and distressing? Yes, Elliot felt that he was definitely distressed—"and distressing," he added with conviction. "If you would be so very kind as to explain a few things to me, I would so appreciate it."

He was going for a combination of shy and winsome. As he had never tried to act like this ever before, he wasn't sure how well he was succeeding, but the elf maid unbent further. So he couldn't be doing too badly.

"Certainly," she said, and offered him her arm. Elliot, a quick study, accepted it with a sweet smile. "The council course is a course in diplomacy, mapping the lands to this side of the Border, learning about other cultures. Elven culture, for instance, is quite different from that of humans."

"I am beginning to see that."

"War training is seen as more prestigious, and has far more recruits," said the elf.

"That is totally unreasonable! These people are idiots! I suspected it all along."

"You are very forthright for a man," said the elvish maiden. "But I understand that human men are not reared as delicately as elven gentlemen. I agree with you, moreover: both courses should be considered equally important."

Elliot had not said that, but he was already unbecomingly forthright, so he fluttered his eyelashes and remained demurely silent.

He did not think the demure silence thing was going to work out, because he was only able to keep it up for a minute.

"What's your name?"

"Serene."

"Serena?" Elliot asked.

"Serene," said Serene. "My full name is Serene-Heart-in-the-Chaos-of-Battle."

Elliot's mouth fell open. "That is *badass*."

Serene's serious countenance did not change, but Elliot felt a subtle shift of that slim body: he was fairly certain she was preening.

"I'm Elliot Schafer," he added.

"A strange name," said Serene, adding gallantly: "But not unpleasing."

Take that, every jerk at school who had ever laughed at Elliot's name. No badass elven maidens had ever told them that their names were not unpleasing, had they?

"Are you interested in the cultures of the Borderlands?" Serene asked in a courteous tone.

"Super interested," declared Elliot. "When you said peoples, you mean humans, elves, dwarves and . . . ?"

Please say mermaids, he thought. Please say something cool with wings.

"Mermaids," said Serene. He could have kissed her. (He would have been really delighted to kiss her.) "Trolls. Harpies. Centaurs. Dryads, and various other peoples."

"Badass," Elliot whispered again.

That was when they both noted that the woman in odd clothes was there again. She turned out to be called Captain Woodsinger, and she was collecting them all for a roll call, which Elliot thought was ridiculous considering they had just lined up to sign into the Border training camp.

He cheered up when she started reading out names, and Blondie turned out to be called Luke Sunburn.

"Sunborn," hissed Surfer Dude, once Elliot was done loudly making fun of this. "He's called Luke Sunborn. Of the Sunborns, you know!"

"I don't," said Elliot. "And I don't want to."

"Centuries ago, the first humans came across the Border to the otherlands," Surfer Dude recited, as if this was a lesson he had learned long ago. "Humans settled in this country near the Border, and lived among the creatures here, and brought peace to the Borderlands."

He eyed Serene as he said "creatures" which Elliot thought was an odd way to look at the most beautiful and badass girl in the world

Elliot glanced at Serene, then back to Dale. "So this place is the otherlands?"

"Depends on your point of view," said Serene. "Some people call where you come from the otherlands. It is, after all, on the other side of the Border."

Though Elliot enjoyed debate, he was currently on an information-gathering mission.

"This country is called the Borderlands, though," he said. "And the Border means the giant magic wall?"

Surfer Dude nodded and smiled his happy smile. "Yes."

"And humans came from across the Border," Elliot said. "Did we invade?" He leaned forward. "Tell me right now, are we engaged in a system of colonial oppression?"

The boy's happy smile melted away, like ice-cream in relentless verbal sunshine.

"I don't know . . .," said Surfer Dude helplessly, "what most of the words you just used mean."

"There are small communities of humans all over the Borderlands," said Serene. "They call the communities villages. And the Border guard established a law that must be kept throughout the land, and enforce that law. Elves consider the humans useful allies. Certainly more to be trusted than the dwarves. Or the trolls." A dark look crossed her face. "Do not get me started on the trolls."

"I want you to talk to me about trolls at length, but perhaps another time," said Elliot. "So elves call this country the Borderlands as well?"

A small smile, almost imperceptible, passed across Serene's face. "Not in elvish."

Elliot thought it was possible she was messing with him. What a babe.

"And this is a training camp for the Border guard, the people who made up all the laws and enforce them. This Border guard is partly kids from across the wall and partly kids from the Borderlands villages, but mostly . . . ?"

Surfer Dude's smile resurrected itself. "The backbone of the Border guard are the families who settled in the fortresses built along the Border itself centuries ago, and have protected it ever since, raising their sons in the tradition."

He buffed his nails on his leather jerkin. He and Captain Woodsinger and Luke Apparently-Not-Sunburn and many of the other humans were dressed like that, in a lot of leather and straps. It looked pretty ridiculous to Elliot, especially compared to Serene's form-fitting clothes, soft and green as moss.

Especially if all the leather-clad people were colonial oppressors.

"I'm a Wavechaser, you know," Surfer Dude added proudly. "Dale Wavechaser."

"Ha!"

Dale Wavechaser frowned. "Sorry?"

"Nothing," said Elliot. Mocking people who didn't get it was kind of pointless, like throwing sharp weapons into pudding.

Dale returned to his favorite subject.

"Of course, the Wavechasers aren't anything compared to the Sunborns," he said. "They were the first family. They held the Border on their own for a generation. There are songs about them: the shining ones, the golden guard, the laughing warriors. The Sunborn family is an army unto itself. Even their women are all soldiers, and a Sunborn woman is as good as any man."

"Cool, no video games *and* outdated gender politics," Elliot muttered.

Serene looked totally perplexed.

Dale continued making cheerful oblivion an art form. "Whenever there is a Sunborn acting as Commander of the Border guard, we cannot lose. Luke is the great Trigon champion Eleanor Sunborn's nephew, you know. He was taken to his father Michael Sunborn's last post with him and trained by him personally for three years. They say he's shaping up to be the best Sunborn of his generation. I was so excited to meet him today!"

Elliot raised his eyebrows. "Congratulations. I'm sure you will be very happy together."

So Blondie was basically the scary warrior equivalent of a trust-fund kid, the kind who had their pictures in the paper on the regular. One of life's born winners, with golden luck to go with the hair. No wonder he was glaring over at Elliot, looking betrayed and unhappy as a wet cat, as if nothing like being laughed at had ever happened to him before.

"The elven clans do not pay much heed to the brief fame and even briefer lives of men," remarked Serene.

She was a stone-cold elven fox.

"Tell me about your clan," Elliot invited her.

Elves apparently lived in the four woods that stretched across the otherlands, in linked family groups never more than a day's ride from another clan. Of all these clans in all the woods, if you believed Serene—and Elliot absolutely did—the Chaos clan was the most notorious.

Serene launched into a long tale of bloodshed, kidnapping gentlemen, highwaywomen, and foresworn oaths. The Chaos clan were rogues. Elliot was so into it. Dale Wavechaser wandered off at some point early on, which was his loss.

Serene was actually laughing at one of Elliot's jokes, her pale face bright as sun on snow and her dark hair swinging into her face, when Captain Woodsinger approached them and said, her voice very dry: "Schafer. Chaos-of-Battle. Have you made any decisions about whether you are staying or going?"

Elliot looked around the clearing, which was largely empty. Most of the kids in jeans and hoodies like him were long gone. He vaguely recalled seeing the kid who had cried over video games leading the way. Sadly, a group of kids Elliot's age remained, mostly the ones wearing leather, with Luke Sunborn at the head of the group and Dale Wavechaser circling him like an excited moon.

"It is a very different world to the one you are accustomed to," Captain Woodsinger observed. Elliot thought she was talking to him until she added, "We have never had a female elf wish to join the Border camp, though of course we have heard of the elves' legendary prowess in battle. You may be surprised and dismayed by the reactions of those around you, which you will consider unnatural. And your lady mother has expressed serious reservations about your behaviour in joining up."

Serene tossed her dark hair. "My mother was the wildest elf in the woods until she met my father," she said. "I can have an adventure of my own. Anyone who thinks I am not equal and more than equal to any human challenge will soon realize their mistake."

Elliot regarded her with his chin propped on his fist and sighed dreamily.

"And you, Schafer?"

Phones exploded here, and there was way more nature than Elliot was comfortable with, but there were mermaids and harpies and also true love.

Besides, it wasn't like there was much to go back to.

"I'm in," said Elliot. "For the non-fighting course. I want to read books and never, ever to fight. I'm a pacifist."

"A what?" asked Dale Wavechaser.

Elliot stared at him, then over at Blondie. "What I am attempting to communicate," he explained to the captain, "is that I want to be anywhere that guy is not."

He pointed to Blondie, who he felt was a helpful illustration of everything Elliot did not like in human form. Luke Sunborn stared at him in outrage, and Elliot used his pointing hand to give him a little wave.

"I think that can be arranged," Captain Woodsinger said dryly. "Welcome to the Border camp, Cadet Schafer."

"Cadet?" Elliot repeated. "Ahahaha. Okay."

Elliot began to regret his decision as soon as he was separated from Serene and sent off to his sleeping quarters.

His sleeping quarters were a large bare wooden cabin with several bunk beds and chests full of clothes and—oh good—weapons. There were already other boys there, and two of them were conducting a fight with daggers. Elliot saw no evidence anywhere of plumbing, and it was freezing cold in magic land. Elliot had never given much thought to the importance of plumbing and indoor heating, and he had never wanted to long passionately for double-glazing.

Magic lands in books had always seemed close to nature, but in a nice way, without all the unpleasant details.

A dagger landed in the wall, far too close to him.

"Oh no," Elliot moaned, and sat down heavily on his bunk bed. "This is magic Sparta."

Forget fancy luxuries like telephones and toilets. The Border camp did not even have writing implements.

In his first class, Elliot was presented with a quill, which he promptly broke in two and threw against a wall. He'd brought a pencil with him in his pocket: he clung to it as his only hope and insisted on using it to take notes on the parchment provided. (Magic land also did not have notebooks.)

The first class Elliot took was—somewhat ironically—geography class, though they called it mapmaking, but the maps were of a world Elliot had never seen before. He stared, fascinated, at the lines and circles that formed strange mountains and lakes: at the alien names that he would learn, and the places he was suddenly determined to go.

He still would have been happier with a pen.

He would also have been happier if he'd been able to keep his hoodie and jeans, but this morning he had woken to find his clothes stolen and had thus been forced into the uniform of those in council training. The others called his clothes a tunic and breeches: Elliot called them a dress and leggings, and it looked pretty terrible combined with the fact that Elliot's wild curly hair needed cutting and there was no hairdresser apparent in this magic land. If anyone from his old school had seen him, Elliot would have been destroyed on sight.

What would have made Elliot happiest of all was if he could see Serene, but she was nowhere to be found. The council course were being taught mapmaking, arithmetic, history, basic dwarvish, all about different species and their cultures, and several different types of law: for treaty making and property disputes and military discipline.

The council course seemed to have almost entirely different classes to the war-training course. Elliot looked for Serene in every class, and saw her in none. He had no idea how to find her, so at the end of the day he stuffed his new books (they were awesome) and his parchment (it was stupid, and nobody had listened to his impassioned speech on the topic of notebooks) into his bag, and went in quest of her.

The Border camp was all cabins, tents, a few stumpy towers like a couple of broken gray teeth in an otherwise toothless mouth, and endless fields. It was very difficult to navigate.

Elliot was fairly certain that he had gone around the same cabin twice, so in order to prevent the same thing happening for a third time he took out his house keys and made a small notch in the wall.

"Hey!" said a voice behind him. "You can't vandalize the camp!"

"I do what I want," said Elliot.

He turned and beheld the most horrible sight imaginable: his beautiful Serene and Luke Sunborn. They were actually walking together and obviously getting along, their arms brushing, their gold and dark heads bowed together. They were both wearing the uniform of the war-training cadets, and Elliot had to admit the leather and straps actually looked good on Serene. They looked like a natural pair, a matched set. They looked like a couple from a storybook.

Elliot's despair was put on pause when Serene's mouth turned up slightly at the corners and she said: "Oh good, Elliot. There you are."

Elliot beamed. "Here I am."

"You," said Luke Sunborn. "Why are you still here?"

"I'm sorry," said Elliot, and paused. "Who are you?" he asked. "Have we met before? What's your name?"

Luke opened his mouth and no sound came out.

Elliot grinned. "Sorry. I guess you're just not very memorable."

"This is Luke Sunborn," Serene informed him efficiently. "Luke, Elliot Schafer. Did I say that right?"

"Perfectly," Elliot assured her.

"I know his name; they said it at roll call," said Luke. "How do you know this guy, Serene?"

"He's a new friend of mine, like you," Serene answered, and Elliot was torn between delight and disgust as she continued: "I was hoping that you would both accompany me to Commander Rayburn's rooms and support me as I make my petition."

Elliot had several questions, like: Who is Commander Rayburn, how are we supposed to find these rooms, how are we supposed to find anything, what is your petition?

He did not voice any of them. He went to Serene's other side, taking her offered arm and privately vowing that he would be amazingly supportive. Way more supportive than Luke.

"I wish to be enrolled in both the war-training and council-training courses," said Serene. "I cannot be content with simply taking one. There is no such thing as too much learning and both have too much of value to offer me."

"Absolutely not. Get out of here," said Commander Rayburn.

Captain Woodsinger, Commander Rayburn's silent, reliable second-in-command and the lady with a constantly serious expression and cornrows who had kidnapped Elliot, gestured them toward the door.

"With respect, sir," Serene began.

"No," said Commander Rayburn, a big burly guy in the standard excessive leather. He had an actual candle burning much too close to a stack of parchment on his desk. "The war-training course demands total dedication and extreme discipline. It leaves no time for anything else, certainly not another course. The council-training course also, I have no doubt, takes up considerable time. You would not be capable of studying both."

Elliot noted the commander's obvious deep commitment to the council-training course.

"With respect, sir," said Serene. "And meaning no offence to you or my fellow cadets, but while it might certainly be too much for the delicate, I am a woman, and scientifically we have more endurance than men—"

Commander Rayburn's face grew darker. Elliot tried to gesture to Serene to cease this line of reasoning.

Which turned out to be a terrible mistake, because the commander's eye lit upon him. "Do you have something to say, cadet?"

"No," said Elliot prudently. Then his actual personality reasserted itself and he said: "Well, actually yes. Okay, I've only been in the otherlands for a day, and so far it's all horrible and confusing, but this much I understand. Serene is the first female elf to join the Border camp, and the women of her kind are more highly valued socially than the men. She's also of a very high rank. If you send her home saying that you doubt her capabilities, you will be insulting the elves, and they are one of the few nonhumans the humans actually have an alliance with. Why insult the elves when you do not have to? Moreover, Serene is extremely intelligent and by all accounts really good at stabbing stuff and whatever. You should want to have gifted students who may excel in both courses, and you should be encouraging students when they show interest in their studies. Do you not want warriors who are brilliant, and diplomats who are brave? The war-training course is also obviously the command-track course.

Do you want the next generation of commanders and captains to be idiots like Luke? If the coursework proves too much for Serene—which I do not anticipate—she can always make a choice between the courses, and at that stage it will be a choice made with more information than she has now, and with mutual goodwill." He took a deep breath. "Also, that candle so close to your papers is a fire hazard. I thought you should know."

Captain Woodsinger gave Elliot an appalled look. Elliot suspected she had never forgiven him for the child-predator remark.

Commander Rayburn's lip curled. "You'd be in the council-training course, I assume."

"Yeah, you can tell by my pretty dress," Elliot snapped.

"Well, your deluge of slippery words and Chaos-of-Battle's burgeoning insubordination fail to convince me, for some reason," Rayburn said drily.

"My mother always said men's minds were unsuited to the rigors of command," Serene murmured. "With respect, sir."

Captain Woodsinger smiled faintly. The commander did not.

"What did you say?" Commander Rayburn thundered.

"I agree with them," Luke Sunborn said loudly.

He had not spoken before, only saluted and stood to attention, hands clasped behind his back and listening seriously to what his commander was saying. He stepped forward now.

"I beg your pardon, Sunborn?"

"I agree with everything Serene and Elliot are saying," Luke said. "Except the stuff about guys, obviously. Serene, you have to remember the cultural differences."

Serene inclined her head. "My apologies."

"And the fact that Elliot insulted me, which was completely rude and uncalled for."

Elliot smirked.

"Aside from that, sir," said Luke, "it does no harm to let her try. She's amazing with a bow. You should see her in the ring. If she was asked to choose between courses, she might not choose war training, and she would be a real loss to the camp."

Elliot did not miss Luke's implication, as clear as the commander's, that council training was useless.

"She has a brain, you know," Elliot said. "She'd be right not to choose war training."

"I speak for myself," Serene announced, her arms crossed. "And I am brilliant with both a bow and my brain. But if you do not know how to value a daughter of Chaos, that is your loss."

She walked over to a chair, which she flung herself into, and sat in a rebellious slouch. Elliot looked at her with love and joined her in sitting down, though he didn't think he had quite Serene's élan. Luke remained standing, but he moved to the other side of Serene's chair.

It was Serene's absolute refusal to be cowed or to submit that changed the commander's mind, Elliot thought. But he figured the support of a Sunborn and Elliot's statement of some shatteringly obvious facts about diplomacy didn't hurt.

"You can take both courses," the commander said eventually. "On trial. For a year. If you do not perform satisfactorily in both, you will be asked to choose at the end of a year, whether you wish to or not."

"Thank you," said Serene.

"And I hope I don't regret this."

"I intend you will not," Serene informed him. "I intend to excel."

They left the tent with Serene striding in the centre and both of them flanking her.

"Well, Serene, you were amazing," Elliot told her. "Now, you'll want to learn what you missed in council training today. Come with me to the library and we will go over the lessons. Good-bye, Luke."

"Right," said Luke. "See you in archery at dawn, Serene?"

"Indeed," said Serene.

Elliot was calling that one a draw. For him and Luke, that was: obviously Serene had triumphed in her altercation with the commander, because she was wonderful.

Serene was obviously in way over her head.

It was not her fault. She was brilliant and amazing and perfect, and if anyone in the world could have done it she could have, but there simply were not enough hours in the day. Those in council training were meant to burn the midnight oil (literally; God grant

Elliot patience, but he would rather have electricity), and those in war training were meant to rise at dawn.

She was not getting enough sleep.

Elliot came forcibly to this realization when he was reading to her aloud in the library about the adventures of a dwarf prince and the elven commander of his armies. It was also an interspecies romance, because Elliot's courtship was both intellectual and sneaky.

Their burly elven librarian, Bright-Eyes-Gladden-the-Hearts-of-Women, walked over and coughed pointedly as Elliot was reading.

Elliot ceased doing the voice for the dwarf prince. "Am I talking too loudly—" he began, and then saw that Serene was asleep, her dark head cradled in her arms. "Oh."

He shut up the book, slipped off his chair, and went into the stacks where he could give himself furiously to thinking. He had only been brooding there for a few minutes when he was interrupted by Luke.

"What are you doing here?" Elliot demanded.

"I'm worried about Serene," said Luke.

"No, I didn't mean why did you come here," Elliot explained. "How did you even know how to find this place? Did you get somebody to show you the way? Do you know what these objects on the shelves with all the words in them are called?"

Luke did look somewhat out of place in the library and mildly uncomfortable about it, but in response he stopped looking uncomfortable and started looking annoyed.

"We were having an archery competition this morning."

"How is that different from having archery practise every other morning?" Elliot asked. "Wait, don't tell me, I just remembered I'm not interested. So?"

"Serene missed every bull's-eye," said Luke. "She could barely focus on the target. She still did better than a lot of the other cadets, mind you," he added with notable pride: it almost made Elliot have a positive feeling about Luke.

"Who won the archery competition, then?"

"Me, of course," said Luke. Ah, there went all positive feelings. Status quo restored.

"Okay, loser, quit bragging," Elliot commanded. "We have a real problem here. This has been made deliberately impossible for Serene. They won't go any easier on her. We have to coordinate our efforts."

"I don't understand," said Luke.

"I don't know how to express the depths of my surprise," Elliot told him. "How would it be if Serene skipped the earliest classes, and you remembered the lessons and trained her? And while you train her, I could read to her and try to catch her up in our lessons so she won't have to study late. She'll have to multi-task, but she won't be too exhausted to do it."

Luke thought this over, and then nodded. "All right. So we'll work together on this. Truce?"

"For the year," said Elliot hastily. "We're not friends."

"I'm not confused on that issue," said Luke. He spat in his hand and held it out. "Deal?"

Elliot backed away. "Ugh, no, I'm not touching your spit. That's disgusting."

Luke flushed and wiped his hand off on his trousers. "It's a totally normal—"

"Save the performative manly exchange of bodily fluids for the people in your military training, loser!"

"Why are you helping her?" Luke asked abruptly, and loud enough so that Bright-Eyes the librarian elf gave them a sharp warning look. Of course Luke had no idea of appropriate manners in the library.

"Why are you helping her?" Elliot shot back.

"She's my comrade-in-arms," said Luke. "And this isn't fair. But you hardly have a code of honor, so why are you helping her?"

So Luke was saying that he was helping Serene out of the goodness of his heart, but naturally he assumed Elliot had no goodness to speak of. Because if Elliot's code of honor wasn't the same as Luke's, it might as well not exist at all.

Elliot did note that Luke had not mentioned any romantic interest in Serene, so he chose this time to stake a prior romantic claim.

"If you must know, she is the one soul destined for my own, and we are going to be together forever," he declared loftily.

"That's weird," Luke told him. "We're thirteen."

"I don't care what you think!"

"Elliot, don't yell, we'll get thrown out," Serene grumbled, appearing rumpled in the stacks. "Merciful goddess, Luke, what are you doing in the library?"

Luke looked betrayed.

That was how the study-slash-stabbing lessons got started. Elliot made Luke sign them up for one of the good practise rooms in the towers, because the war-training kids didn't let the kids in the council course sign up for practise rooms, and people had been known to scribble out the elf girl's name, but nobody was going to scribble out a Sunborn.

There were a few benches at the back of the practise room. Elliot sat on those and perfected his lesson plan. It had to be sharp, short bursts of information: purely aural and oral learning, striking enough so that Serene would remember what she needed to.

One method was to quiz her at the same time as Luke and Serene were fighting with quarterstaffs: using the clash of wood on wood as a rhythm for belting out questions, like a song.

"Name the lake where mermaids have historically murdered the most sailors."

"Lake Atar," said Serene, whirling and striking her staff against Luke's.

"Correct! You're the greatest. The place where the largest host of the harpies resides."

"The Forest of the Suicides," she said, whirling away as Luke struck back, her plait flying.

"One thousand percent correct. You're amazing. The richest dwarf mines?"

"The Edda mines," Luke chimed in, circling Serene.

"No, no, shut your face, these questions are not for you," Elliot said sternly. "But actually that is the correct answer, thank goodness, because if you had confused Serene with another wrong answer there would have been consequences."

Torchlight caught Luke's grin before he lunged forward and met Serene's defence.

One night, Serene fell asleep in the practise room, and rather than wake her and deprive her of yet more sleep, they let her sleep.

Luke covered her with his jacket. Elliot found that offensive showing off, since Elliot's uniform did not come with a cool leather jacket.

"I have to say," said Luke as they were walking back to the cabins. "I would've thought you'd give up well before now."

"Really," said Elliot. "Because kids from my side of the Border don't have any follow-through or honor? Or just because you think I don't?"

"You did say you were only helping because you . . . had a crush on Serene," said Luke.

"Excuse you," said Elliot. "I worship her. Do not underestimate my feelings. My devotion is intense and will be enduring!"

"I was *trying* to say something nice," Luke said crossly.

Elliot imagined that anyone else in the camp would have fallen all over themselves at receiving a compliment from a Sunborn, however grudging or double-edged.

"Yes," said Elliot. "Very flattering that you assumed I was inferior to you in commitment. You really seem to think you're something special, Luke Sunborn. It's strange. I don't see it myself."

He went into his cabin, leaving Luke standing speechless behind him. Once he was in the darkness and relative privacy of the cabin—given that all his annoying roommates were doing was begging him to "get into bed" and "stop torturing us like this"—Elliot allowed himself to smile.

Spending time with Luke was not actually as painful as Elliot had assumed it would be. Not that Elliot intended to let him know that.

A few more dark weeks followed, in which Elliot was tired enough to snap at a couple of people who couldn't take it and make them cry, and he and Serene and Luke ate dinner standing up over lessons rather than around their separate council and war campfires every evening, and Elliot passed out in his cold uncomfortable bunkbed every night without noticing the cold or the discomfort until morning, when he woke aching all over.

It was worth it, because Serene and Luke were both getting rather good, Elliot thought. He would've thought about being a teacher when he grew up, but Elliot knew himself, and he knew that the impressionable and tenderhearted should be protected from him.

When Luke and Serene both got merits in the two classes the council and war courses shared, and Serene merits in every other class, Elliot felt like he could finally relax.

Then it occurred to him that he was spending all his time with Serene. Of course she was his heart's chosen darling, and every moment spent drowning in her eyes was bliss, but she was also—it was unfortunate, but it could not be denied—a sporty type. In the occasional times when Elliot had daydreamed about having friends, they had not been sporty.

Besides, he was a modern independent man who intended to have his own interests and circle of acquaintances, even if he had found his soulmate young.

One day when he was not too tired, he came to mapmaking class—the last class of the day—early and carefully studied the maps everyone was working on. There were not that many. The council-training course was far, far smaller than the war-training course. Apparently they needed ten swords to every brain.

The other students seemed disturbed to have their work surveyed and commented upon.

"Do you *mind*?" snapped a boy from Elliot's cabin who had already taken against Elliot because of his "endless whining" over "central heating or whatever."

Elliot beamed. "Not at all."

That boy's map was distinctly substandard. Elliot let him know.

Then he stationed himself at two desks pushed together, where the two best maps in class lay on proud display. The owners of the desks were cadets Elliot vaguely recognized—a human boy called Peter, and a girl called Myra.

There were not many girls in the Border camp at all, and Myra was special. Elliot had wonderful suspicions about Myra. She was very short and had dark hair on her upper lip. Elliot had seen dwarves on the day people had signed up for training camp, and never after: it made sense to him that they had been seeing off someone who had signed up.

Also, Myra had an elaborately carved axe under her desk. Not that Elliot was making any judgments based on that fact. Elliot did not judge.

"Hiiii," Elliot said ingratiatingly as they approached.

Myra and Peter looked surprised to see him, but—Elliot thought—not unhappy. Elliot was an expert in people being unhappy to see him.

"Can I sit with you guys?" Elliot asked.

"Of—of course!" said Peter.

Elliot felt his winning smile widen into a real grin. He had not expected this to be so easy. He'd always had to chase the kids down the road to make them keep him company.

"I'm Elliot Schafer," he added.

"Oh, I know," said Peter mysteriously. "I'm Peter Quint." He seemed to feel his introduction needed further explanation. "I was born in the otherlands, but my dad is from your world across the Border. He kept his name."

"Why shouldn't he?" Elliot asked.

"Most people don't," said Peter. "My mum hates it, thinks it's really embarrassing."

"In my world," said Elliot. "Surnames like Waggletwig are embarrassing. Let me tell you that."

Peter nodded eagerly. "I bet in your world, your name is really cool."

Elliot examined him for signs of sarcasm, and found none. "Yes," he said at length.

"I'm Myra of the Diamond clan," Myra said. Her chin was raised, and she had drawn herself up to her full height. She might be the only person in the camp shorter than Elliot.

"So you are a dwarf!" Elliot said. "I mean, dwarves—the species with axes and mines and so forth—I'm not being offensive, am I?"

Myra studied him. "My mother's a dwarf, and my father's human," she said in the same defiant tone.

"And you have a clan system!" Elliot said rapturously. "How is it different from the elf clan system? Wait, let me take notes."

He dragged a desk over to join the other two. Its legs squeaked on the floor. His classmates regarded him with expressions of exhaustion that Elliot found hurtful. They had only known him for a few weeks. People as young as they were should have more stamina.

"Before I take notes about the clans," said Elliot. "I have a few quick suggestions about both of your maps."

He was interrupted by the arrival of their teacher, Mr Dustlaid. Teachers in the council-training course did not have any military rank, and Elliot had heard the war-training cadets call them "Mister" and "Miss" with a sneer. Teachers in the council-training course had the sad desperate look of old biscuits dunked in tea, who wanted to crumble but were too soggy. All the councilors Elliot had seen so far had the same defeated look. Elliot wondered what that was about.

"Cadet Schafer," Mr Dustlaid said in a sad, wet voice. "To your desk."

As soon as class was over, Elliot leaped up to resume sharing his thoughts with Peter and Myra.

"Sorry," he said at length. "Am I boring you?"

He usually was, and he usually realized it about now: twenty minutes too late.

"No," Myra told him. "It's really cool that you want to hang out with us."

Elliot beamed. "Really?"

"Usually you pal around with Luke Sunborn," said Peter.

Elliot stared at Peter in shocked betrayal, then transferred his gaze to Myra, who he now felt was his favorite of the two. Myra was also treacherous: she was nodding, her dark eyes shining.

"To which of the students in this learning establishment do you refer?" Elliot asked haughtily. "I am not familiar with that name."

Myra and Peter stared at him. Elliot stared challengingly back.

"You know, Luke Sunborn!" Peter said.

Elliot shook his head firmly. "Not ringing a bell, sorry."

"He's famous!" said Peter. "His whole family is famous!"

"How nice for him," said Elliot. "Whoever he may be."

"And he's *very* handsome," Myra said softly.

"I don't know anyone handsome," Elliot lied, and demoted Myra from her position as favorite.

"He's the tallest boy in our year, and he's the best at everything in the war-training class, and he's . . ." Peter, already babbling, descended into an incomprehensible mumble.

"Satan line dancing?" Elliot asked. "Peter, are you drunk?"

"Standing behind you," Myra said in a low, clear voice.

"What—oh my God," said Elliot, turning to find Luke lurking behind him like a terrible blond iceberg. He almost fell out of his chair. "Don't do that! Why would you do that?"

"Hi," Luke said awkwardly.

A terrible thought occurred to Elliot. "Is Serene all right? Has she been injured in one of your reckless training exercises?"

Luke frowned. "She's fine. Captain Woodsinger offered to give her extra lessons, to smooth her transition in taking on two courses."

Elliot had thought he saw a trace of sympathy in Captain Woodsinger's face during their interview with the commander. If the captain was on Serene's side, he decided to forgive her impatient attitude toward Elliot himself.

If Serene was fine, though, that raised the question of what Luke was doing here. Surely he would prefer to be doing something sporty with his terrible sporty friends.

"Where's Dale Wavechaser?" Elliot demanded.

Luke blinked. "Who's Dale Wavechaser?"

"Your friend!" said Elliot.

"I don't know what you're talking about," said Luke. "Which is life as usual, I guess."

Just because Luke, Serene, and Elliot had fallen into something of a routine did not mean that Luke had the right to describe that routine as "life as usual." He was giving Elliot's new friends entirely the wrong impression.

"Dale's about this tall," Elliot said, waving a hand haphazardly far above his own head. "Very good-looking."

"*What*?" said Luke.

"Elliot is right," said Myra, which Elliot enjoyed hearing, so Elliot made her his favorite again.

"I've just never heard him say anything positive about anyone before," said Luke.

"That's absurd. Serene is an avatar of elven perfection, and I praise her every day," Elliot snapped. "Anyway, Dale Wavechaser has the disturbingly happy face of someone who doesn't think very much."

"That's more like you," said Luke. "Also, I don't know this person."

"He followed you around all through the first day of camp!"

"Oh," Luke said, and frowned again, this time in concentration. As if people following him around worshipfully was such an ordinary state of affairs he barely noticed. "I think I remember. I don't know him, though."

"Well, good news!" Elliot declared. "He wants to be your friend!"

Luke did not look especially pleased by this revelation. Of course, he was probably used to people wanting to be his friend.

Elliot remembered his new friends, and also his manners.

"My new friends, meet," Elliot said grandly, "some guy."

"Luke," said Luke.

"We know," Peter and Myra chorused.

Elliot noticed that Luke did not ask Peter and Myra's names, and Peter and Myra did not volunteer them. Everybody clearly had a strong opinion about who the important one in this social interaction was.

Elliot refused to accept other people's version of reality. He debated asking Luke what he was doing hanging around, and whether it was actually Luke's intent to sabotage Elliot's life because of their rivalry for Serene's heart.

It sounded a bit terrible in Elliot's head when he thought it, though, and when things sounded terrible in Elliot's head that was a bad sign. Elliot thought it was probably bad manners to actually tell people they shouldn't be where you were. It was not something that had ever come up in Elliot's life before. Usually people took extreme care not to be where Elliot was.

Elliot decided to accept the situation, with ill grace.

"Since you're here, make yourself useful," he commanded. "Hold all of these."

He gave Luke his bag.

"Do you have rocks in here?" Luke asked.

"I have all my books with me, obviously, and several library books," Elliot answered. "What if I wished to consult a book and did not have the relevant volume on hand? Think about it. Now if you are carrying my books, I can take the atlas back to my cabin with me and inspect it."

The atlas of the otherlands was not a globe, but a square flat stone, smoothed into shape like a tile. The forests of the otherlands were drawn out, and villages, and the seas beyond.

"Elliot!" Peter said, his voice slightly high. "I'm not sure you're supposed to take that."

"Nobody ever said I wasn't supposed to take the atlas home for private study," Elliot told Peter. "Did they? By the way, do people think this world is flat? Is it flat? What happens if you try to cross the sea?"

"If you sail into the deepest ocean, you are killed by giant mermaids," Peter said flatly.

"Fascinating," Elliot sighed. "You've made me very happy."

He contemplated the atlas in his hands, which also made him very happy. There was a place where the actual words HERE BE DRAGONS were written, and it was probably true.

"I don't want to help you steal stuff," said Luke.

"You are talking nonsense, Luke. Obviously I am going to give it back. Besides, is Mr Dustlaid going to punish me? Really? He can barely summon up the will to live. I don't know how any of the councilors get any treaties written."

"Well," Luke said pityingly. "They don't exactly write the treaties. They used to, but the Border guard is too large and too vital to the defence of the otherlands now. Councilors advise on the treaties, of course, and help put them into the proper language, but Commander Rayburn or—if the situation is important enough—General Lakelost decides what goes into the treaties."

"Reeeeeally," said Elliot. "Under those circumstances, I might lose the will to live myself."

The system of war training and council training in the Border camp made more sense now. Once, perhaps, there had been no general, and no colonels beneath him, and only a few fortresses with commanders and their trusted councilors running them together. Now there were fortresses dotted across the otherlands, a general placed over them all, everyone thought they were too important and military to listen to councilors, and the commander who ran the Border camp was under orders to produce more warriors.

No wonder the council course had shrunk down to nothing, and all the councilors taught in a despair fugue. They had given up.

Giving up was not Elliot's style.

He waved a cheerful good-bye to Peter and Myra. The atlas, held in only one hand, wobbled. Peter gulped. Myra, Elliot's favorite, stayed cool.

Elliot went back to holding the atlas in both hands. Luke punched him in the arm.

"There you go," he said. "Hang on to it."

Elliot stumbled slightly and glared up at Luke, waiting for the next blow. It did not come. Luke stared down at him.

"Don't hit me," said Elliot.

"I didn't!" Luke exclaimed. "I didn't—*hit* you."

"Oh, no?"

Luke flushed. "Other boys punch—people they know in the arms all the time," he said. "I've seen them do it."

"Yeah, I've actually been punched before," said Elliot. "I don't like it."

"Who punched you?"

Elliot waved this off as irrelevant. "This is part of the truce," he explained.

"The truce," Luke said. "Oh."

"No violence. No hitting, no kicking, no throwing my bag over my head, no shaking trees so I fall out, no shaking the jungle gym so I fall out, no shoving me out of windows so I fall out—"

"Elliot!" said Luke. "I'm not going to—"

"No interrupting!" said Elliot. "That is doing violence to my train of thought and verbal flow."

"That is ridiculous," said Luke.

"So you insist on perpetrating acts of wanton brutality on the helpless?"

"No!" Luke exclaimed. "Okay, fine. No violence. That's fine. Since I didn't hit you."

He glared at Elliot. Elliot glared back. Elliot returned to studying his atlas.

"On one side is the ocean, and on one side is the wall," said Elliot thoughtfully. "But were the otherlands part of my world once? Who built the wall that marks the Border?"

"Nobody built the wall," said Luke. "It's always been there."

"Someone built the wall," said Elliot. "Because it's a wall, and not a rock. Rocks are always there. Walls are not. Someone has to make a wall. Nobody has to make a rock."

"Says who?" asked Luke.

Elliot squinted. "Luke, are you being metaphysical?"

Luke looked alarmed. "I don't think so."

"Pity," said Elliot. "I would have been very impressed."

"I doubt that somehow," said Luke.

Elliot disregarded this cheap shot and regarded his atlas. He tried to think of a way to ask Luke not to talk to him in front of Peter and Myra, since it might ruin Elliot's reputation, but that also seemed a terrible thing to say out loud.

"What is being metaphysical, exactly?" asked Luke.

Elliot gave up and tried to explain. This took several hours, and by the time he surrendered in frustration, Serene had returned to him. She really seemed to like him, Elliot thought. It was amazing. He was pretty sure it wasn't just about the help he gave her. He was pretty sure she hung around him voluntarily.

He was almost happy in the Border camp.

Until, naturally, Luke ruined his happiness by rudely reminding him what the Border camp was actually for.

"We could help you, you know," Luke said over lunch one day.

Both the courses shared lunch in one of the larger buildings, around small tables and benches like picnic tables and benches but inside. Elliot always sat with Serene, naturally, and had to put up with Luke.

Elliot looked to Serene for translation, but she was nodding, so it was one of those military things they both understood and felt he should too.

"I don't need or want your help, loser," he said, rather than betray any uncertainty. "But I will take your pudding."

He took the pudding. Luke let him. To reward Luke for this, and also because Elliot did not trust green food, he pushed across his apple.

"Because basic self-defence training is going to start up soon," Luke said. "Even the people in the council-training courses have to do it. You signed up to fight when you signed up to guard the Border. You don't have a choice. I mean, what if the camp was under attack?"

"I hope you and Serene would have the decency to protect me!"

"Yes, of course," said Serene, and Elliot smiled gratefully at her.

"I'm not saying this to upset you. I'm trying to tell you what you absolutely have to do. What if we were both dead?" asked Luke.

Elliot looked at his pudding and was very sad about his life and his choices. How had he wound up here, in a place where all he had was pudding—Elliot would have sold his soul for a chocolate bar—and awful people who at the age of thirteen asked questions like "What if we were both dead?"

"Amazing choice of mealtime conversation, loser," he said. "Now I'm not even hungry."

"Give back my pudding then."

"No," said Elliot, on general principles.

"Your gentle nature is unsuited to war," Serene told him. "It's all right to be frightened. I think you have a valiant spirit and you will rise to the occasion."

Elliot glanced up into the steady light of Serene's eyes. She might sympathetically express her opinion of men's weakness at every turn, but she had this belief in Elliot, despite the fact that she was the best cadet warrior in the Border camp and based on what Elliot did not know.

She had misunderstood the situation, but her faith in him meant a lot.

"I'm not frightened," said Elliot. "And I know just what to do."

He finished his pudding.

Elliot had been to the practise grounds before, when Serene and Luke wanted to do their fun pretend murder outside. The other kids from the council-training course had not, and they were all looking at the cleared dirt with what seemed to be nervousness and excitement. Elliot always sat with Peter or Myra when Serene was not there to sit with, and he had hoped for better from them.

"Don't worry, you guys," said Dale Wavechaser, coming up with a giant box of throwing knives. "All of the war-training class are going to come and help you learn, since it's your first time."

Dale was exactly the type a teacher would trust with equipment: he could lift any heavy things, and he was reliable.

Elliot smiled at him winningly. "Hello."

"Oh, hello," said Dale. "Elliot, right? I bet Luke will teach you."

"How thrilling for me," said Elliot. "Actually, I know how to throw knives."

"Really?" Dale asked. "That's great."

"So great," Elliot agreed cheerfully. "So can I have them?"

He looked around, and from the cluster of cabins, coming across the grass, was Captain Woodsinger and other students from the war-training course. Including Serene and Luke. Now was the time to act, or never.

Dale blinked. "Have them?"

"I like to pick my own," said Elliot, and seized the box.

Dale did not actually resist his grab, which was excellent as the box was horribly heavy and Elliot almost tipped over and right into the big container of knives. He dropped it into the dirt instead and clung possessively to the side.

He smiled reassuringly at Dale, and across the field he saw Luke break into a run. He picked up the first knife that came to hand.

"Watch this," he said, and threw the knife at Dale.

Dale stumbled backwards, and Elliot grabbed up several more knives and hurled them in random directions. The council-track class let out screams and scattered.

Elliot grabbed more knives.

"Forcing groups of teenagers to learn how to use deadly force is really weird and disturbing!" he announced, throwing another knife, and another, and then one over his shoulder. "Everyone has a choice, if they choose to make one, and I choose not to do this. The value of people does not rest on their ability to hurt others."

He threw the knives down viciously, as if they were grenades. Puffs of dust rose when they hit the ground.

"I am not winning any arguments because I know how to hurt someone. How does that prove that you're right? How does being stronger or more vicious prove anything, except that all this talk about honor is stupid? Where's the honor in being better at hurting somebody? Telling me I have to do this is insulting, as if I can't win any other way. As if I can't win in a better way."

Luke and Serene got to him just before the captain did. Elliot threw the last knife at their feet.

"He said he knew how to throw knives," Dale Wavechaser said, faint and traumatised, somewhere in the distance.

"I do know how to throw knives," Elliot said. "I can already do all I want to do with knives, which is throw them away."

Luke and Serene were both pale, breathing hard, staring around and visibly pleased that nobody had been accidentally knifed. They were also wearing looks of deep apprehension . . . about Elliot's fate, Elliot assumed, since the knife box was empty.

"Yes, your point was extremely clear," said Luke. "You're just making the whole thing laboured and awkward now."

Elliot rolled his eyes as he was dragged off to the commander's rooms, where Commander Rayburn walked in and said, "Oh, the elf's little ginger boyfriend" in a despairing and, Elliot considered, unprofessional manner. "What have you been doing now?"

"Staged a pacifist protest," said Elliot. "Also, Serene and I have not defined the parameters of our relationship yet, though I have high hopes."

"He staged a pacifist protest by hurling knives all over everywhere," reported Captain Woodsinger from her place at the door, throwing the commander a snappy salute.

"Unusual," said Commander Rayburn. He sounded very, very tired.

Elliot shrugged. "I've been called worse."

He got dishwashing duty for the next three weeks and was sent away, possibly so Commander Rayburn could have a soothing nap. Serene and Luke were waiting outside. Once they had established that Elliot was not expelled, they told him very firmly that he should have been expelled.

"Your behaviour was very rash," Serene said. "And you called enormous amounts of attention to yourself, which is not the way my mother taught me gentlemen should behave." She was wearing her tiny smile, designed to be missed, except that Elliot never missed it. He smiled at her, and she told him: "If the camp is attacked, I swear to protect you."

"And if we're both dead, the odds are pretty good you'll annoy people until they chop off their own heads in sheer frustration," said Luke.

Elliot was pleased by this tribute. Luke and Serene stopped leaning their overly tall leather-clad selves against one of the endless fences surrounding the endless fields, and they walked away from the commander's tower back toward their cabins as Elliot told them about his actual punishment.

"Oh, what?" Luke said. "You're going to miss my first Trigon game."

"Is that the stupid game with the glass ball and the weird hills that some of the war-training guys keep playing?" Elliot asked. "Oh no, do you play that? The others have been playing it for ages."

"It's a good game," said Luke. "But I didn't really have time to play until we got into the swing of helping Serene. She's more important."

Serene shoved Luke's shoulder with her own in a rough affectionate gesture. Elliot regarded Luke with deep dislike. Everything had gone downhill so fast.

"So, what, they just kept a place for you on the team?"

Luke blinked. "Sure. They were upset I couldn't play, of course: they know they won't win against the other years without me."

"But with you they will?" Elliot inquired sweetly.

"Well," Luke said. "Yeah."

"He displays great prowess in every physical activity," Serene said in her measured way, and Luke buffeted her in the shoulder in the same way she had just done to him.

"I have no idea why you would think I might want to go and watch your ridiculous game, loser," Elliot said. "The truce doesn't extend that far. I have no interest in the game or you, and I already see your face more often than I would prefer."

"Suit yourself," Luke snapped. "Have fun washing dishes while I'm winning and everybody else is cheering for me."

Washing dishes, or literally anything else in the world, sounded better than that. But when the day came, Serene appeared and announced that she had got Elliot off early.

"That's so great, Serene," said Elliot. "Except I don't want to go."

"I want to go," said Serene. "You have both made a sterling effort to support me, as my true and trusted comrades, and I wish to show support for you in my turn. And if I appear at an event without a gentleman by my side, people will assume that I couldn't get one."

Trigon was as stupid a game as Elliot had imagined it was. It involved a lot of jumping—someone was going to sprain an ankle, if not break a leg—and grabbing at a giant glass ball. Someone was going to get hit in the head and get glass shards embedded in their skull.

At least nobody was actively trying to hurt each other, and Luke was good at jumping, if you considered that something to brag about. For about five minutes, Elliot almost wanted him to win.

But then Luke looked over at Serene a few too many times and the crowd leaped up and cheered for him a lot too many times, and Elliot retreated to his book and sulked because Serene did not understand his jokes about Tigger.

Luke won. His team carried him around on their shoulders, his hair shining in the sun, their glad shouting rising up into the sky. Dale Wavechaser and Darius Winterchild gave Luke many back-pats and fist-bumps, so Elliot presumed Luke had at last found his sporty brethren. Luke still, rather to Elliot's surprise, came over to them later.

"So?" he asked, grinning with what Elliot found to be offensive bashfulness. "What did you think?"

"I do not see the point of this game, but you were excellent," said Serene.

Elliot looked up from his book. "Is it over?" he asked. "Who won?"

It wasn't that Luke caused all the terrible things at the Border camp to happen. It was mostly just that he was the one who told Elliot about them, and so it seemed like they were all his fault.

Elliot chose to blame Luke anyway.

"What is the point of parents' day?" he demanded at yet another Bad News Lunchtime.

"Men are naturally attached to their homes," Serene said sympathetically. "I believe that parents are allowed to visit to ease their hearts and assure them of their familial affection. I have been going on hunting expeditions away from home since I was a squire, of course, so a visit from my parents will not be required. Are your parents not capable of crossing the Border?"

"Nope," said Elliot, whose father believed he was at military school and whom he would never have dreamed of asking to come to his school anyway.

"My parents are coming," said Luke.

"Okay."

"So's my sister, Louise."

"Good for you," said Elliot.

"Serene's going to come with us," Luke said. "We're going to have a picnic."

"This is a very boring story, loser," said Elliot, instead of saying "Quit rubbing it in." "Did it sound different in your head?"

"You can come if you like," said Luke. "Since nobody else is going to ask you, and everyone should have something to do on parents' day."

"That's all right," said Elliot. "I actually can't imagine anything worse than having to attend an all-Sunborns-all-the-time parade."

On parents' day he went to the library, because it was amazing in the library and he loved it there, and today he had promised himself a special treat: he was going to read a contemporary account of the great harpies battle over the Forest of the Suicides.

He had to put on special gloves and turn the pages carefully, under Bright-Eyes the librarian's watchful gaze.

It was a really enjoyable half hour until Luke showed up.

"So sorry," said Elliot politely to Bright-Eyes, and then to Luke: "Are you *lost*?"

Luke was giving the library a look of unhappy mistrust. In fact, now Elliot was paying attention, he looked more downcast than usual: it probably could not be attributed to the library. Possibly someone had made fun of his hair.

"You have to come to the picnic," he said.

"Why?" Elliot snapped.

"My parents are expecting you," Luke said reluctantly, as if each word were a tooth that had to be pulled.

"Why?" Elliot repeated inflexibly.

"I don't *know why*, Elliot!" Luke snapped back. "I didn't tell them you were coming. But they asked where you were, and I said you were in the library, and they said to go fetch you then."

"How did you know I was in the library?"

"Oh, come on," said Luke.

The whole thing seemed very mysterious to Elliot, but he trailed after Luke out to the fields—oh, lovely, Elliot could never get enough of fields. Even if Luke had not known where he was going, it would have been easy to spot the Sunborns: every one of them was tall and the kind of person you looked at, with golden hair that shone as if a whole host of tiny suns had congregated on a picnic blanket. Serene sat among them looking very dark and pale and solemn indeed, but if you knew her you could tell she was happy to be there.

There was a man who had to be Luke's father with shoulders basically the size of a mountain range, they should probably have a name, and a girl Serene was sitting beside who Elliot assumed was Louise. She was very grown-up looking—she was *eighteen*, Luke had said—and her hair was all done up in a coronet of braids, and she was about the most beautiful person Elliot had ever seen. Weird magic land might not have electricity, but he had to admit it was full of hotties.

The other woman stood up, her bright hair flying like a flag, as they approached.

"Well, here the boys are at last," she said and gave Elliot a hug.

"Oh my God," said Elliot, somewhat muffled, into Luke's mother's bosom. It was not entirely covered, and she was wearing a very large, very ornate golden necklace. Elliot was not sure if he should be worried about being suffocated or having his eyes put out by one of the jewels.

"I'm Rachel Sunborn," said Luke's mother. "You must be little Elliot."

She released him, and Elliot reeled back, breathing in deep grateful lungfuls of air.

"I may be slightly below average height at present, but I am the same age as Luke," said Elliot. "I'm very sorry for being late. I didn't realize you were expecting me. I think Luke must have confused the issue somehow. His command of the English language is not what it could be. Well, you must have noticed that for yourself."

"Nice command of the English language you have there, genius," said Luke. "Very appropriate way to talk when you're a guest."

Elliot took a deep breath. Rachel Sunborn laughed.

"You are just like I thought you would be from Luke's letters," she said. "Come sit by me, Elliot, and tell me how you got Luke to actually learn facts about ancient history."

"*Mum*!" said Luke.

"And he knows his way to the library and everything!" said Rachel Sunborn, rumpling Luke's sunny hair as he went by her on a quest for consolation and sandwiches. "My little man. It's a miracle."

She patted the place beside her. Elliot cautiously went over to it and sat beside her. She ruffled his hair, too, and pulled him in occasionally for another suffocating hug. She asked him to tell her the story about the throwing knives in his own words and laughed when he did.

Elliot got the impression, due to the laughter, that she didn't take him particularly seriously. But she was a very lovely lady, he decided after a while. He felt guilty, since she obviously assumed he was friends with her son, but he could not explain the truce to her. He sat with her and tried to make her laugh instead. It must be nice, to have a mother like that.

"And you don't have to worry about your safety if the camp is attacked," Louise Sunborn added, with a lazy stretch like a lioness. "We'll protect you. None of us have ever missed a target with a knife. Except Luke."

"I was six!" said Luke.

Louise laughed, and they had a casual wrestling match, there on the picnic blanket, which was only interrupted by Michael Sunborn asking about Luke's Trigon games. Elliot bore nobly with this subject and was relieved when it turned to the fact that Luke and Serene were going to be sent on their first mission, accompanying a new captain and a band of the third and fourth years to witness the signing of peace treaties between a small village and the dryads who lived in a wood near them.

"You're going into the forest?" Elliot asked. "To talk to dryads? I want to go!"

"Right, Elliot, but you can't," Luke explained. "Because only those in war training go on missions, since they are the ones who can protect themselves. Those in council training stay where it's safe in camp, and go over the papers."

"All we want is your safety," Serene contributed.

"Do you hear what I'm saying, Elliot?" asked Luke. He sounded anxious. Elliot thought that was very wise.

"I do, Luke," he said, so earnestly that it made Rachel Sunborn laugh again. "I do hear what you're saying."

He didn't know why Serene and Luke had to act so surprised when they uncovered the supplies wagon on their mission and found that he had stowed away in it. He understood everyone else wandering around saying that they couldn't believe his behaviour, but he'd hoped they were coming to know him better than that.

He forgot that disappointment, and stopped paying attention to the lecture Captain Whiteleaf—who seemed a dull and unimaginative man—was giving him, when he looked around at the woods.

This far from the Border, there were harpies, like lion-sized eagles, pinwheeling in the sky. He could hear water trickling somewhere, and if he followed the sound he might find mermaids. There was light brimming around and wind rushing through the leaves of the trees, and as the leaves rustled together Elliot heard a few words in the wind, and knew it was not his imagination. He knew it was dryads.

Elliot forgot about the wonder of the woods when they bullied him into helping with the tents, despite his protests that he'd turned and walked out of the Boy Scouts when they told him that he had to make his bed every day.

Elliot spent a good deal of his time on the mission explaining that these living conditions were too horrible to be borne, and speculating on who would die of a chill first because nobody had proper medical care available in the otherlands.

Eventually Captain Whiteleaf gave him the treaties between the dryads of the Aegle Wood and the nearby village to shut him up, with the air of someone offering a toy to a child. "See, council-course people like papers," the captain might as well have said. "Lovely papers!"

"I wrote them myself," the captain said proudly. He was about twenty, and apparently thought swagger was the perfect cover for inexperience.

"After listening to the wisdom of your appointed councilors?" Elliot asked.

"Ah," said the captain, who Elliot heard had a very important father, a war hero in the fight against the evil saltwater mermaids. "Sure."

Then Captain Whiteleaf nodded happily and went off to hunt rabbits with the rest of the mission. Serene always brought home more than the captain or any of the others did: the older boys, Elliot noted, had grown more and more polite the more they saw her use her bow.

Elliot was huddled by the fire reading the papers over and over when he saw them coming back. He tried to make a note on some parchment, but that was when his pencil was finally reduced to nothing but splinters and a smear.

That was the last straw. He had no pencil, and must scream.

"Something's very wrong," he announced as Serene and Luke sat down.

"You're not going to die of a chill," said Luke. "I will give you my cloak if you promise to shut up."

"I may well die of a chill, I refuse to shut up, and I'll take your cloak," said Elliot. "But this isn't about that. Look at these papers."

Serene drew close to him and began to read them with some interest. Luke stared blankly.

"They're the treaties for the dryads and villagers to sign," he said. "There's one treaty, and there's the other. What's your point?"

"Sometimes people like to do this cool thing with words called 'reading them,'" Elliot explained. "These treaties say different things."

He looked toward Serene, who he had faith would understand, and saw the pin-scratch line of a frown between her dark eyebrows. "Considerably different," she observed.

"There are all sorts of restrictions in the dryads' contracts," said Elliot. "Conditions for this peace, ceding territory to the villagers, agreeing to stay off the villagers' paths while the villagers can go into their woods and chop down their trees."

"Well," said Luke. "Naturally they're going to be a bit different. The villagers are human, and the dryads aren't. I mean—it's not like the elves, who are practically human—"

"Speak for yourself," muttered Serene.

"The dryads are our allies, of course," Luke said hastily. "And they're not like—like the beast kind, like mermaids and harpies, they're good mostly, but they're a bit . . . well, different, you know?"

"They'd better be really different," said Elliot. "If someone gave me this treaty to sign, I wouldn't do it. I'd be insulted."

"You are insulted by people saying 'good morning,'" Luke pointed out.

Elliot paid no attention to this slander, thought for a few more minutes, and climbed to his feet. "I'm going to talk to the captain."

Serene got up silently to join him.

Luke said: "Oh no, no you are not."

"I am simply going to reason with him," said Elliot extremely reasonably.

"You chose to come on this mission, so you're a soldier. You cannot disobey your commanding officer on a mission."

"I'm not a soldier," said Elliot. "Not ever."

He looked around the woods, listened to the snap and crackle of the fire and the rustle of leaves that was dryads talking just beyond the cusp of human hearing. He let the magic calm him, and then he spoke again.

"I'm just going to talk to him and point out a few things that may have escaped his notice," he said. "There's no harm in that."

"Fine," said Luke. "Then I'm going with you two, to make sure that's all you do. This is no time for your stupid games. I mean it."

Elliot started to wonder whether they were brainwashing everyone in the war-training course to think alike when Captain Whiteleaf listened to Elliot's description of what was wrong with the two treaties and said: "Why do you think this is a good time for your stupid games?"

Elliot stood in the centre of the captain's tent, which Whiteleaf had set up to look like a miniature version of Commander Rayburn's office, complete with desk and candle, and stared.

"We want peace between these two peoples," he said. "A peace achieved like this won't hold."

"And how would you know?" the captain asked. "You're a child."

"I know because it's . . . really obvious?" said Elliot, and Luke gave the cough which was a signal for "Too insubordinate! Back up!"

"Look, one person chops down the wrong tree, and they're at war again," Elliot tried.

"Then they will break a peace negotiated by the Border guard," said Captain Whiteleaf. "And the guard will march back to deal with them."

"Right, okay," said Elliot. "But then people will die."

Captain Whiteleaf said: "So?"

Elliot stared some more. The captain was talking about how the guard kept the peace through their willingness to defend it with blades, and about how battle was a regrettable but necessary consequence of disobedience. Luke was coughing as if he actually had caught a chill. A beautiful peace was descending on Elliot: he knew precisely what he had to do.

He looked back at Serene, who was standing at the mouth of the tent. She met his eyes with her own tranquil gaze, drew her bow, and fitted an arrow to it.

"What are you doing?" Captain Whiteleaf snapped.

"If you call for someone to help stop him," Serene explained apologetically, "I will shoot them. In the leg, of course. I do not wish to murder any of my comrades."

"Stop what?" the captain demanded.

Elliot stepped forward and shoved the two treaties into the candle flame. The fire caught the parchment, curling it up with a rich thick crackle, and the flame leaped to show the sudden fury in the captain's eyes.

"You little brat," the captain breathed, raising his fist, and Elliot lifted his chin.

Luke drew his sword. The sharp edge glittered in the light of the burning papers, pointed across the desk at the captain. "Don't touch him."

Elliot took a deep shaky breath, relieved not to be hit and annoyed at how relieved he was.

"You pack of stupid, traitorous children—" Captain Whiteleaf began, and then he cut himself off and just glared at them, as if he was memorizing their faces and thinking of punishments to visit upon them.

Elliot knew what he saw. Serene at the tent with moonlight in her dark hair and her bow steady in her hands, Luke and his sword glinting in the candlelight, and Elliot. Elliot held firm. The treaties were ashes in his hands by now.

"Listen to me," said Elliot. "You don't bring councilors on your missions. So you don't have anyone who can write up a new treaty. Either you go back and admit you've failed in your mission, or you let me and Serene write up new treaties. We can do it."

"Elves remember everything that they read, down to the framework of the sentences to insure that treaties are binding," Serene observed. "Elliot tells me that is a helpful skill."

Captain Whiteleaf stared at the ashes, and then at Serene, and at Elliot.

Matters might have gone very differently, but this was the captain's first mission. He let them write out the treaties. The villagers signed theirs, and seemed to think the restrictions about not cutting down certain trees perfectly fair.

The dryads were beautiful, green-gleaming wraiths who leaned out of their trees like gorgeous women leaning casually out of windows. Elliot could not stop staring at them, or the way their leader smiled when she read the words he had written. She had not been smiling before: it was like sunlight dissolving mist when she did.

"We expected something quite different," she said. "I would be happy to sign this."

Elliot did not miss the faint emphasis she laid on *this.* It seemed like Captain Whiteleaf did not miss it either.

"You're still a pack of impossible brats," said Captain Whiteleaf on the ride home. "But I suppose you meant it for the best. This once, I will not report your wild behaviour to the commander."

He spurred his horse and rode to the front of the company.

"'Oh, thank you for saving my first mission,'" said Elliot. "'No, no, Captain Whiteleaf, it was my pleasure, please do not mention it, all this fulsome gratitude is so embarrassing!'"

"Shut up. That was really good of him," said Luke. "And the mission would have been fine if you hadn't destroyed the treaties like a maniac."

"Oh, *would* it?"

"I'm not saying—" said Luke. "You did the best you know how. You did a good thing. But they're just bits of paper, in the end. The

Border guard enforcing peace is what will keep people safe. Either way, the mission would have been successful."

Of course Luke didn't agree with him: Luke wasn't really his friend. It was all a bargain they had made.

Elliot looked to Serene for help, but her expression did not betray anything. Least of all whom she really agreed with, when it came right down to it.

"I'm glad we're not expelled," she said.

Neither of them seemed to realize how different it would have been if the spoiled son of an important man hadn't wanted their mission to go smoothly, or if the treaty had affected the Border camp directly—if they'd had something to gain—rather than involving a village and a community of dryads. Neither of them seemed to realize that an idiot like Captain Whiteleaf should not have had the last word on the treaty.

They had both stood up for what was right, when it counted. Elliot just wished that one of them would share his dark misgivings once in a while. He sometimes felt like the kid in the magic book who was always whining along the lines of "*Should* we go to find that giant ruby of ultimate magic, though? Isn't it dangerous?" Everyone knew that kid eventually turned evil.

Elliot did not have long to brood about how misunderstood and undervalued he was. As soon as they were back at the camp, everyone was panicking about exams, even Serene and Luke, who should really have known better. Elliot had to forcibly shepherd them to the library and make piles of what he'd decided was the assigned reading.

"Now, loser, let's start with the basics," Elliot added kindly once he was done telling them the list. "This is a book. You open it like this, see? Not along the spine. That's very important."

Luke made an impolite gesture behind his book.

They all did extremely well in their exams, and Elliot was happy until he heard Serene making plans to come stay at Luke's over the summer holiday.

"You can come too, if you want," said Luke. "My mum will probably be expecting you. I don't know why."

"I guess if Serene's going to be there," said Elliot. "And since the year's not up yet, the truce isn't quite over."

"Fine," Luke snapped.

"Great," said Elliot.

First, though, he had to go home. Captain Woodsinger escorted Elliot and the very few other kids from the human world who had stayed back through the hole in the wall. She left them to walk down the steps on their own, down and down, until they reached the real world.

Elliot lifted his eyes to the horizon of the real world, a line of tall buildings standing against the sky, all metal and glass. He realized he had become rather used to the endless fields.

At home every day was the same, just as it had always been. His dad would come home late, when the day was already getting dark and cold, and put his briefcase down neatly on the table in the hall. They would sit at either ends of the polished rectangular table, and eat dinner. Conversations would stop and start, escaping from Elliot's hands like a balloon in the wind. That was how conversations with his father made him feel: as if he were a little kid, surprised every time at the loss.

Elliot had become all kinds of dumb and unguarded at the Border camp, though, because one day when his father went and poured himself his first glass, Elliot did not go away to his room and read a book.

It wasn't that his father ever got angry, or ever hit him. It was just that it was like sitting in a room where all the air was escaping, to stay in a room with a man who was grimly, methodically drinking: to know that he had once been happy and never would be again.

"What was Mum like?" asked Elliot, who had truly grown stupid at the camp if he was asking that.

His father looked out the window, where gray shadows were snatching away the very last of the light.

"She was the first thing I saw when I walked into a room," he said at last. "And once I saw her, I never wanted to look anywhere else. She would speak, and whatever she said was brilliant and startling. She was like that, a constant bright surprise. She was always talking, always laughing, always dancing, and she was never what I expected. I was even surprised when she left." He looked over at Elliot, who was sitting with his hands clenched tight around his knees. "You're not like her," he added. "You're like me. Nobody will ever love you enough to stay."

His father was very thin. Even his hair was thin, gray strands so fine that it seemed as if it had been worn away, as the grooves in his face seemed to have been worn in. Elliot wasn't sure, sometimes, if he was like his father: the patient, desperate ghost who had waited until all hope was worn out. He couldn't imagine his father going to school and antagonizing everyone in sight, being too short, too smart, too awkward, too unguarded, too wildly unused to company, until it was easier eventually to antagonize people on purpose.

His mother had stayed with his dad for ages. She'd left pretty soon after Elliot had arrived. Elliot could do the maths.

He supposed it didn't matter if someone left because you weren't good enough or left because you actually drove them away. The result was the same.

He left the room quietly, went and sat on the stairs, pressed his hot face against the cool banister. He could see through the staircase at this angle, could see the front door, flanked by windows that shone with gray light. He sat and looked at the door as if someone were coming home.

Nothing changed, not permanently. Elliot had known that even when the miracle happened, and he was taken away to somewhere fantastical. Every bit of reality in the fantasy reminded him that miracles were not for him.

Even if you found yourself in a magical story, there were no guarantees that you were the hero, or that you would get the things you dreamed of. Elliot knew no way, being who he was, to deserve that.

No questions were raised about him going to the Sunborns' house. Elliot's father was too glad to have him go to ask questions. Elliot caught his father looking at him measuringly a few times in the days before he left. He suspected that his father might be puzzled at the idea of anyone wanting Elliot's company: that was fair.

Luke had drawn Elliot a map for how to get to the Sunborns' ancestral home once Elliot came over the wall. Luke had offered to come get him, but Elliot had haughtily declined and said that he could certainly find his own way.

This meant it was absolutely crucial to Elliot's pride that he not get lost.

It was meant to be half a day's walk—walking the way you do, Luke had said, which was insulting and unkind—so Elliot started the walk early in the morning. That meant leaving his father's house before his father was awake, which was a bonus.

Before he left, he packed a bag. He put in pencils, pencil sharpeners, pens, and highlighters. He gave it some thought, then added Sharpies, Post-Its, and a glue gun. Just in case. He considered bringing flash cards, but he knew he was going on holiday and not to a place of education, and he didn't want to go overboard.

He had to double back when he realized he'd forgotten to pack clean underwear.

Elliot took a car down to the wall. He paid the cab driver, who looked dubious about leaving a child alone in a field, but Elliot had spun him what he felt was a very convincing story about rare rock formations and being a keen geologist. The cab driver certainly seemed convinced he did not want to hear any more about rare rock formations. Elliot put his hands in his pockets and watched him drive away.

Then he climbed the wall on his own, took the trip into the clouds and back down to the otherlands. It felt strange walking past the track that led to the Border camp: Elliot's feet seemed to want to go there, against all reason.

He walked on through the woods nevertheless. He looked around for dryads and harpies, but found nothing. He darkly suspected Luke of plotting a boring route to his house, just to spoil Elliot's fun.

Being annoyed at Luke was a good distraction from being nervous about going to Luke's house. Elliot did not know how to be around a proper family. He might have managed all right at the picnic, but he was meant to stay here for days. They would all realize that he had no idea what to do.

He followed the directions, which came with helpful drawings of trees, almost mechanically. He was worried enough that he almost did not realize when he arrived.

In the midst of moors and woodland was a tower, in the same brief, round style as the towers at the Border camp, looking like nothing so much as the rooks in the chess set his father had gathering dust in a cabinet. There was ivy climbing up it in cascading green profusion over places where the stone was jagged and worn. Elliot stuffed Luke's map into his pocket and climbed the broad, flat steps.

From within the Sunborns' tower came the loud sound of swearing. Elliot broke into a run.

The swearing was coming from a cavernous kitchen, where Rachel Sunborn was wrestling a stewpot. Half the stew was already on the wall.

"Um, let me help you with that," said Elliot, and grabbed the other handle. The pot tipped dangerously down to Elliot's level, but they got it on the ground.

"Thank you, Elliot," said Rachel. "I bloody hate cooking, but Michael's on campaign, and what are you going to do? Welcome, by the way."

"If Mr Sunborn is gone, aren't we going to be a lot of trouble?" Elliot asked apprehensively.

"Oh no," said Rachel. "We all go on campaigns, and the one on leave gets the kids. We always have Louise's friends over, and this summer we have my sister's boys, Adam and Neal, staying too. You guys can distract each other. And frankly, it's my turn for a houseful of kids: Michael had Luke at the Northmark fortress from when he was nine to when he got sent off to camp. I was on an expedition to traverse the entire otherlands. It was meant to be a two-year mission, but it ran long."

"The DeWitt mission, led by the explorer from my world," said Elliot enthusiastically. "The one that improved all the maps! How was finding an entire lagoon full of mermaids? I wish I could meet a mermaid."

"Kid, they drown people."

Elliot waved this off. "Is it true that the river mermaids have a common tongue but the mermaids who live in lakes have all entirely separate languages, though they can usually speak the language of the people who live near the lakes, and the saltwater mermaids seem to only speak the languages most common to sailors? Do you think the sea mermaids do have their own language but only use it in the deep? Because that's what I think."

Rachel threw back her head and laughed. "How would I know, funnyface? But I can harpoon a mermaid at a hundred paces from a moving boat. Not bad for an old lady, eh?"

"How old are Adam and Neal?" asked Elliot.

Rachel frowned in thought. The expression was not made for her face: it slid off the golden surface like water. "Close to your age," she said. "A year and two years older, about." Elliot must have made a face without meaning to—he'd been hoping for as old as Louise, which was old enough to not bother with Elliot much—because Rachel laughed at it. "Don't worry, you'll like them!" she said. "They're just like Luke."

"Oh," said Elliot. "That's fantastic."

"Bit more outgoing than my shy boy, but that's all to the good," said Rachel. "I think it's nice for Luke to have his own friends here. You're all going to have fun! Don't let anyone dare you to jump off a tower, though."

"Don't worry," said Elliot. "Luke's not shy. Everyone likes Luke." "Except me," he would have added, but it seemed rude when he was a guest.

Rachel frowned again, this time more deeply, a woman even less used to explaining herself than frowning. "Maybe that was the wrong word," she said. "But you know how he is. My point is, Neal and Adam are lovely lads. I'm sure you'll all get on. And Serene, when she gets here. Luke's crazy about Serene."

"Serene's not here?" Elliot asked. "Where's Serene?!"

"Oh, her mother took her on a hunting party for a magical stag, or somesuch."

This was a complete disaster. Elliot wondered if he could claim that he'd left the oven on at home and make his escape.

This fragile, beautiful hope was crushed when Luke barreled into the house, calling for his mother and attended by vicious animals.

"Mum!" said Luke. "When do you think he'll get—oh. Hi."

"Hi," said Elliot. He should probably, as a guest, not insult Luke in front of Luke's mother.

"Why are you wearing those clothes?" Luke asked. "They're weird. The Border camp gave you proper clothes."

"Because, A: these are my clothes," Elliot said. "B: the Border camp gave me ridiculous clothes, and C: I cannot believe that you, a loser who I have literally never seen wear anything but leather, are setting yourself up to be some sort of fashion expert and critiquing jeans and a hoodie. Worst host ever!" He glanced over at Rachel. "Not you, you're a very charming hostess," he added hastily.

"Thank you, Elliot," Rachel told him.

The two wild beasts Luke had brought in with him—into the house, in fact into the area of the house were food was prepared—wandered over to Elliot. Their long, plumy tails waved cautiously: their long, sharp teeth were bared.

"I haven't had my rabies shot," said Elliot, circling. The dogs circled after him in what he considered was a menacing fashion.

"How can you be scared of the puppies?" Rachel asked.

"I am not scared of them," Elliot replied with dignity. "I am just not accustomed to them, so I do not trust them."

He had to admit that the dogs did not seem currently interested in devouring him whole. However, this might change at any moment.

"Cavall, Culaine," said Luke, and the dogs backed off a little. "You like mermaids and centaurs and stuff, though."

"They're not animals," said Elliot. "I can talk with them, so they're people. I enjoy intelligent conversation. You know, the polysyllabic kind. I realize you're still at monosyllables, but I have faith you'll get there one day."

"Uh-huh," said Luke, not doing anything to justify said faith.

Elliot regarded the dogs with suspicion, then glanced up at Luke, who was looking at him. It was a moment of mutual embarrassment: they were not used to being without Serene, and yet they should obviously pretend to be friends, or Luke's mother would wonder why Elliot was here.

"The thing is," Elliot announced. "I think I left the oven on in—"

"Mum," said Luke, rudely interrupting. "Can we have the key to the library?"

"The library?" Elliot asked, diverted from his purpose.

"My Great-Uncle Theodore was wounded in the Wars of the Rainbow Serpents and couldn't fight again, so he spent his whole life collecting books," Rachel said. "Poor old boy. Don't let the dogs in with you, Luke."

She took a ring, heavy with keys, off the wide belt slung around her hips, and tossed it to Luke, who caught it easily, and Elliot followed him as he went out of the kitchen and round and round and round the stairs to the very top of the tower, where they stopped at a large oak door.

The library was as big as the one at school, but quieter, with the air of long disuse. Sun streamed through half-closed curtains, and the air was thick with sunlight and silence, with gold and dust. Books rose to the ceiling, which rose to a point, with ladders that leaned against the walls.

"Is it OK to touch the books without gloves?"

"Why would you need gloves to touch a book?" Luke asked. Elliot decided that meant yes.

He climbed one of the ladders to get to one glinting embossed spine, to see if it could possibly be what he hoped it was going to be. It was.

He climbed down the ladder to display his prize to Luke.

"*1,000 Leagues Across a Sea of Blood*," Luke said. "That's a good title."

The subtitle was *Sea Monsters Demanding Sacrifice, Fanged Octopi & Murderous Mermaids I Have Known.*

"It's the account of a famous exploring party told by Maximilian Wavechaser. This voyage is how his family got their name," Elliot explained, going over to the window and pulling the curtains open. He climbed onto the broad wooden windowseat built into the window, which was many-paned and also rose to a point, like a window in church. Luke climbed up to sit on the other side, and Elliot turned the pages until he found some of the drawings of the great naval battle four hundred years ago, made out in cerulean and gold, which he thought Luke would like.

In return Luke said that he did think it was possible that the mermaids of the deep sea communicated through hand gestures rather than speech, and asked Elliot to read the awful bit about battle tactics again. There were accounts of notable seafaring voyages undertaken in the last century at the end, including the journey led by Captain

Whiteleaf's father twenty years ago. It was a long and fascinating book, and Elliot was surprised when Luke said that he had to set the table for dinner.

"Have you boys been in the library all day?" Rachel asked, amazed. She ruffled Luke's hair as he went by with the cutlery. "Who are you?"

"Elliot found a good book," Luke said.

"I didn't miraculously find the only book in there that was good," Elliot argued.

Luke gave a tiny shrug. "I don't know that. I've looked at other books in that library, and they're boring."

"You don't know anything," Elliot told him severely. "Statistically, you have to see that book being the only good one is not at all likely. The problem is you don't get books. You tend to be an auditory or kinesthetic learner."

"Hey!" said Luke.

Elliot was going to tell him that it wasn't an insult, but then he decided it would be more hilarious not to. "I wish I had a radio," he said. "They do readings of the classics on Sunday afternoons."

"What's a radio?" asked Rachel, while Luke sulked about being called a kinesthetic learner.

Elliot gave some thought about how to describe it. "It's a magic box that says stuff and plays songs."

"A music box?" Luke asked, scornfully. "We have music boxes."

"No!" said Elliot. "It plays quite different songs." He thought about the classic hits he listened to at home, filling his whole empty house with song, something that a mother might like, and sang a few lines of "When I'm Sixty-Four." Rachel beat time on the lid of her pot.

"You have a nice voice, kid," she said. "You could be a minstrel."

"Oh, thank God, there are other jobs for people besides being a weird conscripted soldier on the Border camp," Elliot said. "Logically there had to be, someone has to make the food, the world would be stupid and make no sense otherwise. But I was terrified it was all dumb killing people in the face."

"Excuse you?" said a voice from the door. "Being a soldier is the noblest profession in the world."

"Killing people in the face is a downside," Elliot said. "You have to admit that. I'm Elliot Schafer, by the way."

"Adam Sunborn," said the boy, marching in. "And this is my brother, Neal."

The two boys clattered in, walking as if they owned the room and possibly the world. They were Sunborns, clear as a fine day: big and blond and blue-eyed. They looked like practise sketches of Luke, before the artist had got him right. They spent all of dinnertime talking about how they hadn't gone to the Border camp because they had been born and raised to fight, and Luke shouldn't have either but should have come to serve in one of the lesser fortresses with them and learned through action.

"He could have been our comrade-in-arms," said Neal.

"I've got one," said Luke. "Her name's Serene."

"A girl?" Adam sneered.

"I think you should meet her," said Luke, deceptively mild.

"I don't think you need any more of this delicious stew, Adam," said Rachel.

"I deplore violence in all its forms," said Elliot. "But she'd kick your ass."

"Why wait until Serene's here?" inquired Louise, coming in late and mussed with her dark-haired friend, who would have been very pretty standing beside anyone but Louise. "I'll kick both the brats off the tower as soon as dinner's over."

Louise spoke with friendly menace, and Rachel hit Adam's hand when he reached for more food with a spoon. Neal and Adam didn't pursue an argument, but Elliot saw their darkling look at him when he spoke, and knew they did not like him.

He hadn't expected them to.

The next day Elliot figured that Luke would probably wish to do one of the awful things he enjoyed, something outside involving weaponry, and so like an excellent and considerate guest he decided to entertain himself.

Since he was pretty sure Luke would expect him to be in the library, Elliot acquired a book and cunningly hid out of doors. He wandered around the woods for a little while until he found a tree that he thought looked appropriate and comfortable, then carefully stowed his chosen book into his hoodie and climbed up into it.

He was reading peacefully for an hour or so in the green-glowing quiet, until he heard the sound of twigs snapping underfoot and bodies shoving through the undergrowth. He looked down and saw the glint of two blond heads, and Adam Sunborn looking up at him.

"Well, well," he said. "Look, Neal. There's a snotty little bird up in a tree."

"That's not a terribly good insult," said Elliot. "The mixed metaphors, with the bird and the snotty thing, it doesn't work. Maybe if you'd just called me obnoxious. Wait, I'm sorry, should I define obnoxious for you?"

He was not terribly surprised when Adam grabbed one of the lower-hanging branches. He expected him to climb up, but instead Adam shook it violently. Elliot clutched his book protectively and fell out of the tree.

Falling out of the tree was extremely unpleasant. A branch bashed him on the face on his way down, he hit his head, and his whole body felt jarred by the stupid ground. Elliot levered himself up on one elbow.

"Wow," he said, tasting blood in his mouth. "That was a witty retort. I certainly have learned the error of my ways, and that I should hold you in far higher regard!"

Adam strode toward him, and Elliot was just considering whether he was going to get punched or kicked when Luke emerged from the trees and knocked Adam off course.

"Where have you been?" Elliot demanded.

"Looking for you!" Luke snapped back. "How was I supposed to know you were off hiding in trees, you lunatic?"

"Don't be rude to me when you're rescuing me, loser," Elliot told him. "That's terrible manners. You're the worst."

Luke made an incoherent sound of rage, which for some reason seemed to encourage Adam Sunborn, who moved toward Elliot. Luke held up a hand.

"You're not doing it!" said Luke. "Where's the honor in hurting someone who's not as strong as you? What does that prove?"

"It might stop him being such a brat," Adam suggested.

"Doesn't," Elliot contributed. "This is not the first time somebody's ever wanted to punch me in the face."

Luke frowned for some reason, but supported him by saying: "That is obviously true. He's extremely annoying."

"See, you two are not original souls. Kids at my old school used to hit me all the time, I have collected the data on this subject, and I am in the perfect position to tell you that it has no useful results whatsoever. It just means I'm bleeding as well as annoying."

"Also, the value of someone does not rely on their ability to hurt others," said Luke. "You guys aren't proving you're better than him if you knock him out of a tree."

Neal's lip curled as he looked down at the ground where Elliot was still lying. It didn't seem a great idea to get up, when the two Sunborn cousins were obviously dying to knock him down again, plus his head and his face hurt. Elliot touched his mouth, and his fingers came away red.

Neal said: "What value does he have, exactly?"

Luke had to give it some thought, which Elliot found offensive. Eventually, he said: "He's clever about some things. And he makes up songs."

"No, I don't," said Elliot, even more vastly offended.

"Yes, you do," said Luke. "You sang the song to me and Mum."

"That was not my song," said Elliot. "That song belongs to the Beatles."

Luke rolled his eyes. "Elliot, beetles do not write songs."

"Uh, do you guys *mind*?" Adam demanded.

"Oh, I'm sorry, are we not paying enough attention to you loathsome weasel bullies?" Elliot inquired. "Do you feel your dignity as someone who pushes little kids out of trees is somehow being slighted?"

"You're not a little kid, Elliot," said Luke.

"I'm considerably below average height!" Elliot snapped.

"Oh my God, what a little snot," exclaimed Adam, and surged forward. Luke was suddenly in his way, pushing him back with a small shove that obviously made Adam more mad.

Violence was like that, Elliot had noticed. One move toward it and all at once everything was allowed: anyone could be hurt, out of a mix of pride and anger and stupid disregard for the fact that you could be hurt as easily as someone else.

"You think you can take both of us?" Adam asked.

A corner of Luke's mouth kicked up. "Yeah," he admitted. "I really think I can."

Neal started forward, then stopped abruptly because the end of a whip had sailed out from among the trees and curled itself around his wrist.

"I do not like to hit a gentleman," Serene said, emerging from behind a screen of leaves, "but since you are responsible for shedding the blood of the defenceless, I am prepared to make an exception."

"Serene!" Elliot exclaimed. "You're here! And you're my hero!"

He was fully prepared to swoon.

"You're the elf girl, then?" asked Neal Sunborn.

"I am Serene-Heart-in-the-Chaos-of-Battle. Keep a civil tongue in your head or lose it."

Neal and Adam stared at her.

"Are you going to make your name known to me, knaves?" Serene asked dangerously.

"Neal Sunborn," said Neal, getting a look that Elliot had seen before on the faces of boys in the war-training course about to be soundly beaten by Serene: both hunted and smitten. "This is my brother, Adam."

"I've been meaning to ask," Elliot said conversationally to Luke. "If they're your mum's sister's kids, how are they Sunborns too?"

Serene frowned. "It makes perfect sense. Of course the children bear their mother's name. The woman is the strong one, who bears the child and begins the family. You can't be sure who any child's father is."

Elliot considered. "That's a good point, actually. It's why the Egyptians married their sisters."

"I don't know that family," Serene said, "but that does not seem to me like a good solution."

Adam and Neal looked defeated by the whole situation—having to fight a girl who was looking pityingly down on them, and the way people kept having conversations without including them. When Luke began to explain that while actually a lot of men took the Sunborn name when they married Sunborn women—having met Rachel and Louise, Elliot thought he understood—his mother and father were both born Sunborns, from different branches of the family, because the Sunborns were a vast clan and long might their glory shine, so on et cetera. Which made Serene start talking about the house of Chaos.

At which point, Adam and Neal gave up and simply slunk away.

The rest of the stay at Luke's house, graced with Serene's shining presence, was rather nice. There was sunlight and the woods and Rachel Sunborn, and the dogs proved to be all right after all—Culaine was Elliot's favorite. Sometimes everybody would get together and play terrible games, like throwing knives at trees who had done nobody any wrong. Elliot would fetch a book at those times, but he was obscurely gratified to see that either Luke or Serene always won.

The only real problem came at the end of the holiday, when Rachel and Louise Sunborn had to ride away with a border patrol in order to deal with a gang of brigands who were waylaying people on the northern roads.

She and her men were gone all day, and still gone when it was time for bed.

Elliot finished his book in bed and pondered going to get another one. He only had so much time left, and he had so many books to get through. He slipped out of bed, and as he was making his way to the library he stopped to investigate the fact that a candle was still burning in Luke's room.

"What are you doing here," said Luke in a flat voice, who was staring at the ceiling. Elliot didn't see why he needed a candle to look at the ceiling. It wasn't going anywhere.

Elliot came to a decision. "I've come to bother you."

"Isn't it enough to bother me every day, all day? Do you have to bother me through the night as well?"

"Yes. You shouldn't sleep with animals, I'm sure it's unsanitary. Come here, Culaine," said Elliot, and when both dogs shuffled over across the bedclothes to be patted, Elliot pushed Cavall gently away. "Not you. Culaine's my favorite."

Luke sat up. His blond hair was sticking straight up: he looked like an offended dandelion. "They're both good dogs. You can't have a favorite."

"Of course I can, loser," said Elliot. "I'm very judgmental."

The door creaked open and Serene stood in it, looking severe and beautiful in her sensible black pajamas. "Oh good, you're here," she said to Elliot. "You can administer manly sympathies and sweet comfort."

"I could," said Elliot haughtily, "but I have no intention of doing so."

"I was worried that you would be fretting, Luke," Serene continued. "I know how boys do."

"Get out of my room, both of you," said Luke, and put a pillow over his own face.

Serene climbed up on the bed as well, and entered into an argument with Elliot about which was the finer dog. Serene thought Cavall was the best at hunting: Elliot was firm in his conviction that he did not care.

When the riders came home from battle it was so late the darkness was turning to light again, as if the moon had dissolved in the sky and flooded it with pale radiance. They rode home victorious, and Serene and Luke ran downstairs with the rest of the household.

Elliot stood at Luke's window and saw the torchlight falling on triumphant, desperate, and grieving faces alike, saw Luke, Neal and Adam in a cluster of children relieved their parents were safe. He saw Rachel Sunborn with her gold-ringed fist raised in triumph, and Louise with her hair shining like gold on the horse beside her mother. He saw the empty saddles of those who had not come home.

He said, aloud into the night wind and with no one to hear: "I find war very annoying."

Everyone else seemed to think that the whole situation was perfectly all right, because the Sunborns had prevailed. It put Elliot into a terrible mood.

Not too long after, it was time to go back home. Rachel talked cheerfully about how much she was sure they would enjoy the second year of camp at the Border: more swordplay, larger bows. There would be piles of weapons, which was about as enticing a prospect to Elliot as piles of cat poop.

Everyone sat around the table and discussed how much they were looking forward to weapons. Everyone looked happy, looked excited: looked as if they could not ask for anything more than a battle won.

This world was stupid, and everyone in it was stupid. Elliot was stupid, too, for being happy in this house full of stupid people who were all going to get themselves killed. He shouldn't even be here. Luke wasn't even his friend.

"And are you looking forward to camp, dear?" Rachel asked Elliot, beaming but vague. Elliot suspected she had no idea what went on in the council-training course at all.

"Sure," said Elliot, and when Rachel was no longer paying attention but Luke still was, he added: "Truce is over then. I'll finally have peace and quiet."

11

ELLIOT, AGE FOURTEEN

Elliot had to go home before he could go back to the Border. He spent another week with his father in his chair with his constantly empty glass, the kids down the road still on holiday, and his bags already packed.

It wasn't just because he wanted to go, though he did want to go. His packing was also extremely complex. Elliot had decided to think bigger than Sharpies.

It was a long week. Even though the Border camp was a heathen hellhole dedicated to martial law, and even though he was carrying way too much stuff, Elliot felt his shoulders relax under his heavy burdens when he went over the wall and walked until he saw familiar fields, short towers, rough wood cabins and brown and blue tents.

He felt in a good enough mood to wave to some of the students he recognized. Myra and Peter gave him a weird look and a wide berth, but Elliot thought that was more because some of his bags were starting to crackle and pop than that they didn't like him anymore. His back was starting to feel uncomfortably warm: Elliot hoped it was his muscles being overtaxed, but he twisted his head around to look. Maybe the smoke was rising from a nearby campfire or something.

He looked back around and up into Luke's face.

"Elliot, give me that bag," said Luke.

"Why are you bothering me, loser?" Elliot demanded imperiously. "Especially when I clearly have everything under control."

"People can literally see you for miles," said Luke. "Captain Woodsinger is clearing the area!"

Elliot waved his hand, partially to indicate his airy lack of concern and partially to dissipate the smoke. "I'm not responsible for other people being fussbudgets."

"You look like a snail that's about to explode," Luke said and made a grab for one of his bags. Elliot gave a pterodactyl screech of protest.

Luke stepped out of range of Elliot's grab and studied the bag. It did seem to be melting at the bottom a tiny bit. "What have you got in here?"

"None of your business, loser. You know, you are not the first bully to ever snatch my bag from me, and I think keepaway is a terrible game, so—"

Elliot had noticed that referencing his previous schooldays often made Luke give him his way, but apparently not this time.

"Bet I'm the first bully who snatched your bag that was *about to explode*," said Luke, and started to spin the bag by its strap.

"Don't throw it!" Elliot wailed as Luke whirled it over his head and threw it with all his might.

As soon as the bag hit the ground, it loudly burst into flame.

Elliot winced. "That'd be the microwave. In retrospect, the microwave was a mistake."

"What's a microwave?" Luke asked.

"Clearly some kind of volatile explosive weapon," Serene deduced, strolling up to them and eyeing the small fire in the distance with her usual aplomb. "Elliot, you really must leave handling weapons to the experts."

After the explosions and everything, it seemed odd to remind Luke that according to the terms of the truce he could now stop hanging around so much. Besides which, sometimes Elliot said stuff when he was annoyed that he later didn't mean as much as he'd thought he did at the time. Elliot realized the truce was working in his favor; he had no confidence that if Serene had to choose which of them to hang out with, it would definitely be Elliot. And Luke and Serene were both excelling in all their history and geography and mathematical courses, and if he didn't watch them they might slip. He supposed he didn't mind so very much.

Being fourteen wouldn't be so different from being thirteen, Elliot thought.

~

It took him less than a week to realise how very wrong he was.

The absolute worst thing about being fourteen was that almost everyone else's interest in girls had caught fire and caught up with Elliot's at last, and thus Elliot was no longer the only one actively wooing Serene. Though he did flatter himself that he had got the head start, and made real progress. Plus he was easily the most cunning person in the entire training camp, and had several cunning courtship plans.

He put one of them into action at one of their lunchtimes, when Serene had once more been waylaid by other boys. They were always offering to teach her how to do this or that warlike thing which Serene already did better than them, it made Elliot feel extremely unwell. But Serene was very patient with them. She even seemed to like it.

She was standing near the food buffets with her tray empty and the small discreet elven smile on her face directed toward other men, and Elliot decided he could bear it no longer.

"When Serene gets here," Elliot informed Luke, "you have to compliment her."

"What?" asked Luke blankly.

"I'd do it," said Elliot. "In fact, I'm going to do it, I doubt I can restrain myself, she's a perfect elven being. But I compliment her all the time; it doesn't have the same impact coming from me."

"What?" asked Luke, even more blankly.

"Do you want her to leave us?" Elliot asked. "Is that what you want?"

"What?" said Luke. The blankness was now inscribed, as on a white page with red pen: "What horrifying thing are you saying, Elliot? What are you trying to imply?"

"What if she wants to sit at someone else's lunch table?" Elliot asked. "Some other table where she receives the adulation that is her due. If I am deprived of my only love and have nothing to do but stare at your stupid face, I'll stop eating and probably go into a decline."

"Serene's not going to leave us," said Luke. "She and I are sword-brothers. Well, you know what I mean. We swore an oath on a blade and shared blood. It's a warrior thing. You wouldn't understand."

Elliot understood enough to feel hurt and left out, so he said: “Please do not discuss swapping bodily fluids with Serene in public. She is a lady! And ladies need to be wooed with soft words.”

Luke made a face. “I’m not randomly complimenting Serene. That’s weird.”

“It isn’t weird, it’s an ingenious scheme in which I thought outside the box and decided that the devilish competition I know and can keep an eye on is better than the devilish competition I don’t. Why are you being so difficult, Luke? I know you like Serene, so what is the problem with verbally expressing your appreciation? Why are you upsetting me?”

“Why are you upsetting *me*?”

“Why would flawless logic upset you, Luke? That makes no sense. If you don’t want to do this simple thing for me, I don’t think I want to eat my extra pudding anymore.”

“Fine,” said Luke. “I don’t want you to keep taking my pudding anyway. I never said you could. I like pudding.”

Elliot was Boy Scout levels of prepared to argue the matter further, but just then Serene arrived with her lunch tray, arrayed with the usual elvegetarian fare of lettuce, various vegetables, and flowers, plus her own pudding, because Serene had been corrupted by their disgusting human ways.

“Hello, flower in the garden of my heart and nightlight of my soul,” said Elliot.

“Elliot, Luke,” said Serene.

Elliot was pleased: he privately kept track of when Serene said Elliot’s name first. But then Serene chose to sit on Luke’s side of the table, which cancelled out the names and left them at a draw.

“Hi, Serene,” said Luke.

Elliot coughed and ostentatiously pushed away Luke’s pudding.

Luke rolled his eyes and frowned. “Serene. Your, um, dagger work was seriously exceptional today.”

“Why, thank you, Luke,” said Serene, gracing him with a small smile. She and Luke fist-bumped: Elliot supposed it was a *sword-brothers* thing.

“Really, daggers? Really? You are useless. You are entirely without use,” Elliot announced, but since Serene seemed satisfied with Luke’s pathetic effort, and he believed even pathetic efforts should be met with rewards to encourage improvement, he deigned to reach over and draw the pudding back to his side of the table.

Serene still got lessons with Captain Woodsinger occasionally, when the dark, serious captain felt they were required. Every time Serene went to see Captain Woodsinger, she came back a little steadier and more certain of her course. Elliot could not grudge Serene that, and could not be anything but grateful to the captain, even if he missed Serene's company.

Luke was still oddly around at those times, when he didn't have Trigon practise. Elliot wanted to question why Luke was hanging around, but he remembered Rachel Sunborn calling Luke her shy boy and thought it was true that Luke did not like his familiar routines changing or spending time with anyone but familiar people. Elliot supposed it was habit, even though Luke had a dozen other places he could be. He refrained from pointing this out to Luke and instead kindly spent their time together educating Luke about history. Luke was learning very little about it in his warrior training.

"The Border guard were initially a far less military operation," Elliot explained. "Records indicate that long ago the relationship between the military and their councilors was mostly equitable, with diplomats and soldiers working together to find solutions for their people."

"So that didn't last?" said Luke. "Because it didn't work?"

Elliot's eyes narrowed. "It was only as time passed, and the other species militarized in response to the humans, that councilors became the largely useless and disrespected body they are now. Basically, the military *crushed* their *spirits*."

He stopped declaiming from his position on his bunk to give Luke an accusatory glare.

"Yeah," said Luke. "I can see the spirit of every future councilor I know is really crushed."

Elliot hit Luke in the head with a pillow. Elliot was not used to administering violence, and he slightly misjudged the force he needed to use. Feathers exploded everywhere: all over the floor, the beds, themselves. Everywhere. It was like a feather-based apocalypse.

"This would not have happened if I were in my own world," said Elliot sadly. "In my world we have pillows and mattresses made of foam."

"I like feathers," said Luke calmly.

Elliot scowled at him. "That's a weird thing to like, loser." He sighed, thinking of the lost luxuries of civilization. "The best kind of foam is called memory foam."

Luke frowned. "How does foam remember things?"

"Don't make me talk about it," said Elliot. "I will only get upset. I am upset enough that I am going to be finding feathers in my hair for weeks. Maybe months. Maybe years. You don't understand what it's like. It's not just that it's bizarre and pumpkin colored. It has the texture of a tangle of fried worms."

Luke suppressed a smile. Elliot thought smiling when other people were suffering was a terrible sign of sadism and Luke should be ashamed. Though Luke did win some points back for mercy, since he helped Elliot with the emergency feather removal.

"It's okay that it's—bright," said Luke. "It means I can find you, when you're in trouble."

"I don't know why you would suggest the possibility of me being in trouble," said Elliot. "Because I am a retiring and bookish individual, and I don't like being in trouble, in danger, or in proximity to weapons. You will never find me in trouble. You will find me in the library. If you can remember where that is."

Luke looked prepared to argue this, though Elliot was so clearly in the right, but just then Elliot's roommates came back. They all greeted Luke with smiles and welcome, and when Luke was gone they all said very firmly that he was not allowed to come back.

"No more weird scenes with your friends," said Richard Plantgrown. "No more weird stunts with knives. We are all very tired. None of us slept well last year. This year we need to be sharper in battle, and we need to be able to focus on important things, like impressing the ladies."

"I don't know why you think it's my fault you can't impress the ladies," said Elliot. "Much more likely to be your personalities, or possibly the way this world has no way to disguise persistent body odor. Have you considered that?"

His roommates clearly did not feel Elliot was being helpful.

Being fourteen meant that if Elliot wanted to spend more time with Serene—which obviously he did, since she was the rose in the flower crown of the world—or Luke—which, all right, he did, though it was an embarrassing admission to make even in the privacy of his own mind—he had to do it outside his cabin. Elliot gave up on making friends with anyone in his cabin, and spent even more time in the library.

Their advanced age meant they were accorded certain privileges, like access to the lake that had been out of bounds for thirteen-year-olds. Elliot wanted to ask if fourteen-year-olds were really much less likely to drown than thirteen-year-olds, but Luke and Serene had urged him not to do so.

Apparently they liked the lake.

Elliot did not like the lake.

He would have liked a different lake, full of shadows and with leaves hanging above the water and whispering secrets to each other. This lake was crowded with people, and they were barely wearing any clothes and celebrating their discovery of hormones.

The first Saturday they were allowed to go down to the lake, Serene was immediately separated from them and surrounded by a crowd of boys clamoring to get to be the one who taught her how to swim. Apparently the elven way was more about floating and communing with the spirits.

Serene laughed and held court to indulge the forward human boys. Elliot sniffed and skulked off to secure himself a sunbed (sunbeds in this backward land were basically old wooden bedframes, but beggars could not be choosers) in the shade. He had cleverly chosen a large and fascinating-looking book about mermaid customs, and planned to be wrapped up in it all day. He had been saving it for just such an occasion.

The way girls did their flirting was different.

There were far fewer girls than boys in the Border camp, and they seemed to want to gather in groups, not around a lone boy like the boys crowded around Serene (like lions around an antelope that had been cut off from the rest of the herd, Elliot thought bitterly). The herd of girls looked at the boys, selected one, looked at him and discussed him. And the boys didn't quite dare approach the whole group of girls, so they formed their own group and then the two groups were in a stand-off that involved a lot of casual hair-tossing and muscle-flexing.

Presumably rebels from both sides would break away and unite at some stage. Elliot's plan was to do his reading.

None of the girls were whispering or staring at *him*: stupid war training had given most of the other guys a lot more to flex, and even the few other guys in council training did not have the short issue, or the ginger issue, or the prickly-like-the-unholy-offspring-of-a-hedgehog-and-a-cactus issue to contend with. And Elliot's heart was pledged to Serene forever, anyway, so he didn't care. But he still wasn't taking his shirt off so the girls could actually make flexing comparisons.

Luke, of course, was the clear winner in the who-the-girls-were-staring-at Olympics.

"He's always lovely to me when we talk, but he never stays. If I could just get him to stick around," sighed Adara Cornripe, who was golden of skin and hair, the best at daggerwork of anyone in the war-training course, and considered the prettiest girl in the Border camp. Though Elliot figured this gave him his fifty-second piece of proof that people were blind, stupid, and prejudiced against elves.

Elliot was suddenly struck by another cunning plan.

"I find that telling him to go away helps with that," Elliot offered. "He is very contrary."

Adara stared at him. "Who asked you?"

"You were speaking quite loudly, and I'm a yard away," said Elliot. "If you wanted to keep your conversation a secret, may I suggest whispering about it on some lonely midnight? And if you wanted me to politely pretend about anything, I'm sorry, have you met me? But suit yourself. I'm sure tossing your hair as if you're a pony being bothered by flies will work eventually."

Adara made a face at him, but looked thoughtful. Elliot had noted already that she wasn't stupid, or he wouldn't have spoken up at all.

When Luke left Dale Wavechaser and the rest of the admiring posse of war-training guys (Elliot thought of them as a kind of armed

Greek chorus), Adara straightened up on her sunbed, threw her hair back, and called out with sultry daring: "Go away, Luke!"

Luke's eyebrows hit his forehead, backed up, accelerated, and then hit his forehead again. "Ooookay," he said, and carefully skirted around the girls' sunbeds, giving Adara the widest berth possible and also some serious side eye, until he reached Elliot.

"Aren't you coming in?"

"Don't bother me now, loser, I have a very serious and important question to ask Adara," said Elliot. "Now, Adara, you said that, and it actually worked. How did you do it? Was it like this: Go *away*, Luke? Or was it more like this: Go away, *Luke*?"

Adara shot him a look fit to kill.

Luke lowered his voice. "Maybe you shouldn't talk to her? I have no idea what I did to upset her. She seems a bit touchy."

Which was Luke-speak for "she seems weird and mean."

"Also kind of weird and mean," Luke continued, speaking even lower and keeping a wary gaze on Adara.

Adara was hiding behind a curtain of golden hair. This was obviously not the way she'd been hoping to get Luke's attention.

"I just want to know where the stress should lie," said Elliot. "Like, extra scorn on his name, or extra force behind the 'go'? I wish only to learn. Teach me your ways, master."

"Come on," said Luke, and reached for his arm.

"No!" said Elliot, and batted him away. "We've discussed this, Luke. No using your superior physical strength unless it's an emergency. This dumb lake is not an emergency."

"Can't you swim?" Luke asked. "I'll teach you."

"Of course I can swim!" Elliot snapped.

His father had made sure he had many lessons so he would not be underfoot all the time: Elliot could swim, ballroom dance, speak French and Italian, and play three musical instruments. He was way more accomplished than Luke.

"I can't swim," Adara put in. Elliot admired her tenacity.

"See, Luke?" he said. "Your expertise is needed. You go teach Adara to swim. I will sit here and read my book. Everybody's happy."

"Everybody?" Luke asked. "Really?"

"You don't count."

That came out a little meaner than Elliot had intended, so he looked up and checked on how Luke was taking it. Luke didn't look upset exactly, but he was frowning, face slightly troubled under his sunny wet hair.

"Why do you look like an unhappy turtle?" he asked.

The problem was that Luke wasn't stupid either. Elliot didn't see why Luke couldn't do him a favour and be distracted by the blonde Elliot had thoughtfully provided.

"Are you dripping on my book deliberately?" Elliot demanded. "That is just like you."

Elliot hunched protectively farther into the neck of his dumb dress-slash-shirt and looked yearningly over at Serene and her knot of admirers. She laughed, her laugh like the ripple through leaves, and called over to them.

"What do you think, Luke?" Oh pardon, Elliot, she wasn't calling over to them at all, but to her *swordbrother*. "Would I like swimming?"

"Give it a try," Luke called back, grinning.

Luke could have literally any girl he wanted. Adara was right there, and Elliot had specially selected her as an excellent option. Why did it have to be Serene? Elliot glanced over at Adara, and she looked like she completely agreed. He felt some fellow feeling for the poor girl.

"I shall," said Serene, laughing again.

She stretched like a young, thin birch tree swayed by a wind, pulled her tight leather top over her head, and tossed it on the ground, leaving her smooth, pale skin entirely bare from the waist up.

There was an echoing silence all around the lakeside suddenly, as jaws dropped in such perfect unison Elliot thought they should have made a tiny collective creaking sound.

It was broken by Luke snapping: "You dropped your book."

He ran from Elliot's side then and was with Serene in two strides. He knocked two boys away, flat on their backs in the grass, while Serene was still looking mildly puzzled.

Elliot scrambled off his sunbed and got there at the same time as Mal Wavechaser, Dale's cousin, and one of the older boys who was on supervisory duty. So when Mal insisted that Serene was going to Commander Rayburn's, they were both there to insist they were going too.

"You can't say she was in a scandalous state of undress and punish her for it when she was in the exact same state of undress as more than half the people there," Elliot shouted.

Commander Rayburn was looking fixedly at the carpet and not at Serene. Captain Woodsinger, who had come upon their procession as they headed for the commander's cabin, had announced she was duty-bound to accompany them as the highest-ranked woman in the camp. She was looking at Serene, though very deliberately at her face. Serene was still naked from the waist up. Elliot had offered Serene his tunic, even though that meant Luke and half the censorious Border camp would see his clearly not-athletic physique, because love meant sacrifice. Serene had refused his sacrifice with obvious astonishment.

"I am mystified by everyone's behaviour!" Serene exclaimed. "My breasts are not so large as to need supporting garments, so why should I wear anything on my upper half? Don't worry," she added. "I'm not self-conscious about the size of my bosom at this time. I am still very young, and I will develop further. Besides which, I do not subscribe to the superstition that says the larger a woman's breasts, the greater her courage on the battlefield and prowess in the bedchamber."

She saw everyone's startled looks.

"I beg your pardon," she said. "Obviously that is an elven superstition, and besides which you are, in the main, men. You do not have any masculine attributes that could be compared to other men's: it would be ridiculous if you did, since you could have only the most minuscule difference between one man's attribute and the other."

"What do you mean by miniscule?" burst out Commander Rayburn, and at Captain Woodsinger's sharp look he said: "Ahem. No. Sorry, sorry. Totally inappropriate question for a student. But I'll have you know, young lady, those rumours aren't true."

"I don't understand," said Serene.

"You know, she makes a good point," Elliot said. "Generally and without specifically thinking of anybody in particular at all."

"Is there some kind of taboo against seeing a woman's breasts in human culture?" asked Serene. "Breasts are functional. They feed children. Whereas I know many men cultivate their shoulder and abdominal muscles merely to attract the opposite sex. Their chests are the ones that are more decorative and which it is less modest to display!"

"You know, she's making another good point," said Elliot.

"Both of you stop," Luke urged, his arms now wrapped as tight around his chest as Serene's were about hers. "The commander is going to think you're crazy."

"Sing it, cadet," Commander Rayburn muttered. "Sing it loud." Captain Woodsinger coughed, and he looked guiltily at her. "Don't let this happen again," he said. "Your job is not to question orders but to obey, and we have already permitted Cadet Chaos-of-Battle enormous liberties in her studies."

"I strongly object on principle," said Elliot, and Luke elbowed him viciously.

Elliot understood why, even: the threat that they could take back last year's leniency and force Serene to choose between war and council training was fairly obvious. But these people were meant to guide them and teach them, were meant to be fair and not show obvious double standards because it was easier to do that than to question what they were thinking and change how they behaved.

"If you do not obey, there will be consequences. There should be consequences for your behaviour today, but"—Commander Rayburn again caught Captain Woodsinger's eye—"I'm prepared to be lenient this once," he finished feebly.

"I will obey," said Serene, pale and determined.

"Yeah," said Luke, just as determined. "We'll obey. None of us will go down to the lake again, and none of us will appear in a—in a scandalous state of undress again."

"That's right!" Elliot exclaimed. "We'll have a lake boycott."

The commander and the captain did not seem to care about the lake boycott. They were sent away, and once they were out Serene stopped abruptly in the dark outside Commander Rayburn's cabin and sat down on a dank grassy hillock. Elliot sat down beside her, and Luke sat on her other side. Luke put his arm around her, and Elliot rested his cheek against her naked back.

"The way," Serene said, after a pause, her voice fierce so it would not shake, "they *looked* at me. As if my skin were sin, and theirs never could be, and I should have known."

"They're jerks," said Luke.

"I'm sorry," Elliot whispered.

He meant more than sorry for the others: he meant sorry for himself as well. He'd looked too. Stared, for an instant forgetting who she was and what she meant to him. He'd been a jerk as well, and Serene was so unhappy.

"Told you the lake sucked," Elliot muttered, and Serene laughed a small broken laugh.

"It's the eppy tomb of suck," Luke said.

There was a pause. "The what?" Elliot asked.

"The eppy tomb," said Luke. "I read it in a book. It means, like, the very definition of—"

"I know what it means," said Elliot. "And it's pronounced *epitome*."

"Leave it out," Serene said. "I know you men must squabble, but not right now, okay?"

"Yeah," Elliot sighed, oddly comfortable even though he was sitting out on the grass at night, already chilly, and still angry. "Okay."

They all sat together in the cool darkness of the night, silent for a little while. Serene's hair blew into Elliot's eyes, black ribbons against a black sky.

"I realize this is hypocritical, and I do apologize. I have been struggling against it and trying to keep my composure as a lady should," Serene said at last. "But I am in an emotional state, and I must admit I do find myself somewhat uncomfortable in such close proximity to an unclothed gentleman."

"Yeah, Luke, you shameless hussy," said Elliot, and cackled.

They did not go down to the lake again. Instead on their days off they spent time in the fields around the Border training camp. Sometimes Luke and Serene wanted to do weapons practise or a sport, and Elliot sat in the grass and read a book. Sometimes Luke made Elliot do exercise, which was simply bullying and he should be reported. Sometimes Elliot told stories or read aloud or sang to Serene and Luke, and sometimes they lay in the long grass and got into vicious arguments about the shape of clouds. Nobody ever took their shirt off, by silent mutual agreement. The others would come back from the lake wet and flushed and happy. Elliot wasn't the least bit jealous, but he wondered if Serene and Luke were.

Fourteen wasn't horrible, but it was more complicated, and sometimes that felt like the same thing.

Naturally the authorities, in their infinite wisdom, had decided that now they were all tiny pressure cookers of hormones it meant they were "ready to become men." Or in Serene's and Adara's and Delia Winterchild's and the other girls' case, women.

The way to do that was apparently more military manuevers and weapons training, with a view to taking the second years on their "first skirmish" soon. "You know," Elliot said loudly and often, "just a mini battle."

So all the fourteen-year-olds could be just a tiny bit killed.

The first step was a foray to mining land in which the Border humans hoped to find gold, and which the Border guard thus planned to claim as human territory.

A troop of those in war training was sent, but since Serene was going Elliot petitioned to be allowed to go as well. Elliot presumed he was permitted to go because he had made such a powerful and inarguable case for himself, though he also heard Commander Rayburn mutter "the brat will just stow away again or do some other awful thing, why not just let him go and shut him up? Can nobody shut him up!"

So the trip started off pretty well and went dramatically downhill, or rather uphill, from there. The first day, they climbed a mountain. The plan was to then go down a mountain and go up another mountain, and then repeat the process. On the second day, when Elliot was on watch, he left Luke sleeping as a hilarious prank to enliven the mountainous monotony, and laughed and laughed when they saw Luke's furious face peering over at them from the mountain path miles above them.

Then Luke jumped. The moment in which he was outlined against the blue sky, making an impossible leap, burned itself into Elliot's vision even when he shut his eyes in horror.

He opened them to see Luke landed, safe and sound and with Dale Wavechaser clapping him on the back.

"Oh my God," said Elliot, and sat down abruptly on a rock with his head in his hands. "Oh my God, *your* whole life just flashed before my eyes. Blond annoying smugness, weapons, weapons, annoying smugness, little kiddy weapons, right back until you were a fat smug baby. Oh my God."

Luke cleared his throat and gave Elliot a brief pat between the shoulderblades. "I'm okay."

Elliot thought Luke might be pleased that Elliot was upset. Elliot found this outrageous.

"I don't care!" said Elliot. "I care about gravity and how it doesn't work that way! Does nobody else care about gravity? Why isn't your leg broken? Why aren't *both* your legs broken?"

"Sorry to disappoint you," Luke said dryly.

"I've seen Luke jump from many similar heights before," said Serene. Elliot thought he might actually have a heart attack. "Is that an abnormal ability for humans?"

"*Yes*, you heedless elven wretch!" Elliot exclaimed. "No, Serene. Forgive me, Serene, I didn't mean that, I'm overwrought. But seriously, are none of the rest of you the least bit concerned? Do you think people can defy gravity through, like, *being awesome*? Do you not know that's ridiculous?"

Elliot kept demanding answers until the entire troop, apparently finding the subject of Luke defying the actual laws of nature very dull, demanded he switch conversational topics.

"The dwarves say that this area is both barren for mining purposes and, get this, structurally unstable," said Elliot obligingly. "Isn't that amazing? I'm so glad we're going on this life-threatening field trip."

"Nobody asked you to come," muttered Darius Winterchild, Delia's twin.

"Nobody asked you to breathe out IQ-lowering air in my vicinity," said Elliot, and glared at him until he went away.

"Yeah," Luke said, ignoring this byplay. "But come on, you can't always trust dwarves."

Elliot gave him a look of withering scorn. Luke, used to it at this point, did not seem unduly affected.

"You're from the human world and maybe you don't know," he said. "But they're—I mean, some of them are nice, obviously, I've met some very nice dwarves, but there's a tendency to be a bit cunning? My dad says so."

"It's true," said Captain Briarwind, who was really young for a captain, a bit spotty, and had a distressing tendency to look heroworshipfully at Luke. "They're a low and cunning folk." He did not seem to be making a pun. "They'd lie, cheat, and steal for gold."

Elliot could not believe that idiots like Captain Briarwind and Captain Whiteleaf got missions while Captain Woodsinger hardly ever did.

Both Luke and Captain Briarwind seemed blissfully unaware that one of Elliot's friends from council-training course, Myra, had dwarf blood.

"Don't either of you talk to me," said Elliot, and stormed off.

Serene went with him. "The dwarves were our allies once before humans were," she remarked. "And perchance will be so again. Moreover, I have observed that humans speak of elves in a similar fashion."

"Perchance they're total idiots," said Elliot. "Well, at least this is a fool's mission."

"Not necessarily," said Serene. "Trolls often occupy the territories dwarves have deserted. They eat sediment, you see." She reached back and gave her bow a slow, disturbing caress. "I think there is an excellent chance of a good fight."

"I'm sure trolls are also lovely and misunderstood," said Elliot, and started violently when the rushes to the non-cliff-edge side of the mountain path rustled. "Luke!"

The rushes parted to reveal that their opponent was very small, but definitely not a dwarf.

"Oh dear, a child," said Serene, moving backward with more alacrity than elven grace. "Could someone fetch a man to see to it?"

The group stared at her, as one.

"In elven society caring for the children is considered a task for the menfolk," said Elliot, sighing and wondering why nobody else ever bothered to read a book.

"Of course it is," said Serene. "The woman goes through the physically taxing and bloody experience of childbirth. A woman's experience of blood and pain is, naturally, what makes womenkind particularly suited for the battlefield. Whereas men are the softer sex, squeamish about blood in the main. I know it's the same for human men, Luke was extremely disinclined to discuss my first experience of a woman's menses."

Luke stared ferociously into the middle distance, obviously trying to visualize himself somewhere else, having an entirely different conversation. Serene patted him on the back.

"Perfectly all right, I should have had more respect for your delicate masculine sensibilities."

"Thank you," said Luke, sounding very far away.

"What, you people expect women to tear apart their bodies and then go to all the bother of raising the children? That takes years, you know," Serene remarked sternly. "The women's labour is brief and agonizing, and the man's is long and arduous. This seems only just. What on earth are men contributing to their children's lives in the human world? Why would any human woman agree to have a child?"

"The more she talks the more sense it all makes," said Elliot. "Has anyone else discovered that?"

"No," said several of the cadets in unison.

Elliot wanted to please Serene, so he looked to the child. Her hair was sticking up in tufts, and her face was stained with the juice of berries. She seemed altogether a sticky proposition. Elliot was not accustomed to the company of any children younger than himself, but he'd read that you were supposed to praise them and pat them on the head.

"Well done for not eating any poisonous berries," he said, gingerly patting. "Unless they were slow-acting poison, of course."

The child opened her mouth and gave an earsplitting howl. Elliot snatched his hand back and jumped away.

"Elliot," said Luke. "You're not supposed to pat children on the face and ear."

Luke knelt down and whispered in the child's ear, then smoothed her hair back from her sticky face and did something where he pretended to produce a dandelion from her ear. She beamed at him, and he smoothed her hair again.

"There," he said. "You're safe now. I'm Luke. You're safe with us. Let's go find your people."

Serene looked significantly from Luke to the others. "You see," she mouthed.

Elliot turned away with a loud sound of irritation. He was feeling exceedingly uncomfortable. This realization had come to him a time or three before, but the sight of Luke comforting a lost, lonely child made it hard to push away: that Luke actually was good and noble and kind and honest and true, that he was obviously a better and wiser choice for Serene than Elliot ever could be, and that Luke would never bully anyone.

He should probably say something nice to Luke once in a while. And right, absolutely, he would. The very next thing he said would be something nice. He could say something nice any time he liked.

"You may take the child in charge, as long as it isn't for too long. If we still have her by nightfall we will have to make different arrangements. A Sunborn is a bit too valuable to waste on babysitting, ha ha," said Captain Briarwind.

"Cadet Chaos-of-Battle and Cadet Schafer will help me, sir," said Luke.

"Ahahaha, wait just a minute," said Serene.

"Speak for yourself, you big traitor," Elliot hissed.

"May I say, it's an honor to have Michael Sunborn's son in my troop," Captain Briarwind continued.

To one side, Elliot could see Dale Wavechaser nodding earnestly.

Luke ducked his head and said, "Thanks."

No, Elliot decided, on the other hand it was probably good for Luke to see how the other ninety-nine non-worshipped percentage of the population lived. Besides, he had other things on his mind as they resumed the march.

"A moment, I wish to speak to Luke in private," Elliot said hastily to Serene, and fell back to the end of the procession, where Luke was walking with the child's hand in his.

Elliot automatically came to the child's other side, as he and Luke always walked with Serene in the centre. She lifted up her other hand for Elliot to take, which Elliot supposed was forbearing of her considering the patting incident. Elliot accepted her hand. It was, as he had feared, very sticky.

"Luke, Luke," Elliot said urgently. "Will you look after mine and Serene's children? I'm starting to have some real worries about Jasper and Smooth-Skin-Like-Finest-Porcelain's well-being."

"You've named your children," said Luke, with extreme and offensive skepticism.

"Yes, one elven name and one human name. I wish to be fair."

"You've named them Smooth Jazz?"

"Look, apparently I'll be raising them, let me have my fun," Elliot snapped. He had known about men's place in the home in elven culture, but it had not really sunk in until this moment, and he was feeling agitated. He was pleased, however, to see that his many lectures on the subject of human music had been attended to. "I'm sure I will get the hang of it, but for the first while I might need some assistance. Will you do it or won't you?"

"I might if they're like Serene," said Luke. "Not if they're like you." He grinned. "I'm not dealing with five-year-old you. You're a brat."

"I'm a delight," argued Elliot, and when Serene hove into view he appealed to her. "Serene!" said Elliot. "Do you think I'm a brat?"

"You're a bit of a minx," said Serene. "But in an insouciantly charming way, I think."

Elliot was so pleased by this compliment, he did not realize until too late that when Serene summoned Luke to the front of the group, Elliot was, so to speak, left holding the baby.

Elliot swore and then said, "No, I didn't mean that. Don't tell Luke I said that."

The child eyed him. He felt she had a mistrusting gaze, the gaze of someone who would definitely rat him out to Luke at the first possible opportunity.

"Couldn't we establish a bond in some way?" Elliot asked. "Can I bribe you?"

"Back, Schafer!" barked Dale. Hearing that tone from normally good-natured Dale, Elliot's eyes snapped to the front of the line. The cadets had their weapons out: someone had seen some sign of a troll then.

Elliot stepped back and felt the child's hand slip out of his. He looked for her and saw she was edging away, farther and farther, as if his alarm had been communicated to her through their linked hands.

Except she was now at the very edge of the path, and Elliot saw pieces of earth falling away at her heels.

"Careful!" Elliot said, and realized he had spoken far too sharply. The child stumbled back another step, and Elliot saw the ground beneath her crumbling.

Elliot looked toward the others for Serene, for Luke, for help, but they were marching on and no one else was close enough to get here, and so Elliot swore again and dived for the child.

He meant to knock her away, knock her back to somewhere safe, but he couldn't even manage that. Instead, as the ground fell sickeningly out from under them, Elliot curled around her, trying to protect her head, as rocks and earth and both of them went flying. Elliot heard someone shouting his name and was briefly annoyed—how was that going to help?—before everything went dark.

He woke up to a small finger poking him in the forehead. He moved, and a shooting pain went up his arm.

"Ow, I think my arm's broken," said Elliot. "Ow ow ow, the pain is excruciating, I hate stupid military camp, ow." He remembered what Serene or Luke would have thought of first, and said belatedly: "Are you damaged, small child?"

"I'm not hurted," said the child.

"Oh great, you can talk, that's excellent!"

"Of course I can talk," she sniffed. "I'm almost six!"

"Is that a normal age for people to talk at?" Elliot said. "I didn't know. I think I was talking at that age, but to be honest with you, I'm extremely advanced, and I got on the talking train fast because I was in a hurry to reach cutting-repartee station."

The child was silent.

"Um," Elliot added. "Don't—don't worry. The other people in our group are highly trained experts in tracking and using pointed objects, and they will find and protect us."

"Will the pretty one come?" asked the child.

"Undoubtedly!" said Elliot. "I'm glad you noticed her. She's called Serene, and she is the most beautiful creature I ever beheld. She has ebony hair and porcelain skin, as I'm sure you observed. She is also an elf, and they have excellent eyesight and can track people by a single blade of crushed grass, and she is the best with a bow in the whole camp, including the teachers."

"The boy," the child said after a pause.

"Oh," said Elliot. "Luke. Well, he's okay too, I guess."

He didn't want to crush a child's dreams.

"He looks like a prince," she continued wistfully.

"Well," said Elliot. "The monarchy are historically inbred."

The child was silent again. Elliot was sure he was getting this very wrong.

"Luke will come," he assured her after a moment. "I know he will. He always comes, and he always protects people. He won't stop until you're safe."

There was a little content hum in answer, and Elliot felt slightly better. He sat up, in the darkness and the sliding shale, and was relieved to find that he could sit up. He stood up, swaying with the pain of his arm and the necessity of keeping hold of the child, and found he could do that too.

"According to my memory of the maps of the mines, we should emerge somewhere if we keep heading south," he said. "Don't worry, small child. I am extensively acquainted with the geography of this area. Can you walk with me?"

He had hold of her sleeve. She tugged it away and after a moment he felt her hand creep into his.

"How did your hand get even stickier in a rock fall?" Elliot asked. "Never mind, I don't mean to criticize, it's just a habit of mine."

They walked, for what seemed like a long while, through the dark holes. Elliot kept being afraid more rocks would fall, or they would be met with a rock face or a space so small they would not be able to continue. He kept talking, despite his fears about oxygen, and tried not to show the fear that was choking him.

Instead of narrowing, the tunnel opened, light shining and rays reaching out to them, as if the sun were fixed directly onto the mountain like a badge. Elliot and the child stumbled out into it. The light still seemed bright, even when they were out of the mines. The green world below the mountain wavered in Elliot's vision like a dream.

"Awesome," said Elliot. "See, we didn't need anyone at all. We're safe as houses."

That was when he saw the party of trolls coming up the mountain track toward them. They were big, seven feet tall, bigger than even Luke's dad, and their skin was gray. Elliot saw the leader's head jerk up, and he knew they had spotted him.

"Safe as houses that are currently on fire," he amended to the child. "Run!"

He ran, and she ran with him, but the trolls picked up speed in response and Elliot knew they would catch up with him soon and did not know what to do. He forced the child, sobbing and stumbling, out in front of him so at least his body would be between her and them.

He glanced over his shoulder to see if they were gaining, and saw the first one fall.

He had an arrow in his throat.

Elliot stared and saw, so far ahead on the curving path that it was on another mountain entirely, a black fleck that must be Serene. He saw it moving toward him, faster than humans could move, and saw another troll fall. He knew she was running and firing arrows and never missing, all at the same time, all from so far away.

She shot every troll but one, and that troll thundered toward them, his shadow falling on them, and Elliot knew the creature was so close to them Serene might be afraid to shoot.

That one troll might as well have been all five. He could crush them just as easily. Elliot pressed the child against the crag, pressed himself against her so hard he heard her cry out in protest. He reached up a hand, and he said: "Stop, we're no threat, she's a local child," and saw the troll frown, an expression of incomprehension on that unfamiliar face, and Elliot thought, if he could figure out some way to talk to him—

But then the troll raised his club, big as a tree, and the next moment Luke jumped, made one of his impossible leaps from an impossible point high above them, and landed crouched before the troll with his sword already drawn. The blade blazed in the sunlight, and so did his hair, and the child behind Elliot gave a glad cry as if recognizing a prince come to save her.

Luke caught the troll by surprise. He rushed at him, and ran him through. Through the belly, and when the troll fell to his knees Luke wrenched the blade out of his belly and drove the point home to his heart. The troll crumpled forward, a dead weight, and tumbled into the dust.

Luke pulled his sword free, leaned his face and his free arm against the rock, and was suddenly sick.

Elliot realised, after a stunned instant, that though Luke was past master at any number of instruments of death . . . he didn't think that Luke had ever actually killed anyone before.

That was how all Luke could do, all he was celebrated and adored for, ended up: these dead bodies in the dry path before them.

Elliot grabbed the child's hand tightly as Luke was gripping the hilt of his sword and went over to where Luke stood braced against the wall. He leaned against Luke, rested his cheek against Luke's arm. He could feel Luke shaking.

"You saved her," he said. "You did it. The child's safe. They didn't hurt her, because of you." It probably didn't matter much in comparison, but he figured it couldn't hurt to add: "I'm safe too. You did everything you could."

Luke took a deep shuddering breath. "Yeah?"

Elliot took a step back and nodded nervously and so vigorously his hair tumbled in his face, a blinding red tangle, and he had to shake it out. By the time he had, Luke was smiling faintly—Luke thought Elliot's total inability to deal with his hair was really funny, which Elliot resented usually but was grateful for this once—and then Luke swiped a hand over his eyes. Elliot decided they would have a manly understanding that he'd never seen the tears gleaming in Luke's eyes and would thus never have to discuss them.

"C'mon," said Elliot. "Let's go find Serene."

Half of the troop had gone looking for Elliot and the child, and the other had found the nearest neighbouring village that would supply healing and shelter. Serene sat with him while the village medic bound up Elliot's arm.

"Luke's outside," Serene said in a low voice. "Might you want to go out and say something to him? He's a bit torn up." She looked off into the distance. "Your first one's the worst. It gets easier after that."

Does it get easier? Elliot thought, looking at her still pale face. Or is it just that you shut doors in your own heart and never open them again for fear of what is behind them?

Serene had killed for him too. Serene was a child soldier, created in the same way Luke had been. The only difference was that Serene had killed before she ever met Elliot, had been damaged like that before he ever saw her. He remembered thinking that the grave, older air she had was beautiful, was something elvish and wonderful, and felt sick of himself. He wanted nothing more than to lift the sadness forever and see her smile, uncomplicated and happy, the child she should still be.

"Was someone with you for your first?" he asked.

Serene nodded. "My mother. She said—she said she was proud of me, and that I was brave."

"Hey, you are brave," said Elliot at last. "And I'm proud of you too. Always. Thanks for saving me."

"Any time," said Serene. He thought she might have liked to smile but found herself not able to do so. "Always."

Elliot wanted to ask Serene to go out there. She'd obviously be better at comforting Luke and be the one he wanted to see, but he understood that he was the least hurt of the three of them, even if he did have a broken arm. He stood up, and stood looking for a moment at her profile, like that of a marble bust, all set perfect lines, and her gray eyes fixed on a private vision. He swept her dark hair off her face with his good hand, kissed her brow, and walked away. It wasn't how he'd wanted their first kiss to go, but it had weirdly seemed like the right thing to do.

He walked outside and found Luke sitting on a low wall outside the tent, his bright head bowed. He looked up at Elliot's approach.

"Hey, it's you," he said. "Are you—doing all right?"

"Fine," said Elliot. "They say I'll play the piano again. Well, they didn't, they didn't know what a piano was, but I'm going to be fine anyway."

"That's good," said Luke.

"How about you?" asked Elliot.

"Oh, you know me," said Luke. "Great. Always great. Why wouldn't I be?"

"Sure," said Elliot. "Absolutely, you should be. I'm certain it seemed like there was nothing else to do at the time."

Luke's face changed. "Seemed like?"

"Well, ideally we would have been able to reason with the trolls, and there would have been no bloodshed," said Elliot, sinkingly conscious that he was saying the exact wrong thing but not sure what else to say, now they were talking about this.

"Oh yeah?" Luke demanded. "You think you're so smart. Did it seem to you that those creatures were going to listen to reason?"

"Well, I mean, maybe," said Elliot. "We're never going to know now, are we?"

Luke was white under his tan. "Are you serious? I know what you think of me," he said. "You're always really clear on the subject. But is this the time to have a go at me?"

"That came out wrong," said Elliot. "Obviously, there were extenuating circumstances. There was the child—"

"You know what, Elliot?" Luke demanded. "Could you shut up for once in your life and leave me alone?"

He pushed himself off the wall and shoved past Elliot, fairly hard, on his injured side. Elliot went and leaned against the wall until the jolted pain in his arm subsided, and by then Luke was long gone.

Elliot blamed himself for trying. He was not a comforting type of person: it was stupid, like a hedgehog trying to be a hot-water bottle. Of course he was only going to make Luke more upset.

The village, which the child belonged to—her name turned out to be Aysha, and everyone asked silly questions like "you were trapped with her in a rockslide and never even found out her name?"—had a party to celebrate Luke saving one of their daughters. People made speeches and clapped, and the popularity of the Border guard received a significant boost.

Elliot mainly sat in the corner and sulked over his broken arm. Eventually Serene and Luke came to sit with him, and they were all pretty quiet together.

The incident with the trolls was, they were told, not a skirmish but merely an *encounter*.

However, the Border camp leaders assured them that there would soon be a real skirmish. It was discovered by the Border guard that the dwarves were occupying several rich mines on land that was rightfully the property of the elves. The elves, a territorial people, were outraged once they were informed and shown the documentation proving their ownership. The guards and the cadets from warrior training were set to ride out in the space of three sundowns.

Elliot supposed you could tell the difference between a skirmish and an encounter by counting the number of corpses. Apparently nobody but him thought it was at all suspicious that as soon as the humans had decided they wanted the land, this conflict between the elves and the dwarves had arisen. He bet some of the land would be granted to the Border humans by the elves as thanks for their aid in battle.

This meant the official neutrality and private distrust between humans and dwarves had now become open enmity. Myra took to wearing her hair loose, hiding behind it like a veil, and slinking around the classrooms as if expecting to be hit.

Elliot might at this point have slightly broken into Commander Rayburn's office and found a large file of deeds and treaties that he confiscated and took with him to the library, where he sat studying them and trying to project an air of innocence. This worked until Serene came to drag him out to Luke's next Trigon game.

"I have no time to bother with Luke's stupid game," said Elliot.

"Sure, all right, we're going anyway," said Serene, who was the most wonderful girl in the world but sometimes did not listen. She went over to grab Elliot's arm, and as she did her eye fell on the papers. "Elliot," she asked after a moment's pause, her voice heavy with foreboding. "What are these, and where did you get them?"

"Ahhh . . .," said Elliot, reluctant to incriminate himself, and then stuffed the document he had been staring at for ten minutes in her hands.

The treaty which sealed the alliance between the elves and the dwarves, in which the dwarves pledged treasure and the elves pledged land. The very land which the elves were now claiming was theirs.

Everybody had seen the deed that proved the elves had originally owned the land. Nobody had seen this treaty.

"My people believe the land rightfully belongs to them," said Serene. "They would go to war for nothing less. We will not break any word, once given. If we knew of this document, we would never have agreed to fight. This war would bring us dishonor."

"Yeah, I kind of figured," said Elliot.

"Perhaps this treaty was overlooked by mischance."

"Yeeeeeeah," Elliot said. "Perchance. Would you bet your honor on it?"

"I would not," Serene replied at last. "Would you go fetch Luke?"

"Why can't you go fetch Luke?"

"I'd rather someone found me with the documents than you," said Serene, and smiled a wolfish smile. "They can't take them from me. Well, they'd be welcome to try."

"Okay," said Elliot. He got up and dashed for the Trigon pitch, hoping against hope that Luke had been knocked out early.

Of course Elliot could never be that lucky. The Trigon game was in full swing, the stands full, and Luke still playing. Elliot had to dodge several interfering people in order to make his way onto the pitch.

"Uh, you're not meant to be here . . .," said Dale Wavechaser. "Uh, maybe you could wish Luke luck after the game, or something . . . ?"

Elliot waved him away.

"Only we're really close to winning . . .," Dale said, and his voice was faintly pleading. "Against the *fifth* years."

"That's nice for you," Elliot remarked. "Also disappointing for you in a minute, I suppose." He whistled. "Oi, Luke!"

Luke looked around, smiled to show his appreciation for the support, and gestured for Elliot to get off the pitch. Elliot shook his head vehemently to indicate that he was not supporting at all, and beckoned. Luke looked upset and shook his head. Elliot nodded insistently, beckoned again, and walked off.

He heard the chorus of groans and booing as he left the pitch, suspected he was going to be even less popular from now on, and was not terribly surprised when Luke caught up with him outside the pitch, breathing hard and disgustingly sweaty.

Elliot wrinkled his nose and pushed at Luke's shoulder. "Please stand farther away from me."

"This had better be important," said Luke. "Do you have any idea how embarrassing it is to let down the whole team, in front of everybody, because you whistled and beckoned? I'm not your dog."

Elliot suspected the whole camp would blame him and still love Luke, so he didn't see what Luke's problem was.

"And yet you came," he said. "Come on, Serene's waiting in the library. It actually is important."

"The library," said Luke, and sighed. "Wonderful."

He stopped complaining when they got to the library and Serene showed him the treaty.

Luke did not even suggest that the commander might have missed seeing the deed, and they should point it out to him and trust the matter would be settled. Maybe the commander *had* missed it, but they couldn't be sure.

"What would happen if we showed this to Captain Woodsinger?" Elliot ventured.

"She's loyal to the commander," Serene said. "We can't risk it."

They had to go to someone who had something to lose.

Luckily, Serene had a plan.

"I've been thinking since you were gone. We need to get quickly to someone who will believe us. One of my kinswomen is in a troop to the far north of this wood."

Elliot met her calm gaze, glanced at Luke, saw them glance at each other, and they all reached an accord.

"Then it's settled," said Elliot. "We go to the elves."

They left as soon as they had gathered up a few necessities: rolled-up blankets and dried provisions and one or two books Elliot could not be parted from. It was barely dark when they went, but Elliot hoped it was dark enough that they would not be missed until morning. They left pillows arranged in the shape of bodies under their sheets, which was fairly basic subterfuge, but the captains didn't check the younger ones' beds as carefully as they did the older ones', on account of indecency and lewd behaviour.

"I would have thought the girls of the camp would be more careful not to dishonor the boys," said Serene when Elliot explained this, deeply shocked. "The boys are already fighters, which cannot be pleasing to prospective wives, and if they are ruined on top of it, who will marry them?"

There was an embarrassed silence in the hush of the woods as they walked along.

"Kind of works differently for humans, again," said Luke.

"Is human biology so different to elvish, then?" Serene asked with interest.

"Beg pardon?" said Luke.

"Well, elvish women are driven by powerful lusts that men cannot understand," Serene said in matter-of-fact tones.

"Let's just leave it at that, shall we!" Luke implored.

"Please go on, Serene, don't stop, this is very interesting," said Elliot.

"Once a woman's passion is roused it can be very difficult for her to stop until the act of love is completed," said Serene. "Preferably several times over. How can an innocent man understand such desires? As I understand it, men are completely exhausted when they complete the act of love once."

"Well, not completely!" said Elliot.

"After the first flush of youth," Serene said sadly, "men are only able to perform the act once a night."

"Please talk about something else or maybe kill me," said Luke. "I don't want to live in this world any more."

"Thus, necessarily, a man must perform attentions upon a woman when he is no longer aroused, which is why for a man such acts are more about feelings of the heart than of other areas," said Serene. "Else how can a woman be satisfied with just one man? Of course, the elves in the eastern woods have different arrangements—"

"You know what would be amazing?" Luke said. "If we were kidnapped, bound, and gagged—the gagged bit is really important—and put to death by brigands like right now. Right now. Brigands!"

He looked around. The woods at night offered the hoot of an owl, and the rustle of leaves in a breeze, but no brigands.

"We're sharing differing cultural points of view and information," Elliot remarked. "No need to be such a prude."

"Come now. It's natural for a young pure gentleman to be abashed by such discussions," said Serene. "Forgive me for being so frank with you and putting you to the blush, Luke."

"I am not blushing!"

Elliot peered in the gloom. "He's definitely blushing," he reported to the night air.

"I'm just going to go wander into the undergrowth all alone," Luke said in a flat voice. "If I'm lucky a warg might eat me. I hope so. Don't come looking for me."

"Okay," said Elliot. "Can I have your cloak before you go get eaten by a warg? I'm freezing."

Serene undid the clasp of her cloak and handed it over. Elliot accepted it with profuse thanks. Luke selfishly kept his cloak and did not wander off to be eaten by a warg, but nothing in this life was perfect.

They went to sleep snuggled into the roots of a vast tree. Elliot woke up first in the early morning because his teeth were chattering, despite the fact that Luke had donated his cloak in the night. Stupid magic lands, stupid nature, his stupid body and its learned dependence on central heating. Serene and Luke were still sleeping soundly, holding hands, Serene's long dark hair caught up with the tree roots.

There was a little bird perched on the lowest branch of the tree. It had bright button-black eyes and a yellow beak and had tilted its head in an adorable manner. It looked as if it was definitely considering covering Serene and Luke with leaves.

"I'm watching you, little bird," Elliot said darkly. "Don't even think about it." He hugged his knees to his chest and waited for the others to wake up.

When the others did wake, it was still early morning but a little brighter, the sky the colour of peach juice with light shining through it. Elliot could not believe he was drinking juice and eating fruit so much he thought about it in similes: he yearned for the food of his people, wrapped in foil and basically made of chemicals. Oh lost Coca-Cola, he mourned. Oh pizza, gone but not forgotten.

First Luke yawned and stretched and rolled away from Serene, then Serene's eyes opened. Her eyes were clear and she was alert in an instant, whereas Luke had to spend a whole lot of time looking dopey and rubbing his eyes. Elliot nobly refrained from teasing him.

"Are we far enough away, do you think?" Serene asked Luke. Nobody asked Elliot's opinion, Elliot noticed. Far enough away for what? What were they planning to do?

He found out when Serene rummaged in her bag and brought out a horn, made of bone and delicately carved. She blew on it gently, and the sound went rushing through the trees as if there were wind-chimes hanging from every bough.

In a few moments, sooner than Elliot would have dreamed possible, came the response. Through the trees in a shining cavalcade and a patter of hooves lighter than falling leaves, wheeling and turning in a perfect circle like birds whose flight patterns were guided by sheer instinct into absolute smoothness, came the elves. In the lead was a woman beautiful as the dawn and calm as a lake nobody had ever even breathed on. Her gray eyes widened as she recognized Serene.

"Hail, kinswoman, Swift-Arrows-in-the-Chaos-of-Battle!" called Serene.

"Hail, kinswoman, Serene-Heart-in-the-Chaos-of-Battle," Swift returned, and then a smile split her grave sweet face. "Out in the woods with a couple of *boys*?" she asked. "Why, you little rogue!"

"Ma'am, it is not at all what you assume," said Serene. "They're decent gentlemen, I assure you. Human ways are different, and besides, this is an emergency."

"That's what all the young girls say when it comes to dalliances in the woods with trollops," said one of the other elves, and Elliot gave an indignant squawk.

"Two of them, as well," said Swift, who had Serene's fine bones and translucently pale skin, though her braided hair was chestnut, much lighter than Serene's, and her expression was mischievous. "Certainly your mother's daughter. Chip off the old wood block."

"Ma'am, Luke Sunborn is my *swordsister*," Serene said severely. "We swore the holy oath, over a tree trunk by moonlight."

"What, a boy?" said yet another of the elves, the youngest by all appearances, with rippling gold hair, and she let out a rippling laugh to match it. "Who ever heard of such a thing?"

Elliot was even more indignant about this evidence that the ritual had been extremely complicated and meaningful than he was about being called a trollop.

Luke sidled closer to him and murmured in his ear: "Can you understand them? I do not like the way they are looking at us!"

"Of course I can understand them. What, you don't even know elvish?" Elliot asked. "Fine swordsister you are."

"What?" Luke asked, and Elliot snickered. After an exasperated pause, Luke said: "What are they saying?"

"Are you sure you want to know?"

"Yes."

"Quite, quite sure?"

"*Yes!*"

"Well, if you're really sure," Elliot said blandly. "That one with the black braid just said you were a pretty, pretty thing and looked like you'd be a fun afternoon."

Luke went a slow, horrified scarlet. Elliot beamed.

"But the undersized one," said Swift. "I'm not sure of the appeal. With the wild garish hair—carrots, my dear—and the squinty look."

The blond elf snickered and said a single word.

"*Deh'rit*," Luke whispered, triumphantly. "She looked right at you and she said it! What does that mean?"

Elliot thought about lying and saying that it meant "totally awesome, very handsome, in a respectful way," but he was hoping Luke would submit to elvish lessons very soon and lying was no way to begin teaching him.

"Uh . . . the closest translation would be that she called me a bluestocking."

"What does *that* mean?"

"Um . . . like, a nerd," said Elliot, and sighed. "Something along the lines of, someone who always has their nose buried in a book and who nobody wants to marry."

"Oh," said Luke, and grinned. "Well, they're not wrong on all counts then."

Elliot ignored him and concentrated on what the elves were saying. Tragically, Serene was still apparently involved in a conversation about whether Elliot and Luke were her wanton floozies.

Swift continued eyeing Elliot in a way he found upsetting and insulting. "He must have a really great personality," she said at last.

"You know, I really don't," said Elliot, impatiently and in elvish.

Swift looked a little rueful about being caught out, but not as embarrassed as Elliot had expected. She was still looking at him as if, after all, Elliot should accept that of course he'd hear comments like that about himself.

The blond elf snickered and said: "Told you he was a bluestocking." Luke perked up at the one elvish word he now knew. Elliot scowled at everybody.

"Smile, sweetheart," called the elf with the black braid.

"Uh, I'm a total stranger and my whole family could've just died in a unicorn stampede," said Elliot. "You don't know. I don't feel like smiling. What right do you have to tell me to?"

Black braid rolled her eyes and sent her horse turning in a playful little circle. "Might want to get your boy to loosen up, Serene, or how is he ever going to be any—"

At this point, Serene lost her temper and strung her bow. She held an arrow poised to fly at Swift's face, her hands and her gaze steady.

"They are my comrades," she said. "I hold their honor as my own. One word more said to defame it, and I will consider that word a challenge."

The elvish troop stopped grinning and snickering. Elliot was briefly furious that it was Serene's anger that got them to stop, but then he recalled how Luke could quell the boys at camp when it came to Serene in a way Serene herself could not. It was an uncomfortable thought and he did not like it, so he reached for the roll of parchment in his bag instead.

"We actually come on a question of honor," he said. "Unless you'd rather sit around and laugh at young boys all day long."

Swift's face hardened. She jumped off her horse in one smooth motion and came striding through the grass toward them.

Serene did not put her bow down. "First you apologize to my friends."

Elliot had the sudden crushing realization that the adults were not going to be adults about this. Human adults had already messed things up by being greedy liars, and now elvish adults were going to be stubborn, and Serene was too good a friend to back down, and Luke did not understand what was going on and would be too direly embarrassed to be helpful if he did.

Being obnoxious was not going to work.

Elliot got out the treaty and waved it until Swift's eyes went to it and her attention was on him.

"I'm sorry if I was short with you," he said, as if the elves hadn't started it all. "It's just that I'm *so* worried about this, and I thought that if we found you, you would know what to do!"

Swift visibly wavered, to Elliot's secret amazement.

"I only want to do the right thing," Elliot proceeded, and fixed Swift with a limpid gaze.

"Of course," said Swift, almost reluctantly. "Poor dear."

Elliot nodded with conviction and felt his stupid hair wave about all over the place. "Honor's so important," he said wistfully. "I wish I understood this paper better. But I am such a silly thing! I need guidance."

"What is Elliot saying," Luke whispered to Serene, "and why does he look so weirdly upset?"

Serene, clever girl and mistress of Elliot's heart as she was, shushed him.

"Oh," said Swift. "I suppose we were a bit rough with you. Lot on our minds, you know? Womanly things. I'm sorry about that, little gentleman."

"Apology accepted," said Elliot, and tried to smile in a winsome fashion. Serene put away her bow.

Swift glanced from Serene to Elliot and back again. For a moment Elliot thought it was all over, but Swift grinned, as if Elliot being manipulative was only to be expected and a little charming.

She slung her arm around Elliot's shoulders. "Don't you worry your pretty head about a thing," she said consolingly. "The women are here to take care of you. How about you sit down with me and explain this piece of paper?"

Elliot sat down on the bank with a beautiful elven warrior in the heat of the afternoon sun, and he explained the treaty as clearly and with as much detail as he could. He reminded himself to bat his eyelashes a couple of times.

The rest of the elves set up camp around them, and the blond elf, Silent-Arrow-in-a-Clash-of-Swords, after asking if Luke fancied making the meal and receiving a polite stare of incomprehension, began to prepare some food.

At one point Elliot forgot himself and told Swift that she was an idiot with no grasp of politics, but Swift rumpled his hair and told him he was a little spitfire.

"I am a rough and simple soldier," she said eventually. "I follow my clan leader and do not become involved in such intrigues. But I can see well enough that you three have done us a signal service. My thanks to you, Serene-Heart-in-the-Chaos-of-Battle."

"Oh wow, thanks," Elliot muttered.

Swift smiled at him. "And to your charming companions as well. Redheads," she murmured. "I get it now, Serene. He's a taking little thing, in an odd way. Grows on you."

"That was maybe my first ever compliment from a lady," Elliot said. "Thank you for making it absolutely awful. Oh my God."

Luke and the black-braided elf, whose name turned out to be Rushing-Waters-Bear-Away-our-Enemies, Rush for short, even had a brief spar with short swords. Luke beat her, and for a moment Elliot thought that Luke would now be honorary member of the elf-warriors-club and Elliot was going to be gently condescended to by everyone all evening.

But then Rush winked at Luke and said: "I like a boy with spirit," and Elliot felt torn between amusement and annoyance that there was apparently nothing you could do that would make you good enough to enter the club.

The most annoying thing, perhaps, was that the elven troop were obviously good people and were being kind to them, and yet Elliot felt subtly wrong-footed at every turn. He wondered if this was how Serene felt all the time, and he promised himself to bear it as well as she did.

He sat by the campfire, warm in its flickering orange glow, even the dark trees seeming to form a sheltering shell around him. Swift had placed him protectively at her side because she said that some of the younger elves hadn't seen a boy in weeks and their hands might wander.

Rush and Silent immediately started canoodling with each other, so their hands were wandering but not anywhere near Elliot.

"They're swordsisters," said Serene discreetly. "Their warrior bond is very beautiful. Some think that no bond could ever be as strong, no love ever as true, as that between two women who fight side by side."

"Swordsisters," was all Elliot managed to get out, in a voice strangled by jealousy. He hadn't realized that meant—that meant Luke and Serene already—

He looked over at Luke for some confirmation of this on his stupid smug face, but Luke was busy looking away from Rush and Silent with his ears gone red.

"The bond is different for every pair," said Serene casually.

"You definitely did not mention anything like that to me when we agreed to do it," said Luke.

Ha! Elliot thought, and rejoiced in Luke's disappointment.

"There are also simply some women, warriors and not, who can never be tempted by the shining hair and alluring chests of men," said Serene.

"Sure," said Elliot. "Guys too. I mean, by women."

Serene frowned. "Are you sure?"

"Yeah, a guidance counselor gave me a ton of pamphlets over this guy called Simon," said Elliot. "I'll show you some."

"It just seems so unlikely, given that men cannot truly feel the pulse of desi—"

"It's true," Luke said abruptly, "and if you two start talking like you did last night in front of strangers I will put my head in the fire."

"The pretty blond one may dress like a harlot, but I think he is truly a modest gentleman," remarked Silent, whose name Elliot thought was ironic. "Look at his sweet blushes."

She shut up about Luke's blushes when Rush tickled her. Elliot felt pleased by the success of their mission and in charity with everyone, amused by all the stories the elves had about the wild escapades of Serene's childhood.

"She would've gotten away with it too if she hadn't boasted about it to a pretty little boy who went running to tell his papa," Rush finished.

"Golden-Hair-Scented-Like-Summer is a judgmental boring goody-two-shoes," said Serene, flushing.

"I heard Serene tried to kiss him and he slapped her," said Swift, and burst out laughing.

"THAT DID NOT HAPPEN," yelped Serene, like any kid teased by her big cousin, and Elliot found himself liking the elves after all. It wasn't just Swift. They all treated Serene like family. He wanted her to have a home where she was safe and warm and loved.

"Oh, you come by it honestly," said Swift. "Before he met your father, your mother—Sure-Aim-in-the-Chaos-of-Battle," she added, nodding to Elliot. "She was a devil with the gentlemen. Ruined two gentlemen in the west woods. I heard one of them was married off to a goblin! Of course Sure is settled now. The love of a good man will steady you one day too, you firebrand. Running off and joining the Border camp, of all the mad things to do! Your mother was raving about it for days. But proud too, you could see it. Of course she'd have the wildest daughter in the woods. All the careful fathers had best seal their virtuous sons in the nearest tree!"

Serene crossed her arms over her chest. "I am nothing like my mother."

"Whoa, you have like, daddy issues about your controlling parent whose exploits inflame your desire to be like him but whose reform and new steady reputation makes you even more rebellious," Elliot crowed in English. "And all the elven beauties are warned to stay away from you because you're mad, bad, and dangerous to know. You're a bad boy! Right, and Luke's the good boy—golden boy, boring, you know the drill. This is such an enlightening night."

"Maybe you could stop defining us by, like, literary tropez," said Luke. "Bluestocking."

"Tropes, oh my God, loser, of course you can't speak elvish, you can barely speak English. It's pronounced like tropes, not like St Tropez."

Luke looked a little frayed around the edges, but Swift provided a distraction by asking Elliot what gods he kept calling on, and Elliot had to try and explain being Jewish but not practising to an elf. He wasn't sure if Swift understood, but while they were talking about cultural differences he asked her if she knew anyone who spoke troll, and she promised to send him a troll-elvish dictionary.

"Write to me anything you learn about trolls!" Elliot said. "Or mermaids. Please write to me about mermaids."

All in all, it was a successful day.

Later that night Luke grumpily rolled his blanket over to Elliot's and said: "Fine then. Teach me a few words of elvish."

Elliot grinned triumphantly in the dark. He'd thought the sword-sister guilt trip would work.

An alliance with the dwarves and elves followed the surprise discovery of the treaty, extremely cordial on the elves's side since the dwarves were graciously forgiving of their territory faux pas. The only thing to do was for the Border guard to form an alliance with the dwarves themselves.

All the people who had been talking about the low cunning of dwarves were shut up. And Serene managed to be attending her kinswomen at a conference and mention that since she, an elf, was training with the Border guard, it should be made clear that full-blood dwarves were welcomed there too.

After being away for a few weeks on a family trip, Myra came back. She was no longer hiding behind her hair.

"Oh, hey," said Elliot, stopping and standing by her table at lunch. "You look great."

He smiled. She didn't have the beard most dwarves wore, but she had a mustache, dark, shining, and clearly carefully shaped, and her painted-pink mouth curled beneath it as she smiled back.

He knew a compliment wouldn't mean as much to girls coming from him.

"Luke!" Elliot commanded. "Tell her she looks great."

Luke looked at Myra as if he'd never seen her before, and at Elliot as if he wanted answers. Elliot made an impatient gesture.

"Yes . . . ?" said Luke, questing.

Myra beamed and looked so happy that Elliot permitted Luke to seize him by the arm and drag him away without reminding him of the rules about physical force.

"Who was that?" Luke hissed in his ear.

"What do you mean, who was that?" Elliot asked, offended on Myra's behalf. "That was my friend Myra. She's in council training with me. She doesn't look that different!"

"You have a friend called Myra in council training?" Luke said, as if it was news to him. "Since when?"

"For the whole two years I have been in this godforsaken place, Luke!"

Luke looked unconvinced, but at least he was only being self-centred instead of prejudiced against dwarves.

"I wish I could grow a moustache like that," Elliot said wistfully.

"Probably a bad idea," said Luke. "You can't control the hair you've got."

"Besides," said Serene, joining them, "I know it's natural and everything, but don't you think it looks weird if a man has hair anywhere but on his head? I mean, can they not be bothered to put in the time and effort to look good?"

The only problem came when they were all summoned to the commander's office, and General Lakelost was there, a man with a white moustache so huge that comparing it to Myra's was like comparing a white whale to a dolphin. General Lakelost and Commander Rayburn asked how exactly one of them had happened upon the treaty in the first place.

It had not occurred to Elliot before, but it was very clear to him suddenly that breaking into the commander's office was going to get him expelled. Elliot took a deep breath.

"I found it," said Luke, and the whole room went silent, either in surprise or in total shock at hearing Luke lie. "In my library at home. The Sunborns have a very extensive library. Then Cadet Schafer and Cadet Chaos-of-Battle realised its full significance."

The story was extremely plausible, especially since nobody wanted to discuss where the treaty had actually been. And nobody was going to expel a Sunborn.

Commander Rayburn looked beseechingly at the general. Elliot knew that the papers had been in Commander Rayburn's office, and that meant the commander would be blamed for hiding them, even if the rest of the guard had known exactly what he was doing. The Border guard would want to avoid a diplomatic incident. The commander would be in even more trouble than Elliot if the truth came out.

"The Sunborns do have a big library," the general rumbled out at last, as if weighing the words for believability. "But . . . why on earth would you be in there reading, lad?"

"Improve my vocabulary, sir," said Luke.

From the corner of the room where Captain Woodsinger had placed herself, she coughed. "He does read a lot," she contributed. "In the space allowed him around performing his duties. I have often seen him with his head in a book."

Elliot stared at Captain Woodsinger. She gazed back, her face impassive.

"Oh, oh, very good," responded General Lakelost. "Er . . . commendable." He lowered his voice to what was essentially still a dull roar and said: "Is the boy not any good at fighting?"

"He's excellent, sir," put in Captain Woodsinger in her quiet voice. "One of our finest."

"I don't understand it," the general announced. He squinted at Elliot. "That child can't be old enough to be in the camp. He looks about ten."

"Fourteen, sir," said Captain Woodsinger. "Undersized, sir."

Elliot scowled but refrained from comment, since it was for the best to have everyone distracted from issues like "technical treason."

"Besides, it doesn't really matter, does it?" asked Luke. "We all want peace. Don't we? Sir?"

They couldn't say they did not. Not one of them could actually say that.

General Lakelost did stop Luke at the door, put a fatherly hand on his shoulder, and say: "Maybe ease up on the reading, lad, all right?"

"All right, sir. I know a lot of long words by now anyway."

This was too much. Elliot broke.

"Oh, really, you do? Like what? I want you to be somewhat acquainted with the definition of this word," Elliot demanded.

Luke cast him a sidelong glance. "Provoking," he said. "And I am pretty well acquainted with the definition of the word."

Elliot beamed. "Aw."

Elliot thought it was settled, that they'd done the thing, and there would be no more talk of skirmishes and battles.

Until the trolls and the harpies, alarmed by all these alliances, made an alliance of their own. The harpies encroached on dwarf territory, and the dwarves called on their new allies.

And it was happening again, as if everything they had struggled to accomplish had just been to give themselves an escape route that led around in a circle, right back to where they had been before. Right back to the looming nightmare of war.

Luke and Serene were posted to Lieutenant Louise Sunborn's troop, the 15th, Luke's sister's first command. They were given their marching orders and collected their weapons and bedrolls, all the standard military equipment.

Elliot meant to sit and sulk over the pointless waste of it all in his cabin until the very last moment. There was a knock on the door at one point, but he wasn't done sulking and he ignored it.

He did not make it to the very last moment. When he emerged from the cabin, it was to see the dust of the troops leaving: it was to find Serene and Luke already gone.

Then the news arrived that the trolls had come in far greater force than anyone expected. That the Border guards were hopelessly outnumbered, and the tide of war was turning against them.

Elliot went to pay a call on Captain Whiteleaf, the most senior officer left in charge of the camp. His father had asked for the honor to be granted him. Command did not suit Captain Whiteleaf. He already looked wild about the eyes before he spotted Elliot, and when he did he almost jumped out of the commander's chair.

"Cadet Schafer, what do you need me for?" Captain Whiteleaf said nervously. "I mean, I don't want a repeat of the—burning incident last year, and the commander has, has warned, I mean prepared me, for all your tricks. Just don't . . . just don't do anything. Go back to class."

"Why, Captain, you wrong me," said Elliot with the sweet smile he'd used on the elves. It seemed to make Captain Whiteleaf nervous, which would work just as well as charm. "I thought, as most of the trainees whose duty it is to wait on the officers are off at war, that I would volunteer my services to assist in bringing cool water and snacks to our valiant leaders."

"Let *you* in the council rooms?"

"People need drinks and snacks, Captain," Elliot said in dulcet tones. "It's a totally normal reason for me to be there. I mean, if you don't want me to go there—"

"I don't want you to go there!"

"—for that reason," Elliot continued. "I can certainly find a different reason to go. I'm very resourceful." He smiled again, this time less sweetly but very wide. "You'll see."

None of the councilors were actually allowed in the council room. They sat in an antechamber, and documents were sent out to them to put into proper language. After the big decisions were already made.

Elliot was allowed to bring water and snacks to the officers in the council room. He peeped at the dispatches sent in. He could usually manage to read the ones for Captain Whiteleaf and edit the replies, since the captain was scared of getting things wrong and maybe a little scared of Elliot. He only got glimpses of the most important dispatches sent to General Lakelost. The general seemed suspicious of him, which was understandable but inconvenient.

When he wasn't in council, he was writing long ardent love letters to Serene and trying to work his way out of feeling so truly horrible.

He'd thought he might enjoy spending more time with Peter and Myra, but he was in a slightly ruffled condition and during one lunch made Peter go off somewhere, he suspected to cry, and reduced Myra to staring at him with stunned eyes.

"Sorry," he told her, banishing himself from the lunch room for being an unacceptable human being. "I'm in a filthy mood. Sorry."

He hadn't even said anything so very bad. Luke would not have been reduced to tears. Everybody needed to work on not being so thin-skinned all the time, he told himself, and went off to deliberately pick a fight with the remains of the Trigon team.

He didn't even realise that was what he was doing until he spat out another mouthful of malice at Richard Plantgrown.

"Look," snapped Richard, "you can be as much of a little snot as you want. Luke Sunborn told us if we laid a finger on you while he was gone, he'd have our heads."

"Luke Sunborn needs to learn to mind his own business," snapped Elliot, and at least the others looked like they agreed with him there. "Besides, who's going to tell him? Or are you all just such cowards the mere idea of Luke has you quaking in your—"

Richard did hit Elliot in the face then. Very hard. Elliot hit the wall, and hot pain and blood bloomed, his own flesh breaking open against his teeth. He spat, and this time it was not malice aimed at someone else, but blood hitting the stone. It was still awful.

"Wow, it's been a while, hello old friend being hit in the face," Elliot said, putting his tongue out and tasting the blood, feeling the split and swell of his lip gingerly. "Yep, turns out I still hate pain and think violence is pointless. Sorry, I think I was attempting emotional catharsis, but this is dumb and you people are stupid."

"You're not going to hit me back?"

Elliot blinked. "And prolong this special encounter? No, thank you. Oh, but don't hit me again, I don't want you to, and besides, how do you know I'm not going to tell Luke? I wouldn't trust me. I'm a shifty character."

He took advantage of either their pause for thought or their pause for confusion and slipped away.

Elliot went to the hallway outside the commander's office, since the commander was gone with everyone else. Nobody stopped him: it was as if their camp were a ghost town. He went and sat in the dark hall, leaned his hot face against a stone wall, and shut his eyes.

This magic land was all wrong. In the books, you had to destroy an evil piece of jewelry or defeat an evil-though-sexy witch or wizard. In the books, people did not hide documents and steal land and try to cheat dwarves and dryads.

The whole world was stupid, and now he was stupid too. He didn't understand how this could be happening, how they might be dying. He'd fixed everything. He'd done everything right.

Whenever the dispatches came or the next lot of wounded soldiers were carted in, Elliot went shoving through to the forefront of the crowd—he had very pointy elbows, which was a natural gift he felt called to utilize to his advantage—and asking if anyone had any word of a supremely beautiful elf in a human troop under Lieutenant Louise Sunborn. Or anyone else in that troop. Anyone at all.

Eventually, he heard a familiar name.

"Sunborn?" Elliot repeated, a chill going through him. "Luke?"

"No," said Captain Whiteleaf. "Louise Sunborn, the sister. She's one of the wounded, being carried into the tent now."

Elliot turned and ran. He made it to the largest of the brown tents and stood for a minute just inside the flap, plotting a subterfuge to make his way inside.

A grumpy voice, with that Sunborn ring of expecting absolutely to be listened to, rang out. "Will someone bring me Little Red?"

Or the direct approach might work.

"Hi," said Elliot, darting in and around some medic trying to interfere with him. "You mean me, right? You wanted to see me?"

Louise stared up at him from her cot, her blond hair tangled and filthy. There was a bandage covering half her face: under the white stretch of cotton Elliot could see an open and darkly gleaming wound.

Louise saw him looking. "Yeah, kid, I'm going to have a big scar. You think nobody'll marry me now?"

"I don't think any of them are going to mind," said Elliot matter-of-factly. "Mal Wavechaser says that you have the most rocking bod in the otherlands."

Louise let out a peal of laughter, then put her fingers to her jaw and winced.

"Sorry, sorry!" Elliot said. "I don't know the force of my own wit."

"You're a trip, kid," Louise informed him. Something about the way she looked at him just then reminded him of her mother, Rachel, and he loved her for that alone. "My little brother asked me specially to look in on you. He seemed to think you might be getting into trouble."

"*Me* getting into trouble?" Elliot asked. "That is so unfair. I'm the only one not on a battlefield getting pointy weapons of death jabbed at me."

"Well, he seemed to think you could manage anyway," Louise said. "Are you being a good boy?"

"Yes," said Elliot positively. "I have nearly got these treaties worked out. Captain Whiteleaf almost completely messed up a codicil the other day, but I set him right."

Louise's eyes were half-lidded, he suspected not with sleepiness but with pain. "Whatever keeps you amused."

Elliot hesitated. "Are . . ."

"They're both okay," said Louise. She must have seen the mute appeal on his face, because she continued: "The first battle's never easy, and this is the first battle and the first campaign all rolled into one. But they're tough kids, and they've got each other." She smiled a tiny bit. "They like your letters. You should write them more."

"Luke's been reading my letters?!" Elliot exclaimed.

"Well, we all do," Louise said. "I mean, they read them out at the campfire."

"What," said Elliot.

"No, they're great," said Louise. "They really give everyone a boost. They're hilarious."

"They are not hilarious. They are touching and private love letters for the eyes of my lady alone," Elliot told her severely. "They are addressed to Serene! They begin with a greeting to Serene! They are extremely personal!"

"Ah, you're so much fun," said Louise. "Write Luke a letter tonight, okay? He's nervous about taking over command."

"Ahahaha," said Elliot. "Now you are the one who is being hilarious, because you did not leave a fourteen-year-old in command of armed forces."

Louise hesitated. "You have to understand. They're doing better than okay. Better than all the grown men I have under my command. I couldn't have left my men with anyone else. They wouldn't have followed anyone else when there was a Sunborn to lead them."

"Obviously you're delirious from some sort of medication," said Elliot. "Or maybe I'm delirious, because you talk and all I can hear is la la la suicide mission la la la your fourteen-year-old brother!"

"Serene's there to help him," said Louise. "I left the command to both of them, really."

"Serene is, what's the word I'm searching for here, oh yes, ALSO FOURTEEN."

"What about you, Little Red?" asked Louise. "Getting tired of fiddling with those treaties? Going to leave it all to the grown-ups?"

Elliot opened his mouth to argue. He knew that Luke and Serene were exceptional. He had been told that and had seen that over and over again. But shouldn't the adults, if they loved them, if they were responsible for them and cared for them more than for anything else, the way adults were supposed to . . . shouldn't they try to stop them saving the day, even if they could do it? Unless Elliot's father was only the most honest of the adults, and all adults were willing to betray children if offered an incentive.

Surely there had been other soldiers, not as good as Luke but grown, with strength a kid could not have and experience a kid could not have. For a fourteen-year-old to come to the fore as the obvious leader, others must have made the choice, conscious or not, to step back. Elliot did not know how they could live with letting this happen, letting someone this young be the leader and the sacrifice.

But this was Luke's sister, Rachel's daughter. She had led while she could stand. She was a grown-up, but lying there with her face bandaged, she did not look so very old. She looked tired and hurt.

Elliot leaned his chin sulkily on his fist. "I'll write."

"That's a boy," Louise murmured. "He'll like that."

"Do you want me to stay with you? Can I fetch you anything?"

Elliot was thinking of grapes or something, but one of Louise's eyes popped all the way open. Luke's eyes, kingfisher blue, but with a wicked expression.

"Yes, you can," she said. "This Mal Wavechaser you mentioned."

"Uh . . . what about him?"

"How old is he? And, don't lie to me Little Red, is he good-looking?"

"Well—yes, one of the best-looking guys at school. And he's a fifth year. He only stayed behind to be Captain Whiteleaf's aide-de-camp," said Elliot. "So seventeen, I guess?"

"Close enough," said Louise. "Send him to me. Tell him that a lieutenant with a rocking bod needs her . . . pillow smoothed."

Elliot's mouth fell open.

"Go on!" said Louise. She leaned over to the next cot and stole one of the pillows, ignoring the patient in that cot's feeble protest, and fired it at Elliot's head. "I'm an invalid and I need to be cosseted. Besides, Sunborns, we're a family with great enthusiasm for living, if you know what I'm saying."

"I don't," Elliot lied firmly, and backed away.

"We're like lions on the prowl," Louise shouted after him.

"Don't speak to me like that, I'm an impressionable child!" yelled Elliot.

"Would both of you please stop shouting, this is a place of healing," snapped the redheaded medic.

"Why, Little Red, when I was fourteen—" Louise shouted, and Elliot did not hear the rest because he had wisely departed, which was to say fled. He admired Louise Sunborn's style, but she was a grown-up and Luke's sister, and it was too weird.

Mal Wavechaser hunted him down at dinnertime and professed his eternal gratitude, which was extremely embarrassing.

Elliot was already embarrassed about the letters he had written to Serene, which he had not meant to be as hilarious as everyone had apparently found them. He wanted to tell Serene off for reading them aloud, and at the same time he was too embarrassed to show he cared, since she hadn't thought it was important.

And he didn't want to write something that would make them feel worse. He didn't want anger to be the last thing he ever wrote to them, and he had no guarantees. Any letter could be the last.

So after dinner, he went and wrote a letter for both of them, full of all the news he could think of. It began: "Luke, you miscreant, since apparently you've been READING SERENE'S LETTERS . . ."

In the morning, the dispatches said that Commander Rayburn was dead.

Word after that trickled in agonisingly slowly: word of what had happened, and who had died. Word of Captain Woodsinger seizing the flag before it fell and leading the army: "A *woman*!" said General Lakelost, and yet did not dare send orders that she be removed from command in case those orders were not obeyed.

Louise Sunborn's troop, now Luke's, had been in the thick of the battle.

Elliot did not sleep for two nights, not until the list of survivors arrived. He had always wanted to be taller, and now he was finally growing a little and realized it was not worth the price. He was experiencing shooting pains in his legs, which was super fun and so conveniently timed, and he was staying up reading and thinking until he could neither read nor think any more. Until his mind, the only thing that had never failed him, failed him and he was left lying in his bunk having nightmares with his eyes open.

Of course Elliot was scared sick for Serene, but lonely in the night, at the coldest quietest hour, he had to make certain admissions. He had to admit that he was desperately worried about both of them: he had to admit that Luke was Elliot's friend.

It was so embarrassing. Luke could never know. Elliot decided that he was just going to be Luke's friend very sneakily.

So he tried to be terribly nice to Louise. He visited her every day and stayed with her a long time telling her stories about how annoying other people were, despite the shushing the medics did, and he bothered the medics about her care.

"Have you no ways to make her better faster?" Elliot asked. "This is a magical fantasy land. Have you no mystical unguents?"

The medic gave him a flat look. "What."

"Be straight with me here," said Elliot. "Do we have aspirin?"

"No," said the medic.

Elliot was relieved she knew what aspirin was, at least. She must come from his world. Elliot wondered if she had become a medic hoping for mystical unguents, and that was why she seemed so disappointed with life.

He tried to touch the bottles in the grouchy medic's box and read the labels. "What does that do?"

"Kills you," she said. "And that one makes you vomit for twelve hours straight."

"Cool," said Elliot.

"Not cool, young man," she said. "No touching."

"You're a healer. You should be filled with ineffable goodwill and radiate an aura of peace."

"Get out of my infirmary," she said. Elliot decided he liked her, and bestowed a smile on her as he ambled over to Louise.

Louise took the opportunity to thank Elliot again for recommending Mal Wavechaser, and said that Elliot had excellent taste. Elliot had dark visions of being sent to Captain Whiteleaf's office and scolded for being the world's youngest procurer.

Louise had fever one night, and Elliot sat with her and held her hand. She called out for her mother, but only once. Rachel Sunborn was such a nice mother: Elliot supposed it made sense to still want her, even if you were grown up.

Elliot also came to Louise in order to vent his frustrations when his fury was clearly scaring Myra and Peter: when the offer for a truce came that made the dwarves happy but which gave nothing to the humans and the elves, and the plan was to summarily reject it as an insult.

Elliot sat with Louise that night still furious, thinking: just say yes, just bring them home. Later when he could not sleep and he was thinking about it as if it were a war in an old book, long fought and which he could regard as a game, he realized that if the elves and the humans were both unhappy, the peace would not work. He would not have them given back to him only to be inevitably snatched away.

"It's a question of the size of the territory!" said Captain Whiteleaf the next day, raging imbecile that he was. "And the honor shown us!"

"Oh, well, I don't think that's true, is it?" Elliot asked in his sweetest, least argumentative, talking-to-the-elves voice. He poured General Lakelost his water. "Trolls want rock, so if they're ceded something we think of as a barren wasteland, like for instance here . . ." he gestured pretend-carelessly at a map. "And elves want the woods. In fact, I happen to be in correspondence with a well-connected elven captain, Swift-Arrows-in-the-Chaos-of-Battle, who mentioned a particular bit of woodland her people had their eye on. Here it is. Humans want farmland and gold, and if the trolls switch us this little space here where there's meant to be gold in exchange for the barren wasteland . . ."

"What about honor?" snapped Captain Whiteleaf, weak chin quivering with indignation.

Elliot gazed, wide-eyed. "I'm sure that's important too."

"Indeed, indeed, but forget about it for a second," said General Lakelost. "What were you saying about gold, lad?"

"My friend Myra's part of the Diamond clan," said Elliot. "She seems pretty sure. I mean, I'm not saying she has insider information . . . Oh dear, the jug is empty and you fine officers need to be refreshed. Gotta go refresh!"

He raced away.

The next day, Captain Whiteleaf was too ill to come out of his room and take part in the negotiations.

"You did this," he croaked to Elliot when Elliot went to check this was in fact the case.

"Don't know what you mean, sir," Elliot said. "But I'm sure you'll be better in, oh, twelve hours."

He shut the door and went to bring the general more juice.

"I don't know what it is, lad," said Lakelost, ruffling Elliot's hair—Elliot was pretty sure the general still thought he was ten—"but I think much more clearly with you bringing me apple juice."

"Important to keep refreshed so your mind is at peak performance, sir," said Elliot, and pushed a treaty he'd selected as a good new model into the general's hand.

He wasn't poisoning or drugging General Lakelost. Brandy was medicinal.

In the time it took for the new treaty to be delivered, there came word of another big battle: at the pass in Tharnapyr, trapped between the harpies' Forest of the Suicides and the trolls' Roaring Cliffs. Where the 15th were stationed, and no other troop close enough to reach them. When Elliot heard about it, he was sitting with Louise. She had to be strapped down to her bed to stop her from rising, commandeering a horse, and riding off to a fight that was already over.

Elliot sat with her all that long, cold night.

Word came in the morning, not slowly as before, but in shouts piling on shouts from every messenger and passerby, like the sound of victory bells. They heard of how the 15th had held the pass, their young leaders never faltering, and how Michael and Rachel Sunborn had led an army of their own people from across country and crushed the trolls' force from behind.

The name was repeated so often it began to seem like a thousand candles lit one by one and illuminating night into dawn; it began to seem like a hosanna: Sunborn, Sunborn, Sunborn.

Rachel Sunborn did not stay at the pass long. She got a fresh horse and rode for the Border camp and her daughter. She came in laughing and sweaty, dirty and bloodstained, and stood framed in the entryway of the tent. Rain glittered in her golden hair like diamonds.

"Alive?" snapped Elliot and Louise as one, the sound instinctive as crying out when hit.

"The whole family," said Rachel. "By which of course I also mean that gorgeous elf girl. She stood on the cliffs and fired until we had no arrows left, and every arrow hit a mark. Her kill count is in the hundreds. I'm kidnapping and adopting her."

"Only daughter right here," said Louise.

Rachel strode over to Louise's bed and began to undo the straps. Louise let Elliot's hand go.

"I thought you might be pleased to know the new treaty's getting signed today, little funny face," Rachel said over her shoulder. "You like all that kind of thing, don't you?"

"It was a pretty good treaty," Elliot said.

He was not heard, but he did not mind. Rachel was sweeping Louise's hair off her forehead, looking at the stark wound on her face, and Elliot liked watching her until he heard what she was saying and the cold that had been freezing him all night long trickled back into his blood.

"Never mind that you missed out on the last bit of the fun, baby," Rachel murmured. "There's always another war."

Now the treaty was signed and Rachel was with Louise, there was nothing to be done but go to class, so Elliot went because learning was imperative and he worshipped at the temple of knowledge.

"Could you stop looking out the windows, Cadet Schafer, and listen to the question?" asked Mr Dustlaid, his voice hopeless.

"The Wavechasers discovered the island a hundred and twenty-four years ago," Elliot snapped. "I read extra materials. And looking upon greenery makes the mind relax and absorb information better. That's science. *Brain science.*"

Well, he would worship at the temple of knowledge if the rest of the class would catch up with him and stop being so boring.

The lesson Elliot already knew droned on. The trees shook fistfuls of leaves in the wind like impatient customers waving sheaves of crumpled bills, and the wind whooshed and rustled and carried no other sound.

Until it did. Until Elliot heard, faint and far away, the sound of an elven horn.

He'd imagined such sounds before, but he saw Myra's head jerk up. She'd heard it too.

Elliot's desk and chair went crashing onto the floor, the desk before him and the chair behind.

Mr Dustlaid was startled enough to shout.

"Sit back down, Cadet Schafer!"

Elliot considered this, said: "No," and raced out the door. There was nobody in sight yet, no sign of armies in the fields or over the hills. Elliot went for the woods, which would screen sight, climbing over the rise of a hill as he went around the last few clusters of trees.

He wanted to see them, expected to see them, and was yet not quite prepared for the sight of them, the small band of faraway figures, little more than black dots in the green. Elliot squinted, hand over his eyes to block out the glare of the sun, to make sure it was them: he saw Luke's hair shining like a helm, and then knew that the figure standing farther off from the troop but closer to Luke than anyone else must be Serene.

In another moment he was sure of it, and sure she had seen him. She began to run, faster than any human could, racing elven-fleet across the grass. Elliot ran down the hill toward her, stumbling as he went, lent speed by the slope and not caring if he fell.

He fell into Serene's arms. She flew at him and he stumbled into her, and her hands held on to the back of his shirt, clutched handfuls of it as if he were trying to get away. He wasn't. He clung to her, felt her slim and strong and safe against him. He buried his face in the crook of her neck and the sheltering dark veil of her hair. And he heard the sound of Luke's panting and running footfalls, indrawn hesitant breath and hovering warmth. He grabbed hold of his jerkin and drew him in. Luke's hand caught Elliot's arm, and his free arm went around Serene's waist, and Elliot could hear them all breathing, could almost hear their heartbeats, had proof they were both alive and returned and whole.

Elliot lifted his head and looked into Serene's eyes. Serene drew in a shaky breath, Elliot knew so as not to cry and be unwomanly, and said: "You're taller."

"Am I?" Elliot asked. "I missed you."

Someone was going to cry, he was fairly sure, but then the war-training classes arrived on the scene, every boy and girl who had not been sent to war, all of the younger ones, and they rushed them. Elliot stepped out of the way basically in order to avoid getting trampled down as by wild horses. People were already chanting, the same refrain: "Sunborn, Sunborn!"

"No," Luke said loudly, and the boys paused in the very act of pulling him onto their shoulders. He offered Serene a hand, courtly as if he were helping her into a carriage. "Serene was with me every step of the way. I did nothing she did not do as well, and better. Serene too."

Serene took his hand. Boys swarmed around her too, lifted them both up high into the air. Their shouts seemed to echo off the sky.

Elliot was left to trail behind. As he did, he thought about Luke talking about literary tropes—the fearless hero, the valiant heroine, and where did it all leave him? Sidekick: a horrible indignity, Elliot refused to accept it. And the other idea was some sort of lurking, jealous figure: an Iago, a pathetic pseudo-villain waiting in the wings to plot and bring the hero down. He wasn't going to plot against Luke, who had dumb daffodil hair and said "tropez," for God's sake.

Delia Winterchild had come back from the war. Her twin, Darius, had not. She trailed alongside Elliot, dragging her feet as the crowd raced triumphantly ahead. He looked at her and was almost ashamed that he was so glad his people had come home safe.

"I'm really sorry," he said.

"He was a brave soldier," said Delia, squaring her shoulders as if that gave her some comfort. "And he's lying in the ground while everyone cheers for the untouchable Sunborns."

Elliot reached for her hand. She looked surprised, but after a moment she let him. Her hand was chilly in his. They walked back to the camp together.

Elliot didn't know why he was bothering to think about roles and stories. Any of their stories could end, any of them could stop being a hero and be put in the cold ground at the very next battle. And Rachel Sunborn had said there would always be another war.

The feast went on for a long time. Elliot had a place near the centre of the action, which he hadn't asked for and didn't want, and so he had to hear all the battle stories, over and over. There were songs and toasts, but worst of all were the stories. The one where Serene stood at the top of a cliff and Luke at the bottom, bow and sword at the ready, until their troop stopped their retreat, was the worst. Serene proudly showed a notch in one of her beautiful ears, and someone had one of Luke's old shirts, with a tear and blood on it, which they waved like a flag.

"Aren't you proud?" asked Dale Wavechaser at one point, and everybody looked at Elliot.

He understood that Luke and Serene were both very good at using weaponry, this had been made very clear to him, but he didn't really see what there was to be so impressed with about that.

Elliot made a face, and said finally, weakly: "Doesn't really have anything to do with me."

Which wasn't great, but wasn't "No, not proud at all, and also if anyone tells another of these stories I think I might be sick."

"And then the treaty was signed and all our brave boys and girls could come home!" thundered General Lakelost, distracting people. Elliot was grateful. Captain Woodsinger, now Commander of the Border camp, had to get up and take a bow, and Elliot clapped along with everyone else.

"Did you get a chance to see the treaty?" he asked Serene, leaning over to her under the cover of the noise.

"Oh, well, no . . .," said Serene. "Not yet."

"Uh, she'll get around to it," Luke said, his eyebrows raised. "She has more important things to think of right now."

"More important than the terms of the treaty that got the other side to agree to peace?" Elliot asked.

"But of course they would have signed no matter what, after the beating we gave them," Luke said, casting an approving eye around, and his scattered troop preened at his praise.

"Oh, of course," said Elliot. "Because the astonishing fact that some people got *killed* in a *battle* would definitely have stopped everyone in their tracks."

"Elliot," said Serene. "I will of course be most interested to hear about such matters another time, but you have to be aware we almost died."

The hall was much more quiet than Elliot would have liked. Elliot felt like everyone was paying attention, weighing him in the balance, and finding him unworthy.

"I am," said Elliot. "Very."

"Treaties are important, just—"

"Just not as important," said Elliot quietly.

The General reached across the table and tugged at Serene's sleeve. Serene made an apologetic face at Elliot and turned to him. Elliot didn't even know why he was surprised. Serene had always been a little more inclined to war than council, though brilliant at both: he just hadn't wanted to see it. Now she had been away at the wars and knew viscerally that war was a matter of life or death. Now she was closer to Luke than she had ever been before; it was easy to see, even in the way they both reached for their cups in tandem. He didn't know why he had expected Serene to be on his side.

He got up from the table murmuring about the privy, abstracted a book and Swift's latest letter from one of his many book hiding places, and went back to his cabin. Everyone was at the feast, so he wouldn't have to deal with the annoying people he was forced to sleep with, and he could read properly. Swift was an oddly excellent correspondent, and Elliot had to figure out where the next war would break out and how to stop it.

Clearly, he had forgotten that his days of occasionally not having to deal with annoying people were over. He'd only just settled down on a pillow on the floor beside his bed and begun reading Swift's latest, which began somewhat horrifyingly with "My dear little red-headed seeker after knowledge" but continued with a list of common troll phrases, when Luke came in the door.

Elliot thought of several things to say, including "I see we need a refresher course in how to knock" and "It was so lovely and peaceful when you were gone," but he didn't particularly want to be accused of callous indifference to heroes who had almost died again. He said nothing.

"Are you not coming back?" Luke asked. Elliot made a noncommittal gesture. "I know that parties aren't much fun," Luke went on. "But it's a tribute to bravery and sacrifice."

Obviously Luke was very proud of all his bravery and sacrifice and enjoying being showered in glory. Elliot failed to see why he had to participate, but he didn't say so.

"This is just like you," said Luke. "Are you seriously going off to sulk over nobody wanting to talk about your dumb treaty? I know you think violence is a stupid last resort, but it was our only resort, and we did well. And you might not want to hear about anything we did, but other people do. People died, and you should show a little respect. And shut up about how unnecessary and useless war is for one night."

"I hope you're enjoying your fight with Imaginary Elliot," said Elliot. "Because I haven't said a word since you came in."

"Well, why are you being so quiet?"

"I can't believe you just asked me that question. Are you aware that nobody in the history of time has ever asked me that question?" Elliot demanded. "Has it struck you that you are being a *little hard to please right now*, loser?"

"What," said Luke, and suddenly looked confused. "Are you trying?"

Elliot had to admit that probably, from the outside, leaving a party early in a huff and then administering the silent treatment did not seem like he was trying especially hard. He considered Luke. He looked a little older than when Elliot had seen him last, and a lot more tired.

"I am a bit," Elliot said eventually. "I'm glad you're both not dead, and I don't want to fight."

"Oh," said Luke. "Okay."

That seemed to be that. Luke stopped his righteous looming and came to sit on Elliot's bed.

"What are you doing, then? Who's the letter from?"

"Serene's cousin Swift," said Elliot. "She's teaching me troll."

"You're penpals with Serene's cousin?"

"She's a very nice lady, and she says she gets lonely out on patrol, on the long, cold nights." Elliot stopped and frowned. "Actually, now I say that out loud it sounds like something I should report to my chaperone. But I don't have a chaperone, and besides I'm really getting a handle on troll vocabulary."

"So you haven't changed, then," said Luke, who was sort of drooping with tiredness like a sad dandelion.

"I've been told I'm taller."

"Still kind of titchy," observed Luke, which was offensive, and then put his head down on the pillow.

"Get up and go back to your celebration, you lump," said Elliot.

The one eye Elliot could see rolled. "I thought you were trying to be nice."

Elliot gave up on being nice. "Ugh, you're the worst, leave and never come back."

Luke fell asleep instead. After about six minutes, there came a knock.

"Who is that rapping on my chamber door," Elliot murmured to himself. "What elf could it be? And when shall I read my letter? Nevermore. Come in, Serene!"

She came in, looking a little abashed to be in a gentleman's bedchamber.

"Sorry I'm late," she said, and came to sit on the bed. "I had to stop and have a look at a treaty."

Elliot almost hated himself for being so pathetic, but knew he was glowing just the same. "Yeah?"

"It's pretty good," Serene told him, in her measured way. "I love the bit about the trolls cooperating on farming in the south fields in exchange for help with mining equipment."

Elliot shrugged modestly instead of saying "Oh baby, talk treaties to me." "Well."

"How'd you do it?" asked Serene, lying down next to Luke, who stirred and slid his arm around her, with what even Elliot could tell was the ease of familiarity and long loving habit.

"I poisoned Captain Whiteleaf," Elliot announced proudly.

Luke opened his one visible eye. "No," he said. "No poisoning captains. 'm drawing a line."

"I poisoned him, and I got the general super drunk," Elliot boasted in a rush.

"That was very enterprising," said beautiful Serene, who always understood him, or at least understood him better than anyone else. She shut her eyes.

"Okay, no, guys, now I'm drawing a line," said Elliot. "This is my bed. I have boundaries. I have a personal bubble. Get off. Go away. I'm serious."

They lay curled around each other like two leaves in the forest, and about as responsive to demands. Elliot looked at them, so comfortable and close, and felt a jealous pang that wanted to turn to fury or despair. He'd always known where this situation would wind up, he supposed, if he was honest with himself. He knew how life worked. He could call Luke a loser as often as he wanted, but that didn't make it true.

Elliot sighed and opened his book. It had a map on it that he wanted to refer to.

After he memorised the map, he looked back at them, legs tangled, their slow breathing in sync. Luke was filthy, Elliot noted disapprovingly, and even Serene looked slightly disarranged. Elves did not seem to get as smudgy as humans. They did not look like heroes but like sleepy, dirty children. Elliot felt like a little kid himself, confused and helpless, not able to deal with the world at all. Their heads were leaning together on his pillow, the gold and the dark, ruffled and mingling. Elliot felt like he should maybe smooth them or something.

There was a noise at the threshold. Elliot snatched his hand back. Rachel Sunborn stood at the door. She was in jewels, with her hair neatly braided, and looked as magnificent as she had battle-stained in the rain.

"Hi there," she said. "I was wondering where you'd all got to."

"I'm here," Elliot told her, perhaps unnecessarily. "They stole my bed. They have perfectly good beds of their own."

Rachel seemed unmoved by her son's thieving ways. "Little rascals, all tuckered out. And what are you up to?"

"I've decided to put an end to all war," Elliot announced.

Rachel blinked. "That might take a while."

"I know. I probably won't be done by the time we're out of school," said Elliot. "That's why I figured I should get started right away."

Rachel threw back her head and laughed. "That's good thinking. Well, me and my man and Lou have to get going. There's clean-up to be done." Elliot understood that by "clean-up" she meant more killing, and not cleaning up at all. But she leaned over him in the candlelight and looked at him so kindly. "Tell my boy to take care of himself. See you this summer, funny face?"

"I don't know," Elliot said awkwardly.

Rachel tweaked his nose and departed. "See you there."

As the door banged shut behind her, Elliot glanced to the others, wondering if the noise had woken them. He saw Luke had his eyes open, watching the door. There was a certain expression on his face which made Elliot remember that he must have watched his mother leave to go somewhere dangerous hundreds of times.

"You can come if you want," Luke said. "We're having a big thing. I mean, whatever."

"Yeah," Elliot said. "Okay."

"Okay," murmured Luke. He sighed and turned his face into the pillow, covered with Serene's dark hair. He burrowed against her, and she said something indistinct with Luke's name in it, and they both fell back asleep.

Elliot felt a little Iago-ish, but mainly he was so terribly glad they were alive. And the school year was almost over, with so much work left to be done. He turned back to his books.

Elliot was meant to go to Luke's in late summer, so he could go straight back to camp with the others. That meant spending a lot of time with his father beforehand. He tried to call the kids up the street, Tom and Susan, but they were off backpacking with their friends through the countryside. He left a message saying he'd join them, if they thought that would be fun, but he didn't expect a call back. He started hanging out a lot at an old music shop called Joe's, run by Joe himself, a grizzled old guy who talked a lot about his nephew who might come to visit him soon and played Elliot vinyl records. He was clearly as lonely as Elliot was.

Elliot bought a lot of old radios, even ones that played tapes, which he thought were hilarious and quaint. He went searching the shops and found a cracked camera that filtered out real paper photos with a whirring sound a little while after you'd taken them. He'd noticed it was the most modern stuff that did worst at the Border. His heart cried out for a proper phone, but the situation called for experimentation.

He came home late from the record shop one day and almost collided with his father going to bed. His father looked at him. He seemed very mildly startled, as if at a near-stranger whose existence he had forgotten, encountered unexpectedly in the street.

"Getting quite tall, aren't you," he said, with a faint note of accusation.

Elliot held on to his tape deck and tried to smile.

"I suppose," he said. His father slipped softly and silently by him, like a ghost whose haunting of this house had been only briefly disturbed.

He was glad when the time came to go. He left a note on the table for his father rather than say good-bye to him, and he climbed the steps to the wall lightly, even though he was somewhat laden down.

The sun was shining on the other side of the wall. Only one of Elliot's bags went on fire, and he disposed of it behind a tree because it seemed bad guest behaviour to bring a lovely fire for the whole family to share. There was a distressing smell of melting plastic, but Elliot elected to ignore it.

The wood was like a green net of light, leaves capturing the sunshine and leaving it to blanket the grass. One of Luke's dogs, Culaine, came racing through the sunny dust toward him.

Elliot knelt down and fondled his ears. "Hey," he said. "Do you remember me?"

Culaine tried to lick his face, which seemed very familiar and indicated to Elliot that he did.

"I think you must be unusually intelligent for a canine," Elliot observed. "Who's unusually intelligent for a canine? Is it you? Yes you are!"

He patted his head a final time and stood up, looking around a bit warily to see if anyone had seen him being silly with a dumb animal. But there was nobody there, and Culaine danced at his heels all the way to the Sunborn tower.

He pushed open the door to the hall, then wandered into the kitchen and almost tripped over Rachel Sunborn lying prone on the floor.

"Oh my God!" said Elliot.

Rachel opened her eyes a slit. "Aw, welcome," she said. "I was just catching a quick nap on the floor. There's so much work on with the whole trial."

"Trial?" asked Elliot.

"Luke didn't tell you?"

"He said there was a—" Elliot made a gesture with the tape deck, which was excitingly and totally intact. "Big thing. It wasn't illuminating."

"Strong silent type, my lad," said Rachel. "Well, don't worry about it, you don't have to participate. I just have to set up some obstacle courses and hang some bunting and so on."

"Have you been doing it all morning?" Elliot asked, appalled.

"Well, no, to tell you the truth I had breakfast and then got a bit overcome by the thought of all the work to be done and had a kip in the sun instead," Rachel said. "If I went outside Michael might find me and make me do something. Put down your things, kiddo, and give me a kiss."

Elliot put down some of his bags on the big tabletop and knelt down, then gave her a quick kiss on the cheek, near her pink-painted mouth. She smelled like grass and perfume. He hesitated as he did it—he'd never kissed a mother-type person before, and he wasn't certain that she wasn't making a joke, that she didn't really mean him to—but she didn't seem to be joking. She patted his hair with her heavily ringed hand, and he hoped she had not felt him tremble.

"What have you got there, lad?"

"Oh," Elliot said, scrambling to his feet. "You'll like it, I promise. It's a tape deck. I brought tapes for it. I brought some Beatles, and Joe says the Sex Pistols are really good too."

Rachel laughed. "Love the name."

Elliot selected a tape at random and put it in the tape recorder. "I super apologise if there is a fire," he said, and pressed play.

Tinny and small, the music began to play, singing an urge to dance. Rachel sat up on the floor, hugging her knees to her chest. "Oh, look at that, it's a minstrel in a box."

"Yes, exactly!" Elliot said enthusiastically, and then looked up at a sound in the hall to see Cavall bounding in, Serene and Luke clattering in after him, looking rumpled and sun-warm. Elliot beamed and beckoned to them. "Guys," he called. "Come see."

They came in, both grinning, though Serene looked slightly worried.

"Why is the box telling us to dance?" she asked, and came over to give him a hug. Elliot was stunned to find he was actually slightly taller than she was. "Is it a command we must obey, or a geas?"

"Yes," Elliot decided, and grabbed her hands. A certain amount of scuffling followed. "Why are you trying to lead?"

Serene stared at him. "Why are you?"

"Fair enough," Elliot decided, and let Serene take charge, her steps guiding his.

Serene frowned, her face very close to his and sweetly concerned. "Do you want a turn?"

Elliot rubbed his nose against hers. "I don't mind, as long as I'm dancing with you."

"I admit I'm rather an expert. My name can be found on every boy's dance card back home," said Serene, and instantly Elliot knocked into Luke, who was hovering. Luke tried to save them both and ended up tripping over his mother, and then everyone was on the floor but Serene, who leaned somewhat smugly against the wooden counter. "Elves have a certain natural grace," she added.

Elliot glanced at Luke, who nodded, and Elliot held up three fingers, then folded them quickly down one by one, counting down until the moment each of them grabbed one of her legs and brought her crashing to the ground.

Everyone was laughing by then.

"Do you hear it," said Elliot. "Isn't it great? I am bringing technology to the Border. Next step, the Industrial Revolution."

"I wish you would not start a revolution," Luke contributed.

"Don't tell me what to do, loser, I'm going to and it's going to be awesome," said Elliot firmly.

"When the revolution comes," Luke said, "I am still not going to wear the funny clothes from the weird world."

They all looked at Elliot's clothes.

Elliot glanced down at his Pink Floyd T-shirt and jeans. "I am wearing totally normal clothes. Plus my T-shirt is cool and retro."

"Luke's right, it is a little provocative," said Serene. "Not that I wish to question or shame you. You should wear whatever clothing you feel most comfortable in. Being comfortable in yourself is the best way to be attractive to others."

"Firstly: thank you, you're as wise as you are totally gorgeous. Secondly: I've said this before and I'll say it again: I will not be lectured on my fashion choices by a pair of fetish-gear enthusiasts." Elliot added to the severity of this proclamation by pulling Luke's hair. Luke batted his hand gently away.

"You're in a good mood," he said, smiling.

"I love revolution," said Elliot, instead of saying something embarrassing like that he was happy to be there.

Then Elliot grabbed the kitchen counter and levered himself upright so he could fiddle with the tape deck and start the song again.

He put out a hand to help Serene up, saw Luke and Serene both reach for the hand, reconsidered and reached past them to lift Rachel to her feet. Rachel grabbed his hand, laughing, and dipped Elliot with a look over at Serene as if to check she was doing it the elven way. Elliot laughed and laughed, and spun her when she let him up, and then they both shimmied at each other, circling each other with their palms up before they linked hands again. Sunshine painted them all in warm strokes, the song told them that fantasy could never be so giving, and Elliot sang along. Luke and Serene were leaning and tapping time against the kitchen counters.

Culaine barked once, a quick warning, and Elliot looked over to see Adam and Neal Sunborn at the door, watching them. He stopped dead, letting Rachel's hand slip from his.

"Oh, hey, boys," said Rachel casually, and beckoned them in.

"Hi, Aunt Rachel," said Neal, coming over to kiss her while all the time undressing Serene busily with the corners of his eyes, sly as a vicar feeling up a choir mistress in church. "Wow, Serene, you look amazing."

Simple fact. Neal could mention it if he felt he must. Elliot knew that Serene was used to the admiration of men and it would not affect her feelings. Besides which, he was slightly distracted by Adam Sunborn. Adam was still standing in the doorway, looking at Elliot. Elliot made a face at him: he was not going to put up being teased about his Pink Floyd T-shirt by awful Adam.

"Hey," said Adam, and grinned. "You're never little Elliot."

"Have you tipped too many kids out of trees to be able to remember them all properly?" Elliot inquired, and withdrew to the counter as Adam advanced.

"What's that?" said Rachel, her head turning sharply.

Elliot glanced at Luke. Elliot loved tattling on people. He thought it was amazing fun, and if people were dumb enough to put Elliot in a position where he could get them into trouble by opening his mouth, they deserved what they got. The code of not telling tales was the usual stuff where stronger people tried to impose their rules on weaker people so they could get away with everything. But Luke really believed in it, and this was his house, his mother, his cousins. Elliot had promised himself that he was going to be nice to Luke now Luke was his friend.

"Haha," said Elliot unconvincingly. "Just a boyish lark, or whatever."

"Yeah, I didn't mean anything by it, and no harm done, right?" Adam asked. He had crept up on Elliot somehow: Elliot hated all people with warrior training. "Wow, you've changed."

"I haven't," Elliot said flatly. "Just taller. Still extremely annoying."

Adam laughed as if Elliot were making a joke, as if Elliot wanted to joke around with awful Adam. "I like your shirt."

"Oh, that's mature and intelligent," said Elliot.

Mocking someone's clothes in front of a mother. Well, it was about what Elliot expected of those two.

Fortunately Luke's dad came in, and Adam and Neal had to follow him around like terriers yapping for a bigger dog's approval, while Michael's actual son gave him a nod which Michael returned because they seemed to have a silent understanding. Elliot had possibly heard them exchange two words ever, but he was pretty confident that Michael would drop Adam and Neal in vats of boiling oil rather than let anyone harm a hair of Luke's head, so he figured Michael's priorities were in order. Louise came in with her dad and said, "Little Red, you got so big!" and Elliot had to attend to the important business of showing her the tape deck.

After dinner Elliot sat in a window seat away from the main gathering on the cushioned chairs in the parlor. Louise and her dad were telling a war story, while Neal whispered sweet nothings to Serene and she looked amused.

Adam offered to fetch Elliot a drink, as if Elliot had not got wise to the whole spitting in a drink and handing it to someone when he was five. Elliot called in reinforcements and beckoned Luke over.

"Come sit," he ordered. "Protect me from your cousin."

"He's not exactly fearsome," said Luke, but he sat willingly enough and kicked up his legs, boots propped against the other side of the frame, so his whole body formed a barrier between Elliot and possible Sunborn cousin incursions.

"Why are they here again?" Elliot asked.

"They have to be here, for the thing," said Luke.

"Strangely, your wildly unspecific words convey no information to me."

"Oh, it's like a trial?" said Luke. "For Sunborns? It's a family thing. We have obstacle courses and tourneys, and there's banners, and afterwards there's a big celebration."

"Ugh," said Elliot.

"I know, parties," Luke commiserated.

"I more meant all the physical exertion," said Elliot. "But your mum says I don't have to participate."

"No, you can't," said Luke. "It's for Sunborns. Also, no offence, you'd be killed."

"No offence taken. I don't want to participate in your horrible sounding family rituals. I also think it's creepy that your family has private bonding rituals with bunting."

"Calling my family rituals creepy is a bit offensive."

Elliot waved a hand dismissively. "Well, I'm sad your cousins are here. Your cousins are the worst."

"They're not the best," said Luke, which Elliot decided meant he agreed and he hated them too. "What are you reading?"

"A troll history written by one of their preeminent scholars. Did you know that trolls are naturally a very peaceful people?"

Luke found this difficult to believe, and had some purely anecdotal story of a troll trying to pull his head off and seemed to believe that proved something. Elliot disagreed vehemently.

"You are wrong and stupid and wrong about everything," Elliot said. "Someone save me from this conversation."

"Hi," said Adam.

"Do you mind?" said Luke.

"Get lost," Elliot told him.

"Oh, hey, reading again?" asked Adam, as if a) he knew Elliot at all, b) it was a funny hobby like compulsively making papier-mache rabbits, and c) Adam was being indulgent about it. "What's the book?"

Elliot smiled at him charmingly. "Oh, it's a great book, it's called *None of Your Business* by *I'm Not Going To Tell You.*"

"This is a private conversation," Luke added.

Elliot tapped Luke approvingly on the knee with his ballpoint pen. Adam eyed the object as if it were a tiny firework. Elliot still refused to use quills like everyone else because he found them inefficient and personally upsetting. Nobody understood. He had tried to share his awesome stash of office supplies from the other world, but Serene claimed she had an allergy to plastic, Myra had poked herself in the eye with a Sharpie, and the one time Elliot had felt pleased enough with Luke to award him a pen, Luke kept it like a souvenir rather than ever actually trying to use it.

"What," Elliot said, as Adam finally backed off, "is wrong with that guy?"

Adam was a real problem. Neal was also dreadful, but at least didn't bother Elliot directly. He seemed to be invested in staring at Serene with his mouth open. Because Serene was sadly susceptible to flattery from pretty boys and did not wish to be discourteous or hurt fragile male hearts, she permitted him to waylay her and ply her with compliments all the time. Adam, in contrast, was constantly underfoot. Elliot supposed Adam was lonely but did not see why that had to be his problem.

His attempts to make Adam Luke's problem instead were only partially successful, on account of Luke was a monster.

"Take him away," Elliot said when Adam invited himself along to an outing with Luke, Elliot, and the dogs. "Play a sport with him!"

"Play a sport?" Luke repeated.

"Yes!" said Elliot. "You know you love a sport."

"Why are you sending me away? How is that fair?" Luke demanded.

Elliot stared at him. "Send you away from what? You big *baby*," he said severely. "What's so great about this grove? Let me tell you, you can get trees and grass literally anywhere. Take him to another grove, it will be just as good."

Serene had the kindest and sweetest heart in the world, so she offered a solution.

"I have noticed that when I wear shirts that bare more skin, human boys become quite obviously distracted."

Elliot would never have asked her to do such a thing, but he was deeply touched when she did. Unfortunately for his plan of sneaking away from the Adam menace, Adam did not seem particularly distracted. Neal walked right into a door, though, and that brightened everybody's day. Adam had to tend to him as well, and so that did take him away for a while.

Elliot raised his arms in victory, king of all the grove he surveyed and not bothered by the annoying and unwelcome. "Concussions are hilarious! Concussions are the best!"

Serene and Luke, lying in the grass with the dogs, mumbled protests, but Elliot knew they agreed really. They spent the day using Elliot's camera to take pictures. Serene looked beautiful in every single one, Luke managed to accidentally take an up-the-nostril shot of himself, and Elliot decided to save them all.

In spite of Adam, the summer was nice. Until more and more Sunborns started arriving, and talking about the trials, and a joust, and lances, and bows and arrows and riding and who had broken bones last time and then mentioned poor Harry Sunborn, dead before his time, but it was the way he would've wanted to go. That was when the full horror of the situation burst upon Elliot.

"Are you telling me this is a huge dumb competition to pick the *best* Sunborn?" he demanded.

"Our champion," said Luke, frowning.

"And people die because of a pissing contest?" Elliot further demanded. "Are you kidding me? Is this a joke?"

Luke frowned. "Well, the contest doesn't have anything to do with—"

"Don't be nervous," said Adam, slinging an arm around Elliot's shoulders.

"Don't be handsy," Elliot snapped, and elbowed him. He did not enjoy Adam's touchy bro ways. They were not bros.

"Hardly anybody is ever killed," Adam continued loftily. "And they're only held every decade, so very few Sunborns are lost to the world. Besides which, Ellie Sunborn has had long enough as both Sunborn and Trigon champion. Time for the young blood to have a turn. The Sunborns want to have a hero and a new hope for every generation, and I think I've got a pretty good chance. Did I tell you what my arms commander said to—"

"Did I mention I don't care," said Elliot.

Adam was always telling them about his exploits or someone saying that he was good at some awful thing to do with weapons or him winning something and making everyone else look a fool. He was so vain.

"I agree the contest is terrible," said Serene, and Elliot brightened until Serene continued: "I can't believe only Sunborns can participate."

The day of the trials was, despite all Elliot's hopes, sunny and dry, as if the sky wanted to wave one of the Sunborn flags of gold and blue. Sunborns were camped through the woods, their tents peeking out amongst the leaves. There was nowhere to hide: there was a family living in the library. Elliot saw a Sunborn baby sucking on the edge of a tome and had to go sit down. He did not get up again until Adam appeared and Elliot had to give him the slip, claiming that he wanted to wish Luke good luck.

Elliot was sure Luke was lurking somewhere in the equipment room, being very conscientious about his gear or something. Luke was good at dealing with people, but he was also truly excellent at receding from them. Sometimes Elliot thought about Rachel calling Luke her shy boy.

Luke did not look particularly shy, though, when Elliot looked around the door of the equipment room. Elliot might've got a bit taller, but Luke was really tall for his age, and strong. He didn't look afraid about facing down grown-ups. He had, Elliot supposed, done it before.

"Hey," he said, looking over at Elliot with a small smile and continuing to strap weapons on.

"You know I hate violence in all its forms," Elliot announced. "And if you wanted to sit out this stupid contest, I would be supportive."

Luke tilted his head inquiringly. "What would you being supportive even look like? I'll pass. It would be too much of a shock to my system."

"Okay, that token protest made," said Elliot. "You're better than Adam at everything, right?"

"I'm better than Adam at some things," said Luke. "Though I don't feel the need to boast about it all the time."

"I know, we hate him," said Elliot, delighted. "Also when you say some things, can you name anything that Adam is better at?"

Luke was modestly silent.

"Great!" Elliot declared. "Can you beat him in this stupid contest so that we don't have to hear about it for the rest of time? By an embarrassing margin, if you can manage it. Please and thank you."

"Yeah," said Luke, still smiling. "I think I can do that."

"Cool," Elliot told him, and ducked back out. He and Serene had a date to watch the Sunborn trials together, and she had saved him a seat on the stands.

"Hey, are you Elliot?" asked a woman on the stands with them, in a Border guard uniform. Elliot thought she was Rafe Sunborn's girlfriend. Serene looked at her with recognition: they reached across Elliot and shook hands, but the woman was still looking at him and smiling. "I was in Louise Sunborn's troop. I loved your letters," she told him. "They were hilarious."

"Oh were they, hey, that's great, *kill me*," Elliot added urgently to Serene. She patted him on the back.

She did a lot of patting him on the back that day, as the heat haze rose from the ground and the Sunborns went into the ring. Dust rose, choking in his throat and stinging his eyes. Rachel was in that ring. Louise was in that ring. And Luke.

He opened a book and leaned against Serene. He'd thought he might be able to watch, but he wasn't able to at all. When Neal Sunborn, who Elliot actually disliked, broke his leg and the snap cut through the air, Elliot shuddered against Serene and knew she felt it, was helpless to do anything else. He refused to even look up when

Luke was in the ring. He only knew he was because of the ripple of sound that was his name, the hum of approval that Rachel and Michael's son was doing so well. He hated literally everyone around him. Except Serene.

"Hit her again, Luke!" Serene yelled.

Occasionally also Serene.

Rachel Sunborn got struck out with a lucky blow to her helmet—she told him afterwards, Elliot obviously did not see for himself—and Elliot hurried off to the kitchen, where they had set up a makeshift infirmary.

"Oh, honey, go back, you don't want to miss all the fun," said Rachel, but Elliot refused, held her hand, and tried not to wince at the clash of swords, the twang of bow strings, or the thump of bodies on the ground filtering through. Neal was moaning in pain. Adam, for once, didn't bother Elliot but rushed to his brother when he came into the kitchen, and Elliot supposed that meant Adam had been knocked out of the contest.

Elliot waited for Luke and Serene to come into the infirmary, either to find him or because—if Luke was hurt, but they did not come. Eventually there came a great roar from outside, Elliot knocked something over, and Rachel got up despite the fact that her head was bandaged and she'd told Elliot he was holding up seventeen fingers. Elliot went with her, letting her lean on him, and for the second time in a handful of months, he saw Luke being carried away on people's shoulders. He heard the chants of 'Sunborn!'

They were all so pleased with themselves. They had set this up like a game, they acted like it was all a game, like honor or glory was an acceptable exchange for a life.

The Sunborns thought battle was a game and choosing a champion was reason for a party. They lit a bonfire and roasted a pig, set the minstrels playing and the torches burning. Elliot made himself busy carrying stuff and setting up places for the wounded, and it was not until the sunlight was nothing but a slice of orange between dark hills and darker sky that Luke found him.

"Hey," said Luke. "Did you see—"

"No, wasn't watching, don't tell me about it, don't want to know," Elliot said hastily. "Oh, but—good job."

"Right," said Luke.

"Hi, Luke," said a blond girl who looked Sunbornish. Elliot hoped she wasn't a very close relative, given the way she was twirling her hair around her finger. "You were fantastic today."

"Oh, thank you," said Luke.

"Do you want to dance?"

"Oh, uh, no," said Luke. "I don't really dance."

"I like to dance," Elliot offered helpfully.

"Um . . .," said the girl, looking both disappointed and disgruntled. Elliot could not quite work out how to withdraw his offer. "Okay."

The girl was a bit taller than Elliot, despite his recent strides in that area, and her hands in his felt like unenthused dead fish.

"Have you known Luke long?" she asked as Elliot spun her and the sparks from the fire flew upward.

"Two years."

"That must be amazing," said the girl.

"Every day a gift," said Elliot.

"He's so brave and strong. And so good and kind."

"Also his hair," Elliot commented. "Very shiny."

The girl glared. "Are you making fun of me?"

"Can you blame me?" said Elliot. Apparently she could: she pulled her hand away and stomped off to her friends.

Elliot looked around hopefully for Serene, but she was sitting across the fire letting Neal Sunborn pity-hold her hand. Stupid lucky people with broken legs.

"Hey," said Adam.

"You," said Elliot flatly. "Fantastic."

He looked around for Luke, but Luke was hidden by a crowd of admirers. Elliot eyeballed the sky wildly for answers. He couldn't see where Rachel was, and Louise was sitting in some boy's lap. There was no help anywhere.

"Want to dance?" asked Adam.

Elliot stared at him. He couldn't quite work out the joke. "Um," he said, and felt a touch on his hand. He looked down and saw Culaine. "I think I'm going to take the dog for a walk."

"I'll come with you," Adam said promptly.

"Uh, wow. I guess I . . . walked right into that."

It was stupid to walk Culaine, since he lived in a world composed largely of fields and woods where he could roam freely. It seemed Elliot was doing it anyway. Stumbling in the dark, almost falling down a hill, walking a dog that didn't need to be walked with Adam Sunborn. What an adventure. Maybe he'd break his neck and wouldn't have to suffer the company any longer.

"So, it's been cool to get to know you better this summer," said Adam.

"But imagine how fun it would be to do something new and different," suggested Elliot. "Next summer, we could not see each other at all."

Adam laughed. He did not ever seem to understand that Elliot's jokes were not for him. "I know I had you all wrong last summer, when I thought you were just a snotty brat," he said. "I didn't realise until the kitchen, with the dancing, that you liked to have fun. That you were fun."

"Sure," said Elliot. "Barrel of laughs, that's me. A joy forever. Anyway . . ."

Elliot was still trying to work out what exactly Adam was doing when Adam grabbed him by the arm. Elliot tried to jerk away, but Adam held on fast. Elliot was pulled in and pressed against him, and then Elliot was being kissed.

"Wait, are you trying to express *romantic feelings* for me?" Elliot demanded. "God, what a terrible day."

Something about Adam's face told Elliot that he had been less than tactful.

"Sorry, um. It's not you, it's me," Elliot said. "I don't like you."

Elliot was beginning to suspect he was not smooth in these situations. He truly did not like Adam, but it was flattering, he supposed: he couldn't quite get his head around the idea that it might be possible for him to hurt somebody, but if it was, he didn't want to.

"The thing is that I'm in love with Serene," he announced.

There. Surely liking someone else was an acceptable and not too insulting excuse.

"What?" said Adam. "Not seriously? You don't have a chance with her."

"Wow, keep wooing me with your sweet words, lover," Elliot snapped.

Adam laughed and used his hold on Elliot to pull him closer. "Come on, I know you like me."

Elliot tried to twist his hand away again. "I have a serious question to ask you. During today's trials, did anyone hit you on the head really hard? Did you have a fall? Are you feeling all lost and confused?"

"Stop messing around," said Adam, his face darkening, and Elliot recognized the expression on his face: that of a spoiled child not used to being denied anything he wanted.

That expression had always spelled trouble for him in the past. It seemed worse now, in this unfamiliar and confusing situation: Elliot pushed Adam away again, to very little effect, and tried to yank his arm away, only succeeding in wrenching it. This felt like a fight. "Let *go.*"

Culaine, who clearly thought this was a game, went yapping and winding around their legs, and Elliot shoved as Culaine wound, and Adam tripped backward over the dog and ended up flat on his back. Elliot looked down into his angry face.

"You *are* still the same snotty brat," Adam snarled.

"Finally you get it," said Elliot, and ran.

By the time Elliot reached the fire and the festival, Luke had sneaked away somewhere, but Elliot was pretty sure he'd know where to find him, so he made his way to the house.

"Luke," Elliot called. "Luke, I have something really funny to tell y—ohhhh."

Luke was not in the equipment room. Rachel Sunborn was, wrapped in the arms of a man who was not Michael Sunborn: who was not Luke's father.

"Oh, I'm so sorry," said Elliot, and shut the door fast.

Then he leaned against the wall and tried to focus all his energies on not having a heart attack before he turned fifteen.

"Elliot," said Rachel, emerging from the room a moment later. "It's not what you think."

"Okay," Elliot said numbly.

"Michael knows all about it," Rachel said. "We have an understanding. On a festival occasion, like this, or when we're apart on patrol, it's all right for us to have—other friends. Lovers. It's grown-up stuff, so you might not be able to understand completely—"

"You have an open relationship," said Elliot, deeply relieved. "I read a lot."

"Something like that," Rachel said. "But the thing is . . . It's not that Luke doesn't know. I'm pretty sure he does. But he's kind of bashful—I don't understand it, he didn't get it from my side of the family, and if you said anything to him he might be unhappy or embarrassed. So if you didn't . . ." Rachel raked her fingers through her tumbled golden hair. "I sound like one of those people who sneak around and make excuses. I'm sorry. Never mind. You can talk to whoever you like."

"No," Elliot said slowly. "I trust you."

Rachel gave him a small, worried smile. "Sorry if I upset you, kid. I don't know how they do things in your world. Probably all a bit more civilized there."

"No," said Elliot. "I'm okay. I don't mind. I . . . like it here. I like you."

"You're always welcome, kid," said Rachel, and ruffled his hair. "Except obviously right now is grown-up time. Off you go. I think Luke is practising archery."

Luke was indeed in the archery ring, stringing a bow as Elliot approached. The target glimmered like a tiny moon, far off in the distance. After doing awful sports and violence all day, Elliot did not see how Luke could wish to do more, but he supposed that if the other Sunborns were being lions on the prowl Luke probably wanted to be discreetly elsewhere.

"Hey, I was looking for you," Elliot said.

"Yeah?" Luke smiled. "Here I am."

"Why are you doing the archery again?" Elliot asked. "I heard you beat everyone."

"I wouldn't have if Serene had been allowed to compete."

Elliot was pleased by this tribute to Serene until it occurred to him that she would probably be able to participate in the trials when she and Luke were married. Luke lifted the bow, arms steady and able to master it in a way he hadn't quite been two years ago, and hit the bull's eye. He aimed and fired again, three times in a row, and every time the arrow he fired hit the arrow before it and split it, so every one landed in the bull's-eye.

"So I came to tell you something hilarious," said Elliot, sitting on one of the low wooden benches surrounding the ring and bored by all the martial prowess. Culaine came to his arms with a soft whine, butting against Elliot's chest for praise and petting. "And also, Culaine is a hero!"

"My dog is a hero?" Luke looked confused but amused.

"Blind people have, like, seeing-eye dogs," Elliot continued. "I think Culaine could have a real future as a sexual harassment preventing dog."

"Wait," Luke said. "What? Who was . . . getting sexually harassed?"

"Me!" said Elliot.

"What," said Luke.

"I know!" said Elliot. "I was surprised too! It was Adam! Can you believe it! That was what all his hanging around annoying me was about, apparently. He is such a smug blond idiot. He kissed me, and I could barely manage to stop myself from laughing in his face."

"Yeah," said Luke. "I'm amazed that you had that much restraint myself."

Elliot looked up from Culaine, startled, at the flat sound of Luke's voice. He wasn't frowning and laughing at the same time anymore, in the way where he felt he should disapprove but secretly was on Elliot's side. His face was like thunder.

Elliot suspected he had gone wrong somewhere, but he wasn't sure where. He knew Luke could be kind of prudish about these sort of things, and wondered if he was being judged as a floozy, which seemed massively unfair.

"I never liked him," Elliot said uncertainly. "I always made that very clear."

"Oh, you always do," Luke said. His voice was savage.

"What?" Elliot asked. "I should have taken it as a compliment?"

He got up and walked away, back to the house. He didn't have to deal with Sunborns and their monstrous egos for a moment longer.

Luke probably thought it had been a compliment. Just because Adam was a Sunborn, and at the last, when their loyalties were tested, Sunborns were loyal to each other. Sunborns thought they were all so much better than everybody else, and their attention must be an honor.

"Yeah!" Luke said, coming after him, shouting the word at his back. "Maybe! It would've been better than acting the way you always do!"

"Wow, sorry that everything I ever do offends you."

The Sunborns were so stupid, and Elliot was done with it. They were so stupid they thought having a champion just turned fifteen was a glorious thing, instead of a target painted on Luke's back. Now he was the Sunborn, instead of just a Sunborn, he was going to be someone people looked for in a war: his death would now be someone else's trophy. Luke and all the other Sunborns seemed too stupid to realise that or too stupid to care. Luke's own mother had cheered for something that was likely to get Luke killed.

"Do you hear yourself?" snapped Luke. "Do you actually hear yourself saying these stupid things? No, I guess you never do."

"Everything I ever do and everything I ever say, apparently," Elliot snapped, storming into the house. "You didn't have to invite me here if you think I'm so unbearable."

"I barely did," Luke shouted back, slamming the door. "I had to, to be polite! Who wanted you here, asking people to do things and then not even watching when they do? You are the rudest person in the world. And you didn't have to come running because of an invitation I didn't mean, all because of Serene and your stupid idea of a stupid *truce*."

"Stop calling me stupid!" Elliot yelled.

"You are stupid!" Luke yelled back. "You don't understand anything!"

"Luke?" said Rachel from above, sounding stunned.

She was standing on the balcony that overlooked the hall, wrapped around with a bedsheet. Elliot looked up and saw the shadow of a man at her bare shoulder, and had a sudden moment of fear on top of distress: he wondered how he could possibly get Luke away without Luke seeing.

But it was Michael. Luke glanced up at his parents, threw up his hands, and walked away, making a disgusted sound in the back of his throat.

"Teenagers yell sometimes," Rachel said, as if she was testing out the words. "Even Luke. This is normal."

"Haha," Elliot said. "Yep. Normal stuff. People are always yelling at me. It's fine. I'm vexing. Go about your business. I will try to keep the vex down."

"Okay," said Rachel.

"That kid is a weirdo," Elliot heard Michael mutter as Luke's parents both walked away from the balcony and back toward their bedroom.

"I know, I'm crazy about him," Rachel returned.

It pleased Elliot in a distant way to hear it, but it didn't matter, not really. He kept his head high in case Rachel looked back, and he walked away, outside the Sunborn tower in the opposite direction to the one Luke had gone. He couldn't come be Rachel's friend. Rachel might like him, but she loved Luke. Nobody had ever loved Elliot, but he was really smart. He was smart enough to know the difference.

It was dark. The stars were out, smudges of brightness in a dark sky that seemed to be running, like streaks of white paint on a black background. Culaine whined and tried to lick the tears off Elliot's face, but Elliot shoved him away. Good-bye to the stupid dog, good-bye to the tower and the nice, grumbling, easy, warm ways of a family. He couldn't come back. He had been stupid, he supposed: just because he'd decided he was Luke's friend didn't mean that Luke was his.

"Elliot?" said Serene's voice, behind him. Elliot jumped and scrubbed at his face with both hands, but it was a futile gesture.

Serene looked very uncomfortable, which made two of them. "What are you doing here?" Elliot snapped.

"I came looking for you," Serene said slowly, approaching and sitting down by his side. "It was rather sad for me to be left without male company."

It was good of her to come and sit, even awkwardly. She edged closer, and her warmth seeped through Elliot. She liked him better than anybody else did, or probably ever would, and Elliot loved her best of all.

"Uh, you do have Neal," said Elliot. "Can't shake him, last I checked. And plenty of other Sunborn suitors, I'm sure."

"Ah," Serene said. "But not the male company I prefer."

Luke, Elliot supposed, and glanced bitterly over at her. Serene was looking at him, her face pale in the moonlight, her eyes grave. She looked remote as the moon, but she was very close.

She leaned in. His breath left him in a shocked rush, replaced by a feeling of light-headed disbelief, and the brief sweet warmth of her lips meeting his.

Serene leaned away, eyes still serious, still meeting Elliot's without fear or wavering. She did not speak. She stood after a moment, and left his side without saying another word.

Elliot sat and stared after her slim retreating form until she disappeared into the night, then up at the stars. They were suddenly brilliant and clear.

The next morning was ungodly awkward.

Luke was very quiet, staring at his porridge with his arms crossed over his chest. Serene was also very quiet. Elliot could not tell from Luke's face if he was upset at still having an intruder in his home, or from Serene's face if she regretted any rash acts of pity-kissing that might have happened last night. He concentrated on being a good polite guest: he didn't steal the little container of jam Luke had for his own porridge, even though he was used to it and the porridge tasted awful without it. He passed several excellent-guest remarks about how delicious the awful porridge was, and how nice the weather.

Everything became even more hideous because people kept stopping by the table, one of a dozen little makeshift tables out on the lawn, to congratulate Luke on his shining victory.

"Guess that Woodsinger wench is teaching you something, at that," said Eric Sunborn, Adam and Neal's father.

"Like my mother and my sister taught me before her," said Luke, speaking mildly but also basically uttering treason. Sunborn women were meant to be regarded as an exception.

"Commander Woodsinger is not a wench!" snapped Elliot. "And I'm sure she's very proficient at teaching weaponry and other terrible things."

"How would you know, you sissy?" Neal hissed.

Elliot was about to snap back that he only had to examine the evidence—Luke was champion, and what was Neal?—but then he remembered that he couldn't insult Sunborns while under a Sunborn roof. He bit the inside of his cheek and sulked.

Luke did not look in the least appeased by Elliot's noble self-control. He glared at his porridge.

"Do humans call *women* wenches?" Serene asked. "That's very humorous."

Elliot jumped and stared at her. She looked just the same as ever, a beautiful enigma with no discernable thoughts about kissing.

Eric Sunborn gave Serene a squinty suspicious look and drifted away. Luke kept glaring at his porridge. Serene ate dried apricots and continued to be a lovely mystery. Elliot wanted to be back at school, very badly.

The one bright spot of the day was that Adam was sitting at another breakfast table with a broken nose.

Elliot disapproved of violence, but obviously Adam had decided to sexually harass someone else, someone who was totally okay with violence. That was what you got for having wandering hands, Elliot thought with satisfaction. Not everybody was as kind and forbearing as he was.

He beamed at Adam. Adam flinched away as if he were about to be hit again. Whoever had hit him, Elliot thought cruelly, it served Adam right.

III

ELLIOT, AGE FIFTEEN

Being back at school was marginally better, though Serene and Luke were off spending a lot of time together. Serene stopped by Elliot's cabin once late at night by herself and Elliot's heart leapt, but it turned out she only wanted to study some pamphlets to broaden her understanding of the human world.

Over the summer, a tavern had opened for the farming community around the camp and the Border guard alike. It was called the Elven Tavern. There was a sign outside that showed an elven warrior, though in oddly revealing armor that Elliot had never seen any elf warrior wear and striking a strange pose. Elliot brought the matter of the sign up with the tavern keeper.

"It's empowering, innit?"

Elliot examined the sign some more. "What . . . putting your back out and getting stabbed in the midriff?"

"You have to strike a balance between being empowering and, you know, gettin' actual customers," said the innkeeper. It did not seem all that balanced to Elliot, but he added: "Tons of students come down bringing their sweethearts. That blonde cadet Adara, she's brought three men in the last week."

"She lives a life of daring and adventure," Elliot agreed.

So the Elven Tavern was the hot new place to take a date. Elliot gave the matter deep thought, and then some more thought than it needed because he was very nervous. Finally he glanced across the library table at Serene, who was making a study chart like the babe she was, and mustered up the courage to ask: "Do you want to go to the Elven Tavern with me?"

Serene looked up from her task, gray eyes like the dawn. "Absolutely," she said. "What a good idea."

"Oh," said Elliot, stunned by his good fortune.

Maybe Serene had been trying to do things the human way, he thought, as he sometimes tried to do things the elven way. Maybe she had been waiting for him to ask her.

"Luke could really do with some cheering up," Serene continued. "Let me go fetch him."

"Oh," said Elliot.

And maybe it wasn't Elliot she really wanted, and never had been.

They were not a cheerful group at the Elven Tavern that evening. Luke was sulking as usual, Elliot was dismayed by how terrible he was at romance, and Serene was appalled by the décor.

"I would be extremely surprised if any elves were consulted when the theme for this building was discussed," Serene sniffed. "Ever. At any point."

Elliot did not know what to do about it, when the girl he loved had kissed him and then decided she wished to spend all her time with Luke from that moment on. He did not know what to do about the fact Luke was still furious with him, even though Elliot had been carefully polite to him for weeks.

Trying to appease Luke was not working any more than trying to woo Serene. Elliot appeared to be terrible at manners as well as romance. He should possibly be locked up in a dungeon as one unfit for any kind of human companionship.

Serene excused herself. Silence reigned, a dark tyrant, over the table while she was gone.

"Why are you mad at me?" Luke asked abruptly.

Elliot stared.

"I'm not mad at you," Elliot said. "Why would you think such a stupid thing, loser? Now I'm mad at you."

"There is a statue in the bathrooms that I have strong objections about," said Serene, returning. "Will you come and examine it with me, and then come and speak to the tavern keeper?"

"Sure," said Elliot.

"No, we will not go into the bathroom in a weird group!" said Luke.

Was this, Elliot wondered, how Luke wooed ladies? Not giving them all their own way. Treat 'em mean, keep 'em keen. He narrowed his eyes at Luke, and Luke lifted his own eyes to the ceiling.

They reached a compromise, and Elliot went in with Serene while Luke waited outside. Elliot had to agree with Serene that the statue was physically implausible.

It had also been defaced. Someone had drawn COMMANDER WOODSINGER on it in lipstick.

Elliot kept hearing more of the same kind of thing Eric Sunborn had said about Commander Woodsinger. Apparently Captain Whiteleaf had been suggested to replace her: Elliot thought that was a bad idea, on account of Captain Whiteleaf was a dribbling idiot, but his father, Colonel Whiteleaf, was such a very important man. People said he might be the next general.

Elliot supposed that was nice for Captain Whiteleaf, but the man was still an idiot. He suspected Commander Woodsinger thought so too, since she was now sending out missions with leaders who were actually competent, and captains like Whiteleaf were relegated to training and teaching.

Captain Whiteleaf proved he was an idiot by giving them the worst ever lecture about mermaids three weeks into term, in the military-history class, which was one of the few the war-training and council-training courses took together.

It was always nice to sit beside Serene, and Elliot could admit it was even nicer to have Luke at the desk on her other side. It was not nice to listen to an idiot.

"The hostilities between mermaids and man arose from that incident. Given the draining of their home lake, the Grayling clan of mermaids might thus be said by some to have a legitimate grievance," said Captain Whiteleaf. "But then the sea mermaids began to murder innocent sailors. The only question is, did the sea mermaids join the Grayling clan in their mission of vengeance because they were bribed by the Graylings, because they have some dark purpose of their own to fulfill, or simply because they have an innate love of violence and destruction?"

"Sorry in advance for my insolence and lack of cooperation in class, but you phrased that question incorrectly," said Elliot, and noticed Luke had his hand up. "Luke, put your hand down. This question insults your intelligence."

Luke kept his hand up.

"Your arguments are based on a false hypothesis. The thing is that some mermaids are able to swim in both fresh and salt water," said Elliot. "We don't know for sure whether the Grayling clan are exclusively fresh-water mermaids or if they can survive in both. So you can't say for sure that the Grayling clan weren't responsible for the initial sea attacks. Your father Colonel Whiteleaf, wrote about them: the mermaids who perpetrated them were never identified as being from any clan. And of course after we started attacking all the other mermaids, they defended themselves."

"It hasn't been definitively proven that some mermaids are able to survive in both," said Captain Whiteleaf.

"Almost every in-depth report we have on mermaids suggests it," said Elliot. "Please see Maximilian Wavechaser's *A Thousand Leagues Across a Sea of Blood*. It's an excellent book. It even mentions your father, Captain Whiteleaf, at the end and in some supplementary materials I found in the library."

Dale Wavechaser gave Elliot a thumbs-up for praising the Wavechasers. Elliot ignored this because he was embarrassed to be associated with Dale in history class: Dale was very bad at history.

"In any case," said Captain Whiteleaf. "Cadet Sunborn, I commend you on raising your hand and not shouting out insubordinate remarks. Whenever you have something to say in the classroom, always do so."

"Can I speak now?" Luke asked. "It's not so much of an answer to a question as a personal announcement."

Elliot glanced over at him. Luke looked a little pale under his tan. Elliot wondered if perhaps Luke needed to go to the infirmary and felt guilty about talking so much. People's stupidity could always be corrected another time.

"I'm—I like guys," said Luke, staring at his desk. "Romantically."

Elliot put his hand up so fast he almost dislocated his arm. Captain Whiteleaf was staring and nodded, possibly on stunned autopilot.

"Since when?" Elliot demanded.

Luke put his hand back up. "Since always."

Elliot put his hand up in retaliation. "That's absurd."

Luke put his hand up and waited for Captain Whiteleaf to nod and say apprehensively: "Er . . . Cadet Sunborn . . . is this going to be a question?"

"Yes," said Luke. "*What is wrong with you*? Not you, sir. Cadet Schafer, sir."

"I don't understand your question, and I have one of my own," said Elliot, putting his hand back up as a formality and not looking at Captain Whiteleaf. "If that's true then why don't I know?"

Luke looked mulish about the face. "You do know because I just told you!"

"Excuse me," Dale Wavechaser said. "Excuse me, sir."

Everybody turned to look at him. He had apparently been waving his hand in the air for some time. He was very flushed.

"Yes?" Captain Whiteleaf gazed upon Dale as a shipwreck survivor seeing rescue in view.

"Me too, sir!" said Dale. "I like boys romantically too."

Captain Whiteleaf looked hideously betrayed. Shot through the heart, his pallid demeanour suggested as he looked at Dale. And you're to blame.

Dale blinked innocently at him, and then concentrated a hopeful gaze on the back of Luke's head. Oddly, that was what made Elliot believe it: of course if this was true, then Luke would immediately have someone offer to be his boyfriend in five seconds flat.

Elliot spun to the sound of Serene's small, polite cough. Captain Whiteleaf bitterly nodded permission, having obviously abandoned all hope.

"This is not a question so much as a comment, sir."

Captain Whiteleaf gave a hollow laugh. "Of course it is."

"I wondered, sir, if anyone had attempted to capture a Grayling mermaid and prove Cadet Schafer's hypothesis," she said.

Captain Whiteleaf started, suddenly a man finding hope in a hopeless place. "You have a comment about the lesson?"

"Why yes, sir." Serene nodded gravely. "I had already vouchsafed my comments to Cadet Sunborn on the other matter under discussion in private."

It was true, then. Luke had told Serene.

Elliot put his hand down and was silent for the rest of the lesson. Captain Whiteleaf was almost embarrassingly happy as a result.

Elliot didn't know why he had assumed Luke would've told him. He was such an idiot: he kept forgetting that Luke wasn't his friend.

"Is it true?" asked Peter next class. Peter was excused from some lessons in geography and history because his mother was a master mapmaker, and looked disappointed to have missed the whole thing. "What they're saying about Luke Sunborn?"

"It is true!" said Myra. "I mean, I was there, I heard it all."

"I assume it's true," Elliot said. "Luke doesn't lie."

There was a long, awkward silence. Elliot fiddled with his pens. Myra slowly dipped her quill in the inkpot, and stroked her mustache with the feathery end.

"So you didn't know?" Peter asked slowly. "Isn't that a bit weird?"

"No," said Elliot. "Seems totally reasonable to me. Did *you* know?"

"Well, I, well, no," said Peter. "But that's different. I would have thought you would know."

"Why?" asked Elliot. "He's your classmate too. I cannot be expected to know every little detail about every one of my classmates, Peter. Surely you see that."

He fixed Peter with a severe gaze. Peter nodded humbly.

"People get to choose who to tell their secrets to," said Elliot. "You know—people whom they trust and feel comfortable with. That's all right. That's fine. I understand that. Nobody's owed anyone else's secrets."

"That's true," Myra said, and favoured him with a smile. "I think that's very mature of you, Elliot."

Elliot smiled, comforted, and made Myra his favorite between Myra and Peter for the rest of the day.

He really could understand. Elliot was not sure that he would have told himself any secrets: it wasn't like he was conspicuous for his ready sympathy and emotional depths. And the fight he'd had with Luke about Adam looked different now, when Elliot was not just a guest who was behaving badly but someone who Luke might've thought was judging and condemning Adam for something Adam and Luke had in common.

Elliot was slow to learn, that was all: he always had been, well before he ever came to the Border camp, when he kept hoping that his dad would start liking him and kept doing everything wrong so his dad never did.

Serene might hate him too. Perhaps that was why there had been no repeat of the kissing incident, even though Elliot had waited and watched and hoped and tried. Perhaps they had both decided he was worthless.

It didn't matter what they thought. It was no use Elliot sitting around making himself wretched over it. This wasn't even about Elliot feeling bad: if Elliot had been the one to make Luke feel bad, it was his responsibility, and it was Luke's feelings that mattered. Elliot had to do something. Elliot had to make it up to Luke.

Elliot had to find him first. He searched the halls, the practise rooms, the Trigon field, and finally wound up outside the cabin Luke shared with several other guys who always gave Elliot the disapproving side-eye as if he had grievously insulted their leader. This loyalty was even more impressive, Elliot told himself, on a new quest to be understanding and kind, considering he didn't think Luke knew their names.

Elliot tapped on the door, and when nobody answered he peeked around it. Serene and Luke were the only ones inside. Neither of them had lit the candles, though day was slipping down to night.

"Hi," said Elliot.

"Hello," said Serene.

"Why do you walk inside when nobody's told you to come in?" asked Luke.

"I don't want to spend my whole life waiting outside closed doors," said Elliot. "I wanted to . . . talk to you. I might have been taken by surprise and expressed myself in ways I did not exactly intend."

"Is that so?" said Luke.

"I might have not shown enough consideration for your feelings," said Elliot.

"Sorry," said Luke. "Are we just talking about today?"

The thing about Luke was that he was a secret snarky jerk. Elliot was not sure how Luke kept that a secret: possibly it was a secret from Luke himself. His shoulders looked a little bit less tense, though, and Serene looked a little bit less like a bodyguard standing in front of the bunkbed.

"I'm terrible at feelings, it's like they're knives, I don't really know what to do with them and I end up throwing them with too much force," said Elliot, advancing. "But I have strong views on having a more accepting society, and everyone getting to be who they really are, and so it's excellent that you made your class announcement, and if anyone else had been insensitive about it I would have been extremely vexed and plotted vengeance." He paused. "I don't suppose anyone was insensitive about it later?" he asked hopefully.

Luke shrugged, the last of the tension going out of his shoulders. Serene looked relieved. Elliot knew that she lived in the constant fear that one of them was going to go off into hysterics.

"Just the one guy at first," said Luke, and smirked. Such a secret jerk: it was unbelievable that nobody else had caught on.

"I can't plot vengeance against myself, you must see that," said Elliot. "But I can plot something else! I love plots, you know that."

Luke, grinning a little, looked up at Serene: she looked fondly down at him, and smiled. "How many times have the words 'I love plots' been followed by good consequences?"

"Statistically it has to be very few," said Serene.

"So little faith," Elliot said mournfully.

He closed the distance between himself and them. Serene subsided onto the bunk beside Luke with a little sigh of satisfaction, and Elliot sat at her feet, leaned an elbow against her knee, and looked up at Luke expectantly.

"So," said Elliot. "Is there a boy you like? Tell me."

Luke choked on air and spluttered.

"Elliot, that's inappropriate," said Serene. "Luke has his maiden purity to think of. To be modest and discreet is to be much desired. Although I am not quite sure how it works when two gentlemen desire each other."

"Serene," said Luke.

"Presumably it is a very tactful courtship, and no doubt most chaste—"

"Serene, you're not helping me!" said Luke. "Neither of you is helping me."

"No, I know," said Elliot, leaning toward him. "But I want to help you! I can help you! Tell me who it is."

"Drop it," said Luke, and squirmed across the mattress, away from both of them. His shoulders were hunched again.

This was a clear sign of guilt.

"The fact that you're not answering me makes me believe that there is a boy you like. You can't fool me, because I'm extremely intelligent. Now tell me or I'll keep pestering you to tell me."

"You're supposed to be supportive of me!" said Luke.

Serene nodded. "That's what the pamphlets said. We studied them carefully."

Elliot's pamphlets had been taken from him and used against him, and he couldn't even be angry because this was more important.

"I'm trying to be supportive of you!" he told Luke.

"Then stop yelling at me!" said Luke.

"I will stop yelling at you if you let me support you," Elliot proposed. "Do we have a bargain?"

Luke's shoulders were still hunched in, but he glanced over and down at Elliot: there was a deep flush running along his cheekbones. "You'll laugh at me."

"I won't," Elliot promised. "I'll be supportive. We're going to be supportive, aren't we, Serene?"

"If you wish to tell me, I will be happy to hear your secret," said Serene. "I vow not to mock at you and never to tell anyone the object of your tender maidenly affections, not even if they torture me. A true gentleman's heart is as sacred as a temple, and as easily crushed as a flower."

Elliot and Luke absorbed that in a brief moment of silence.

"See?" Elliot said. "We're being supportive. I promise not to laugh."

"You promise?" Luke asked warily.

"Yes. Trust me," said Elliot. "Tell me."

"Okay." Luke took a deep breath. "Dale Wavechaser."

"Uh," said Elliot, and broke into a grin.

"Elliot, you promised!"

"No, no," said Elliot hastily. "I'm not laughing at you. But that's pretty convenient, isn't it?"

"How do you mean?" Luke's eyes narrowed. "Just because he's into guys doesn't mean he's into me."

"That's not what I meant."

"Then what did you mean? Why did you smirk?"

Elliot had smiled because that was so typical of Luke's life, that everything would go smoothly for him. Confessing to a crush on someone who clearly had a crush on you back was a bit like saying you were hungry with breakfast already laid out before you: expressing a wish that was already granted.

But Luke looked upset, and Luke's life was not quite as easy as Elliot had always supposed—not as easy as Elliot had thought it was when he first saw Luke, not even as easy as Elliot had thought it was this morning—and Elliot had promised to be supportive.

"I didn't mean to smirk," said Elliot. "That's great. You should ask him out!"

"Are you trying to make fun of me?"

"Usually yes, today *no*," said Elliot.

It was ridiculous, how uncomfortable and upsetting this was. Elliot glanced at Serene, but she was looking to Elliot, clearly expecting him to make things right: not only because she thought men were the ones who talked about feelings, but because Elliot was the one making Luke so tense and unhappy. Luke had trusted Serene with his secret, and that had obviously gone well. It was Elliot messing everything up. It was Elliot who always did.

It was clear, from the elves and the council of war and Adam Sunborn, that Elliot needed to learn how to tact, both personally and professionally. Being more tactful was the only possible tactical decision.

Elliot cleared his throat and tried again. "I mean, I like Dale."

"Yeah?" Luke brightened. "He's nice, right?"

"Sure!" said Elliot. "Also super handsome. You should definitely ask him out!"

Serene and Luke both spoke at once, Serene vehemently on the subject of modesty and chastity and Luke even more vehemently on the subject of not being pushed or teased and also it being a little soon.

"I only just decided," Luke finished, as Serene said: "—a gentleman's most private treasure!"

"Oh, you only just decided?" Elliot inquired. "Like, you decided today? *Luke.*"

Well done Dale Wavechaser for putting his hand up, he supposed. He could not help laughing.

"You promised not to laugh at me!" said Luke, but he was laughing a little too, even though he didn't seem sure why.

"I'm trying!" said Elliot. "I'm sorry, but I can't do it."

He wasn't just laughing. He was plotting. And he was thinking, as well, about something that perhaps should have occurred to him earlier: if Luke liked guys, he didn't like Serene, not in that way. Elliot had got it all wrong. Elliot might not have any real competition: Elliot might really, truly have a chance with her.

The next day was bright and clear. The sky was blue, trainees wandering over the grass between classes, luxuriously slow as the wisps of cloud moving across the sky, and Elliot was not in a love triangle.

"Hi. Hi, wait a minute. Hey, wait. Oi, Dale!"

Dale Wavechaser turned around and looked startled to see Elliot bearing down on him. He opened his mouth to speak, but Elliot forestalled him: Elliot was on a mission.

"I wanted to say," said Elliot, speaking fast and fiddling with the strap of his bag. "I'm really sorry if I came off badly in class yesterday? I was just surprised. I think it was brave of you to tell everyone, and I totally support you."

"Oh," said Dale. He smiled crookedly. "Cool."

"Also I like you," said Elliot. "And I want to be friends. Good friends. Can we be friends?"

"Uh . . . sure."

Dale's smile got brighter. Elliot smiled back, and in case it would help tried to add charm to the smile, the endearing air he had used on the elven warriors and on the council of war last year. Oddly, it seemed to work.

"The rest of the guys from the Trigon team are coming to meet me, and we're all going down to the Elven Tavern," said Dale. "Do you want to join us?"

Elliot shook his head gently. He was devoted to his new life of tactfulness, so he carefully did not say that he would rather be boiled alive in a cauldron of fire ants and cyanide.

"I don't want to be friends with them, Dale." He gave Dale the soulful look that he had practised on the elves. "I only want to be friends with you."

Dale looked surprised, and still a bit puzzled by Elliot's behaviour, but mostly pleased.

"You should come hang out with me," Elliot said. "And Luke and Serene and Luke and me. Anytime you see us. Come hang out. Anytime. Also it seems to me that you might need help with your classes. You should come to me about that. Especially about history. No offence meant."

"I think history's kind of boring," said Dale, and Elliot controlled himself and did not flinch. "But that's really nice of you."

"Yes," said Elliot. "We're both nice. This is why we're such friends."

Dale laughed. He was actually nice, not pretend nice like Elliot was being. It was probably better to know how to interpret what everyone said to you as the best thing they could've meant than to know history. Probably he and Luke would be great together.

Behind Dale, Elliot could already hear the clatter of boys coming from Trigon, loudly discussing the many imbecilic intricacies of the game. Escape became urgent.

"I'm looking forward to hanging out," Elliot told Dale earnestly. "But now I must go. Good-bye, friend."

He thought that had gone excellently. Get Luke and Dale together, be very supportive of Luke and Dale together, and get Dale to like Elliot so that almost all of them could be friends. Elliot's plan was fiendishly brilliant, elegant in its simplicity, and bound to succeed.

Elliot was feeling fairly good until two hours later, when somebody attacked the library.

~

Elliot was peacefully looking up facts about mermaids, feeling a thousand leagues away under a cool blue sea, when the smell of smoke and fire made him slam his book shut and jump to his feet. He looked up to the roof and saw it kindle: saw the thatched roof open into a burning hole.

"Don't worry, children, the women will protect us!" shouted Bright-Eyes-Gladden-the-Hearts-of-Women.

The students, mainly boys, looked skeptical but frightened as well. They were mostly young, in council training because those in war training didn't spend much time in the library.

Elliot raised his voice. "Come on, follow me." He strode over to the library door, opened it, and saw fighting in the yard beyond. He slammed the door swiftly shut again. "Never mind that! Let's not go out there. You and you, behind those stacks, you and you, under the table. You two, help me with the fire. If the fire gets too bad, get out and make for the lake—don't go back to your cabins."

A first-year boy helped Elliot pull down one of the heavy curtains and muffle the floor where one burning arrow had hit. The wood smoked and crackled, Elliot coughing in the poisoned air, but he was mainly concerned about the books.

"In my world there's this beautiful thing called running water," sighed Elliot.

The boy looked at him as if he was crazy. "We have running water here too," he said. "In rivers and streams. Where water runs."

Through the tall narrow windows of the library, like windows in a church in Elliot's world, Elliot saw the sudden chaos in the courtyard, saw the Border guards in camp and the warrior-training students running out, their weapons gleaming in the light of the sinking sun. He saw battle joined.

He thought for a moment these were the bandits in the eastern woods whom he'd been hearing rumors about, and realized the next moment that this was much worse than a bandit attack.

The people fighting were all either in Border guard uniform or in the uniform of cadets. The people fighting were all human. It was chaos, even worse than battles usually were. Cadets were being cut down by adult guards, and protected by different guards. Elliot could not tell who was on which side, or why they were fighting.

He saw people in the battle who looked as panicked and confused as he felt.

There wasn't time to hang out the window and stare at the battle, even if Elliot had the stomach for it. He turned away and got back to pulling down curtains.

The skirmish was brief, the newcomers in Border guard uniforms receding as swiftly as they had appeared. Elliot saw the blades sheathed almost as soon as drawn out through the windows.

He still tensed when the door was flung open, but it was Serene, who stood framed in the doorway with her braid flying and in the process of sliding her sword home in its sheath, attached to her belt. Elliot had seen Myra and Adara wearing jewelry on special occasions, but Serene's swordbelt was the only ornate thing she ever wore. She didn't need jewelry.

"Rest easy," she said, and Bright-Eyes looked pleased to be rescued by a lady, even if he did clearly think Serene was only a young whippersnapper. "We have beaten back the foul attackers. You are all safe."

There was a flaming arrow, set deep and burning in the centre of the table. Serene strode over to it and took the parchment rolled around the shaft of the arrow, careless of the fire that licked at her fingers.

She walked out to the threshold of the library, and unrolled the parchment.

It read: HAVE THAT WOMAN GIVE UP COMMAND OR WE COME TAKE IT.

So that was what this was all about. Elliot thought of the whispers about Commander Woodsinger this summer, the captains no longer allowed on missions, the rising discontent. Commander Woodsinger had been the hero of the last war, but people's memories were short, and there would always be another war.

Someone did not want a woman in charge of the Border training camp. Someone had been willing to go beyond whispers and petty vandalism. Elliot wondered who had mounted the attack. Captain Whiteleaf was the only one whom he'd heard spoken of as a replacement for the commander, and Captain Whiteleaf would not have the nerve.

He slowly became aware that beside him, Serene was vibrating with outrage.

"Oh, men are cowards," said Serene. "So afraid of a woman in charge that they would commit treason. They must worry that she will show the world a woman is a far more able commander than any man."

"They're not going to take Woodsinger's command," said Elliot. "Let them come and try."

Serene looked at him. The lights of the torches of war were reflected in her cool gray eyes. She was panting and disheveled from battle, beautiful beyond his dreams, and she held onto his arms with strength far beyond any strength he had.

"When we saw the library roof catch fire . . .," Serene began.

Her tight grip on him made Elliot think that she might be shaking if she were not holding on so hard. He could see her violent distress: Serene always ignored how different human ways were from her own, right up until the point she could not ignore it any more.

"You must have been furious."

"I thought you had been killed," Serene breathed, and kissed him.

They were kissing, they were finally kissing again, and this time Elliot was not too stunned to participate. He curled his fingers around her braid and drew her closer against him, kissed her and kissed her again.

He kissed her until they were both breathless, then he whispered breathlessly against her mouth: "No. Nope, I'm awesome."

She kissed him again, pressing him against the threshold of the door. Her mouth was warm, searching, burning-sweet, and her body against his was lithe, strong, and urgent. Elliot realized her hold on his arms had changed: that she was tugging him downward. He kissed her throat and felt a spike of nerves in his own throat, as if he had swallowed a tiny shark of panic and could feel its fin scraping on the way down. He felt the warm beat of her pulse against his mouth and opened his lips to kiss her again, taste her skin, and to say he didn't know what he was doing.

There was a sound, low and startled: Serene turned to it and let go of Elliot, though he reached out a hand to keep her.

His hand fell by his side when he looked where she was looking, and saw Luke. It was truly terrible luck that both Serene and Luke should make for the library as soon as the battle was over.

Luke had stopped and was staring at them, blue eyes very wide.

"I didn't—" Luke began. "I'll go. I didn't mean to intrude."

He turned around, boots cutting furrows in the mud with the force of his turn, and left. He had hardly been there for more than an instant.

"I should—" Serene began, blinking as if she was dazed.

She wasn't looking at Luke's retreating back. She was looking toward the commander's tower. Elliot filled in the rest of the sentence for her: after years at the Border camp, he knew a soldier's duty.

"You should go," said Elliot. "Show that note to the commander. We can talk later."

He stood in the doorway of the library for a long time, dazed himself, until it occurred to Elliot that he was in over his head, and he needed to find out more about women and how to please them immediately. Fortunately, he knew where he needed to go in order to obtain knowledge.

He was still dedicated to being tactful, so he waited an hour and half so that everyone could put out the fires before he sidled back into the library.

"I need some books full of elven lore," said Elliot urgently.

Bright-Eyes-Gladden-the-Hearts-of-Women gave him a very suspicious look. "What kind of elven lore?"

Elliot gave up on subterfuge, clung to the counter, and said, "All right, you got me. I need some books full of specific elven instructions on how to please an elven lady." Bright stared at Elliot, and Elliot wondered if he had perhaps misunderstood. "Sexually please her, I mean," he clarified. "Very specific instructions, please. Do you know of a book like that?"

Bright drew in a deep breath. "*How dare you*?"

"The library is meant to be a place of learning, not of judgment," said Elliot.

"I suppose you think that just because I am unmarried and in employment I am no better than a hussy peddling pornographic literature!"

"What?" Elliot said. "No. What?"

"I'll have you know, I am dedicated to my passion for the written word," Bright raged. "And one day, my true elven knight will come, and she will understand my love of literature and why I felt called to promote said love among human children. Moreover, I will come pure to my marriage bed, as all true gentlemen should aspire to do!"

Elliot took a moment to assimilate this new information. It was only a moment.

"Okay, cool, good for you," said Elliot. "But what if . . . just for instance. . . a guy didn't aspire to come pure to his marriage bed? Like, if he was no true gentleman, but a hussy? Is there any advice for hussies in this library? I need advice for hussies."

Bright-Eyes-Gladden-the-Hearts-of-Women made it clear the only thing hussies were going to get in his library was detention.

Elliot gave up. There were other avenues to find out these kind of things, he'd heard: you were meant to learn all you needed to know through something called "bro time." What he needed was a little help from his friends.

It was well after dinner, but the tables were crowded with people talking about the attack on the library. Elliot did hear a few people speculating on who had ordered Border guards to go after their own people: some familiar names were being thrown around. Captain Whiteleaf was nowhere to be found, though he had not been sent out on any missions, and all messages sent to Colonel Whiteleaf's fortress received no response.

And yet nobody had come out in open rebellion against Commander Woodsinger.

They could not be sure the Whiteleafs were the ones in mutiny, any more than they could be sure who else was on their side.

They could not tell what side those who had been killed had taken. Nobody alive who had remained in the camp would admit they had fought against the commander. Nobody's accusations of others, or defence of themselves, could be trusted. They all wore the same uniform. They were all supposed to be on the same side.

The commander had given no statement, and no new orders. Elliot did not know if ignoring unrest would make it go away.

Elliot heard Commander Woodsinger's name being spoken, in sympathetic and critical tones, and took note of who was truly on her side and who was not.

On the other hand, there were also idiots busy congratulating each other on their first skirmish or describing it as a "good little fight." Elliot gave up on eavesdropping and surged forward. It was the work of a few moments for Elliot to cut through the crowds, elbowing people judiciously, and separate Dale Wavechaser from the throng.

Dale grinned at him when Elliot grabbed his elbow and forcibly turned him around.

"Hey, Schafer," he said. "I was worried about you. I kind of figured you'd be in the library. But you're doing okay?"

"Excellent, never better, thanks for your concern, pal. I don't suppose you like girls as well as boys?" Elliot inquired.

"Uh," Dale said. "No."

"Lots of people do, you know," said Elliot.

"Not me," said Dale.

Elliot had further arguments to make on the subject, but he didn't want to be offensive.

"That's cool, buddy," Elliot told him, and clapped him on the back. "Suit yourself. It's always a pleasure. But I have to go talk to another guy about something."

He rushed away from Dale, who wore the puzzled but friendly expression that was his default around Elliot, and almost crashed into Luke, who caught him before he hit Luke or the wall or anything else.

"Luke, I need bro advice," said Elliot.

"Oh," said Luke, looking startled. "Okay. Is this about—"

"So, have you seen my friend Peter?"

Luke blinked. "You have a friend called Peter?"

"Uh," said Elliot. "Yes? He's friends with my friend Myra."

Luke was scowling now. "I don't know a Myra."

"I don't have time to discuss the long list of things and apparently people you do not know," said Elliot. "Gotta go, bye!"

Luke looked as though he had more to say. Elliot assumed that Luke had done something super heroic during the library attack. He spun Luke around by his elbow and had his faith justified when the person now facing Luke immediately begin to congratulate him. Elliot slipped away while Luke was still trying to escape congratulations.

Myra had been singled out by another member of the war-training class, who wanted to tell her all about his valor in today's clash. Peter was actually sitting at a lunch table on his own, looking forlorn, which was sad for Peter but useful for Elliot.

"Peter, you like girls, right?"

"Uh . . . yes?" said Peter, looking very startled by this greeting.

A thought occurred to Elliot, briefly distracting him from his purpose. "Hey, do you like boys as well as girls?"

He knew it was unworthy of him to be so concerned about Serene when he should be thinking about the uprising against their commander. On the other hand, as every terrible day in the otherlands proved, life was short and elves were extremely foxy.

"No! Wait, why do you ask?" Peter asked. "Is this about Luke Sunborn?"

"Maybe," Elliot said cunningly. "Would you go out with him if it was?"

Peter looked like he was considering it. This was typical of Luke's life, absolutely typical: now boys who *didn't* like boys wanted to be Luke's boyfriend. On the other hand, Peter was a lot smarter than Dale, and Elliot thought he could talk Luke around on the subject.

"No," Peter said at length. "I mean . . . well, I mean no."

"Why don't you think it over," Elliot suggested. "Luke has many fine qualities."

"I really don't think . . .," Peter said, and hesitated. "Did Luke say he liked me?"

He sounded equal parts disturbed and flattered.

"I can read Luke like a book," Elliot told him evasively. "And I read books extremely well. Speaking of which, do you have any instructive pornographic literature?"

Peter looked like he was thinking of drowning himself in his pudding. "Oh my God."

Again, Elliot noted, not a denial. Just like Luke not denying he liked someone. Once you watched out for what people didn't say, everything became very clear.

"Great, I need to borrow it."

"Oh my God. Elliot, don't you—don't you have some of your own?"

Elliot blinked. "For recreational purposes, do you mean?"

Peter looked around at the milling crowd. "Kill me," he said, which was not something Elliot would have said to a riled-up bunch of people with a selection of various weapons.

"It wasn't necessary for me to have any before now. I have a very vivid imagination," Elliot reassured him. Peter did not look reassured. "But I need some now," he continued. "I need to learn how to satisfy a lady. Really quickly. Let's go get your literature. Can I borrow it right now?"

"Will you leave me alone if I give you some—some, not all—of my educational literature, Elliot?" Peter asked. "Seriously, do you promise not to say anything upsetting to me for like two weeks?"

"Deal. I really think you and Luke should date," Elliot added. "I think you might be soulmates."

"Um," said Peter. "Were you actually in the library when the attack happened?"

Elliot nodded. Peter looked awestruck.

"People are saying that they recognized some of Colonel Whiteleaf's men!"

If that was true, it was the father, then, trying to get the command for his son.

"Are they?" Elliot asked. "Are they indeed?"

Peter's pornographic literature turned out to be not very educational or instructive. The women in it were genuinely enjoying themselves, in Elliot's opinion, about as much as the pictures and statues in the Elven Tavern were genuine elven warriors. Elliot wondered why people liked bad illusions so much more than reality.

It did, however, enlighten Elliot on several key points of mechanics. He dearly wished he had some access to the internet in this land, but this was better than nothing. He looked through them and made some notes in the five minutes every hour he allotted himself between his new task of reading every book in the library.

Commander Woodsinger had not stepped down from her post. People said that the attack on the library had been a mistake, the result of an order given in error, or a band of rogue guards striking out on their own. People said there would not be another attack. Elliot did not believe any of it, and he kept researching.

At one point Luke came and tried to get him to come back to class.

"I won't," said Elliot. "Someone attacked this camp. And I remember reading something odd about Colonel Whiteleaf when I was doing further reading on *1,000 Leagues Across a Sea of Blood.* We have to know more about Colonel Whiteleaf, if he's the one who attacked us."

"The library isn't where you go to win wars!" said Luke.

"The library is where you go to learn more. By the way, what do you think of Peter?" Elliot asked. "To go out with, I mean?"

"For me to go out with?" Luke asked, and looked badly startled. "I don't even know who he is!"

Elliot waved a hand. "He's great. You'd like him!"

Luke began to blush, which was mystifying until he muttered out: "I told you I like Dale Wavechaser."

"I know, I've taken that onboard too," said Elliot. "You can go out with him whenever. I just thought you might like another option. Peter knows four languages and is probably going to be top in the class in mapmaking!"

"I don't care about mapmaking!" said Luke. "Nobody in the world cares about mapmaking! Or about how anyone's doing in class!"

This was very bad news for Elliot. He'd assumed that his scholastic prowess was a huge plus for him with Serene. But Luke was a philistine who clearly cared more about hot bodies than brains. Elliot had proof of this: Luke had a crush on Dale Wavechaser. Probably intelligence appealed more to Serene. Elliot was going to have to hope so.

"Why are you frowning at me?"

"That's just what my face does when I look at you," Elliot said automatically.

"Look," Luke said, raising his voice. "I don't know what you're assuming, but it can't be just—just any guy."

Elliot wanted to argue that someone who was top in mapmaking was hardly just any guy, but he could tell that Luke was about to be annoyed with him for being offensive.

He raised his hands in surrender. "I'm only trying to help."

"Well, your helping is terrible," said Luke. "Everything you do is terrible."

"Fine," said Elliot. "I have more terrible work to do. Please leave."

Luke pushed one of Elliot's books out of the way to uncover Peter's instructive manuals.

"Enjoy your work," he said, and stalked out.

Elliot had to break the news to Peter that Luke was not interested, which led to Peter glaring a lot at Luke for toying with his affections. This was made more hilarious to Elliot by the fact Luke noticed someone glaring at him, but still had no idea why or who Peter was.

"Do you think he might be one of the people working against Commander Woodsinger?" Luke asked in a low voice when he and Serene came to visit Elliot in the library, and Elliot laughed and laughed.

He didn't feel much like laughing, these days. He never saw Serene without Luke anymore.

Elliot had been telling himself that of course he and Serene couldn't pursue anything until the matter of who had attacked the camp was answered. But maybe that wasn't it at all.

Luke didn't like women, but Serene could still like *him.* Maybe the only reason she'd gone after Elliot at all was because she couldn't have who she truly wanted. Maybe she had realized that Elliot was no substitute, and never could be.

Elliot couldn't think about it, or about the way Luke and Serene went out, united in their purpose: the way Serene did not stay in the library the way she used to. He went back to his books.

Myra joined him, pulled up a chair to his table and took one of the books from his unread stack.

"Luke and Serene told me what you were doing here," she said. "And I—I like Commander Woodsinger. She's kind to my cousin, who's all dwarf, and I don't want the camp to have any other commander, and I want to help."

"So you know who Luke is," said Elliot.

"Of course I do," said Myra. "We get on quite well. He's always really nice to me."

Elliot wanted to say: he has no idea what your name is, but he was being a prince of tact these days, so he made a tactful sound instead. "Mmm."

Myra blushed. "He's very handsome. It's such a pity about . . ."

"Awesome luck for the guys," Elliot said firmly.

"That's true, I wonder if he and Dale Wavechaser will go out," said Myra, and Elliot was deeply noble and did not try to get her to make a bet.

Even with Myra's help, they had found nothing by the time the real attack came, the soldiers flooding in under Colonel Whiteleaf's command, calling on Whiteleaf's famous name, intent on replacing Commander Woodsinger with his son.

There were too many of them, and the camp was full of children: Commander Woodsinger and the guards who remained loyal to her had to act to protect the children before they did anything else. The commander sent out messages pleading for reinforcements and then took the field against the invaders.

Everybody knew reinforcements might be slow in coming: that the other fortresses might be hoping that a woman would be replaced, and they would later reprimand the colonel and leave it at that. Colonel Whiteleaf was still honored for his valiant deeds in a battle against mermaids twenty years ago, but apparently no one cared about Commander Woodsinger's valiant deeds last year. This was the reward someone got for being a war hero, if they weren't the kind of war hero people wanted.

That gave Elliot an idea. He went to look for books about war rather than mermaids at the exact moment when Luke and Serene showed up to take Elliot to a place of safety.

"You don't understand," Luke said. "Colonel Whiteleaf has more men. They have already taken the commander's tower."

"You're the one who doesn't understand," said Elliot. "I'm staying here. We can barricade ourselves in here: we'll be as safe as anyone in the camp."

Serene looked upon him with worry and, Elliot thought and hoped he was not imagining it, fondness. She was the only person in either world who ever looked at him like that. "You have a valiant spirit. I will respect your wishes, but you cannot ask me not to worry."

Luke looked tired: he addressed his words exclusively to Myra. "Can we take you to a place of safety, at least?"

"No," Myra said slowly. "I'll stay here with Elliot."

Maybe Myra could be his favorite of Myra and Peter forever.

They kept reading, through the silence of a siege and then when the battle finally broke out: men in Border guard uniforms attempting to take the camp and appoint Captain Whiteleaf as commander. Colonel Whiteleaf had come from his own fortress and occupied Commander Woodsinger's tower. There was still no sign of Whiteleaf Junior. Elliot assumed he would be produced, pretending to be innocent of any rebellion, once Commander Woodsinger surrendered.

Elliot thought it was meant to be a quick coup, and perhaps it would have been. Except Colonel Whiteleaf's Border guard had not expected the cadets to fight back: not so fiercely, not for a woman. They had not expected the commander to fight back so fiercely herself. Commander Woodsinger was not surrendering.

Elliot had not slept for two days and found himself drifting off, even though his bed was a hard chair and his lullaby was the sound of clashing weapons.

It was Myra, leafing through books of genealogy, who gave a soft incoherent sound of triumph and nudged Elliot out of his doze.

"Look at this," she said. "There's something wrong with the dates—there's something wrong about the mermaids—"

That was when lightning struck for Elliot, and he leaped out of his chair as if lightning had set it on fire.

"I can stop all this. I have to see Colonel Whiteleaf right now."

"You can't go out there! It's much too dangerous."

Elliot looked out the window. There were buildings burning out there, cabins and towers where he had been sleeping and playing and learning for years. He had chosen council training; he would have been rubbish at anything else. Most fights were always going to be at a remove from him, but this was his home and that meant this was his fight.

"It is much too dangerous," Elliot said. "It would be really dumb to go out there." He paused. "Well, even I can't be smart all the time."

He got up quickly, before she could stop him, dropped a kiss in her hair, and went out the door into the chaos of a battlefield.

It was obscene, his camp becoming the backdrop for this horror. There was someone dead on the ground, facedown: Elliot could only be thankful. He did not want to see if it was someone he knew. There was a man in chainmail bearing down on him.

"I come on a mission of peace," said Elliot, and got backhanded with a chainmail fist. Elliot tasted blood and saw stars in a gray daytime sky. "Did I stutter?" Elliot asked, feeling his mouth fill with blood. "I said I come on a mission of peace, moron."

The chainmailed guy drew his sword. Elliot hated his life, especially when he saw two of the guys' buddies closing in to help him slaughter an unarmed student. Elliot tensed, wondering if he should run toward the sound of fighting, where there might be assistance, or away.

The chainmailed guy collapsed, spat blood, and dropped his sword: Luke had his own blade out of chainmailed guy's back and in the chest of the second man before the group realized what was happening. In less than three seconds the three men after Elliot were dead.

Elliot tried not to be sick, and tried not to think of how Luke had been sick once, killing someone. Now Luke had been through a war and killed people easily, effortlessly, as if it was routine.

Luke grabbed Elliot's arm, which led to there being blood and dirt on Elliot's arm. This was not routine for Elliot. "What are you doing out here?"

"I need to get to the—"

"You need to get back inside right now!"

"No!" Elliot shouted back, since they were shouting, which he found to be unnecessary and rude. "I need to get to the commander's tower. Take me there right now."

"And if I don't?" Luke bit out.

"Then I'm going on my own!" Elliot snapped. "And I bet I get stabbed, and Serene will be annoyed with you."

He wrenched his arm out of Luke's grip and strode toward the tower. He heard the sound of Luke killing someone else behind him, so he presumed he was protected: Luke caught up with him, and nobody else stopped them until they reached the commander's tower and the four unfamiliar guards at the door.

"I urge you to surrender," said Elliot, and stood aside.

Three guards down, and the fourth had his hands up, weapon loosely clasped in one of them, but his intent clear. Only Luke was a whirlwind of murderous movement: blade shining and singing through the air.

"Not that one," Elliot said, and when Luke didn't listen Elliot had no choice but to eel his way in between the two men and their blades. "He's surrendering!"

Luke was already swinging his sword: Elliot was very glad he trusted Luke to be fast enough to catch his own swing. As it was there was a nasty moment where Elliot felt Luke's sword graze his throat and the other man's swordpoint at his back.

The enemy soldier could have run Elliot through right then. But he put up his blade, and Elliot opened the door and went into the commander's tower, Luke following him.

"Oh my God," said Luke, and sat down heavily on the stone steps, in the dark, his head in his hands. "He could have killed you. *I* could have killed you!"

"No, no, I had every faith in you," said Elliot. "I did think he might kill me, but there was a life to be saved in the balance, so you see it was worth it."

Elliot also found war very traumatizing, but he'd thought that Luke would be more used to it by now. He reached out in the dark, found Luke's shoulder, and patted it.

"I know, violence is terrible," he said. "I'll be more supportive later. I have to go see Colonel Whiteleaf now. Don't let anyone come up these stairs."

He ran up the stairs and into the commander's office, where Commander Woodsinger should have been. Instead there was a man, burly around the shoulders with a fiercely bristling black beard.

"They send brats from council training to offer surrender and command to my son?" barked Colonel Whiteleaf, hand on his sword hilt.

"No," said Elliot, and took the rolled-up pieces of paper from his belt.

He found ripping pages out of books sacrilegious, but not as sacrilegious as letting people die.

"I read this interesting account of your battle with the mermaids long ago, Colonel Whiteleaf," he said. "The one in which you first won acclaim as a military leader. The battle on which all your fame is based. It's funny, because your account of how the mermaids behaved was not at all in accordance with a book I read in the Sunborn library called *1,000 Leagues Across a Sea of Blood*. Have you read it? It's very good."

"What does an ancient book have to do with me?" Whiteleaf snapped, going rigid.

"Moreover," said Elliot. "A few years ago, an explorer from my world called deWitt went on a voyage to the same place you claimed you fought your battles, and he saw there no sign that they had ever taken place. There were mermaids there: their numbers had not been decimated and their habitat had not been destroyed. It was very clever of you, Colonel Whiteleaf. You can't claim to have had a battle with trolls or harpies or elves—people will expect to see evidence, people will expect to see bodies. But a battle with mermaids, out at sea? Nobody but you and your sailors would ever know the truth. Or so you thought."

"No one will pay attention to what a stupid cadet claims," bluffed Whiteleaf, his eyes less confident than his voice. "Or to a stupid book, or to a voyage of exploration, whatever foolish thing that is. I've never heard of one, or this deWitt fellow either."

Elliot raised his eyebrows. "You're right, the voyage isn't very famous, because exploration isn't as exciting as war, and deWitt is regarded with suspicion since he wouldn't even take an otherlands surname. But Rachel Sunborn was one of the soldiers with the explorers. She described what she saw to me very accurately. I think she could do the same for anybody . . . and I think a Sunborn would be believed."

Whiteleaf's face was red as dawn.

"One more thing," Elliot added casually, and saw Whiteleaf turn pale. "I know the birthdate of Captain Whiteleaf. He's not your son. He can't be. By your own account, he was conceived while you were at sea. But you know that, don't you? You and your wife never had any other children. You wanted him to be your heir, and you wanted him to have command of the trainees' camp, which is a stepping stone to real military command. You wanted a lot of things, and you're not going to get all of them. So now you have a choice. I left a letter describing the truth of your long sea voyage, just so I wouldn't get murdered."

Elliot made a courteous gesture to Colonel Whiteleaf's sword, already half drawn.

"If I die, the story gets told. So if you keep fighting, you maybe take the camp, maybe not, but everybody knows that your son is not your son, and he is disgraced and you are both a famous coward and the laughingstock of the otherlands. Or you were overpowered by the brave young heroes of the Border camp and came to realise that your doubts had been wrong and that Commander Woodsinger was a brave and inspiring leader. You stood your troops down, and you and your son declared your support for the commander," said Elliot. "Which is it going to be?"

Whiteleaf's hand clenched on the edge of the desk.

"If I let you live," he said, "and follow your terms, do you swear to say nothing?"

Elliot bit back a smile at the dizzy joy of victory, and said: "I swear."

When he left the room, he found Luke still waiting on the steps, his head still in his hands. Luke leaped to his feet when he saw Elliot.

"Now explain to me what you were doing," he snarled.

"Oh . . .," said Elliot. "Nothing, really. I had an idea, but it didn't pan out."

"Nothing?" Luke repeated. "You risked your life for nothing? Do you realize how short-sighted and selfish and irresponsible you were being? Do you think this is a game?"

"Yes, yes," said Elliot. "My behavior was very wrong. I see that now. But I do have good news."

They held a feast to celebrate the truce between Colonel Whiteleaf and the reinstated Commander Woodsinger. Serene sat beside Elliot at the feast and told him about how she and Luke had argued down students who wanted to go over to Whiteleaf's side.

His friends always seemed to be fighting different battles than the ones Elliot was fighting, and Serene was always fighting on the war-training side. But Elliot liked to think Serene had used her council-training skills when she convinced the vast majority of the camp to keep faith with their commander.

He saw Commander Woodsinger look over at their table occasionally, and once he caught her dark, watchful gaze. It felt like she was trying to tell him something, but Elliot looked away. She was probably looking at Serene.

Elliot did not know, and perhaps could not appreciate, exactly what the war-training class and soldiers of the Border camp had done. But for once, because it was the way to peace, he was happy to let them take the credit.

He let Luke tell him off over and over again for being dumb enough to go out in the midst of a battlefield. He let Serene, and Dale, and Luke tell him all about their adventures. He sent Dale on his way with the sweet smile Elliot used on the elves, and Serene looked at him sharply from her place beside him on the bench.

"What did you do?" she asked.

Elliot smiled a real smile. "I might have helped a little. In my fashion."

Serene said nothing, but she helped him to his feet, and they left the feasting hall together. She paused once they were outside, then stepped up to him and kissed him again.

A lot of the buildings had been torched, but there were tents set up around the Border camp. They found one and tumbled inside it, still kissing, kissing and kissing: Elliot did not want to let her go, not ever, and perhaps he would never have to.

"I have struggled against my passions, and I can struggle no longer: they have me in an irresistible grasp," said Serene.

"Grasp away," Elliot advised her.

"A man cannot understand the force of a woman's desire," Serene continued.

"I'll give it a try," said Elliot.

"And I cannot—I do not offer you marriage," Serene added, the words almost lost between their mouths, kissing and clinging. "You should send me away. You should preserve your virtue. I find I cannot help myself in the face of your charms and I fear if you do not spurn me from your door at once I will besmirch you utterly."

There was no door to speak of, since they were all in tents. Through the rough cloth of the tent, Elliot could hear the murmur of people passing by, the crackle of fires and sound of blades being sharpened and all the other sounds of a battlefield settling back into peace. War was over, at least for a time, and he was warm, his head on a soft pillow, tangled up in soft blankets with the only girl he had ever loved tangled up with him. She hovered above him, murmuring words that only meant, to him, that she did want him after all.

Elliot could not help but smile, and he felt her smile blossom against his mouth in response to his. He curled his fingers around her long dark hair and tugged her down the last fraction of an inch toward him.

"Besmirch away," he said.

He didn't know whether he had Peter's educational manuals or Serene's helpful instructions to thank, but Elliot thought the whole thing had all gone rather well.

He was lying amid tumbled sheets, looking up into Serene's flushed face, when he finally had the courage to bring up a certain matter. Moonlight and starshine were growing faint behind her dark hair, diffused into the pale glow of morning.

"You know," Elliot said, a little shyly, "I used to think that you . . . maybe liked Luke."

Serene was levered up on one elbow, looking at him with pleased soft eyes. She liked it when he was shy: he'd noted that before, on the rare occasions that it happened.

"Luke?" she repeated blankly. "Our Luke?"

She started to laugh.

"Hahaha, I know, so silly," said Elliot, greatly gratified. "Why are you laughing, exactly?"

"Luke and I have always had a relationship that was firmly platonic and based on our shared passion for honor and weaponry."

"Oh," said Elliot. "You were bros the whole time?"

"That's a human idiom, but yes," said Serene. "Moreover I do not find golden-haired gentlemen sexually appealing. They remind me of Golden-Hair-Scented-Like-Summer, than whom there is nobody more infuriating."

"This is awesome news."

"Golden thinks he is so pretty, and so well-behaved," Serene continued.

"Sounds like the worst," Elliot contributed.

"He called me a rogue last summer, you know, in front of his whole clique of snotty friends, and everybody laughed."

"Okay," said Elliot. "I'm no longer worried about Luke, but I am starting to be a little worried about someone else."

Serene glanced over at him, an odd expression on her face. Elliot thought it might be simple surprise: it only lasted a moment, and then was gone, replaced with what Elliot was incredulously pleased to identify as an admiring look.

She leaned down, close enough to kiss but not quite kissing yet, and her dark hair fell down all around him so the dying night was veiled and the only starshine was her eyes.

"You have no need to be worried about anyone," murmured Serene, and kissed him. Her mouth was warm and lingering, her hand tight around his arm. Elliot felt the calluses from bow and sword against the sensitive skin on the inside of his elbow. He shivered.

"Unhand me, you vile seducer, you virtue bandit. I feel sullied by your irresistible yet immoral touch!"

Serene's eyes widened and her grip went loose.

"No, I didn't mean it!" Elliot exclaimed hastily. "I was teasing. Maybe also role-playing a little bit? I'll tell you all about role-playing. I read about it in a book."

Serene's eyes got even wider, and she lunged at him. They went rolling across blankets and grass, her hair winding around his hands, him laughing helplessly and her murmuring amusement in his ear and in between kisses.

"Oh, you did, did you," said Serene, rolling her eyes and smiling so wide that Elliot knew in a human it would have been a laugh. She held him pinned down to the ground. "You are such a minx!"

"You know that's right," murmured Elliot.

"There is something I want to ask you. I was talking to your friend Myra," Serene said. "I had a few questions for her, but as it turned out I find her company most congenial. She too is often puzzled by the strictly human way of doing things. She told me, though, about a facet of human romance, in which people are romantically involved not with the specific purpose of marriage but with the intent of providing companionship for each other. I must say that seems efficient. Everybody's needs are met and neither party is in any way disgraced." Serene paused. "She called it 'dating' or 'being boyfriend and girlfriend.'"

Elliot hardly dared to breathe, in case it interrupted Serene's flow of thought. He knew her better than that, though: knew her serious face when she was intent on a purpose.

"How about it?" asked Serene. "Do you want to be my boyfriend?"

Elliot smiled, and the smile drew Serene down to kiss him, so the smile might have been answer enough. Just in case, though, just to show her how much he meant it, he murmured, "Yes" just before their lips met.

Later, Serene slept through her morning archery practice. Elliot looked at the sunrise, golden rays caught in the treetops and sky catching fire. Warm light spilled over Serene as she slept, her skin illuminated and her shoulderblades golden crests and her back a valley, her bare skin a wonderful and strange landscape. Elliot rested a hand gently at the dip in her lower back, and felt both awed and scared.

He had been wishing for love his whole life, and if he'd had just one wish that wish would have been her. He was not sure how it had happened, or why: but the wish granted, he had to prove he could deserve it. He did not know how to be grateful enough.

"This is my plan," said Serene as they entered the lunchroom, and Elliot gazed at her with deep appreciation of her strategic mind. She steered him toward the table where Luke was sitting. "I will tell Luke of the newfound status of our relationship, for I wish to express that I am in no wise ashamed of you."

"Thank you, Serene, excellent decision!"

"And then I will go get my nourishment and you two can have a longer conversation about feelings. I know boys like to gossip about girls and romance."

Elliot's squawk of protest was cut off when Serene pushed him forcibly onto the bench opposite Luke and said: "Elliot and I are dating now. You have four minutes to gossip about it. Good-bye, blossom!"

She pressed a firm kiss to Elliot's horrified mouth and strode off. Elliot loved to watch her go, but he really hated her leaving.

"We don't have to gossip," Elliot informed Luke. "Let's be strong and silent. In a manly way. That would be awesome, right?"

"So you were . . . serious about . . . all that?" asked Luke Sunborn, secret gossip fiend.

Elliot was disappointed, and then he actually listened to what Luke was saying and took a sharp left turn into being offended. "Why wouldn't I be?"

Luke fiddled with his pudding rather than looking up. "You were always so . . . exorbeetent . . . about it."

"*Ex or bee tent?* . . . Oh. You mean 'exorbitant,' loser. And as opposed to all the other reasonable well-balanced sides to my personality, you mean?" Elliot scoffed at the very idea that he might not have been serious. "Like you'd know anything about how I feel."

"Fine," said Luke. "I hope you'll both be very happy."

"Thank you," said Elliot graciously.

"You know, for about the one minute that it lasts," Luke added, with a smug twist to his lips.

Elliot opened his mouth to say: hey, how dare you, it's going to last forever, but then he shut his mouth. He had been bold when he knew, secretly, that there was no chance at all. Now he had a little hope, hanging in a fragile balance, and he was terrified that being overconfident would upset the balance and he would lose everything. It was terrifying to have something: he wondered if other people lived their whole lives in this strange state between exultation and absolute dread. He'd never had anything to lose before.

"You think so," he muttered as Serene put her tray down, and then there was no opportunity to say anything else.

His feeling of panic eased as he looked at her: beloved and best, her eyes like water reflecting a morning sky and her hair like water shadowed by trees, dark but with a sparkle of light through the leaves.

She smiled at him. "Did you have fun gossiping?"

"I can't describe to you how much," said Elliot. "But I missed you."

He leaned in and kissed her. He hoped it never stopped being so sweet it was almost painful.

"You missed archery practice," Luke remarked, his gaze on Serene. "You never miss."

Serene almost smiled, and Elliot was thrilled. "I was a little preoccupied."

"That's great, everybody already thinks we can't obey regulations because of him," Luke said. "Well, I'm going to practice archery some more. Someone ought to."

He got up, pushing his tray aside. They stared at him in dismay.

"Luke, you have hardly eaten anything!" said Serene.

"I'm not hungry," said Luke.

"Luke, please don't develop an eating disorder," Elliot begged. "We do not have any therapists in this world!"

"What's a therapist? I said I'm not hungry!" said Luke.

Elliot paused. "Don't eat any therapists. That's not what they're for."

"Then I don't know why you brought them up, other than the fact you always want to be talking about something stupid."

Luke fixed Elliot with a look of definite dislike. Elliot reached for Serene's hand, for comfort, but she was looking at Luke, who was now making his way out of the room.

"Okay, I know what's going on," said Elliot. "You said you were best bros with Luke, right? And obviously, as a supportive boyfriend, I respect your close bonds of platonic friendship. When one bestie starts dating and the other's still single, conflict can occur. I read about this."

Serene nodded seriously. "That makes sense."

"Fortunately, I have a solution! You have to spend lots of time one on one with Luke and assure him of your continued platonic affection," Elliot told her. "He just needs bro time."

Serene regarded him with eyes that shone with what Elliot thought was tenderness. She shook her head. "I would never have realized all that. Masculine intuition is a wonderful thing."

"I am pretty intuitive," Elliot said, with beautiful simplicity. "And sensitive. And New Age."

Serene leaned in, the light of admiration still in her eyes, and kissed him. Her mouth was soft and cool, and he felt warm all over.

"I'll go now," she whispered. "But I'll see you tonight."

Elliot's brilliance thus left him alone at his lunch table. Many occupants of the room were staring. He sat smugly radiant until Peter cautiously approached.

"Whoa, you tamed an elf, good job, buddy," said Peter.

Elliot eyed him with disfavor. "I didn't tame her. She's not a pet."

"Oh, so she tamed you? I heard elves were into that."

Myra was definitely Elliot's favorite forever. "Nobody is anybody's pet."

"Um, I'm probably saying the wrong thing. Sorry, man," said Peter. He put down his tray with a glum little thunk. "I don't have much luck with girls myself. My dad says it runs in our family."

"Er . . . how does he explain your mother?" Elliot asked.

"To tell you the truth, I think he means my mother. My mum's family is from the Borderlands—generation of Waterwrits after generation—and you know my dad is from the world outside. It's an adjustment, of course . . . you'd know . . . but my dad couldn't go back, after the Border camp. Things are always a bit strained at home."

"I'm sorry," said Elliot after a moment, and forced out: "I know what that's like."

Elliot put down Peter's view of his romance to his bad home life, but to his surprise, he found most people had a similar reaction: they either wanted to congratulate him or were condescending in his direction.

He was the significant other of an elf, but he hadn't expected to be made into The Significant Other rather than being Elliot. He hadn't thought he enjoyed it when people looked at him with exasperation, but it was infinitely better than being looked past.

Not that people had stopped looking at him with exasperation. That was made very clear a few days later, when the dust of battle had settled in the camp, and the bloodstains in the dust had faded until you might think they were something else, unless you knew better.

One of Elliot's dorm mates, Benjamin Rainfall, had died in the battle. Elliot remembered how he had always begged Elliot to blow out his candle, stop reading, and let him sleep. Elliot wished he had let him sleep now.

Elliot was walking from the library to his cabin, wearing an illicit hoodie against the winter chill and all alone because Luke and Serene were spending bro time together, when he saw Delia Winterchild going for Richard Plantgrown's throat.

"Uh," said Elliot, catching her wrist so she did not stab Richard. "Maybe we could indulge in some cutting repartee instead?"

"He was fighting on Whiteleaf's side, you know," Delia snapped. "I saw him kill Ben."

Elliot was tempted to drop Delia's wrist and walk away, but Whiteleaf and Woodsinger had a truce now. That meant they all had to have a truce as well.

"Fight's over," he said, and held on.

"And the wrong side won," Richard snapped. "Because you sneaked around and made it happen. Don't think I don't know."

Richard lifted his hand. Elliot didn't want to let go of Delia, so he couldn't shield himself. Elliot braced himself to be hit.

"*Hey*," said Luke, swooping down on them. Elliot didn't even know where he'd come from, he'd moved that fast. "Cadets shouldn't fight each other. And they certainly shouldn't put a council-training cadet in the middle of a fight!"

"He put himself in the middle," Richard protested.

"Sorry," said Luke, calmly scathing. "Are you telling me you're having problems handling a council-training cadet?"

Luke regarded Richard with lofty Sunborn disdain until Richard growled something like a negative and slunk away.

"We didn't need your help," Delia barked at him, and stalked off. Luke watched her go with raised eyebrows.

"That girl," he began.

"Delia Winterchild," Elliot supplied.

"She's always bad-tempered," Luke remarked. "Now she's starting fights and dragging you into them?"

She's not bad-tempered, Elliot thought, remembering taking Delia's hand in his when she came back from the wars and her brother did not. *She just doesn't like you.* He thought Luke might have trouble understanding the concept.

He also felt an impulse to explain why Delia and Richard were fighting, but what was the point? Then there would be even more cadets who hated and mistrusted each other.

Elliot shrugged. "I guess she's bad-tempered."

"Oh," said Luke, with a small grin, always pleased when Elliot agreed with him. "So you were standing up for her because you two have a lot in common."

"That's it," said Elliot, and grinned back at him.

"Stop wearing contraband," said Luke, flipping Elliot's hood over his hair. Elliot had barely seen Luke in three days, but possibly Luke had now had enough bro time and was ready to stop sulking.

"I'm a rebel without a cloak," said Elliot. "I know Delia, actually. I like her."

"Really," said Luke, his voice colder.

"What?" Elliot snapped.

"You haven't even been dating Serene a *week*," said Luke, and stomped off.

Now Luke was being protective of Serene, as if Elliot would ever hurt her? Maybe that was what always happened, when you dated someone's best friend. Maybe they would always see you as a potential enemy, always be ready to take their friend's side against you, just in case.

Elliot thought about being on different sides, and those loyal to Commander Woodsinger and those loyal to Colonel Whiteleaf. In his books about magic lands, the evildoers had horns, or at least had the decency to wear outfits composed entirely of black leather. Sometimes there was one traitor on the good side, but he didn't remember any stories about teams who wore the same uniform splitting up and turning against each other. Usually the traitor was banished, too. People did not have to learn how to live with each other again, after trust was broken between them.

Elliot stood staring down the dark paths to the many cabins where the cadets slept. Every year, he thought, things got more complicated, and there were so many ways to lose.

The next day Commander Woodsinger left word for Elliot to come to her office. He found Luke and Serene already there, both standing to attention. Their offensively military posture shamed Elliot into a half-hearted salute.

"Hey, Commander," he said. "Is this about getting medals? Because it's not necessary, really, it was our pleas—"

Luke coughed pointedly.

"Shh, my dear," said Serene, and put her hand on Elliot's arm.

Elliot sidestepped her. "I will not shush," he said, frowning. "When have I ever shushed?"

"Can I see you alone for a moment, Cadet Schafer?" asked Commander Woodsinger. "I trust that I have made my position on this subject clear to both of you."

Serene and Luke cast vaguely concerned glances in Elliot's direction, but Elliot had already figured out that there were not going to be medals, and in fact that he was going to be told off for some cruel and unjust reason.

It was also possible that they were not concerned for him, but concerned about what he might say to Commander Woodsinger once left alone with her. They were right to be concerned, but there was nothing they could do about it.

Elliot smiled at them sweetly as they went out. They both looked deeply apprehensive.

Commander Woodsinger did not start scolding him. Instead she fixed him with dark eyes and barked out a weirdly personal question.

"What do you love, Cadet Schafer?"

"Serene," Elliot replied promptly.

Commander Woodsinger closed her eyes and visibly prayed for patience. She did not reach for any weapons when she opened her eyes, so Elliot figured her prayer was granted.

"What else?"

Elliot sunk down low in the chair, hands linked over his chest, and kicked the desk. To punish the desk even more, he eyed it darkly.

"So long as this goes no further," he muttered. "Luke, I suppose."

Commander Woodsinger breathed out through her nose. This sounded like an irate horse's prayer for patience.

"What else?"

"Well, there's Myra of the Diamond clan," said Elliot. "I think I just like her a lot, though."

"What more?" demanded Commander Woodsinger.

"I mean, I quite like Peter Quint, and Adara Cornripe, and the cranky medic who won't tell me her name, and you," said Elliot, "but meaning no offence, I don't think that I'd classify any of that as l—"

"You're misinterpreting the question, Cadet Schafer!" said Commander Woodsinger. "Fascinating though the complexities of your emotional attachments undoubtedly are. What do you hold allegiance to?"

Elliot frowned. "Well, Serene. And—"

"Do you love your country?"

"What, England?" asked Elliot. "Wow. Am I a poet in 1914?"

"What," said Commander Woodsinger.

"What," said Elliot.

"The Borderlands," the commander clarified.

"I think I'm probably still British on my passport," said Elliot.

"I hoped that after your years of training, you would have come to think of the Borderlands as your home."

"It hasn't been that long," Elliot pointed out. "I'm only fifteen." He chewed his lip thoughtfully. "Can a country be a home?"

"What do you think?" asked Commander Woodsinger.

Elliot tilted his head. "Clever."

"I wish you were more clever," said Commander Woodsinger. "I'd like it if you were even half as clever as you think you are."

Elliot stared with his mouth open. He was ready to be disciplined, but he had not expected to be *insulted.*

"Are you aware that because of your reckless behavior Luke Sunborn left his squad—the squad that he was leading—in order to protect you, as an unarmed civilian?"

"Well, it's not my fault Luke left his squad," said Elliot. "I didn't ask him to. That was his irresponsible decision, and you should tell him off for it."

"I have already disciplined Cadet Sunborn," said Commander Woodsinger.

"How could you?" Elliot asked. "He saved my life!"

"Your position on this matter seems to be slightly contradictory."

"It's not," said Elliot. "We saved the day, and that means that I wish you to overlook any slight irregularities. I would like to complain about Luke, as it is my hobby, but I don't want anyone to be punished. Least of all me."

"I'm afraid you are going to be disappointed, cadet," said the commander. "I want you to tutor some of the first-year cadets in history and mapmaking."

"Well, that's just ridiculous," Elliot said. "We're punishing children now? What have they done?"

Commander Woodsinger did not look amused. In fact, she had the stern countenance of someone who was determined to be oblivious to jokes, impassive as a tree stump or a toadstool. Or as a blank screen: Elliot might be forced to live without technology, but that didn't mean that he had to descend to nature metaphors.

"Your 'irregularities,'" said Commander Woodsinger, a woman who could imply quote marks with devastating clarity, "could have led to your own death and that of others. That it turned out well does not mean that you are exempt from the rules, which are in place for your protection. And that of others."

"It could be the rules need to be changed."

"Or it could be there's a reason I'm in charge, and not you," said Commander Woodsinger.

It was on the tip of Elliot's tongue to snap that without their support, she wouldn't be in charge: but the alternative had been much worse. This was the difference between making a bargain and winning a victory. The other side was not getting punished, and Elliot was not getting rewarded.

Elliot would still rather make a bargain.

It wasn't like Elliot wanted to be in control of a military camp, and he supposed since she did, she did have to enforce some sort of military discipline. Not that he was a soldier, but he was a student here. He'd entered into an implicit contract. He knew the rules.

"Fine, I'll teach the brats," he said. "But it still seems cruel to them, if you ask me."

The commander unrolled a map. It was a map Elliot was entirely familiar with: he knew it from geography class, from Maximilian Wavechaser's book and hundreds more like it.

"These are the Borderlands," said the commander. "This is a land of magic and mystery: this is our charge and our sworn duty to protect. This is a land to be loved and served, because nobody can understand it."

"Well. Nobody has understood it *yet*," said Elliot.

Commander Woodsinger looked as if her prayer for patience had not been answered, and she felt personally betrayed.

"Get lost, Cadet. Time's wasting and I have reports of brigands in elven territory to deal with."

Once he was finished with Commander Woodsinger, Elliot did not climb down the stairs. He climbed up, to the top of the brief tower, and he gazed down at the vast tapestry of the Borderlands. Like green silk spread as far as the eye could see, the grey satin of mist and sea at the edges, embroidered with the delicate blue of rivers.

Nobody can understand it, the commander had said, and the challenge echoed in Elliot's bones, as perhaps the commander had wanted it to. A challenge was more familiar to him than love, and felt close to the same thing, as though one led to the other. He felt his heart beat to the double time of two words.

Not yet.

Teaching was as nightmarish as Elliot had expected.

"I hate children," he announced at lunch after his first lesson, flopping down on the bench and banging his forehead against the table.

Serene patted his back. "I know, sweetheart."

"I hate them all," said Elliot. "I especially hate Cyril, who became overwhelmed by my, quote, harsh tone, unquote, and began to hyperventilate. But I also hate Daniel, who asks stupid questions, and Miriam, who is a little know-it-all, which would be fine if she knew it all, but let me tell you—she doesn't!"

"They will be less annoying soon," Serene soothed, her voice balm. "Children from your world, I have noticed, are often immature and ill-acquainted with the realities of this one. But they grow up fast once transplanted to the Borderlands."

They did seem about ten years younger than Elliot's class, rather than two. It made Elliot uneasy to think about.

"I'm pretty sure all children are just awful," he said. "Cyril also hyperventilated during a reenactment of *Star Wars* I was doing. And I remember that awful sticky creature whom I fell off a cliff with. I never, ever want any."

"I'm certain your tale of stellar combat was riveting," said Serene. "And I'm certain you'll change your mind. Most men long for children, due to their selfless and nurturing natures."

"I don't have one of those," said Elliot.

"What about Smooth Jazz?" asked Luke meanly.

"What?" asked Serene.

Elliot was about to echo her, but then he recalled his conversation with Luke about the hypothetical names for his and Serene's hypothetical children that he'd had before he was acquainted with any actual children and their horrors. He did not think Luke bringing up this evidence of Elliot being absurd in front of Serene was playing fair.

"Ix-nay on the abotaging-say of my elationship-ray," said Elliot, kicking him, but that just made Serene and Luke both look at him as if he was speaking in tongues. He had so much to teach them about the other world: he'd forgotten the crucial aspect of pig Latin. "Anyway," he said hastily. "Do you two have selfless and nurturing natures? I mean, hypothetically: Kids, yes or no?"

"Women have so many other things on their minds," said Serene. "I'll decide when I'm older."

Elliot hoped she decided no. He really had not enjoyed Cyril's hyperventilating.

"I obviously can't," Luke snapped.

"Uh, you obviously can, loser," said Elliot. "We live in a military society frequently torn by conflicts and all. You're telling me that somebody wouldn't hand over a war orphan to a Sunborn and their life partner whose name might rhyme with Sail Cravefacer?"

Luke had looked thoughtful when Elliot started speaking, but by the time Elliot was done he looked only flushed and embarrassed.

"Shut up!" he said. "What if he heard you!"

He got up and stormed away to whatever physical activity he'd decided he simply had to practice at lunchtime that day. He might be on to the javelin by now. Elliot suspected the system was alphabetical.

As if Elliot had not already checked that Dale was nowhere in earshot. Elliot was sneaky and on the diplomatic track. He made a mental note to ask Dale about his opinion on children some time.

"You embarrassed me a little in the commander's office," Serene said, and her voice was soft: loving but chiding, and Elliot truly did appreciate how hard she was trying not to overstep the boundaries of their new relationship, but he actually liked it better when she was being brash and open about her attitude toward men.

It was difficult, this way, to separate out affection and condescension, and he didn't want to reject the affection.

"You know me, Serene," he said, and pulled her hand away from his face, linked his fingers with hers instead. "I'll be embarrassing you a lot soon enough."

She took it well. "Probably," she murmured, and kissed him. "I don't mind it too much."

They had a lovely ten minutes together, until Elliot sent Serene off to practise with Luke.

He found something to occupy himself with while they were being bros. For the times when Elliot was not teaching, there was the library and, surprisingly enough, Myra. The first time he went there outside his usual study hours and found her there, he thought it was a happy coincidence. The third time, he was fairly sure there was something going on.

"Never a bad time to get ahead on your studies," she said when he asked, shrugging it off.

Elliot raised his eyebrows. "And yet."

"Oh, fine," said Myra. "If you must know—"

"I must!" said Elliot. "Because I'm nosy and have no consideration for the feelings of others."

"I'm trying to avoid spending so much time with Peter," Myra told him, a light flush creeping into her cheeks. "I think—he has feelings for me, and I don't feel the same way."

"Why, Myra!" Elliot was delighted, though sorry for Peter. "You heartbreaker."

"I like someone else," Myra continued, her blush deepening. "So it isn't fair to lead Peter on. I'm hoping that if I put a little distance between us, he'll get the message without me having to say anything."

Elliot wanted to know whom Myra liked, but the shadow of her mustache did nothing to hide the firm set of her mouth. He could tell when someone was not going to talk.

"Well, I'm happy to keep you company," he said. "Serene's spending time with Luke, and I don't want to get in the way of that."

Myra frowned. "I thought you were all friends."

"Not technically," said Elliot. "I mean, not reciprocally."

Myra looked even more confused. Elliot gave it up, even though he felt personally that it was perfectly clear.

"Anyway," he continued. "Serene doesn't want Luke to feel left out now that she and I are dating, so I am giving them space."

"Aw," said Myra. "I think that's really nice of you." She paused. "So, you're really serious about Serene?"

"Why does everyone keep asking me that?"

Elliot's tone was more snappish than he'd intended, but Myra didn't seem to take offence.

"You know, you're kind of a dramatic person, Elliot," she said mildly.

"I am not. How dare you!"

"It's not a bad thing," Myra said. "But when a guy calls a girl the nightlight of his soul, other people might be forgiven for thinking he's being intentionally over the top."

"I wasn't being over the top," Elliot argued. "I was way under the top."

Myra giggled. "Whatever you say, Elliot. And hey, it all worked out, didn't it? You're with her."

Elliot looked out the window. "Yeah," he said softly. "Yeah, I am."

"And you were serious about her the whole time," Myra said.

"Yeah," Elliot said, even more softly. "Yeah, I was."

"And she knew," said Myra. "That's what counts. It doesn't matter what anybody else thought."

She smiled at him, and Elliot knew it was an apology for making him feel doubtful and uncomfortable, and he smiled back. She hadn't meant it. And it wasn't her fault if Elliot had expressed his feelings wrong. He always did that, as if life were a dance where everybody else knew the moves but Elliot was constantly and fatally out of step.

Myra returned to her book. Elliot sat and looked out of the window, not dreamily this time but feeling a little cold.

He had to be careful not to drive off Myra. He realized exactly what he had said, earlier, even if she did not: that Luke was not Elliot's friend. And in a way, since Serene was now his girlfriend, she was not actually his friend anymore either. If—something were to happen, if he made too many mistakes and they broke up, Elliot would have nobody.

He had not thought about how dangerous it would be, to have all his dreams come true.

"Come with me," said Luke abruptly one day, turning up at the library and grabbing Elliot's wrist and hauling him out of the room.

Nobody protested this outrage but Elliot himself. Myra said, "Hi, Luke! Bye, Luke!" and waved Elliot good-bye with her little finger, not even putting down her book as her friend was carried off. It was scandalous and heartless.

Elliot grabbed at the checkout desk as he went by.

"Uh, help me?" he suggested. "Abduction!"

"Don't be a silly little thing," said Bright-Eyes. "Men don't abduct people. Just boyish high spirits! You should both channel them into embroidery."

"Maybe I would if I wasn't being abducted!" Elliot hissed, but his grip on the desk proved futile as he was pulled away.

Sometimes Elliot worried that Bright-Eyes-Gladden-the-Hearts-of-Women disliked him intensely for being a hussy and always in the library until closing time.

"I don't want to go with you," Elliot declared. "You seem like a bad man."

Luke glanced at him over his shoulder, and grinned. "That's a shame. I was thinking—"

"I hope not unsupervised," Elliot remarked.

Luke rolled his eyes. "The bandits problem is only getting worse. Their numbers are growing—"

"The bandits are banding together?" Elliot asked.

He knew that the bandits, humans who had reportedly either left villages that were not thriving or gone rogue from the Border guard itself, were not funny. And he was touched by Luke's concern. But Luke had handed him that line.

"You're hilarious. Please keep joking until the bandits kill us all. If you insist on getting into trouble, you could at least make *yourself* less trouble than you currently are, is my point. So your *girlfriend* and I don't have to keep getting disciplined for pulling your insubordinate ass out of the fire."

"I won't learn how to fight!" Elliot said, pulling out of Luke's grasp with abrupt anger.

"It's not that hard," Luke said patiently.

"That's not the point! You don't understand anything."

"As you constantly remind me. Apparently I should understand someone endlessly putting themselves in danger but refusing to learn even the basics of self-defence—"

"Yes!"

"Sorry," said Luke, grabbing him again and recommencing dragging. "I don't understand things that are stupid. All right, look, do you have objections to dodging?"

"What?"

"Sharp objects? If they're thrown at you, would you dodge them?"

"Are you planning to throw them?" Elliot asked cagily.

"How about running away?"

"And back to the library? I am considering that."

"No," said Luke. "Come on. If all you're going to do is dodge or run, you have to learn to do it faster."

They had left the cabins, by which Elliot meant the buildings, by which he meant sweet sweet civilization, behind. Elliot eyed the variety of open spaces around—Trigon pitch, javelin throwing pit, archery section, combat rings, endless fields—with trepidation.

"I have always thought of myself as a brilliant mind to be safeguarded by the physical efforts of others."

"You should've thought of that before you left the library."

"You kidnapped me!" Elliot protested.

"I meant that time you almost got yourself killed and did get all of us reprimanded by our commanding officer."

So I could help us win, Elliot wanted to say, but going into exactly what he had done still seemed like a bad idea. Luke probably wouldn't think that blackmailing people was anything to be proud of.

"Oh," Elliot said. "That time."

He supposed that it did not matter if he'd been dumb or brave. He could have been stabbed either way, and he didn't want to be. It was nice that other people didn't want him to be either.

"We're going to start by running laps," said Luke.

Elliot got Serene a present for Christmas, even though neither of them celebrated it. None of them had ever given the others presents before. Luke and Elliot's birthdays were both in summer and thus missable, and Serene said that birthdays were different for elves, and telling anybody outside your family about the day of your entry into the world was considered dangerous. Elliot had always been glad about their presents rule, since getting Luke a gift would have been awkward.

Now that Serene was his girlfriend it seemed like he should give her a present at some point, however, and though the tradition of Christmas had survived in the otherlands, Valentine's Day had not, so this was Elliot's opportunity. He'd figured it would take up the time they usually spent watching Luke open his many presents from his family.

"I was thinking about why a land full of magic, where the humans lead secular lives and there are no churches, celebrates Christmas," Elliot remarked. "I guess it's a remnant of what humans bring across the Border with them. The ritual remaining, past belief."

He didn't know what the excuse for Christmas was in the story he'd read about the magic land with the important lion. Maybe it was the same deal. He was mostly talking because he was nervous.

Serene unwrapped the gift, and light touched her solemn face. It was a book of the treaties written and long history of cooperation between men and elves. Elliot found it idealized the history too much, but there were detailed and accurate sketches of the elven homeland that the writer had been privileged to see. He knew Serene missed home, sometimes.

"Thank you, petal," said Serene, and kissed him. "I got you something, as well."

She put a bracelet into his hand.

Elliot knew her first instinct had been to buy him adornments, but the woven leather bracelet was the kind of thing other boys at the Border camp would wear too. It was a nice compromise, and it was always nice to know Serene was trying too.

"Thanks, snowdrop," he said, and let her tie it on his wrist, then beamed. "Am I pretty?"

"You'll do," she teased, and put an arm around his shoulders. He snuggled up. "Perhaps next year we could incorporate some of the elvish winter festival into this time."

"I would love to do that," said Elliot.

"Yeah, okay," said Luke, unwrapping a crossbow.

The table in front of him was crowded with weapons, but this one was from Louise and she had her current kill count engraved on it, with an encouraging message that said KEEP UP, LITTLE BROTHER! Louise was a terrifying person, and it made them all smile.

"We can do the thing with the funny lamp too," Luke continued.

"Menorah," Elliot corrected. "We don't have to."

He'd told the others about being Jewish, and tried to explain all that entailed, but he was not sure he understood perfectly himself. They had never practiced. His father had never celebrated anything with him. Theirs was not a house that ever had celebrations.

It was just something that Elliot had understood his mother would have wanted him to know about. He had learned all he could, hoping to please her, in the days when he still believed she would come back. But she had never come, and he had never done any of the things he'd read about. He had never believed in much, once he stopped believing in her.

Serene looked dreamily off into the distance, her fingers lingering on the embossed cover of the book Elliot had given her. "In the winter festival, my mother would wrap my father in a mantle of beautiful snow-white fur. And for that one day, the trees will respond to us and give us fruit once more, their colors like jewels in the frost. Also, of course, there is the blood ritual."

"The blood what now," said Luke.

"Maybe all traditions are overrated!" Elliot suggested.

Luke unwrapped his next present, which unlike all the other terrible pointed gifts of death was a soft blue jumper.

"My dad knits," he explained as Serene nodded with complete understanding and Elliot beamed in astonishment. "He says it's soothing to have something to do with his hands in between battles. When it was just him and me because Mum was on her three-year mission and Louise was in the camp, stationed out in the north, it was freezing. All the men wanted Dad to knit them something warm."

It was a nice note to end the present-opening on, and Elliot did not find one particular tradition overrated. He arrived late to his next class—and Serene went late to hers—due to mistletoe in the doorway of the lunch room.

"Oooh, is the elf giving her girlfriend *jewelry*," mocked Natalie Lowlands, Adara Cornripe's best friend, as Elliot slid into the seat next to her.

Elliot gave her a big beaming smile and pushed his sleeve down a little to better display the bracelet. "Sorry you're lonely!"

In his imagination, being with Serene had been perfect. It wasn't: people were constantly passing comments, insulting either to him or to Serene—and he preferred the ones insulting to him—even the teachers sometimes made comments, he hardly saw Luke, and he had to weigh every interaction between himself and Serene carefully, trying to get each one right.

Sometimes he got it right without having to try too hard, though.

Even in winter, Elliot and Serene spent most nights outside the Border camp so they could not be caught by teachers, camping in a tent out in the woods. Serene made fires, which meant it was just as cozy as in the awful cabins anyway, and there was Serene under the heaped-up blankets to keep him warm. That night they read through the book Elliot had brought, and Serene pointed out all the places she was familiar with from the pictures and told stories of her childhood in those faraway settings. They laughed and whispered, legs tangling, and exchanged kisses every time they turned a page.

Serene for a season: Serene's warm skin, the growing-easy slide of his hands up her smooth back, the fall of her hair all around him, the low approving sounds she made as he kissed his way from the curve of her mouth to the curve of her neck down to all the curves of her slim body. Serene as the world edged toward spring, with moonlight turning her bare skin to pearl and her eyes to diamonds. Lying with Serene in the darkness when it was easiest to speak and murmuring secrets and dreams.

Serene eventually did go with just him to the Elven Tavern, where they wrote up detailed suggestions for how to improve the décor. Serene also accompanied him to the blacksmith's, where the lady blacksmith also had the printing press, and Elliot dropped his old camera on the ground while making loud comments about how exactly it worked and how much the Borderlands would benefit from some sort of daily paper about current tidings.

Being with Serene was worth everything. He could only hope she thought so too.

The first time Elliot managed to run a four-minute mile he promptly toppled over onto his back in the scanty springtime grass. Serene and Luke were waiting for him at the finish line, and Serene applauded.

"Thank you for your support, sunflower of my soul," said Elliot, once he could breathe again. "As for you, I can't believe you're making me do this. I hate you, and I hate your face. I actually think I might be allergic to it. Or maybe that's the lack of oxygen and hay fever talking, I don't know."

"I think you are much improved, my sweet," Serene told him encouragingly.

"I don't want to do this anymore!" Elliot wailed. "Can't I do yoga instead? I could be good at that. I could take deep breaths and find my centre and achieve ultimate zen."

"Serene's right. You're getting a little faster," Luke conceded.

Elliot laid his arm over his face. "I wish only for death."

It was pathetic, that he would actually participate in boring terrible physical activity in order to spend some time with Luke.

"Oh, hey guys," said Dale Wavechaser, coming in through the gate in exercise clothes, looking fresh and fit and ready for anything. His hair was awesome. Elliot hated him too.

"Hello, Dale," Serene said pleasantly. Elliot waved feebly. Luke went red and mumbled something.

Dale looked mildly puzzled. "I would've thought you guys would be with the commander and, uh, Sure-Aim-in-the-Chaos-of-Battle. Did I get that right?"

"What?" Serene snapped.

"Uh, they arrived about an hour ago," said Dale. "Expect the commander wants permission to foray into the elven territories to deal with the bandits. It'd be great to get chosen to go, wouldn't it? Well, you have no worries there obviously, Sunborn."

"Mmm," said Luke, still red and looking away.

"I bet you get picked," Elliot said helpfully, because Luke was hopeless. "You're so great at . . . stuff, Dale."

Dale winked. "Aw. Thanks, man."

"My mother is here?" Serene asked. She was standing very straight, her face a shade paler than usual.

"Er. I guess you didn't know," said Dale.

He looked alarmed at this suddenly awkward situation. He stared wistfully at the track and the prospect of physical exercise. He and Elliot were just extremely different people.

Serene began to move, and when Serene moved, she moved like a storm: unstoppable and so fast you barely saw her until she was upon you. She went over the fence and not through the gate, and Luke went after her.

"Yes, 'sweaty and disgusting' was exactly the look I was hoping for when I met my future mother-in-law," Elliot muttered, scrambling to his feet and following them.

~

They were drawing near the commander's tower when the door was flung open, and the commander's voice heard at rather a higher volume than normal.

"—it is the duty of the Border guard to protect the Borderlands, and where we are not granted entry, we cannot protect!"

It did not seem like negotiations for a foray into elven territory were going all that smoothly.

"It is my duty to inform you, Commander," said a tall woman in a black cloak whose back was turned then, "that the elves can protect themselves very well. Any who doubt it can come and try us."

She must have heard the sound of their running footsteps, her ears elven-keen, for she turned before Serene had a chance to call out.

Sure-Aim-in-the-Chaos-of-Battle's cloak flared as she turned, and her hair flared too, dark as Serene's but shot through with silver. She had a face like a judge's commemorated in marble, beautiful but above all things stern. The very sky seemed to shine brighter behind her than anyone else, as if she were etched on crystal.

"Serene-Heart-in-the-Chaos-of-Battle," she said. "Greetings, kinswoman of my house and daughter of my heart. You look well. I trust you are training hard, despite the soft ease of your surroundings and studies."

"Cadet Chaos-of-Battle is an exemplary student," said Commander Woodsinger unexpectedly. "Nobody expected her to be able to bear the double workload of both council and war training."

"And yet my daughter is excelling, are you not?" inquired Sure in elvish, deliberately cutting the commander out of the conversation. Her lip curled in satisfaction as Serene nodded. "I would expect no less."

It did not seem like much, but Serene glowed.

"May I have the honor of introducing my comrades to my revered mother," said Serene, recalling herself after a moment. She gestured to Elliot and Luke, and Elliot now saw where she had learned her graceful dignity from. "This is my swordsister Luke Sunborn, and my boyfriend Elliot Sch—"

"I don't particularly care about the redheaded slut you're amusing yourself with," said Sure-Aim-in-the-Chaos-of-Battle. Her eyes were gray pools like her daughter's, but Serene's were the pools in spring and in Sure's winter had come.

"Mother, how dare you!" exclaimed Serene.

Sure's icy eyes slid over Elliot as if he was not worth bothering with. They fixed on Luke.

"But claiming that a boy is—that a *boy* could be—your swordsister? That is obscene. That is spitting on the traditions of our house and our people. I wish to hear no more of that nonsense."

Serene put a protective, possessive hand on Luke's arm. "It's not nonsense. And the traditions of my people are wrong. He *is* my swordsister. As soon as we saw each other, we both knew it."

Sure made a noise that in a less poised and commanding person might have been called a snort. "What does a human know? Look at his pretty dimwitted face. He does not even know what we are saying."

Everyone looked at Luke, who tilted his golden head and looked down at Sure for a moment with his arms folded.

In faltering, rough elvish, Luke said: "I got it, actually."

Serene broke into a torrent of elvish so furious and rapid that Elliot had trouble following it himself, and Luke looked completely confused. Sure eyed Commander Woodsinger with an air that suggested the commander was intruding on a private family moment.

Commander Woodsinger eyed Sure-Aim-in-the-Chaos-of-Battle with an air that suggested that moment was happening directly outside her office. Then she rolled her eyes, went back into her office, and slammed the tower door, just as Sure walked a few steps away, summoning Serene with a peremptory nod of her head. Serene came to her mother's side, and because she still had hold of Luke, Luke had to go with her.

Elliot and Sure's bodyguard, Swift-Arrows-in-the-Chaos-of-Battle, were left staring awkwardly at each other. Swift was just as beautiful as ever, tranquil-eyed and chestnut-haired, but after Serene's mother she looked totally normal and comforting. She also looked somewhat abashed.

"Nice to see you again," Elliot said, smiling and looking up—no, actually, across, when had that happened?—at Swift through his eyelashes. "Thank you for all your letters. Elvish life is so fascinating."

"I am glad to amuse you, my dear, though I am but a rough soldier who has no great readiness with a pen," Swift said heartily. "Your dear prattling and jesting missives in return have cheered me on many a lonely night out on patrol."

"Heh, really? Um . . . cool," said Elliot, and looked around for help.

Serene had Luke's arm in a death grip and was now screaming in elvish while her mother bellowed cutting remarks. No help there, then.

"I was saddened to hear Serene had launched a successful attack on the citadel of your virtue," Swift said.

She sounded genuinely grieved. Elliot was grieved to be having this discussion.

"The citadel was totally into surrendering. Also I personally would not have referred to it as a citadel," Elliot observed. "Like, ever."

"No doubt you tempted her. Ah, a man's morals are frail as they are, sweet silly creatures," Swift said. "I do think it was up to Serene to control herself, though. She must have known I was considering you as a bride. Your humanity would not have mattered so very much, up in the wild north where I am stationed, but now you have been sullied, of course it is out of the question."

Elliot gave a shriek that wavered between hysterical alarm and hysterical laughter, and tried to turn it into a coy giggle with very limited success.

"I'm very flattered!" he said. "And taken all unawares by this token of your esteem! But I think you might be a little old for me! No offence meant."

Swift did not look offended, but she did look rather puzzled.

"The woman should really have an advantage when it comes to age in marriage," said Swift. "So that she may guide and educate her blushing bride in the ways of the world. Besides which, men are at their most attractive in the first blush of youth, whereas women only grow more distinguished as the years pass."

"Ha," said Elliot, not terribly amused. "That's so funny, because humans think the exact opposite thing."

Swift chuckled. "I don't see how humans can argue with facts? Do women get—" She used a word Elliot did not quite understand.

"Tureen . . . stomachs?" he said. "Oh! Pot bellies? Well, some women kind of have them. Less than men, I guess."

Swift nodded triumphantly, her point made. "And men go"—she almost whispered the word—"bald." She shook her head sadly. "The beauty of men is a sweet soft thing that passes all too soon, like a bird across the sky."

"Um," said Elliot. "Maybe both our societies are messed up, and they each only think one type of person is really a person. And the type of person they think is really a person is allowed to show imperfections and age . . . whereas the type of person they think is an object should show no signs of being a person. We're socialized to see the imperfections in those objects."

Swift chuckled. "You're still a funny, taking little thing. I think it's a shame of Serene. I hope she treats you well when you're under her protection. I'll ask her permission to continue writing to you."

"Except I don't need her permission to do anything!"

Swift continued blithely, as if Elliot's opinion on the subject did not count, and Elliot knew that no matter what he said Serene was getting asked, as if Elliot were a book to be borrowed or a child taken out for an ice cream. "And if she leaves you forlorn and weeping, remember you can trust me. These young rogues can be heedless, but I'd treat you well."

Elliot stared. "I will remember that. In fact, I have a feeling this scene will come back to me again and again. And again and again and again."

Swift reached out and touched Elliot's cheek. "Ah, sweet soiled dove," she murmured.

"I . . . actually don't have a response to that remark," Elliot said.

"Come on, Elliot!" Serene shouted. "I will not stand here and have my comrades insulted by a small-minded provincial tyrant! I would rather be cut to pieces!"

"We are two souls with but a single thought, baby," said Elliot, and ran after her and Luke as they stormed away.

Serene's mother was the one who got the last word. Sure-Aim-in-the-Chaos-of-Battle did not run after her errant heir, or raise her voice. She stood with her guard at her back, her arms casually crossed, her silver-and-shadow hair streaming, and she spoke clearly and calmly.

"Go and play with your humans, child. When the time for child's play is past, I know you down to bones and blood. When the time comes, you will leave all this and come to my call. You will ride into battle at my side."

The elves might have forbidden them entrance to their territory, but that did not mean the commander was going to give up. One day Serene and Luke arrived at their lunch table looking very pleased with themselves indeed.

"What's the good news?" asked Elliot, reaching for Serene's hand.

"Commander Woodsinger is sending out a personally selected troop which she will lead herself to make a sweep of all the non-elven territory where the bandits have been spotted, hoping to catch a few," said Serene. "And we're in the troop."

"Congratulations, my pearl, my diamond, my tiara of assorted gemstones," said Elliot.

Serene took his hand and squeezed it. "We're even going near the Forest of the Suicides, which is harpy territory."

"Now that's neat," said Elliot, with actual interest.

"It's not," said Luke. "Don't even think about it."

"Who, me?" Elliot asked innocently. "I never think about anything." He changed the subject to avoid discussion, and scowled at his reflection in his fork. "Is it crazy that I keep worrying about losing my hair?"

"You'd have to lose about half of it before anyone noticed," said Luke.

"Age but shows the marks of character being displayed and life being lived," Serene told him. "You live well, and I like your character. So there's no need to worry."

It was adorable how hard she was trying to be sensitive for her human boyfriend. Elliot raised Serene's hand to his lips and kissed it. Richard Plantgrown, passing by, made the sound of a whip cracking: Elliot did not know if it was for Elliot, because of the kiss, or for Serene because of what she'd said. He hoped it was for him. Serene bore enough, and he hated seeing her, proud and not quite untouchable, bear more for his sake.

Elliot had taken much worse than this for no reason at all, and this was for her, for the best reason he knew. He didn't care what anyone did to him.

Luke turned on the bench and looked at Richard. That was all he did. Richard put his full tray down on a random table and fled out of the door.

Serene had not deigned to look at Richard while he could see her, but she watched his retreating back with an expression that boded ill for Richard next time he entered the practice grounds.

"Yes," Elliot said to Serene, electing to ignore the problem. "But how do you explain the baldness issue? Swift made an excellent point about the baldness issue!"

Elliot did not want to be left behind thinking about what could be happening to Serene and Luke out among the bandits. So he stole a warrior-training cloak and accompanied them, slinking in the back so that he could say honestly that neither of them had any idea he was there.

"Honestly, Serene and Luke had no idea I was here," he said when he was discovered and dragged in front of the commander. "You can't punish them, because they had no idea I was here!"

Commander Woodsinger sat on a tree stump in the clearing where the cadets were putting up their tents, and stared at Elliot. Her eyes said that she was considering awful things like execution or more tutoring.

"So I have just one cadet flagrantly disobeying my orders and in urgent need of discipline," said the commander. "Wonderful." She held up a hand to forestall Elliot's protestations. "I believe that Cadet Chaos-of-Battle and Cadet Sunborn are not aware of your presence. I believe this since they are not currently in your presence."

Elliot was about to protest—he was in a protesting mood—but at that point Serene and Luke arrived, looking windblown and worried.

"Right on cue!" said the commander. "I do not have the time to discipline you, Cadet Schafer, but for the entirety of this mission you will be under my eye."

"No problem, Commander!" said Elliot.

The commander's order became a problem the very next day.

That night, though, Serene and Elliot had a tent to themselves, which they moved a little farther away from the other tents, into the trees. Elliot had brought what papers he could on the reported sightings and robberies, and they went over them and whispered secrets in between discussing the movement of bandit groups.

"I don't know why the commander thinks we can get the bandits when the group obviously moves from the elven to the human territories to escape justice from both. The only way to defeat them is to unite our forces."

Except your mum is being a jerk, Elliot did not say.

"I don't know why you came if you think this expedition won't be any use," Serene remarked.

Elliot pulled off his shirt. Once he had the hair under enough control that Serene could see his face, he winked. "Don't you?"

"Don't think you can get around me with your newly improved physique," said Serene, and Elliot was torn between being flattered, surprised, and wondering how much improvement it had required. Serene kissed him, so he settled on flattered, leaning into her and feeling her warm fingers tracing the lines of his abdomen. "Beauty is a delusion and a snare."

She pushed him backward, and he fell laughing in firelight and tangled bedrolls. "Consider yourself snared," he told her.

"It was very wrong of you to come," Serene said later. Elliot's head was resting on her stomach as he read. He heard the smile in her voice as she continued: "But I'm glad to have you here."

Elliot smiled. He was still smiling as he pressed a kiss against her soft skin, then another, in a trail from her belly button and heading down.

Serene was sent up with all the best archers into the trees, where they could surprise bandits from above. Elliot's amazing grace, or lack thereof, meant he stayed on the ground with those best suited to swordwork and lurked behind Luke.

Luke, as usual these days, was in a bad mood.

"—cannot believe you would be such a reckless idiot," he said as they walked through the green hush of the forest. "I mean, I can, because it's you, but—"

"Aw, someone's cranky!" said Elliot. "Did someone not enjoy sharing a tent with the commander? I think she's charming, personally."

"Someone is only cranky because someone else is so full of—" Luke broke off, made one of his incomprehensible military gestures that sent cadets and the commander alike scurrying for cover, and with his free hand grabbed Elliot by the back of his tunic and bore him down into the undergrowth.

Elliot spat out leaves and dirt, lifted his head and glared reproachfully at Luke, who was lying on his front with his eyes scanning the skies.

"Quiet," Luke whispered. "I think it's harpies."

Elliot propped himself up on one elbow in the dirt. "Harpies? Cool!"

Luke shoved his face back into the grass. "Not cool! Harpies are monsters, do you hear me? They are not like dwarves or even dryads: they are death with wings. They are the owls to your mice. They rip with their claws, they swoop, and they kill, and once you are dead they rend the body until it is stinking offal, because mutilation of corpses is their beast's idea of sport. And your dumb hair is a beacon. So don't move a muscle, and don't you dare even think of doing something stupid."

Elliot sulked. He would keep still since Luke was in a tizzy, but if Luke thought that he could persuade Elliot to stay put when he got a chance to see mermaids rather than harpies, Luke had another think coming.

There was a rustle in the grass. Luke's grip on Elliot's nape tightened, but after a moment Elliot struggled free in a burst of relief and pleasure: it was Serene, dropped lightly from a branch. She moved, crouching, toward them. There was something small and dark folded in her hand.

"I thought this might come in useful," she whispered, and fitted a black woolen cap over Elliot's head. Elliot smiled, not surprised by her brilliance but by her thoughtfulness, and she smiled back.

"Thanks, blossom," he whispered, and though she looked puzzled to be called that she leaned toward him as he leaned toward her, for a brief sweet kiss in the crushed grass.

"Serene!" hissed Luke, whose eyes were determinedly fixed on the sky. "Do you see?"

Elliot squinted. He could see nothing except for fluffy non-menacing clouds. No . . . maybe something? Like a fleck on his glasses, if he wore glasses. Or like his imagination running wild.

"Two of them," Serene whispered back. "Scouts. The scouts go in pairs. If we get them, they can't report back. We can't have anyone knowing that we're coming."

Luke and Serene rose to their feet in one smooth matching movement, bows at the ready. Their bowstrings were taut, arms held at the exact same angle. They moved like two parts of a killing machine.

"They'll never make the shot," Dale whispered. "Not both of them. I can't even see . . ."

They all saw then, the meeting of the scouts in the sky, a rush of wings that blotted out the sun for a moment, and at that very instant Luke and Serene took their shots.

The harpies tumbled from the sky, two dark marks growing larger and larger against the clouds as they streaked toward the earth. Elliot only ever saw them as dim, falling shapes: he was sorry for that.

"Ha!" said Elliot to Dale. "That was my girlfriend . . . killing a sentient creature. But for good reason and showing very praiseworthy athletic skill!"

The commander rose and gestured to them all to do likewise.

"Good eyes, Cadet Sunborn," she said. "Good shooting, both of you. We cannot risk both harpies and bandits with a force this size. We will do one more sweep of the forest and return home. Chaos-of-Battle, back in the trees. Sunborn, I want you to take four men and pack up the camp as quickly and quietly as you can."

"Commander!" said Luke. "What about—"

"I don't want to be protected by incompetents!" Elliot exclaimed, and looked around at the faces of the assembled troop. "Uh, no offence, everybody."

"I do not want to see another breach of discipline from any of you!" the commander thundered. "Cadet Schafer, you will stay by my side at all times. Go!"

Luke went. Serene went. Elliot fell in unhappily with the commander.

"Don't be scared," said Dale from behind him, marching in step. "Harpies are awful creatures, but there won't be any more. And we can protect you, just as well as Luke. Well, maybe not quite as well as *Luke*, that was an amazing shot—"

"Serene's shot was amazing too," Elliot said grumpily.

"Um, ah, sure," Dale agreed. "The point is, I'm right behind you, and I have reflexes like a ferret!"

"Go to the back of the squad, Cadet Wavechaser," Commander Woodsinger said, with infinite weariness.

"I'm going to be slightly farther behind you," said Dale. "But not to worry!"

Elliot regarded the softly rustling wood with suspicion as they walked and walked. The swaying leaves and the spring flowers had hidden harpies. He fully expected bandits next.

When he saw something shining among the leaves, he froze, expecting it to be a weapon.

A hush fell on their group as they realized that it was something entirely different.

There in the clearing up ahead was a unicorn.

It had a shape similar to a horse's, but it was closer to the toy horse of a seven-year-old's most fevered imagination than it was to any real animal. Its long, graceful lines seemed chased in silver, its mane and tail rippling in bright rivers and total defiance of gravity, and its horn was pearl. It turned and observed them with one tranquil dark eye, a pool that beckoned as well as shimmered, and Elliot took a step forward.

"Cadet Schafer," said Commander Woodsinger in a low, serious voice. "Be careful. Only people who are eligible may approach the unicorn."

"Uh, because we think an animal is obsessed with a ridiculous social construct of purity based on who's been touched where with what, as if people's moral worth depends on what basically amounts to a game of Clue?" Elliot said. "Sure it is. Give me a break."

He took another step. The unicorn charged.

Elliot ran, and Commander Woodsinger ran with him. Their troop scattered madly in every direction. Elliot ran for another tree, feeling the unicorn's hot breath on his back. He grabbed at a low-hanging branch, pulled himself up, and then leaned down and looped his arm around Commander Woodsinger's waist, lifting her off her feet.

If she hadn't got hold of the branch and helped haul herself up, he might have dropped her on the creature. Accidentally impaling your commander on a unicorn was bound to lead to expulsion.

"Well lifted, Cadet," said the commander in a tone of faint surprise.

"Thanks," said Elliot. "Mean bullies make me exercise."

He looked down at the unicorn. He saw, suddenly, that it wasn't as lovely as he had thought at first. Its shiny horn was too sharp, and its eyes were red with the light of murder. It was the Venus flytrap of pretty ponies.

"I think your censorious attitude is absurd," Elliot told it. "And frankly, it's creepy to be obsessed with other people's sex lives."

The unicorn lowered its head, charged, and rammed the tree. Its horn plunged into the bark and was then withdrawn. The leaves all shook as if they were in a storm, and the trunk shuddered as if it had been struck by lightning.

"Cadet Schafer! Kindly stop antagonising the unicorn!"

"Don't worry!" said Serene from the trees. "All of these young blushing men are unmarried, so I am certain a great many of them are pure!"

There was a long silence. Embarrassment reigned among the trees.

"How about you, Dale?" Elliot asked, desperate.

"Um—afraid I can't help you," Dale muttered. "I met this guy, Adam Sunborn, when we were sent to aid the patrol on the Northern border . . ."

"Adam Sunborn!" Elliot exclaimed. "How could you, Dale? He is the worst!"

"He's not the worst! He's a Sunborn!" Dale exclaimed, shocked in return. "And it's not—it's not as if there's a huge amount of choice in the Border guard, if you like guys."

Elliot shook his head sadly, making the leaves rustle around him. "You can do so much better."

"Uh—thanks, Elliot!" Dale sounded gratified. After a pause, he ventured: "Commander, are you not . . . eligi—"

"I am forty-eight years old!" snapped Commander Woodsinger. "Ladies have needs, Cadet."

"Not everybody wants to indulge in carnal passions at all," said Serene. "Take the sisters of the greenwood, who consider themselves married to the trees. Obviously there are no people dedicated to chastity and guarding the beautiful flower of their manhood in this company, however."

Elliot breathed out hard through his nose. He looked up at the rippling green canopy of the trees, and down at the enraged beast below. It pawed the ground, ripping out chunks of earth beneath its cloven hoof, and the sunlight shining through the trees lent a disturbing glitter to the point of its horn. Elliot looked hastily away.

"I didn't want it to come to this," he informed the leaves. "But could somebody fetch Luke?"

"Cadet Schafer, I'm fairly certain that's not going to help," said Commander Woodsinger. "I mean this in the most impersonal and professional way possible, but have you *seen* Luke Sunborn?"

"Yes," Elliot said irritably. "Believe me, I don't get it either. He doesn't want to do the human equivalent of dedicating himself to the trees and never getting some, because he told me he had a crush on Dale Wavechaser. I have a theory he's repressed as an act of rebellion against his family. I also have this scheme to shut him and Dale up in a cupboard. I admit, it's not a terribly sophisticated scheme. It needs refining."

The unicorn headbutted the tree even more vehemently. Everyone was a critic.

The commander took a deep breath. "Are you quite sure about Luke Sunborn's current state of virtue?"

"Quite sure."

The commander raised her voice. "Could the cadet farthest away from the unicorn descend and request Cadet Sunborn to make his way to this section of the woods!"

The unicorn charged once more. From the heart of the tree came an alarming cracking sound.

"Extremely quickly," the commander added.

It felt like a long time until Luke arrived, even though he came running and out of breath, and Elliot had more reason than anybody to know how fast Luke was.

Luke did not immediately dart to the rescue, though. Instead, when he saw the unicorn, he stopped moving altogether.

"Ah, Cadet Sunborn," said Commander Woodsinger, with amazing aplomb for a woman stuck up a tree. "Thank you for your promptness. Cadet Schafer informed me that you might be possessed of the necessary qualities to deal with this situation."

"Did he," Luke said, after a long, dark pause in which apparently all the blood in his body rushed to his ears. They were practically purple.

Elliot grinned and gave him a thumbs-up. The horror on Luke's face only deepened.

"If you would, Cadet," said the commander.

Luke advanced on the unicorn. He took his time about it. Elliot thought it was frankly reprehensible that he was dragging his feet when there were lives at stake.

"Chop chop," he called out.

"Shut up," Luke ordered.

He edged closer to the unicorn. The unicorn had stopped ramming the tree. The animal was now cropping the grass in what Elliot found to be rather a coy manner. Its shining flanks heaved with another breath, like the movement of living pearl. Luke took one last step, and then rested his hand against the unicorn's softly glowing side.

The unicorn did not turn and make Luke an instant victim of horn-based savagery. Elliot let out a breath in unison with Commander Woodsinger. Even the trees seemed to sigh relief.

The unicorn turned, and Elliot sucked his breath back in, but the unicorn seemed to wish only to rest its chin against Luke's shoulder.

"Oooh, it likes you," Elliot said.

"Shut up now and shut up forever," said Luke.

"Cuddling with the unicorn is not a productive way to spend your time," Commander Woodsinger observed, while Elliot snickered and Luke looked cruelly betrayed by the universe at large. "Can you manage to lead the unicorn away?"

"I can try," Luke said in the hollow tones of one who had nothing but his duty left. He tugged at the unicorn's mane. The unicorn lipped softly at his cheek. Elliot worried about an accidental affectionate skull impaling. "It's not working," Luke said, his voice taking on an edge of panic.

"I know what to do!" Elliot exclaimed. "In books, the virtuous maiden plucks a single golden hair from her head and leads the unicorn as if on a leash."

Luke gave him a look of loathing, and tugged at a handful of his own golden but admittedly short hair. "Thanks for the suggestion."

"I'm just trying to be helpful, loser," Elliot snapped.

"Try harder!" Luke snapped back.

"Perhaps some other article belonging to you?" Serene called out from the leaves. "Loath though I am to suggest you compromise your modesty in any way by disrobing . . ."

Elliot kept thinking that there must be a limit to how scandalized Luke could seem about this situation, on a scale from slight-social-faux-pas to nudist-at-the-vicar's-tea-party. Currently he was at Victorian-aunt-time-traveled-to-a-strip-club.

Luke pulled off the blue jumper his dad had knitted for him at Christmas. It was immediately clear to everyone that it had been almost two years of continuous physical exercise since the time Luke used to go swimming in the lake and get swarmed by girls.

There was a thump and a flutter of falling leaves, like a small localized storm of greenery. Dale Wavechaser had fallen out of his tree.

Elliot began to laugh so hard he was afraid he was going to fall out of the tree himself. He stopped laughing when the unicorn gave an equine snarl and tried to turn in Dale's direction.

"Nonono," said Luke, hastily looping his jumper around the unicorn's pale gleaming neck and tying the blue woolen sleeves tight. "Don't do that. Take deep breaths. Uh, find your center. Nice horsie."

"Wow, he's trying to use my yoga routine on a unicorn," Elliot remarked.

"Come on, please let this be over, nice horsie," muttered Luke, and the unicorn began to trot obligingly to keep up with Luke's fast pace, through the trees and away.

"Well, no harm done except the upholding of harmful moral values by a cranky equine," said Elliot, and slid gratefully from his branch to the ground.

"Cadet Schafer, get back in the tr—" the commander began furiously, but her voice was obscured by the thunder of hooves and the sound of those hooves ripping turf as the unicorn charged back.

The creature was a blur of white and silver, the sound it made a scream: Luke's scream back was almost birdlike. Elliot scrabbled for a branch, but there was none in reach.

Luke was a blur, faster than the unicorn. He had to vault over the animal: he jumped between them.

There was a horrible moment when Elliot slipped out from between Luke and the tree and Elliot saw blood on Luke's shoulder.

"Are you okay?" he asked in stark terror. Even the unicorn was still, as if in confusion.

Luke's eyes had been shut, but they opened. "Yes," he said in a small, tight voice. "Get back in the tree."

The murderous beast danced back an uncertain step, and Elliot saw that what Luke had said was true. The unicorn had stopped its lunge just in time. It was only a graze.

Elliot got back in the tree. They all stayed up in the tree for a long time after Luke led the unicorn away by the rags of his jumper, probably longer than they needed to. The only person who spoke was Serene, who asked Elliot quietly if he was all right.

"He's perfectly well, not that he deserves to be," snapped the commander before Elliot could reply. "Now be quiet."

Luke and his small squad came back, Luke wearing a spare war cadet's uniform top and keeping his head down. Everyone descended from the trees.

"Walk with me, Cadet Schafer," said the commander, and they walked at the front of the troop.

Elliot walked with his eyes on the horizon, watching for the Border camp. The commander spoke to him as they marched, and her words fell like blows. He concentrated on walking and not stumbling.

"You were not supposed to be on this expedition," said the commander. "That is not because I blindly follow military protocol, but because it was necessary that everyone on this trip have military training and be able to defend themselves. Are you able to defend yourself?"

"No," said Elliot, and when the commander gave him an inquiring look he spoke louder. "No."

"That means that other people have to put their lives at risk to defend you," the commander said. "That is why you are forbidden to come on these missions, no matter how clever you think you are or how much you believe the rules should not apply to you. For the sake of other people's lives. Do you understand now, or does someone have to actually die?"

"I understand," Elliot said through his teeth. He thought he might be sick.

"And you will never, ever come on another military foray without my express permission?"

"I won't," said Elliot. His mouth was dry. "I swear."

As soon as they arrived back at the Border camp, the commander dismissed Elliot, and he could at last go find Luke and Serene.

They had not even gone to their cabins yet, but were standing sorting through the weapons from their packs and putting the dull ones aside. They looked up as he approached. Luke's expression was not particularly pleasant. Elliot had been thinking of what he should say, how he could apologize or thank him, but a brainwave occurred to him: something good had happened today, and reminding Luke of that would surely cheer him up.

"So Dale Wavechaser fell out of a tree," said Elliot, making significant gestures with his eyebrows alone.

Luke appeared unimpressed. "I suppose you think people falling out of trees and getting hurt is funny too."

"No," said Elliot. "Well, yes, in this specific instance, because of reasons. Him falling out of a tree is great for you."

"Elliot, why would I want people to fall out of trees?"

Elliot abandoned this clearly unproductive line of reasoning.

"You saved him from a unicorn," Elliot urged. "I mean, in that you saved us all. As lines go, that one's bound to be a winner. It has novelty on its side! Go talk to him!"

Luke turned a baleful gaze upon him. "I have never been so embarrassed in my whole life," he said. "And it's your fault. I am going to bed."

"Luke," Serene said, "you have absolutely nothing to be embarrassed about. Rather, you should feel proud that despite the urgings of your manly nature you have kept your virtue intact!"

"It's like seven-thirty, loser," Elliot pointed out.

"And I may never get up!" Luke shouted over his shoulder.

"What I just said was disrespectful and I'm sorry," Serene said after a moment's pause.

Elliot took her hand, lacing her fingers with his own. "That's okay, baby, I'm pretty comfortable with being a wanton."

He looked over to Serene with a smile, but she was not looking at him. She was looking off into the distance, and the pin-scratch mark between her brows, Elliot knew, would have been frantic worry on a human face.

"Elliot, those other boys on the mission," she said slowly, and Elliot's shoulders relaxed because it was not about them. "None of them were saving themselves?"

"Saving which part of themselves exactly?" Elliot asked. Serene looked put out with herself for putting it wrong, and Elliot grinned. "I know what you meant. Well, I suppose we're all on the young side, but given that they're in military training and constantly exposed to mortal danger—I've read about emotions running high, and life-affirming . . ."

He trailed off. He had never considered that Serene had kissed him for the second and more frenzied time after the library attack, that they had come together after the battle. He had not applied what he'd read to his own life. Elliot glanced at Serene again, nervously, unable to look at her steadily but likewise unable to stop looking back.

Serene still looked worried. "None of them want to wait and be courted?"

"Well, we're all definitely too young to get married!" said Elliot. "But they might get married later on. It's not like you're disqualified from being married if you've dated before."

"Oh," said Serene. "Oh, I see, of course. Of course, that makes perfect sense." She gave Elliot a small smile, dazzling as a single ray of light on snow. "Of course they might change their minds later, and of course nobody should be disqualified."

She squeezed Elliot's hand. Elliot felt the impulse to go with it, to smile at her, to not raise a question or face a challenge, but he had never gone with that kind of impulse before in his life and he did not know how to do it now. He did not know how to let anything rest.

"Change their minds?" he asked. "Do you think that dating is—a whole different thing from courting?"

Serene's head tilted interrogatively, and then he felt her hand in his, her whole body, go still.

"It isn't," continued Elliot, speaking with difficulty. "Dating can be casual, but it isn't always. Sometimes people who are dating get married, and sometimes they don't. It's a way of—testing out a relationship. We have dating instead of courting, not as well as."

"Oh," said Serene, the sound abrupt and terrible, and then with gathering anger: "That shouldn't be how it works. That is totally confusing and inefficient!"

"This isn't a humorous cultural difference, is it?" said Elliot. "We shouldn't be talking about this in public, should we?"

Serene took a breath, and Elliot almost thought that she might brush this off, instead of him. He almost wanted her to. But his Serene had never been lacking in courage.

"No, we shouldn't," she told him, squaring her shoulders. "Let us go discuss it in your cabin."

They went. They did not speak again until they were in the narrow confines of the wooden cabin where he had spent his first night in the Borderlands, wondering what he had done by deciding to stay for Serene. It was so different from being with her at the start of this, with no walls and both of them free under a night sky filled with stars and possibility.

"I'm so sorry, Elliot," said Serene, as soon as she had shut the door on them. "I got it all wrong from the beginning. This was much more difficult than I thought it would be—it should be easier than this."

"Don't be sorry," said Elliot. "I'm not sorry. And don't talk to me about what should be easy. I've never had anything be easy in my whole life. I don't want easy. I wouldn't know what to do with easy if I had it."

Serene was pacing the cabin floor and not listening at all. "You've been insulted because you were with me—not just insulted by my mother, but I made so many mistakes, and I heard people whispering, I know what things my cousin must have—and all the time—"

"I don't care!" said Elliot. "I got insulted a few times? Don't act like it's never happened to me before. I know it's happened to *you* before. As for the other stuff, what your mother and your cousin said, even the stuff you said sometimes, do you think the humans do it any better? Do you think I want to make a girl feel the same way I've been feeling? Relationships are difficult. Every world I know of is messed up."

He spoke as quickly as he could, desperate to convince her. *He* had messed up: in two worlds full of blundering and flaws he was always the one who made the worst mistakes, the one who ruined everything he touched. He remembered how Serene and Luke had read out his love letters to an army troop. How stupid could he be? Had he really thought Serene would do that, if she knew he'd meant them?

She didn't know, just as Luke hadn't known and Myra hadn't known. But he could tell her. He would tell her now.

"I am—I'm serious about you," Elliot said. "I'm not saying that any of this is easy. And you can—there could be years before you decide what you want. There will be more insults and more misunderstandings. I know that. But I . . . I really love you," he said. "And I think we have a chance of making it work. If you love me back, enough to work through every difficulty, the way I love you."

Serene was silent for a long time. Her pallor was alarming: she was white as salt, white as exposed bone. There was so much pain in her face that she almost looked like a different person. She almost looked human.

Elliot felt his heart sinking in that cold silence, as if he had thrown it like a stone into a deep dark pool.

He had to look away. He stared at the wooden walls, which bore the marks of countless knives thrown by countless careless children who had not known what they were getting into.

"You don't," he said quietly.

"I do!" said Serene. It came out as a cry, like someone had hurt her when she was already injured.

Elliot lifted his eyes to her face, but hope died when he saw the expression she was wearing. There was too much pain in it for any possibility of falling into each others' arms.

"I love you very dearly," said Serene. "I would gladly die for you. But the kind of love needed for courtship . . ."

"It's fine if you don't feel ready for courtship," Elliot broke in.

He hated himself for being so pathetic. He wished he could be nobody at all, as long as he could stop being himself and feeling like this.

"I don't think I could ever feel it," Serene continued doggedly, as if he had never spoken.

"Not for me," Elliot finished for her, when she could not seem to. They could both hear the bitterness in his voice. "I'll stop," Elliot said. "I won't be any more trouble. I won't keep bothering you with—with feelings that aren't your responsibility. But I need—I need to hear you say it. Could you just look at me and say it."

Serene was a soldier, before she was anything else. She was brave and never backed down from a challenge. She met his eyes when she spoke, and he saw how sorry she was to say it.

"I do not think I could ever feel that way about you."

Elliot drew in a long shuddering breath. He'd asked for it, as he had asked to be hit once when he thought she and Luke might be dead. "I understand."

He was about to turn away, never mind that he was in his own cabin. He was sick of this whole world. He had flayed himself in front of her, and he didn't have to suffer through this for a single moment longer. He was going to leave.

But something else occurred to him, with a hundred times the force that it had in the library, when it was a fear and not his reality. She said she loved him, and nobody had ever loved him before. He couldn't lose that, even if she loved him so much less than he had hoped.

He didn't have anyone else.

He swallowed: he tasted bitterness in his mouth and felt as though he were swallowing something broken, sharp splinters all the way down.

"Thank you for being honest," he said finally. "That's best, isn't it?"

Serene nodded. "Yes."

This was diplomacy, as he'd played it with the elves and the general. The first yes was the most important. It meant another yes would follow, each one more easy than the last.

"We're friends, and that's what is most important, right?"

"Right," said Serene, and almost smiled.

"So you—made a mistake, and I got—carried away. Better to end it now, before anyone's feelings are too hurt. I don't want to mess up our friendship. I know you don't either."

"Of course I don't," said Serene. "Elliot. You're absolutely right."

Elliot wanted to smash things, wanted to shout things at her until she hurt as much as he did. But he couldn't hurt her as much as she had hurt him. He didn't have that kind of power over her, and that was not her fault: it was his.

He went and leaned against the knife-scarred wall, looked out of the window where night was falling on the Border camp.

He heard her approach him, walking softly. He looked down at her, and she was standing very close to him. She leaned into him and kissed him on the cheek. He put his arm around her waist and thought: I will never hold her like this again.

"I'm so sorry," Serene whispered. "But thank you for understanding."

"What are friends for, am I right?" Elliot asked. He made himself smile: it felt like his face was a stiff piece of paper, and he had folded it sharply in half. "I'm sorry for going overboard. Let's go back to how it was before."

"Yes," said Serene. "It will be just like it was before."

It was nothing like it was before. He had never lied to her before, never acted a part to convince her. She was the only person who had ever liked him before he learned, however poorly, to be tactful and hide some portion of who he was. He felt as if he was losing that, as well as her, as he watched her walk out the door of his cabin.

The next day at lunch, Elliot decided to get the news out before Serene could. Serene was looking hesitant, opening and shutting her mouth like a coy goldfish, and Luke was still sulking over the horrific indignity of a unicorn seeing his bod. Elliot had no pity for either of them. There was an empty space where he might have felt sorry, or amused, or even fond: he just had to keep going despite the emptiness.

"Serene and I decided to call it quits while there were no hard feelings on either side," Elliot said. "Pass the butter."

Luke sat frozen, only his eyes moving. His gaze was flicking back and forth between them, as if there were an invisible racquet sending his pupils bouncing back and forth across the tennis court of his eyes. Eventually, Serene passed Elliot the butter. He accepted it.

"I know what you must be thinking, right?" Elliot asked. "You must be kicking yourself that you didn't place any bets on how long it would last."

"I wouldn't make bets about my swordsister's love life," said Luke. He had been using the term "swordsister" since Serene's mother had denied it to him.

Serene pushed her shoulder gratefully against Luke's and, after an instant, they started talking casually about archery. Luke relaxed. He did not leave and go to practice anything: he stayed where he was all through lunchtime, and he looked pleased, glad to have a situation that Luke-Everything-Goes-Right-For-Me-Sunborn had disliked resolved, smug that his best friend had been restored to him and was now focused on him again. The world was back the way it should be, clearly, as far as Luke Sunborn was concerned.

Serene was sitting on Luke's side of the table. From now on, Elliot supposed she always would be.

Luke and Serene continued to make Elliot exercise, which was the despair cherry on the sundae of misery that was his life, and he had to go along with it because he had promised Serene that everything would be like it was before.

Besides, what was the point of doing anything else? He would just make Serene unhappy, and he could not make her love him. Luke would only triumph and potentially find his unhappiness hilarious. He could freeze them both out and have no friends at all. That would be worse than this.

He didn't know how to be blatantly miserable. He never had, through all the long years of childhood knowing that nobody cared what he was feeling. Even if he worked out how to show what he felt, he would only put people off. He knew, from long experience, that he was too much trouble as it was.

At least the late spring had turned cold, rather than mellowing into summer, so they used the indoor practice rooms and Elliot was spared the outdoors. That meant he took every possible opportunity to sit down and read. It wasn't like that was unusual behavior for him: neither of them would think there was anything wrong with that.

"All I want you to do is watch this and try to replicate it," Luke ordered.

"I'm not going to hurt anyone," Elliot said stubbornly, clinging to his book like a life raft in a sea of violence.

"It's a defensive move," Serene explained.

"Like so," said Luke. "Watch."

Serene grabbed both of Luke's wrists, and Luke hooked a foot around her ankles and pushed forward, sending Serene stumbling backward while bracing his other foot to keep his balance. Since it was Luke, he was able to catch Serene before she fell. Since it was Serene, obviously she had let him accomplish the whole move, and obviously she had trusted him to catch her. She grinned up at him and Luke grinned down at her: both of them content, uncomplicated, secure, and first place with each other forever and ever.

"Were you watching, Elliot?" Luke asked.

Elliot raised his book to hide his face and said cheerfully: "I was not!"

As summer drew in, everyone was always determined to show off their athletic prowess to prove their absolute dedication and that they would not be slack during the holidays. Elliot was so looking forward to being slack over the holidays. He was not going to move a muscle, and he was going to read near a radiator, and he would not have to see Serene's relief that the situation was resolved, and he would not almost get anyone killed. He would not have to try so hard because his father would not notice anything he did, and perhaps he would finally stop feeling cold.

It was odd to think like this. He had never wanted to go back before.

He could not help thinking of Peter's father, who could never go back.

They had a day of contests, showing off what they had learned. Serene and Luke won basically everything, as they usually did. Elliot clapped and cheered for every win of Serene's, as he always had and always would. There were always so many people watching who would not applaud an elf, or who did not like to see a woman win. Everybody always clapped long and hard for Luke, so Elliot felt there was absolutely no need to join in. When it was Luke's turn he made sure to always be buried in his book and not to let anyone catch him when he looked up.

Commander Woodsinger even handed out little prizes to encourage morale, which Commander Rayburn would never have thought of doing. Elliot was amused to see the absolute dismay on Dale Wavechaser's face when given the third prize of a book.

They had an impromptu celebration that night, lighting bonfires and sitting around on log benches chattering about their summer plans.

Luke and Serene were on the bench opposite, talking quietly with their heads bowed together. Elliot was staring into the bonfire when he was startled by Dale appearing behind him and clearing his throat. Elliot turned his head and looked behind him.

"Hey," said Dale. "It's your birthday over the summer, right?"

"Yes?" said Elliot, puzzled, but remembering he had to stay in good with Dale and trying to be polite.

"Rotten to have a birthday over the summer with no one around," said Dale, waving the book vaguely over Elliot's shoulder. "Fancy this as an early birthday present? Believe me, I don't want it."

Elliot actually felt so confused he was almost disoriented. It was a confused gratitude, so he said the right stuff, but he almost stammered: "Y—yeah, thanks, Dale," and he actually twisted around, put his arm around Dale's neck and kissed him on the cheek. As if he were four years old, how embarrassing, but that was how he felt: reduced to being a kid, and with even less idea of how to behave than usual.

Dale looked surprised but pleased. "Glad you like it," he said, and with a friendly nod to Luke and Serene, he jogged off back to his friends.

"That's weird: I hardly know him," Elliot announced, since Luke—who everybody liked—would not understand that Elliot had to make an effort to persuade people to put up with him, and it would be humiliating to explain.

"What a kind action," said Serene, and jostled Luke in a comradely way. "A sweet temper and good looks: all anyone could look for in a paramor."

"He could get the wrong idea," Luke said in a hard voice. Elliot looked up from his book to see Luke glaring.

It was lucky that snarking at Luke was habit by now: Elliot remembered a line from a book he'd read once, that habit was second nature, and nature stronger than the first. It was a comfort, to have a natural expression rather than one he had to pin on.

He raised his eyebrows and smirked. "You don't have to be jealous. I'm not going to steal your boyfriend. I told you, I barely know him."

"If you want a book . . ." said Luke.

Elliot hunched his shoulders. "I've got one," he snapped. He smoothed a hand over the leather ridges of the spine, the uneven cover, and then opened it. It was cheap paper, for a book in the Borderlands where books were rarer and more precious. It was also a history book, and from the very first page Elliot could see that the so-called history was biased and inaccurate. He kept reading.

Nobody had ever given him a birthday present before.

Elliot avoided Myra for the few weeks until the end of the year. She might or might not be sympathetic, and he did not know which would be worse. It took enough energy to pretend for Serene and Luke. Elliot avoided most people. Elliot still had to teach his thirteen-year-olds, though. It was during one of his lessons that he broke for the only time.

He stopped in the middle of talking about the fauna of this new world, and said: "I can't help but wonder . . . why I'm not teaching any of you anything about advanced mathematics."

All their little faces looked blank. Except for Cyril Leigh, who was a bit of a delicate plant, and who already looked alarmed.

"Or German or French or Japanese or any of the languages that might be useful in the real world. You're not going to have evidence you completed school. You definitely won't be able to attend universities. And of course you not only won't learn anything about coding or computer programs, but you will end up hopelessly behind on and possibly alarmed by technology."

There was something savage in Elliot's voice. Even he could hear it. Cyril was swaying.

"Has it ever occurred to you all that the books about magical worlds in our world might be lures? Shiny toys dangled in front of children so we go ooooh, mermaids, oooh, unicorns, oooh, harpies—"

"Nobody goes 'oooh, harpies,'" said Miriam Price. "Harpies kill you."

"Unicorns are no picnic either, but that's not my point," Elliot snapped. "We're shown all this stuff we were trained to want, shown the great adventure, and we jump at it like the dazzled fools we are. We're too young to know any better, to know that we won't triumph and be heroes, that we won't be returned to the other world as if no time had passed, that the lies in the stories aren't about mermaids or unicorns or harpies—the lies are about us. The lies are that we might be good enough, and we might get out. We could fail at everything we try to do here, and we will never be able to go back home. Even if we wanted to."

A silence had descended on the little group. Nobody seemed inclined to make any further helpful points about harpies.

"Look at you," Elliot said softly. "How am I supposed to teach you? We're all in a glittering trap, and too stupid to even realize it."

Cyril wavered and then burst into tears, the sound shattering the scared hush, and then as if on cue Luke's voice came from the door.

"What's a trap? Why is a kid crying?"

"Pull yourself together, Cyril!" Elliot snapped.

Luke strode into the room and went to Cyril's desk. He put an arm around him, sweet and concerned. Cyril immediately flung his arms around Luke's neck and wept into his shoulder. All the other students leaned toward Luke, like plants yearning in the direction of the sun.

Elliot was getting a headache. "Okay," he said. "Class dismissed. I mean it. Get out!"

They did leave, even though they seemed loath to leave Luke with an obvious madman. Luke did not seem especially concerned for his own safety. He leaned back in the chair Cyril had been sitting in and watched Elliot with a frown on his face.

"I thought I'd get you for your training, since we don't want you getting soft over the summer—"

"I'm not going to do that anymore," Elliot said flatly.

Luke paused for a moment, evidently decided there was no point arguing when Elliot was in a mood, and continued: "I thought I'd see what your classes were like. I didn't think there would be children crying!"

"Oh yeah, it happens every class," Elliot lied. "You didn't think it was funny?"

"No," Luke said slowly. "Because children were crying."

"Huh," said Elliot. "Well, no surprise that you have no sense of humor."

He busied himself with cleaning the blackboard, the marks of chalk blurring and then lost against the black. He saw that they were fitting back into their usual roles, Elliot making children cry and Luke comforting them. He had enjoyed being the nice one, the one who could afford to be kind. It was easy to be generous, when you had something to give. He missed being happy.

Luke cleared his throat. "About the summer. If you want, I guess it would be okay if—"

"I don't have any reason to come anymore, do I?" Elliot asked casually.

Luke was silent for a moment, then he laughed shortly. "Wait until you're asked. I wasn't inviting you to my place. I was going to say something, um, quite different."

"Oh?" said Elliot, and left a deliberate, expectant pause for Luke to fill.

Luke did not, but in the pause Elliot found the time to feel ashamed. Luke hadn't hurt him. Luke hadn't done anything wrong. It was nice of him, in a misguided way, to take pity on Elliot.

He wanted to be kind to Luke, even if he didn't feel there was much kindness left in him, and any kindness there was he fiercely wanted to save for himself. But that wasn't how friendship worked, was it?

"Well, whatever," said Elliot, more gently. "I misunderstood. Anyway, it would be a bit awkward, wouldn't it? Better to have some space. And I'll have a lot to do this summer: get reacquainted with computers and phones and jeans"—Luke made a face—"make some sort of large chart with a life plan on it, possibly using a projector—"

"I don't think your life plan should include teaching," Luke remarked blandly.

"You're hilarious, loser," said Elliot, rolling his eyes. "Well, see you next year. I have to go see the commander now."

He headed for Commander Woodsinger's tower, because he did not want to be instantly caught out in his fib. He went up to the top of the tower and looked outside. He'd been sitting there for a couple of hours, thinking, when he heard the sound of firm footsteps on stone, and looked up to see the dark serious face of the commander.

"Cadet Schafer. A few of the students you were teaching have announced that they are leaving the Borderlands and do not plan to return after the summer."

"Whoops," said Elliot. "Sorry 'bout that. I did try to tell you me tutoring was not the best idea in the world."

"I am glad of it," said Commander Woodsinger. "It is true that recruits from the other side of the Border are very valuable."

Elliot nodded. He remembered Commander Woodsinger, the first time he had ever met her, giving money to his teacher so she could test children to see if they could see the wall between them and another world.

"Though they do not like to admit it, many of the proud Borderlands families interbred with the people of the otherlands long ago when there were fewer humans. This means most of them cannot climb the wall from this side. Recruits from the other side mean we always have guards who can travel between the worlds. It has always been our way to find children who can see the Border, and encourage them to adopt Borderlands ways and Borderlands names."

All his suspicions were proving true. Elliot had been sure there was way more interspecies romance going on than anyone would admit to. He instantly believed the Wavechasers had got their name based on forbidden mermaid love.

"No matter how valuable the recruits are," continued the commander, "I do not want to have cadets who are not committed to their cause. I am not in the business of trapping children."

Elliot bit his lip. "I believe that. You're not. *You* wouldn't."

Others in this world might. He didn't know what expression he wore, but he guessed how desolate he must look when the commander's expression changed. He hardly recognized the emotion, it was so unfamiliar on her face. She looked uncomfortable.

"Cadet Schafer, if you come up to my tower for any sort of—reassurance, I have to tell you that I am not a—maternal person. I am a soldier, and I do not desire a personal relationship with any of my cadets."

He must be so pathetic, to make her feel she had to say that. There was no need: Elliot had never thought she liked him or anything.

"Of course, Commander."

Commander Woodsinger cleared her throat. "I will see you next year, Cadet."

She did not wait for a response, but turned and made her way back to her office. Elliot had made no attempt to give one.

He stared out at the expanse of green, at the brimming blue where the mermaids swam and the deeper green of the forests where harpies flew. He thought of the commander saying that nobody understood the otherlands, and thought of everything here that he had not seen. He did not know if it was enough to stay for, mermaids and a challenge.

He'd thought he would always have one reason to stay—but that was not true, because he did not have much anymore.

He saw, down at the dusty ground at the foot of the tower that was their training camp, two figures he could not possibly mistake. As Elliot watched and they walked toward the Trigon pitch, Luke put his arm around Serene's shoulders. That was not usual for them: Serene might be upset. Elliot had no doubt she would get over it.

The other students who were leaving probably had more to go back to than he did. But if he went back and stayed, he could create a life there. He could build something real in the world where he had been born. He was smart enough to make up for the lost time, he hoped, but if he stayed two more years he did not know if he could do it. Time was passing. He was losing hope and losing ground there, and he did not know what he was doing here. Either way, he would lose.

He didn't have an answer, and he did not have it in him to face Serene and Luke right now. He tried to distract himself with a more cheerful thought.

He'd already figured out that he definitely was not made for a life of tragic celibacy. He was so lonely, and obviously no good at friendship. He hoped, with an embarrassed hope mingled with fear, that he was all right in bed. He thought he could pay attention, and see what the next girl wanted and try to give it to her. He thought that quite possibly his previous experience meant he would be uniquely qualified to understand how difficult it could be, being someone's girlfriend, all the small indignities that you suffered when you were trying to be intimate with someone trained to believe you were not altogether their equal. He could be careful not to hurt her, and careful to be fair with her. He thought that he might manage to be really great with his next girlfriend.

Later Elliot was to think this was typical of the way his plans usually went. He had not planned at all for what actually happened next: that instead, he got a boyfriend.

IV

ELLIOT, AGE SIXTEEN

After a week at home, Elliot was more miserable than he had ever been in his life.

The kids down the road—and they could hardly be kids now, any more than he was—were on holiday with their parents, their whole house shut up. Elliot felt as if his house were shut up, too: there was dust in his bedroom, layer upon layer of it. Nobody had come inside it all year.

The first day he was home, his dad did not speak to him or look at him. The second day, he looked up from the meal the latest housekeeper had prepared and said, "Oh, you're back," in a tone of mild surprise.

It was halfway through dinner.

"Of course I'm back," Elliot said in a small, furious voice.

Everyone else *noticed* him. Nobody could help but notice him. He didn't know how to get people to love him, but he knew how to bang on the door of people's attention, lean on their bell until they answered in the vain hope he would go away. He knew how to be inescapably irritating. But the one person he had learned it for was the one person it didn't work on. He barely existed to his father, insubstantial as the dust in his room, only there because nobody cared he was.

He threw his fork down on the table and stormed out. When he came down later to clean up the plates, he saw through the open door his father sitting in his usual chair. Elliot doubted he'd noticed the door slamming or his son being gone, any more than he noticed Elliot being here.

He had lain awake at night and felt alone for years and years, but it was much worse now that he knew about waking up with Serene, how it felt to reach across the bed automatically and have someone warm there, have someone happy you were there. At least when he was in his horrible unheated cabin he had his idiot roommates for company.

Sometimes he woke up happy and reached for Serene, only to grasp a fistful of cold sheets. Sometimes he hardly slept, cataloguing all the ways he'd got it wrong with Serene, not been good enough or lovable enough, thinking of all the ways he could have done better now it was too late to do anything.

The days were unhappy and lonely too, but more than that, he found he was restless. He, who had always been happy being indoors before, was bouncing off the walls of the house, tapping the arms of his chair and kicking table legs and walls. He took several trips to the music store, where old Joe who worked there said he'd grown and was kind enough that Elliot stayed until closing time every time. He went down to the library, where no elves yelled at him for being immodest.

On the fifth day he got up from the window seat in his room, where he was tucked up much less comfortably than he used to be—he could stop growing *any time now*—and drumming his feet against the glass. He flicked the photo of Serene and Luke he had tucked up under the frame of his mirror.

"Thanks for ruining my life, jerkface," he said, and went for a run.

He raced through the streets of the town, under telephone lines that looked like alien, spidery things menacing the clouds, down hard gray roads with cars running alongside. He jumped whenever anyone leaned on the horn, at every screech of tires, but he kept running until his lungs burned and his head was finally empty.

He went home long after it was dark, peeled off his sweat-soaked clothes, and got into the shower. Usually hot running water cheered him up, but he was all alone and his own body had become a strange and treacherous thing.

What had he been thinking, imagining staying here? He wasn't fit for this world. He wanted to go back to where there was one person at least who really liked him, even if she didn't love him. He didn't know if he could last the summer, let alone live here.

Maybe he didn't have to, he thought. If he just showed up at Luke's house, he would probably be allowed to stay.

You didn't have to come running because of an invitation I didn't mean, Luke had said. Elliot did not have to be more pathetic than he already was.

On Saturday, his father was home. It was so much worse to be silent and alone in company. Elliot bore it for a couple of hours, and then went down to the music store. The little shop was dim, but Elliot pushed at the door and found it unlocked.

"Joe?" he called out.

No answer. He figured Joe was in the bathroom or taking a cigarette break, and knew he was welcome anyway.

"Hi, Joe!" he called out. "I'm trespassing! I'm shoplifting! I'm a teen delinquent and I must be stopped!"

He wandered in and over to the corner where you could play songs in privacy, fitted the giant headphones over his ears, and selected an album called *Goodbye Blues.* There was an electronic guitar near the station: Elliot only knew how to play piano, but he picked it up and played with it as he sang along.

The shop only stayed open until four on Saturdays. Elliot was going to have to go back to his house and his father.

Maybe he could go to Luke's after all. Maybe Luke wouldn't really mind.

Elliot shook his head at himself, and switched songs. The next was good, jaunty, with a clapping, swinging beat: Elliot vigorously strummed the guitar and sang at his own dumb feelings.

He looked down automatically at the touch of a hand on his: not in alarm, as Joe had tried to teach him the basics of guitar before.

When he looked down, the hand was definitely not Joe's. Joe did not have barbed-wire tattoos on his knuckles.

Elliot squawked, twisted around, and brandished the electronic guitar in a threatening manner at a total stranger, some blond guy with a goatee and a few more tattoos.

"Whoa," said the stranger. "Hi. Don't worry, I work here."

"What do you mean, you work here?" Elliot asked. "Nobody works here! Where's Joe?"

"He's having a cigarette break," said the stranger. "He's my uncle."

Elliot lowered the guitar as his blood pressure lowered on its own. "Oh. You're Jason."

Jason nodded. "Jase. I assume you're Elliot?"

Oh good, Elliot had now been rude to Joe's beloved nephew, and he was about to lose his last sanctuary earlier than scheduled. "Crap," Elliot added, heartfelt. "I thought you were like ten." He was desperate enough to give the eyes for the elves a try, and willed: *Don't make me leave.* "You could not be left alone with the musical equipment if you were ten. That would be highly irresponsible."

"Well, we're even then," said Jase. "The way Uncle Joe talked about you, I thought for sure you were a little kid. But you look plenty grown up to me."

"That's me," Elliot confirmed. "Mature. Like a fancy cheese. But unlike a fancy cheese, I can be trusted with the musical equipment. I won't—I won't come into the store and mess around unattended again, though."

"You can come in and mess around anytime you like," said Jase.

Victory! Elliot glowed and beamed.

Jase sorted idly through album cases without looking at them. Elliot glanced at the black barbed wire inscribed around his fingers.

"Uncle Joe said you went to a military academy in the north."

"Uh . . .," Elliot said. "Sure, yes. Really north. Very military academy."

Jase nodded and looked at Elliot consideringly. "I can see it."

"What?" said Elliot.

"So, you like music?"

Here Elliot was in a music shop and wearing his Pink Floyd T-shirt, even though it fit all wrong now. Elliot wondered if Jase was simple. But he was on a mission to be allowed free run of the place, so . . . "Love it," Elliot said cheerfully.

"Cool," said Jase. "If you're at a loose end later, maybe you'd like to come see my band practice. I'm the drummer."

The beatific prospect of not having to go home at all opened up to Elliot like clouds to reveal the sun or ice-cream to reveal jelly. "Yes," Elliot breathed with conviction. "I would like that *very much.*"

"Cool," Jase said again, and then gave Elliot another considering look, this one a bit more worried. "How old are you, exactly?"

"Sixteen," said Elliot. "Practically."

From the vaguely startled look on Jase's face, it was clear he'd thought Elliot was older. Elliot wondered why it mattered. Maybe the band practiced in a bar, but unless Elliot ordered a drink he should be fine.

Then it occurred to Elliot why it mattered.

"Oh, well. Sixteen. That's old enough," said Jase at last, relaxing. "'Cause this would be a date."

He looked at Elliot, this time with his eyebrows raised, more challenge than consideration.

"I know, I just got that a couple of minutes ago," said Elliot. "I'm not sure why I didn't get it before. You were being pretty obvious about it. Also slightly clichéd. But I haven't been hit on a lot."

Jase looked extremely startled while Elliot was talking, which often happened while Elliot was talking and was usually a bad sign, but at the last thing he smiled. Elliot was entirely unclear on what he had done right or what he'd done wrong.

"No?" said Jase, still smiling.

"Only once before by a guy," said Elliot. "My friend Luke's cousin. And honestly I hated him and wanted him to fall into a pit of spikes."

"So you've never . . .," said Jase, and did not seem displeased about that at all. "But you are . . . ?"

"You need to learn to finish your sentences for more effective communication," Elliot advised.

"You still wanna go on a date with me?" asked Jase.

"I don't know. I'm thinking about it," Elliot said impatiently.

Jase was back to looking startled. "Well . . . let me know."

The thought of going home was like the idea of voluntarily stepping into an abyss. Elliot felt a sick swoop of horror at the thought of condemning himself to that when he had another option.

But he could hang out in darkened parking lots on his own, he supposed. He didn't have to go anywhere with this guy.

Jason had asked if he'd never, and asked if he was, and even if he hadn't finished his sentences Elliot had understood. Jason was cute, and Elliot was flattered to be asked, and . . . Elliot had always known he liked both, had strongly suspected that his teacher talking about him confusing hero worship with something else was idiocy. Elliot was rarely confused about anything.

Only he'd been really young when he met Serene, and he'd loved her at once, known at once that if he had her he would never want anyone else. He'd thought about guys occasionally, but in the same fleeting way he'd thought about other girls. He'd figured that he never had to work it out.

Except he didn't have Serene. She didn't want him. And somebody else did.

"I've thought about it," said Elliot. "Yeah, I'll go on a date with you."

Jase grinned. "Cool."

Jason really needed to expand his vocabulary, Elliot thought. But that was okay. They could work on that.

Elliot hung around in the shop all day and came to Jase's band practice that night. They really did practice in the upper room of a bar. The group accepted him without surprise, and Elliot was pleased to see that Jase was actually pretty good, though Marty the lead singer was absolutely atrocious. Elliot spent most of the practice talking to Alice, who did the lights and showed him how to as well.

He told her he was really behind on his technology, and she laughed at him, but nicely, as if she thought he was fun and was ready to accept him. They all seemed ready to do that, and it was absolute blissful relief just to have people who would look at him when they spoke to him, who would listen when he replied.

He drank ginger ale at first, but they stopped practicing and went downstairs where the bar was turning into an overflowing room of people drinking and dancing. Alice bought Elliot a drink and Elliot drank it: he'd had mead plenty of times before at Luke's house, so he was perfectly able to handle it. He danced with her: with the whole group. The room was packed enough that it seemed like dancing with a hundred strangers.

"Whoa, you can dance," said a voice in his ear. Elliot looked around and down at a touch that felt deliberate, and saw Jase's barbed-wire-encircled fingers curled in the loop of his jeans. Then he looked up into Jase's smiling face. "Enjoying yourself?"

Elliot smiled back, and Jase leaned in.

Even though he had loved Serene with all his heart for years, Elliot had thought occasionally: I might want to . . . and will I ever . . . ?

Jase kissed him. The question was answered. He would, and he had. Elliot kissed him back, felt the scrape of Jase's stubble against his face and against his fingers as he touched Jase's jaw, slid an arm around his neck, drew their bodies tighter together.

Jase asked him to come home with him at the end of the night, but Elliot said no. He thought maybe that he wouldn't be asked back, but the next day at the music shop Jase was there and made sure to get Elliot's number. Elliot had bought a phone that morning, in case he asked. He saw the band practice over and over, went out drinking and to a concert, and on his sixteenth birthday he let Alice put eyeliner on him and went out dancing again.

Jase asked Elliot to come home with him that night, and Elliot did.

It was so different to his house, Jase's rented flat that he shared with Alice and Marty. The bathroom was filthy, the blinds broken and skewed like teeth in a prizefighter's face, and Elliot did not wake up alone but woke up warm and had the other two laughing at them for sleeping in late.

"So, pretty different from girls, huh?" Jase asked as they made toast.

"Sure," said Elliot, and winked. "You work out a lot less than Serene."

Jase looked slightly vexed, but Alice laughed out loud and Marty said, "You finally caught a live one," and Jase relented and laughed too.

It was nice in the flat. It was nice to go to concerts. He'd never had someone his age—well, within five years was close enough—to talk about music with. He'd hardly had anyone to experience this world with, and this world looked better with someone else.

Elliot started to think, again, about not going back.

Elliot also could not talk to Joe about music anymore. The few times he came to the music shop when Jase wasn't there, Joe was strange and curt when before he had been gruff and kind. When Elliot ran out of patience—which took thirteen minutes—and demanded to know what his problem was, Joe said: "You can't ask me to approve of that sort of carry-on."

"What?" Elliot demanded. "So Jase isn't welcome here anymore?"

Joe looked away. "Jase is my blood."

Elliot wanted to shout at him, but he knew better than anybody that you could not fight people into caring about you or being fair to you. This was the punishment he got for trusting Joe, for thinking that because someone would throw a kind word to a kid that they were kind, that they could be counted on. He took the punishment. He bit down on what he wanted to say, and he walked out.

The closest he got to the shop, ever again, was when he walked Jase there. He told Jase what his uncle had said the next morning, and Jase nodded, hands in his pockets, looking exhausted suddenly.

"Uncle Joe's never been keen on that kind of thing."

"And it doesn't bother you?" Elliot demanded.

"It does," said Jase, looking more tired than ever. "But I'm used to it. I know you're not. You don't have to . . . you don't need to make anything public, if you're not comfortable."

Elliot stared at him, speechless.

"Anyway, I'd better get in to work," said Jase, nodding as if that was settled, and he started down the road, tread heavy and shoulders hunched. It took Elliot a moment to realize he walked as if carrying a burden.

There was a low stone wall running along the pavement. Elliot jumped up on it and ran along the wall, catching up and grabbing a very surprised Jase by the collar of his jacket. Elliot leaned down and kissed him in front of all the tired commuters going to work and disappointed parents bringing their kids to summer school. Elliot held onto Jase's collar and kissed him all he wanted, until he felt Jase smile.

"There's something you should know about me, if we're going to do this," Elliot told him. "I always do exactly what I want, and I never care what anybody else thinks about it."

Jase seemed dumbfounded and was breathing hard, but he was still smiling. "Yeah?"

"Yes," said Elliot. "And I want to see you later."

"See you later, then," said Jase.

Elliot found himself alone at dinner one night, and knew that his father was on a business trip. His dad didn't leave notes or tell him about them: that would be too much acknowledgement of Elliot's presence. The first time it had happened when Elliot was old enough to be left alone without a babysitter, Elliot had been frantic and thought his father had been in an accident. He'd called the hospitals.

That had been years ago. Now he knew what his father's absence meant. This time he called Jase.

"Hey," he said when Jase picked up. "I'm home all alone. Come keep me company."

He thought it would be nice to have a place to themselves.

It was wonderful, to be able to request company and know the request would be granted. Even back at the Border, Elliot either had company or he didn't. Elliot leaned back in his window seat, glass cold against his shoulders, and watched affectionately as Jase prowled around his room.

Jason whistled and plucked Elliot's one picture from the mirror. "Hello, someone is crazy hot."

Elliot beamed. "I know, right? That's Serene. We used to go out. She actually dated me. I don't mean to brag, but we were physically intimate."

It was funny: it would have been agony telling someone that a month ago, and it still hurt, but he was able to say it, and to feel mostly pride and remember being happy.

"Uh, okay," said Jase. "Before you realized you didn't like girls."

"What? I like girls," said Elliot. "I mean," he added, because he didn't want to hurt Jase's feelings, "I like girls as well."

"Sure." Jase rolled his eyes, and Elliot stared at him with mingled outrage and surprise. He wasn't sure why Jase felt qualified to comment on a basic reality about Elliot. "Don't worry about it. You're young yet," said Jase and gave him a wink.

"I can't say that being twenty seems to have conferred enormous wisdom upon you."

"God, Elliot, settle down." Jase sounded absent-minded but fond, which was worth a lot to Elliot: maybe Elliot was going a bit far. He knew he had a tendency to do that. "Anyway," said Jase. "I was not referring to the bird. I was talking about the guy, obviously. Woof."

"What, *Luke*?" Elliot grabbed his own hair by handfuls in despair. "That is a ridiculous picture of him! That is why I kept that one!"

"So you're saying . . . he usually looks better? Jesus."

"This conversation is a living nightmare," Elliot announced.

Jase did not seem overly disturbed by this announcement. It was possible he was getting used to Elliot's grand proclamations. He continued studying the photo. "So this is Luke. You've talked about him often enough. I can't believe you never mentioned he looked like that."

"It's not a national emergency," said Elliot.

"Uh, have you seen him?" said Jase. "It kind of is."

"And I do not talk about him often. I have mentioned him once or twice. Rarely. Hardly ever. Who is Luke?" said Elliot. "Have you noticed this is a terrible conversation? Because I've noticed this is a terrible conversation."

"Does his cousin look like him?" Jase pursued, and off Elliot's reluctant nod said: "And you turned him *down*?"

"He's a vicious moron," said Elliot.

"Who cares when someone looks like that?"

"I do," said Elliot.

Jase made a dismissive sound, but looked pleased too: it reflected well on Jase himself if Elliot was choosy, Elliot supposed. They had chosen each other. Elliot attempted to catch Jase's eye, but Jase was still looking at the photograph.

"I guess he's straight? Luke, I mean."

Elliot tasted something bitter in his mouth. "No," he said at last, feeling prickly all over. "No, he's not straight."

"Ohhhh. Well. Does he, ah, 'like girls as well'?" Jase repeated what Elliot had said in a voice with just an edge of a sing-song lilt, a savor of mockery that Elliot could not quite pin down and be mad about.

"No," said Elliot shortly.

"Sounds like quite a guy. He coming to visit?"

"No," Elliot snapped. "Why, you want to dump me for him?"

It felt like Jase would. Of course, Elliot had never met anyone who wouldn't, who didn't instantly and instinctively value Luke higher. That included Serene. Jase wasn't going to be any different.

Jase laughed, light and pleased, and came over and tipped Elliot's chin up, kissed him with a kiss light as his laugh. "Nah. But I thought Marty might like him. I mean, who wouldn't?"

Elliot let that last bit go in favor of laughing at the rest. "Marty has a lip ring, and Luke would have a heart attack. This is someone who finds jeans scandalous and distressing. He has a crush on this guy back at school called Dale. They both want to play sports and fight stuff all day every day."

"Oh, right, boring and mainstream," said Jase. Elliot was pleased enough by Jase's dismissive tone to let the fact that "mainstream" was a pretentious label for human beings go. "Shame."

"Luke's not boring," said Elliot. "Dale kind of is. But he's a nice person or something, I guess."

"He sure doesn't look boring, I'll give you that."

"I've had enough of talking about Luke," Elliot announced. He got up and whisked the photo out of Jase's hand, tucking it back into the mirror frame. "I get it, you think he's hot. But you're wrong."

Jase tilted his head quizzically. "He's not hot?"

Elliot moved toward him, close so Jase reached out and grabbed his wrist. Then Elliot hooked an ankle behind Jase's foot and sent him flying backward onto the bed. He kept his own balance, and smirked down at Jase.

"I'm your boyfriend," he said. "Only I am hot."

"That was hot," said Jase, wide-eyed and leaning against Elliot's pillows.

"Just a little trick I picked up in the, ah, military academy," Elliot told him smugly, put a knee down on the bed and then crawled over Jase.

Jase tried to lift up to kiss him, but Elliot held his shoulders down against the mattress easily and shook his head. Jase raised a hand, Elliot thought to touch. He grabbed the back of Elliot's shirt and tried to flip him over. Elliot pulled his hand off, though Jase tried to hang on, and held both of Jase's wrists over his head with one hand.

"I really didn't think you'd be like this," Jase said, a little breathless and a little critical. "You seemed so sweet that first day. I thought you would be shy and kind of hesitant and in need of guidance."

"My best friends are war leaders," Elliot pointed out. "Good luck with your thing."

"War leaders?"

"Uh, classic military academy humor!" said Elliot hastily. "Besides," he added, and cast a look down Jase's body and back up to his face, his dilated pupils. Elliot's grasp on his wrists tightened. "You may not have been expecting this, but . . ." Elliot leaned down and brushed his mouth against the edge of Jase's, smiled, leaned a crucial fraction away when Jase tried to chase his mouth, and spoke softly. "You like it."

Jase's whole body had come to attention: he kept surging up and straining against Elliot's hold, trying to get closer. Elliot smiled, leaned down, and kissed him, catching the small desperate breath Jase let out against his smile.

"C'mon!" Jase exclaimed, his voice on a high hoarse edge.

"What," Elliot asked, stroking the inside of Jase's wrist with his thumb. "You don't like it? Oh dear."

"Yes, I like it!" Jase said. "Goddamn it, come here."

Elliot laughed, delighted, and let Jase go. He gave him a long hot kiss with his fingers tangled in Jase's hair.

Later that night, with Jase sleeping in his bed, Elliot went and sat on the window seat, looked out at the streetlights dyeing patches of night orange, and thought again about staying. The moon caught his mirror and made it into a well of light, the photo a small dark square drowning in the silver shine.

He wouldn't see them again, and he wouldn't see mermaids, but Alice said he was getting really good with computers and he was starting to believe he and Jase could make this work. Jase might say ridiculous things sometimes, but Elliot thought it was because he was insecure. Elliot could understand that. He did it often enough himself.

He thought of Jase, thinking that Elliot would be different. He couldn't quite figure out how to say: You met me when I was sad, but I'm not a sad person, and I don't want you to like that sad person who wasn't me better than you like me. Maybe if he stayed, he could figure it out.

He climbed back into bed, kissed the dragon tattoo on Jase's shoulderblade, and said: "Wake up."

Nights with company were awesome, but Elliot might have liked the mornings best. He woke up in his room with light streaming through the windows, and Jase awake and looking down at him.

"Hey," said Jase, and kissed him. "Is there any food? I'm starving."

"Are you in luck," Elliot told him. "Because I can make truly terrible pancakes."

He made the first pancake as Jase fiddled with the radio and turned it to a station that met with his approval. Then he gave Jase the first pancake, and Jase's eyes widened and he went on the hunt for strawberry jam to disguise the taste.

"I know, I'm really not used to electricity when cooking," Elliot said apologetically.

"Jesus, military academy is hardcore," said Jase.

"Heh-heh, uh," said Elliot. "I know, right?"

Jase ate his pancake. Elliot sang along to the radio, using his wooden spoon as a microphone, and Jase beat time on the table with his fork.

"Maybe you should be our lead singer," he said.

"You do need a new one," Elliot said. "Marty is terrible and the band is not going to succeed."

Jase laughed.

"No, I'm serious," said Elliot. "Dropping out of college for the band was a terrible idea."

"Yes, yes, I get it, you love school," said Jase, kissing Elliot's neck. "Sing again."

Elliot swung around and sang, Jase laughing at him as he did so. Elliot pushed Jase, who slid in his socked feet until his back hit the oven, and Elliot pushed the bowl of pancake batter onto the counter and moved in, still singing.

The door opened with a treacherous little creak. His dad was standing framed in the doorway, still and startled. Elliot dropped his spoon.

There was no way it looked innocent. His dad was watching his sixteen-year-old son with a twenty-year-old tattooed guy. Neither of them were wearing shirts. They had clearly been just about to make out. Everything was terrible.

"I can explain this," said Elliot.

"I'm gonna go," said Jase.

He fled. Elliot glared at him for this treachery but had to admit that he would have liked to flee too.

"Do you want a terrible pancake?" he asked his father.

"No," said his dad, but he came over and sat at the kitchen table instead of leaving the room, which was such unusual behavior that it terrified Elliot.

He could not help but wonder if he was going to get kicked out of his house, and then he thought that he would have to go back to the Borderlands. He couldn't go live with Jase, that would be insane and he didn't even know if Jase would want him to, and he wasn't trained for anything in this world.

It was almost a relief, having the decision made for him.

"I didn't think . . .," his dad said slowly. "That you were . . . like that."

It was news to Elliot that his dad thought he was like anything. Had he noticed the photo of Serene, listened to the few things Elliot let drop? Elliot found himself staring at his father, feeling as if he were trying to glean clues about a complete stranger. His father was looking the same way at him, but with an added distance: as if he might look away, bored, at any time.

"I like girls too," said Elliot. "But Jason's my boyfriend."

"That's not what I meant," his dad said. "I meant . . . how you were, with the singing. You looked . . . happy."

Elliot stared at the spoon on the floor. "Did you think I was never happy?"

It was possible that his father had never seen him happy before, had thought of him as nothing but a bitter-eyed, bitter-tongued ghost child among all the ghosts of his memories.

"I don't know," said his father. "I never thought about it, I suppose."

"Great," said Elliot. "That's just great."

"I don't care about that person being a man," his father told him. "That doesn't matter to me."

"What does matter to you?" Elliot asked. His dad didn't answer, and Elliot picked the spoon up off the floor. "Listen," he said roughly. "I'm thinking about not going back to school this year. I mean—I could go to the school here. It might be better for me, to stay here, to live a—a more ordinary life. The other school's pretty intense. I'm not sure about this, but I was thinking about it. What do you think?"

He looked over at his father. His father wasn't looking at him. He was looking at something Elliot couldn't see.

"I think you'll go back," said his father, at last.

He stared off into space for a while longer, then got up and walked away. Elliot poured his pancake batter down the sink.

An ordinary parent would have been more trouble, he thought vaguely, remembering Serene's mother lecturing her. He would have had to answer questions: about how they met, if they cared about each other, what the age difference was. A real parent would have needed to know Elliot was not in a bad situation.

Elliot did not even know why he was surprised. Elliot had been in bad situations before. He remembered being out playing when he was a little too old for a babysitter and yet a little too young to be left alone for the long stretches of time he was left alone for, and breaking his wrist. Dad had come home and found Elliot white-faced and clutching his wrist on the stairs, and driven him to the hospital, and paid for Elliot's care. He'd done all the right things. He just hadn't said anything: asked Elliot what had happened, scolded Elliot for putting himself in danger. He hadn't cared.

Now he'd accepted that Elliot had a boyfriend, Elliot hadn't been punished or hurt, hadn't been subjected to the cruel unfairness of Jason's Uncle Joe. But Elliot knew Joe loved Jason: knew Joe had liked Elliot, more than Elliot's own dad had ever liked him.

Elliot had lost count of all the ways that people could betray you, out of love or indifference. He didn't know which was the worst way to be betrayed. He sat down in a kitchen chair, put his head in his hands, and felt sick.

He knew one thing. His father thought he was going back, so he was staying.

~

Elliot stayed. The day he was meant to go back, he did not go.

He leaped up and packed his bag to go halfway through the day, then forced himself to unpack. He went and leaned against the window, looking out on buildings like strange square traps and the glaring eyes of electric lights, and he thought about never seeing mermaids and never writing all the peace treaties he'd dreamed of. Then he reminded himself of a life without computers, without electricity, without college, a life where he would be absolutely trapped. He was not going to choose something so stupid.

He crossed over to the mirror, picked up the picture of Luke and Serene, and said: "You don't even want me there, you'll be much happier without me," because that had always been true of Luke and it was true now of Serene too, Serene who didn't love him and didn't want to deal with the awkwardness and inconvenience of his love. "It's better this way," said Elliot. "And if I came back—you're probably both going to die. I'd be stranded and you'd be dead."

They were soldiers. This way, Elliot would never know if they died.

He put the photo down. "I didn't mean that," he said. "You're not going to die. I don't know why I said that."

If he stayed here, he would not be forced to worry about his friends being killed. He would be a normal kid in school, with a real life ahead of him, and with somebody who wanted him there. This was the right choice.

He went over to Jase's, but Jase was not there. Alice was, though, and they played video games for a couple of hours until Elliot felt less like he was about to explode out of his own skin and run for the Border.

"You okay?" Alice asked. "Did you and Jase have a fight?"

"No, nothing like that," said Elliot.

He answered quickly because it was true, but Alice clearly didn't believe him. "You're a lot to handle."

"I know," Elliot said, nettled. "Jase doesn't seem to mind all that much."

"That's not what I meant."

Alice looked wary, as if she did not want her roommate's boyfriend having a tantrum in her direction. Elliot leaned over and kissed her on the cheek. "I have to go. Thanks for being kind to me."

The next day, he called up the local school and pretended to be his dad so he could get information on enrolling. He tried to work out which of his classes to catch up on.

He also spent a while working out whether he could go back to the Border for just one more year, say good-bye, see mermaids, sort out what he could, and then come back and catch up and have that normal life with electricity and without mortal danger. He thought he could. Then he forced himself to stop making those calculations.

The next day he packed for the Border again, in a frantic terrible hurry, hardly putting in any electronics at all, wanting to keep his pack light so he could move fast, so he could just go now.

Eventually he left the bag on the floor, and fled to Jase's. It was late enough so Jase was already at a bar, and he met Elliot outside. Jase was barely outside the door when Elliot launched himself at him: backing him up against the large glass window. Jase's mouth opened under his, slick and hot with a sting of tequila, and it was a long time until they disentangled enough to go back to Jase's.

In the morning, Elliot devoted himself to multitasking: buttoning his shirt, making toast, and attempting to tell Jase that he was sticking around.

"I've been thinking that I want to make some changes," Elliot tried out.

"Yeah, I've been thinking the same thing. With your dad knowing and all. It's kind of heavy," said Jase. "I think maybe . . . we should call it quits."

"Oh," said Elliot. He put down the toast and did up his shirt: he only had one task now.

Jase seemed to warm to his theme. "You're a different person than I thought you were, and maybe we don't mesh that well together, yeah?"

Jase had said much the same thing before, but Elliot hadn't paid attention because Jase had clearly liked him. Elliot stared at Jase over the kitchen counter and the cooling toast, and believed two things: that Jase still liked him, and that Jase was a coward. Elliot remembered Jase not wanting to hear about college, about his band, about Elliot liking girls as well, about his uncle, about everything that Elliot had found understandable and forgivable but which taken all together formed a tower of things that Jase had not wanted to deal with.

Jase liked Elliot being the way Elliot was, but he didn't want to like it: he was looking for something that wouldn't push him out of his comfort zone. Jase didn't want to be challenged.

It was strange how different the same thing could feel. Serene had dumped him, and he would've done anything to get her back, had missed her every day for months. Now Jase had dumped him, and suddenly and simply, Elliot didn't ever want to see him again.

"Okay," said Elliot. "Good-bye, then."

Jase didn't seem to like that either. "It's just the way you are," he said. "It'd be difficult for anyone to put up with."

"That's true," said Elliot.

Jase softened, hearing what he wanted to hear, but Elliot saw it now as condescending instead of affectionate. "If you were a bit more grown up, maybe . . ."

"Oh my God," said Elliot. "You can't handle me *now*."

He found himself almost laughing in Jase's baffled face. He knew what was wrong with him: awkward, spiky, occasionally cruel, inherently unlovable, all of that. But he'd always had a certain intense belief in what he could do: write treaties, end wars, throw all the knives away, make people listen to him, accomplish whatever he wanted. He was getting better at it too: by the time he was twenty, someone like Jase would be a haystack in the path of a hurricane.

Jase looked angry. Elliot felt nothing but that strange amusement and cold contempt, for Jase and for himself.

The key scraped in the lock of the front door, and Marty and Alice walked in.

"Oh my God," said Marty, giving Jase a sad look. "Don't tell me you're doing this here."

Jase was a terrible roommate, Elliot realized. They were probably counting the days until they could be rid of him. But that didn't mean they would want to be friends with Jase's latest castoff, either. He didn't have anyone in this world, but he never had.

"I'm just leaving, guys," he said. "Marty, please, please take a course in something that will be useful to you when you are trying to gain employment in the future. Alice, thanks so much for teaching me about lights. Everybody have a nice life."

He walked out. Jase made a discontented sound, almost fretful, as if he'd pictured it all differently, but it was Alice who chased after him, who leaned over the rail to call down to him as he was making his way down the stairwell.

"I really do think you're a nice kid!" she said.

"I'm really not," Elliot called back up.

Alice smiled. "Well, I definitely think you're going places."

"I definitely am," said Elliot.

He stopped off at his house and picked up his bag. He thought about leaving his dad a note explaining where he had gone, but the thought made him laugh. He just went.

He'd already worked it out. He could go for one more year, and see mermaids.

Elliot climbed the wall alone. Usually he saw someone else in the distance, going to the Border camp, or thought he saw someone else coming, but this time there was nobody in sight. Everyone else was already gone.

He climbed high gray stone steps into a bank of cloud that was like a white cliff he could disappear into. When he came walking out of the cloud and down into the Borderlands, the whole sky had changed. It was bright, light blue, sparkling as if it had been freshly washed. Elliot knew it was weird magic sky business, but it felt symbolic.

He went striding through the long green grass of the meadows that led home. It was an easy walk, though it had seemed farther when he was a child. With every step, he was gladder to be back.

There was time to become whoever he chose. There was still time.

There was even time to see if Jase and Alice and Serene and his father and everyone else he'd ever met so far was right, and nobody could put up with him for long. Serene had liked him for a while. Jase had liked him for a while. There might be someone who would like him for longer than that. Thinking of Jase made Elliot remember Jase's reaction to Elliot saying he liked girls as well, and that made his lip curl. The odds were better for Elliot than other people: he could look for a boyfriend or a girlfriend.

Surely he could get this right, one day.

The sun was seeping through the thin material of his shirt, warm as a welcome. He approached the Border camp, the cabins and the tower, the practice grounds where unfortunate souls were hurling javelins and having swordfights, and he checked his watch. It was about time for the first Trigon game of the season. Elliot was so sad that he knew when the games were.

Luke would be playing and Serene would be watching, so Elliot shifted his pack from one shoulder to the other and made a beeline for the pitch.

He could hear the hum of the crowd as he approached the little scooped-out valley, with artificial hills at its center, and saw the filled benches with people leaning toward the game like flowers to the sun. Elliot looked for the people who had been knocked out, and saw there were four gone from the other year's team already. So Luke was winning and all was as it should be.

Elliot was so sad that he knew the rules of Trigon.

On the pitch, a guy was taking off his shirt. Elliot supposed Trigon wasn't all bad.

Then he noticed something much more important. There was someone lurking at the back of the Trigon stands, and Elliot was amazed and thrilled to see that they were taking pictures. He had given technology to this world. He was an industrial revolutionary!

"Hi," he said affectionately to the camera-wielding stranger.

"I'm from the newspaper," said the stranger. "I have permission to be here from the commander."

"That's awesome," said Elliot. "The newspaper. That's so awesome."

"I'm doing a piece on the Sunborns," he continued.

"No," Elliot said faintly. He felt betrayed.

"With a particular focus on the young Sunborn champion!"

"Oh my God, so quickly I see the problems with a free press," Elliot moaned.

The shirtless guy on the pitch was Luke, he realized suddenly, now he could see his hair. Elliot made a face. Everything was terrible. Now he came to think of it, his options were actually no greater than they had been, because what guys were there who liked guys in the Border camp? Luke, obvious emotional suicide, and Dale, obvious violation of the bro code. Maybe there was someone in the council-training course. That would work better for Elliot anyway.

"Do you know Luke Sunborn at all?" asked the worst journalist of their time.

"I don't," Elliot said firmly. "But I have heard that nobody likes him, and he is dull. And he has an unhealthy and morbid attachment to lettuce. Write that down."

The journalist didn't write it down. Elliot looked back at the pitch, where Luke had just viciously fouled someone. Elliot was sad a third time that he knew so much about Trigon, and also sad because of wantonly violent warrior ways, but wantonly violent warrior ways meant Luke was turned in the right direction. Elliot waved, so that Luke would know he was there. He figured Luke could tell Serene. He'd talk to them both later, and unpack now.

He pointed at the reporter and repeated sternly: "Write that down!" Then he headed for his cabin.

He was only about ten steps away from the Trigon game when he saw Myra, walking through the gate of the enclosure around the tower, and she saw him. She started and then ran right at him, smiling all over her face: Elliot caught her as she came. She was small but sturdy, and he was somewhat amazed at how easy it was to lift her off her feet and swing her around. She felt light and he felt light, too, all over.

"Elliot!" said Myra. "You're back! We didn't know what was going on. It's been crazy. I'm so happy you're back."

She eased back a little and he let her, and looked into her sparkling dark eyes. He'd never thought before of how nice dark eyes were, how warm and welcoming.

"Yeah?" he asked. "You're really glad?"

Myra punched him in the shoulder and eased away, entirely too soon. "Of course."

"Well," said Elliot, and put an arm around her shoulders. "Good. Because you're going to be seeing a lot of me this year. I've decided we need outside-the-library quality time. What do you want to do? I want to do anything you want."

"Er, I'm going to be working on the school play," said Myra, looking puzzled but pleased. "Painting the sets and setting up the props.

You'd be welcome to help out if you want, but—are you sure you're a behind-the-scenes kind of guy?"

"Absolutely! I'd love to be behind the scenes with you."

Elliot grinned at her and winked. Myra shook her head and laughed. This play idea seemed ideal to Elliot. He wasn't going to do anything right away, he'd broken up with somebody this morning, but here Myra was—smart, kind, happy to see him—and here was an opportunity to get to know each other better and view each other in a different light. He'd be a fool not to take it.

He wondered whether he should ask her to grab something to eat now, discuss this play, but then they were both distracted by the commotion on the Trigon pitch. Elliot turned and looked where Myra was already staring, her mouth open: the sound was that of a crowd protesting, people spilling off benches and off the pitch. There was the click of a camera under the rising storm of mutters and shouts.

Luke emerged from the crowd, shaking off people as a dog might shake off water droplets, and ran at Elliot. It was not nice, like with Myra. It was mildly alarming. Luke shoved something at Elliot, then grabbed him by the shoulders and shook him. Luke was a mannerless barbarian.

"Where have you been?" demanded Luke. "Where did you go? I thought—I don't know what I thought, you stupid, selfish, irresponsible—"

"Hey, loser, why are you bothering me?" asked Elliot, happy to see him also.

"I'm going to kill you," said Luke. "I am literally going to kill you."

That seemed excessive and mean to Elliot. He pulled away from Luke so he could study what Luke had shoved at him. It was the Trigon ball, its glass surface slick with grass.

"Thanks for this disgusting object I didn't ask for and don't want, by the way."

"What?" said Luke.

Dale Wavechaser left the turbulent throng to join their little group. Summer was always good to people who looked like Dale, who burnished while Elliot went all red and peeled after twenty minutes in direct sunlight.

"Hey, Dale," said Elliot, for Luke's sake. "Great to see you. Had a good summer? Hope so."

Dale looked upset as well as burnished. "Luke," he said. "The game—"

"Get lost and don't bother me," Luke snapped.

"Whoa," Elliot exclaimed. "You do not mean that! He doesn't mean that, buddy. He's overwrought by—winning or losing the—game, I suppose? You know sports. Adrenalin run mad, emotions running high. Sports."

"We didn't win or lose the game!" Dale snapped, proving Elliot's point. All these people, driven mad by sporting events.

"You have to have done one or the other," Elliot informed him, kindly and patiently.

"We didn't, because the game is *not over*," Dale shouted.

"Oh," said Elliot, and looked at the ball he was holding. "Oh wow, you probably need this, right?"

"*Yes*," said Dale. He eyed Luke unhappily, and then his unhappiness eased slightly into appreciation. "I brought you your shirt," he offered.

"Why would you go and do a thing like that," said Myra, the minx, and Elliot glanced at her and grinned.

"Also, you should know that guy with the picture machine took your picture," Dale continued.

"Why would he do that?" Luke demanded. "I told him after the game, when I was cleaned up."

Luke emerged from his shirt, aiming a venomous glare all around.

"Why is everyone behaving in a ridiculous way that makes no sense? Why are you banging on about Trigon when nobody cares? And you! Where were you, what were you doing, why didn't you come on registration day, why are you wearing those terrible clothes? Get rid of them! Come with me, I need to talk to you."

"They're not terrible," Myra said. Elliot beamed, gratified, and she patted Elliot on the back. "Luke's right, you should definitely change into your uniform before the commander sees you, but even though your garb is outlandish I think it looks quite nice."

"Yeah, actually," Dale agreed. "What do you call those?"

"Jeans," said Elliot.

"Would all of you shut up!" Luke snarled.

"What is wrong with you?' Elliot asked. "Why are you being such a moody baby?"

Myra took a discreet step back. Dale aimed an appalled look at Elliot. Luke's shoulders bunched under his shirt. For an instant Elliot really thought, against everything he knew about Luke, that he was going to be hit.

He did not take a step back.

Luke did not hit him. "Elliot, I need to talk to you," he ground out instead. "*Please.*"

"Yeah," Elliot said. "Okay. Of course. Myra, see you later. Dale, take this and go back to the game." He pushed the ball at Dale, and Dale opened his mouth. "No, no don't argue with me," Elliot told him. "You don't want to go and do a rash thing like that. Just run along."

He grasped Luke by his upper arm and towed him toward Elliot's cabin. Elliot really needed to put his bag down, and Myra and Luke were right: he should probably change before the commander spotted him. But he uneasily suspected that he had to hear this first.

Luke was silent as they walked. Dread drew a cold finger down Elliot's spine. Luke had been with his family all summer: something could have happened to any of them.

"You have me kind of worried," he said as they approached the cabin, shrugging off his bag and holding it in one hand, trying to keep his voice light. "What's going on? Where's Serene?"

He looked at Luke. Luke looked back at him, the anger gone from his face. He looked helpless. Elliot let his bag drop from his fingers into the dust.

"Luke," Elliot said, and heard his voice shake. "Where's Serene?"

Luke sat down, heavily, on the step in front of Elliot's cabin. Elliot stood over him, his shadow touching Luke. He could see the silhouetted outline of his hands. They were shaking too.

"She didn't come back to school," said Luke. "I don't know . . . I don't know if she's going to. She's with her mother, fighting in the eastern woods. The brigand problem got worse and worse, and all the elven troops were rallied, but they don't want humans coming. The brigands are human—some people say they're Border guards turned traitor—and the elves don't like humans much right now. I should be with her. We swore an oath so we would always ride into battle together and always have each other's backs. But the elf commanders—Serene's mother—they all say it doesn't matter. The oath doesn't count, because I'm human and a boy. They've expressly forbidden me to go. There are, um, orders to shoot me on sight. Serene felt she had to go without me, for her people. She didn't have a choice. And then you weren't here, and word came back that the fighting had turned—that it was really bad. I haven't had any word from her. I don't know what to do."

Luke put his face in his hands, as if he was tired beyond words. Elliot stared at his bag in the dust, at his shadow. He went and sat beside Luke, leaning against his shoulder. He looked at his own hands, hanging empty between his knees. He did not know what to do either.

Serene, Serene, Serene. If he had never come back, he would always have imagined her back at school with Luke, riding, fighting, laughing her rare sweet laugh. He would have believed she was safe.

He had lived all summer in a world where the idea of death was so far away it was laughable, and now he had come back here. He had wanted to.

The next few days were devoted entirely to an elven outreach program. Elliot wrote to every elf he'd ever met in Serene's company, including Serene's mother, and sent a particularly forlorn yet flirtatious letter to Swift.

Then he made Luke write down every elven contact that Luke or any of the Sunborns had.

Once he'd forced Luke to wrack his brains, Elliot was surprised by the array of results. The Sunborns got around.

In some cases literally. Gregory Sunborn had spent years in the elven woods being a celebrated courtesan. He had a list of contacts that stretched to the sea, and after receiving a nicely worded note from one of his favorite young cousins, he promised to leave no stone unturned until they had news of Serene.

Luke dropped Gregory's letter on the pile. "I don't want to talk about it!"

"Great, because we don't have time," said Elliot. "I'm going to dictate another letter to you. Listen up."

They spent a great deal of time in Commander Woodsinger's office, Elliot going through her correspondence while she shouted at them not to go through her correspondence.

Elliot used a retired councilor's room beneath the commander's to write his letters, so he could bother her with greater ease and efficiency. He sat and wrote there, freezing in the stupid stone room with rickety doors leading to a wind trap of a balcony and thus forced to borrow Luke's jacket, and he counted the days by noticing when the sun lit the windows and when he lit the candles.

"Have you noticed that the teachers for the council courses don't get replaced when they retire, while there are more captains who teach us every year?"

"There are a lot more people in the war-training course," Luke said absently, sitting at the other end of the desk and methodically going through letters from various aunts, uncles, and cousins.

"And why do you think that is?"

"I don't know, Elliot, maybe some people in this world actually want to be useful."

"I know, education and diplomacy is so stupid compared to knowing how to stick the sharp end of an object in someone." Elliot scrubbed a hand over his face. "Though I'm not sure I can talk. I don't remember what happened in class today."

"We didn't go," said Luke.

"Ah. That explains that. When we get word back about Serene, I'm going to take a break and be cultured and educated. I'm going to help Myra with her play."

Luke gave Elliot an interrogative look. Elliot rolled his eyes.

"Myra of the Diamond clan," he said. "She's very nice. You have met her many, many times. And she's working behind stage on a production of *Radiant and Jewel*, which is—I've heard, I haven't read it yet—a genre-defining classic tale of elven love and tragedy, possibly the most influential fictional romance of all time. It will be very interesting to see what approach a human production takes to not only the dialogue but the costumes and setting: this is a real opportunity to present a balanced middle ground for both species through art."

"Wait, I'm confused," said Luke. Before Elliot could express how unsurprised he was, Luke went on, deadpan: "There's something you haven't read? How is that possible?"

"Ha ha, shut your loser face," said Elliot, pleased that Luke seemed to be on a more even keel than he had been on the first day.

Luke looked out the window, where the sun was setting and light was brimming against dark hills, like a vast candle burned down almost to the wick. "When we get word back about Serene," he said softly, "I'm going to—"

There were running footsteps outside the door. Elliot's heart turned with the door handle. The door creaked open and Elliot's ex-student Cyril Leigh came tiptoeing in.

"I, uh, brought you the letter as soon as it came," he offered. "I was watching just like you said."

"Thank you." Elliot accepted the letter graciously.

Cyril lingered at the table, doing a small humble tap dance.

"You did say . . .," he said at last.

"Oh, right. Luke, pay the man," commanded Elliot.

"You're unbelievable," said Luke, reaching for his money pouch.

Elliot found this hurtful. He wasn't paid for going to magic school, and his father obviously could not give him pocket money in the Borderlands' legal tender. He found it hurtful that Luke would think he was so unimaginative that he'd promise the kid money.

Cyril held out the one-page newspaper called the *Border Daily,* with Luke's picture emblazoned on the front. Luke recoiled like a vampire faced with a cross.

"Would you sign it?" asked Cyril.

"Sign it," Elliot said.

Luke opened his mouth to either protest or vehemently refuse, but then he was caught in the depths of Cyril's powerful puppy eyes. He sighed heavily, gave Elliot a filthy look, and signed the paper.

"Thank you so much, Luke," said Cyril, blushing and leaving.

At any other time, Elliot would have teased Luke unmercifully and at length, but as soon as Cyril was outside the door he was ripping open the letter. Luke was up and standing behind his chair, reading over his shoulder.

It was Swift who had come through and written with news. Elliot's careful letter had paid off: he had not let himself betray how serious the situation was, only expressed masculine flutterings. Swift, simple soldier that she was, had in her attempts to soothe his delicate feelings let slip several pieces of information about the elves that Elliot was sure the elves didn't want them to know. She had also said several terrible things about Elliot's stained virtue and presumed availability. She had also mentioned that Serene was in the eastern woods, alive and unhurt, and in fact much admired by the gentle elven nurses on the battlefield for her valor.

"She's okay," Elliot burst out, in case Luke hadn't got to that part yet.

"Yeah," said Luke. "And we know where she is. I'm going to find her."

Elliot twisted around in his chair. "No you are not. Because doing so would be an act of war."

Luke spluttered. "Oh, like you haven't stowed away or sneaked along on every single mission—"

"When did I not stow away?" Elliot asked. "Oh right, when there was an actual war."

"Of course not," Luke snapped. "You'd have been killed. But I'm not like you—I can actually help."

"Really?" Elliot asked. "So you go in, and you get killed, and the Border guard come in to avenge you. Then the elves are fighting a war on two fronts. Or Serene tries to help you, and gets executed for treason. Which of those scenarios is actually helpful for Serene, in your mind?"

"I can fight!"

"I know you can fight!" said Elliot. "The point is, they won't let you. It's not fair. There's got to be a long-term solution. I've got twelve books on elven customs in my room that I need to consult on the matter, but right now you and Serene both signed on to be soldiers, and that means you signed on to obey the rules of warfare. If you've decided to quit being a soldier, then I'm more delighted than I can say. Have you?"

Luke looked away, toward the window, where there was almost no light left. His jaw worked for a moment, then he shook his head. "All right. But the second I can go after her, I will go after her."

Elliot sighed. "For now, get used to being useless."

Elliot felt useless, even now when he was limp with relief. It was a horrible anticlimax to have information and not be able to use it, no matter how glad you were to have it. Now that he knew Serene was all right, he had to learn how to live his life in the Border camp without Serene and thus without Luke. He had his plans: getting to know Myra better, doing this play. He was even looking forward to it, but it did feel very strange.

"Well . . .," Elliot said. "See you later."

"Uh, okay," said Luke. "See you later."

Elliot put the plan for his new life into action the moment he entered the lunchroom, and swooped down on the table where Peter, Myra, and various other council trainees were eating. "Hello, Myra. You look very pretty today. Is this seat taken?"

Myra beamed at him. "No, please sit. Where's Luke?"

"I'm sure I don't know," said Elliot. "Can you pinpoint the location of every random classmate we have?"

"Hey," said Luke, and sat down beside Elliot. He got some serious side-eye from the girl sitting on his other side, Carla Summersong, but he didn't seem to notice because he was giving Elliot some side-eye of his own.

Elliot despaired.

"There you are!" said Myra.

Elliot double despaired.

"Guys, I don't mean to be rude, but we're in the middle of talking about our play," said Carla. She turned to Luke and adopted a kindly, patronizing air. "Do you even know what *Radiant and Jewel* is?"

Luke blinked. "A genre-defining classic tale of elven love and tragedy, possibly the most influential fictional romance of all time?"

There was a silence. Elliot was surprised, because he would have thought the sound of every atom in his body exploding with indignation might make some noise.

"Oh, wow." Myra looked impressed. "I had no idea you were a theatre buff, Luke!"

"That's so cool," said Carla. "I wish my boyfriend was interested in the arts."

Another girl, this one from the year below, leaned forward and made a grab for one of Luke's hands. Carla and Myra were already holding onto a forearm each.

"Luke," said the new girl. "Do you think the play is too challenging for us to produce? Be honest. I truly value your input."

"Um, no," said Luke. "I think it'll be . . . interesting to see what approach a human production takes to not only the dialogue but the costumes and setting."

"I so agree," said Carla Summersong.

"I agree more," said the new girl.

"I'm plotting your death," said Elliot.

"Um," Luke said. "If you think about it, this is a real opportunity to present a balanced middle ground for both species through art."

An almost cooing sound broke from three throats. Elliot was stonily outraged. Those were his insights, even if they would not have got the same reception from his mouth. Elliot was helping Luke be irresistible to all women, which was unfair and unnecessary.

"Think of the different ways *Othello* has been produced," Elliot said to Natalie, who was originally from the other side of the Border like him.

When everybody was engrossed in a conversation about the evolution of drama, Luke elbowed Elliot hard and whispered: "Why are we sitting here?"

"I don't know, Luke," Elliot said, very reasonably. "Why are *we* sitting here?"

Luke frowned. "I don't get it."

"That seems true!" Elliot exclaimed, but then Myra appealed to him on a point about set design in the human world, and they could not speak on the matter any further.

Elliot thought about it later, and thought he could understand. Elliot remembered Luke slinking away from parties, and remembered what Rachel Sunborn had called him: my shy boy. He remembered Luke punching him, and talking about what other people did as if he'd never had any friends before he came to the Border camp at all. Elliot still didn't think Luke was shy, but Luke *was* wary of people he did not know well. He'd been raised in a fort with enemies without and impatient soldiers within: he had learned to be no trouble, a pleasure to have around, and to melt away long before anyone wished him gone. Elliot didn't understand it himself, but if Luke needed someone to be obtrusive, Elliot could do that.

So the next day at lunchtime, Elliot grabbed Luke by the elbow when he came in and marched over to where the sporty types sat. "Can we sit here, you guys? Awesome."

"Absolutely," said some idiot with teeth that stuck out. "Over here, Luke."

"Sit down by me and let's talk about those moves in Trigon," said another one, this time with an overbite. Elliot did not have the time to learn the names of all these people with dental problems.

It did, however, seem as if integrating Luke into this merry band would be simple. It was possible Elliot could simply slink away . . .

"Sit with me, Elliot," said Dale Wavechaser, crushing Elliot's dreams. He patted the seat beside him, which Elliot had mentally earmarked for Luke.

Elliot shot a desperate look at Luke, who was being pulled down like an antelope by three annoying lions. "Okay," he said darkly. "Why not?"

Dale beamed and Elliot sat down. Dale put a hand on his back. "Are you doing all right?"

"Ahahaha," said Elliot, squirming away. "Never better, buddy."

"I'm glad you're both here. I saw you guys at the drama kids' table yesterday," Dale said, looking honestly concerned. "You can come sit with us anytime, you know."

"Gosh," said Elliot. "What an honor."

"Oh, don't even worry about it," said Dale. "You're welcome."

This immunity toward sarcasm must mean Dale had such a peaceful life. It also meant he and Elliot were basically speaking different languages.

"I mean, theatre, boring, am I right?" asked Dale. "It's just a bunch of pretending stuff."

"You're so right, Dale," Elliot told him nobly, for Luke's sake. "I mean, the history of art, basically a lot of idiots wasting their time."

"And that dwarf girl sits there."

"I like her," Elliot bit out, stabbing Dale with the twin icicles that his eyes had become.

"Oh no, I'm sure she's nice," Dale said hastily. "Sorry, that was—I didn't mean to offend you. Hey, so you missed most of the Trigon game the other day, didn't you?"

"I was thus tragically deprived," Elliot said flatly. "Yes."

Dale began to outline the events of the game.

What a nice person, Elliot thought. What a wonderful chat he and Luke could be having about their mutual love for physical exhaustion and hatred for culture. Also he was really handsome, the curling ends of his hair turned to summer gold. Elliot was so bored he wished harpies would attack.

Elliot was accustomed to being a gleefully abrasive and unpleasant personality, and he did not feel temperamentally suited to extended periods of tedium. He was used to telling people they were unintelligent and leaving at speed.

But he couldn't do that to Dale. It wasn't just Dale and Luke's destined future. Dale had given Elliot his only birthday present: Elliot didn't forget that. Elliot would rather hurt himself than Dale, if it came down to it.

Luke was on the other end of the table, looking twitchy and attempting to rise despite several hands on each of his shoulders. Luke too clearly wished he was the one speaking to Dale. Everything was terrible.

If Elliot said he had to go to the bathroom, he would be expected back. He set his mind to the problem of finding a good excuse to leave the table for the entirety of lunchtime.

"It actually reminded me of classic games such as the one played by Eleanor Sunborn eleven years ago," said Dale. "Do you know that one? Never mind. Let me tell you about it."

"How fascinating, please go on," Elliot encouraged Dale gently, and stabbed himself in the arm with a butter knife. "Whoops, butter fingers. Butter knife . . . fingers."

Dale and Elliot watched with incredulous dismay as the gash on Elliot's arm widened and a lazy trickle of blood became a rushing river.

"As you can see, Dale, and desolate though I am to say it because our conversation was riveting, I have to go see a medic."

"Will I come with you?" asked Dale.

"No," said Elliot firmly. "No, you should stay and enjoy your lunch. If your Trigon prowess suffered because of a lack of proper nutrition, how could I live with myself?"

Whoosh! went the bluebird of sarcasm, zooming miles above Dale's head.

"Oh," he said. "Okay."

"What did you do to him?" Luke asked, looming over them and eyeing the blood, which was now all over Elliot's arm and the table, in horror.

The sporty types with dental problems were in a routed heap at the other end of the table. They were also staring at the blood.

"I did it to myself!"

"What did you let him do to himself?"

"It's not his fault," Elliot snapped. "Why would he assume that I couldn't feed myself without incurring injuries? Which by the way, ignoring current evidence, I obviously can. I've been doing it for years. It was a simple accident. A slip of the knife. It could've happened to anyone."

Luke yanked him up off the bench by the back of his collar. "Come on, we're going to the medic."

"That's a really good plan, Luke," Elliot said. "I commend you for it. However, if I might suggest one teensy, eensy adjustment? I could go, and you—since you're not injured—could stay!"

Luke continued dragging. "Yeah, I'm really looking forward to Serene coming back asking me why she hasn't found you in one piece the way she left you."

If Serene was so concerned about his well-being, she could have not dumped him with a dull thud.

It wasn't fair, so Elliot didn't say it. He let Luke drag him to the infirmary tent, where at least his day was brightened by being whisked away and tended to by the cruelest medic of them all.

"I'm having a crisis," Elliot told her.

"A crisis where you forget how to use your eating utensils? I noticed," she said, bandaging with efficiency and no effort to spare him pain.

"Do you know, at lunch there's one table for kids who like drama, and one table for kids who like sports?"

"Amazing, it's like you're going to a school."

"But this is a school in a magical land!" Elliot protested.

"People are awful everywhere," she told him. "Not just kids. Everyone. They tell you people outgrow it, but they don't. Everywhere you go, you see dynamics just like the petty gangs of youth. Which isn't to say that school is not a very special hell, as people haven't yet learned to hide how awful they are."

"I don't have a special table," Elliot protested.

"Uh, you, the murderous, man-hating elf girl, and the intense gay kid?" asked the medic. "You're the weirdo table."

The infirmary tent was hushed for a moment, with nothing but the sound of the medic humming to herself and clinking through her instruments, as Elliot worked through this awful opinion.

"Well, I just don't think that's true."

"You're the intense weirdo table. I don't care what you think is true."

Elliot gazed at her with admiration. "Will you tell me your name?" he asked. "Can I eat my lunch in here with you from now on?"

"Get out of here. I don't want to spend time with you."

Elliot wandered out of the tent feeling vaguely more cheerful.

"Did you do any serious damage to yourself, you idiot?" asked Luke, falling in step with him.

"No," said Elliot. "But apparently it was a nasty cut. I admit I might have stabbed myself harder than I intended."

"You what?"

"Nothing," said Elliot. "I misspoke. I certainly did not intend to stab myself. Who would intend that? I'm not crazy."

"Debatable," said Luke.

Elliot's shoulders sagged. His arm was throbbing. "I just want to sit somewhere and read, please."

"Well," said Luke, and frowned. Elliot believed that Luke was allergic to the library. "I could use some javelin practice."

"Okay," said Elliot, all the fight stabbed out of him. He brought a book and sat on the sidelines.

"You're not *watching*," Luke said crabbily later.

"You're not wrong!" Elliot called back. Luke was doing fine.

The next day Elliot, in no mood to stab himself, just went to the intense weirdos table and sat down in a state of gloomy surrender to the inevitable.

"Well, thank God you've stopped being so weird," said Luke, sitting down across the table from him.

"What you just said is very ironic, but you don't know it," Elliot observed. "But then there's so much you do not know, loser. About irony, obviously. Also about literature and art and drama. Also about computers and music."

"I know about computers," Luke claimed, which was such a lie that Elliot stared at him openmouthed.

"Really, Sunborn? No, really. All right then. Tell me about computers."

"Well . . ." Luke said, and looked shifty about the eyes. "They're boxes . . . but you can write things in them. And read things in them. And there are cats in them who are funny for some reason. They're like—boxes of infinity. And! You keep the wikipedia in them!"

"Elliot," Myra said from behind him. "Can I talk to you?"

"Absolutely, and I'm glad you asked. Come to me for any reason whatsoever," said Elliot, but before he twisted around he pointed at Luke. "And you, hold that thought, because it might be my favorite thing you have ever said. It might be my favorite thing anybody has ever said."

He jumped off the bench and looked down at Myra, who seemed upset. He wondered if Peter had done something, and wondered exactly how one went about defending one's soon-to-be lady.

"Everything all right?" he asked. "Tell me what I can do to help you."

"Are you sure you still want to help with the play?" Myra asked. "Because if you are, we could use you right now. Adara Cornripe is having a diva moment."

"You can rely on me immediately," Elliot assured her. "Except give me a minute. I'll meet you in the hall."

"Right," said Myra, looking relieved but still under pressure. She turned and fled.

This was a perfect opportunity to win her heart that should not be missed, and an opportunity to keep himself busy and not thinking about Serene. Elliot rapped on the table to get Luke's attention. Luke eyed him, unimpressed.

"Gotta go see about this play. Myra needs help and I can't abandon her."

"Ugh, okay," said Luke, and got up.

"So I'm going to go . . .," Elliot said, as Elliot went and Luke went with him, "to the hall. Where they're putting on a dramatic production."

Luke sighed as if incredibly put-upon. "I wish you weren't making me do this."

"I don't know how you think I'm making you do this, Luke. Do you think I'm an evil wizard?"

"Uh," said Luke. "Obviously not. Wizards are not real."

"Good," Elliot told him. "I don't like wizard stories all that much. Stories about witches are better, because witches are morally ambiguous and traditionally disempowered. And of course my very favorite is—"

"I swear, if I hear one more word about mermaids," said Luke as they walked into the room and heard Adara Cornripe shouting.

"I will break all the props over your head and then beat you to death with the shards! I've waited to play this role since I was a little girl, and now everything is ruined. Tell me, what is my motivation . . . to not kill you?"

The hall where Elliot had once served General Lakelost doctored drinks looked very different from how he remembered it. Someone had removed the table and chairs, and a small stage was in one corner of the room. A sheet was pinned up over the stage, and wooden buckets of paint were lined up like hopeful petitioners beneath the sheet. There were also a huddled group of people, including Captain Whiteleaf, listening to Adara. She had her hands on her hips and murder in her eyes.

"Maybe I could step in and play—" began the captain tremulously.

Adara snorted, which sounded like a horse shooting a bullet out of its nostril. "Can you really see yourself as Jewel? No, wait! You've decided to turn this piece into a comedy." Her eyes narrowed so much they almost slammed shut. "Well, I'm not laughing!"

It was hard to note anyone besides the pillar of flame that had been Adara, but Elliot saw Myra with her arms curled around herself, looking ready to stop, drop, and roll.

He wanted to be her hero, so he stepped forward.

"Nobody's laughing, Adara," he said soothingly. Adara's head snapped around to face him. Elliot lifted his hands in a gesture of peace. "Just here to help, you dazzling apricot of artistry, you. Excited to help out, build sets, see you perform. Can I fetch you a glass of water?"

Adara did not immediately bite his head off and spit it out of the window, which Elliot counted as a win until he noticed that Adara was not looking at him, but over Elliot's shoulder. Elliot glanced behind him, and saw Luke had stepped back and hit the door he'd just come through.

"Jewel," Adara breathed.

"Can I have a word with you, Elliot?" Luke asked between his teeth. "I have a strong feeling that I should be somewhere else."

Elliot leaned back against the door as well. "No. Nope, I think I want to stay and see this one play out."

Luke stared into space. "Awesome."

"So here's the issue," said Adara briskly. "Mr Fleetwood—"

"Was his first name Mac?" asked Elliot.

"No, why would you ask that?" Adara snapped.

"No reason," Elliot told her, disappointed. "Continue."

"Mr Fleetwood retired last year," Adara resumed, "and there was no teacher on the council course willing to replace him. Several students have quit since then, and the best male performers graduated last year and have not been replaced. The drama group has always been primarily female. It's something the very few women in the camp can do together! It's why we put on elven plays, because that means that there are more women with bigger and better parts. But it's also why the boys don't want to join! And this idiot isn't any good at recruiting, due to having the charisma of a rotten leaf."

Captain Whiteleaf looked deeply wounded.

"We need men," Adara continued. Elliot figured there was never a bad time to hear things like that from a beautiful blonde. "Specifically, we need someone to play Jewel-in-the-Crown-of-Beauty, our protagonist's love interest and the most beautiful and virtuous elf in the four forests. Luke, you saved the whole production by coming here. You would obviously be perfect, and you are cast. And you! You're a boy, sort of," Adara went on.

"Oh, thanks," said Elliot.

"More of one than Captain Whiteleaf, anyway."

"Oh, thanks!" Captain Whiteleaf exclaimed indignantly.

Adara's indifference was supreme. "Someone throw Schafer a script. Does anyone think that he could play Red Rose?"

Elliot stared.

"Red-Rose-Blooming-in-a-Dark-Garden," Myra put in helpfully. "He's often played by a red-haired actor, though some people argue that the name symbolizes the carnal sin and temptation he represents in his place as a minor agent on the side of evil."

"Sorry, what?" asked Elliot. "Are you telling me that Luke is cast as the maiden fair and I am the bit-part evil floozy?"

There was a pause. Myra was cute, but there were some things Elliot could not put up with.

"How dare you," Elliot exclaimed. "Come on, loser, we're leaving."

"Thank you, Elliot," Luke said devoutly. "I do not want to be here."

"Red Rose actually has a very interesting backstory!" Myra burst out, jumping to her feet and shoving her handwritten script in Elliot's direction. "He was in love with our hero, the valiant knight Radiant-Blade-Washed-With-Blood. That's Adara. They went to school together, but Red Rose is embittered his beauty is fading with the years, and Radiant's heart has been stolen by Jewel's loveliness and purity, so Red Rose turns to evil!"

Myra gazed beseechingly at Elliot. Elliot flipped through the pages.

"Uh, why is Radiant described as a young woman in the prime of her youth and strength while Red Rose's beauty is fading with his years? Since they went to school together, aren't they the same age?"

"Eeesh," said Myra, making a dismayed face. "Good point."

"Cry me a river of blood tears, you ginger whiner!" Adara exclaimed. "This is a play that will involve a mostly human cast and be played in front of a mostly human audience, and this is not how humans see men and women! It might be good for them to think about how our situation gets flipped around by the elves. I'm not going to have my play ruined by someone who finds it too traumatic to even pretend to walk in someone else's shoes."

"Good point," said Elliot. "You seem really into this play. Why don't you sit around at the table with most of these fine students discussing the dramatic arts? Not cool enough for you?"

Adara sniffed. "I hardly need to have my habits at the lunch table criticized by someone who fell on his butter knife yesterday!"

Elliot felt he'd won that round since Adara had descended from the philosophical to the personal so rapidly. Adara seemed to feel differently. They glared at each other. Elliot thought she was going to be terrific in the role.

"I think you two would play off each other well," said Myra hopefully. "And obviously, Luke looks just right to play Jewel."

Luke looked like a man in a nightmare.

"Elliot's not hot enough to play Red Rose," Adara sneered.

"Excuse you, I am a tornado of recently matured sexuality," Elliot told her. He flipped through more pages. "Oh, Red Rose gets two dance numbers and a song!"

"Elliot," Luke hissed. "I thought we were leaving. I was happy to be leaving!"

"I'm reconsidering," said Elliot. He flipped a few more pages.

"I thought we were meant to help Myra with the props and scene painting," Luke said more loudly. "I don't want to leave her doing all the work."

Myra looked touched.

"Fabulous," said Adara. "You'll play Jewel and Red Rose, and help with the sets. Thanks for volunteering, Luke. I wish I could help, but my part is very taxing and requires all my concentration."

"Wow, I can't believe you volunteered us for double duty," Elliot remarked disapprovingly. "Thanks for nothing, loser."

Luke looked torn between weeping and punching Elliot. Elliot understood that this was an eternal struggle.

And that was how they got cast in the school play.

Dinner was a less important meal than lunch in the camp, usually eaten around the fires. The war-training and council-training courses had separate fires and tended to keep to their own.

Elliot left his fire that night and went to find Luke, who was surveying a cut of meat as if he would never have any appetite again due to being in a play.

"Hi, I need something," he said.

"Will something be another living nightmare?"

"It's a tiny thing!"

"Is it a tiny living nightmare?"

"I simply need you to put your name down for one of the practice rooms so I can learn these dance routines."

Luke frowned. "You can put down your own name."

"Yeah, totally!" said Elliot. "Except no, not at all. People in war training will scratch off my name."

"Nobody would do that!"

"They have been doing it for literally years," said Elliot. "Also, they come and beat people up if they don't take the hint about the name-scratching."

Luke looked upset. "Why didn't you tell me about this?"

"I thought you knew," said Elliot. "Everybody knows. Um. Sorry. So will you put down your name? If you do, I'll come to your Trigon practices. I swear I will."

"Sure," said Luke. "Of course. I'll come to the practice rooms too. You're not getting beaten up. Nobody's getting beaten up again."

Elliot raised his eyebrows. "That's excellent news. Wait, since this is a moral stand you're taking—and you would take it anyway on account of your principles—I don't actually have to go to the Trigon practices, right?"

Luke shook his head and did not look sorry. "You do," he said. "You said you would, and now you have to."

"Ugh, fine," said Elliot.

He turned away while Luke turned to the ring of war-training students, like a ring of crows in their black leather and picking over their meat. Luke raised his voice so Elliot could still hear it over the crackle of fire and of meat on the spit.

"All right, guys," said Luke. "Listen up."

~

Luke's name written on the board was not scratched out. A tall black-haired boy in the year above them did see Elliot come in one day, and followed him in, but he found Luke already sitting on the benches on one end of the room, reading a book on elven customs.

"Problem?" Luke asked with deceptive softness.

The boy started. "No! No, but great to see you, Sunborn. I just remembered that I have to go back to my cabin and get something—"

"Was it your self-respect?" Elliot asked.

"I hope we can catch up sometime soon!"

"You'd better hope we don't," said Luke. The boy just ran.

Since Luke had come through so resoundingly in the name of truth and justice, Elliot actually did feel obliged to go to Trigon practice. It was even more shameful than going to the actual games: the stands were almost empty. It looked as if Elliot had a real interest in Trigon.

Even if Luke had not insisted, though, Elliot did not know if he could actually have forsaken him. Serene had always come to Luke's Trigon practises. Elliot knew how much Luke missed her, as much as Elliot did himself. He felt like going to Luke's practises was something he could do for Serene, when he was so desperately worried about her and there was nothing real he could do to help her.

It was not only for Serene. He hated the idea of Luke looking up into the stands and seeing nobody there for him at all.

"Hey, Schafer, good to see you," said Dale, making his way down to the pitch. "Came to see the new swing I was talking about at lunch?"

"I definitely remember that part of our excellent conversation very clearly," Elliot said. "And that is absolutely why I am here."

He sidled over to Carla Summersong, glad to recognize someone with a functioning brain. "Here we are, isn't it terrible?"

"I know, Trigon, so dull."

"I think I love you," Elliot said. "Don't leave me, but why are you here?"

"My boyfriend's on the team," said Carla, giving every indication of pride.

She waved, and the guy with the sticking-out teeth who'd cornered Luke at the sporty table waved back at her, beaming.

"That's your boyfriend?" Elliot asked. "And this is a voluntary situation for you?"

"What?" said Carla.

"Personally, I am here under protest as part of a dark bargain."

"Okay," said Carla, and her accepting attitude made Elliot realize that the cruel medic was right and everyone totally did think he was weird. "Well, Sam likes me to be here to support him. Besides, my man looks great in the uniform."

Elliot left her to her delusions. It seemed kinder. "Elbow me when it's all over," he said, taking out his book.

"But if you're reading your book, how will you see the game?"

Elliot favored her with a smile for her swiftness on the uptake. "Exactly."

He did look up occasionally. Luke appeared to be better than everyone else, as usual, so Elliot felt it was foolish and unnecessary to practice at all, and yet here they were. Elliot was being wronged by the universe.

Elliot felt a great deal more wronged by the universe when Dale Wavechaser intercepted one of Elliot's occasional glances from his book. He waved.

"Hey, Schafer!" he said. "Check this out!"

He threw the large glass ball in a fast, curving arc. Even to Elliot, it looked impressive.

Even to Elliot, it was obvious nobody else was expecting Dale to throw. People were taking a time out, talking amongst themselves. Richard Plantgrown, who was meant to catch, turned and gestured helplessly as the ball sailed far out of his reach. The Trigon ball hurtled through the air—suddenly Elliot remembered how heavy it had weighed in his hands—and connected solidly with the back of Luke's head.

Luke went down, face forward in the dug-out earth.

"Call for a medic," said Elliot, dropping his book. "Now!"

Carla Summersong had hysterics because of the blood. Dale had hysterics because of the guilt. Elliot had hysterics because of the rage. They, Sam who was holding onto Carla, and Richard were put in the cabin by the infirmary and told they would be informed when there was news. It was more of a corralling than anything else.

They all sat at different points of the room.

"I'm really sorry," said Dale.

"Don't speak to me," Elliot said coldly. "You raving imbecile."

"Do you think he'll be okay?"

"Oh, yeah, no doubt, since he got a giant glass bowling ball to the head!" Elliot snapped. "Try not to be more stupid than you can help."

"There was too much blood," Carla murmured, with her head in Sam of the Sticking-Out Teeth's lap.

"I know, baby, I know," Sam murmured back, and glared at Dale, who looked as if he was going to cry. "How could you be so careless!" he hissed. "She's from council training! They're very sensitive and delicate!"

"If you gave Luke brain damage, I am going to ruin your life," Elliot announced.

Richard shot him an unfriendly look. "Schafer's in council training. He's not exactly a tender little flower."

"Schafer is crazy!" Sam exclaimed. "Everybody knows Schafer is crazy!"

"You haven't seen anything yet," Elliot promised.

Luke had told Elliot in so many words that he was protecting Elliot, so Elliot would be safe when Serene returned. But who had looked after Luke? Nobody had. What was Elliot supposed to do when Serene came back? What was he supposed to do anyway?

Elliot rubbed a hand over his eyes, and continued staring out the window instead of at Dale Wavechaser's idiot face.

The door opened, and all of them jumped. The mean medic stood in the doorway.

"Well?" Elliot snapped.

"My job would be easier if people would let me get the words out instead of yelling at me," she observed. "He's fine. He just has a concussion from your dangerously stupid rough-housing."

The world lost its tunnel-vision focus, and Elliot remembered he was meant to be nice to Dale.

"It was nobody's fault!" he announced. "Just one of those accidents that could happen to anyone." Dale looked extremely surprised but extremely pleased. "Can we see him?" Elliot pursued, and made a gesture to Dale that might have been reminiscent of a mad scientist displaying his latest experiment. "This is Dale Wavechaser. If you mention his name, Luke will want us to come in."

"Nope," said the medic. "He's asking for Elliot. That's you, right?"

"Right," said Elliot doubtfully. "But are you sure you should be listening to someone with head trauma? A large object hit him right in the noggin. I don't mean to tell you your job, but he's probably deeply confused."

"Are you coming or not?"

"Oh my God, go!" said Dale. "Tell him I'm really sorry! Really sorry! Tell him you're not mad at me! Put in a good word for me! I'm so sorry!"

It appeared Elliot had no choice. He trailed disconsolately out of the cabin after the medic. It wasn't that he didn't want to see Luke, but Elliot had some serious doubts about his ability as a ministering angel.

"Could Dale not come too? Luke is, like, totally in love with him. I am sure he would want to see Dale."

"Terrific idea," said the medic. "I can see you know a lot about head wounds. Lots of company is ideal. Let's bring in the whole class."

Elliot appreciated her dark sarcasm but was still left desolate. "Dale has a very soothing personality."

"Are you sure you're not the one in love with Dale Wavechaser?"

"Let me tell you, you wouldn't be asking me that if you saw his test scores," said Elliot. "They are obscenely dreadful. But, you know, okay, the thing is—"

He didn't quite know how to say, I have the opposite of a soothing personality and only ever upset Luke and I should probably be kept away from everybody and put in the cruel-repartee dungeon.

The medic who did not care about anything did not care about his problems. She shoved Elliot inside the tent and departed, Elliot thought maybe to kill everyone left in the waiting cabin.

The day was drawing down to evening, but there was only a single candle guttering in a little bronze cup, lending the tent a flickering glow so as not to hurt Luke further. Luke was lying on a white pillow, looking dazed and helpless: his eyes unfocused and half open, trying and failing to prop himself up on one elbow. It was horrible to realize that Elliot had almost bought into the myth of the untouchable

Luke Sunborn, found himself thinking about Luke the way everyone else did.

"Elliot?" Luke asked thickly.

"Shhh," said Elliot, because it seemed like the right thing to say. He wasn't sure it was: nobody had ever been there when he was sick. He hadn't been taught what to do.

He poured Luke a glass of water and carried it carefully over to him, helping him sit up and putting the glass to his lips.

Luke drank the water obediently, then laid his head against Elliot's shoulder with a little sigh. "Don't be mean to me, okay?" he whispered.

"No," Elliot promised. "I won't be mean."

After that evening, Elliot kept reminding himself that Serene wasn't there to watch out for Luke. He reminded himself of all the reasons he'd been willing to go to the awful sporty table and all the reasons Luke had not wanted to be there. Luke did not like crowds of people, did not like new people, and did not trust anyone easily, even if everyone seemed to like and trust him on sight. Luke always tried to be good to people, and someone had to be good to him in return. There was nobody else: Elliot would have to do. Just until Serene got back.

The next morning, Elliot finally got a letter from Serene herself. He nobly did not read it, but carried it to the infirmary and Luke so they could read it together. Apparently Serene had been severely reprimanded, and also robbed of many privileges including writing implements, due to what her commander had described as "berserker frenzies." Serene seemed rather proud about the whole thing.

They had a lot of things to do behind the scenes for the play. Myra turned out to be a harsh taskmistress. They had to paint all the scenery, help with the costumes, and build a balcony for the big romantic scene between Radiant and Jewel.

Luckily, Luke seemed to quite like painting scenery. This meant that Elliot was not abandoning Luke, nor forcing him to do anything that made him actively miserable. It also meant that Elliot could spend lots of time with Myra and earn her eternal gratitude. Two birds, one stone, thrown by a strategic genius who had no interest in throwing actual stones or harming actual birds.

When one of them was high up on the ladder painting, someone else on the ground had a rope tied to the paint bucket and their wrist so they could catch it and the person on the ladder could catch themselves. They had to implement this policy because of the time Myra was on top of the ladder and wobbled, tried to catch the paint and ended up falling right off.

Luke had caught her. Elliot had caught the bucket of paint with his face.

"You cannot be mad about that forever," said Luke, painting the starry night of the balcony scene.

"It's funny you should say that because being mad about it forever is my exact plan," Elliot told him, and carefully painted the front clump of Luke's fair hair dark blue. Luke ducked his head and grinned.

He had been extremely grateful that Luke was there to catch his lady love, because Elliot definitely could not have done it. He was, however, still going to punish everyone for the cruelty of the universe in directing the bucket of paint at him.

He had been painting odd bits of Luke and Myra for days. It was possible that was why Myra had gone up to the top of the ladder again. She looked down at them laughing, though, so Elliot didn't think she minded. She was very fetching with scarlet paint streaked down one side of her face.

"Terrific," said Adara, coming in to inspect their handiwork. Her tone, as always, was deeply sarcastic. It was one of the things Elliot liked best about her.

"Oh no, we need more blue paint, I'll get it," said Luke, and bolted.

Adara looked vexed. "The sets aren't done and you're all wasting paint. Getting in character already, Elliot?"

She referred to scandalous elven men who were no better than they should be and used cosmetics to adorn the contours of their chests.

"Is that a request for me to take my shirt off?"

"It's a request for you not to mess things up. Do you think you'll be able to pull off the dance between Radiant and Red Rose in the ball scene?" Adara asked.

Elliot grinned at her, charmed, and put down his bucket of paint. The rope was still tied to his wrist, but he had plenty of room to maneuver. He glanced up at Myra, who gave him a thumbs up. "Let's see."

The ball scene was when Radiant suspected Red Rose of turning to the side of evil, but was not sure, and Red Rose tried to seduce her—to get information or because Red Rose wanted to seduce her. Elliot thought it was both. He had made extensive notes and had many opinions about Red Rose by now: the way the world had told him he was useless until he seized on being evil as the only possible purpose, the charm and strangeness of Red Rose, which had once attracted and now repelled Radiant, and how the unfairness of that, of being first loved then hated simply for being himself, enraged Red Rose so completely.

Adara bowed and held out her hand, with Radiant's wary chivalry: Red Rose sank to the floor, eyes sparkling up at her from the direction of Radiant's ornate belt buckle.

"It's been a long time," said Radiant, and helped Red Rose rise. They began to move across the floor, Radiant leading but Red Rose making moves that he should not have.

"Have you missed me?" Red Rose asked, laughing softly.

There was a set of boxes to represent the table and chair that Radiant and Red Rose danced across: Adara had not proved able to catch Elliot when he leaped from the table, so instead they leaped together: neither of them could stumble or both would fall. The world whirled by and narrowed to the press of their bodies and the clasp of their hands.

"How would you desire to be missed?"

"I would desire to be missed like the remembered and desperately sought fragrance of a strange flower that grew in your garden: missed like a riot of color gone from your eyes, missed like the sweetest of feasts lost from your lips, missed like a carpet of the richest and most gorgeous silks, which you long and long to lay down on the floor once again."

"You desire too much," said Radiant. "But you always did."

"As a flower drinks the sun, as the earth drinks rain, I know that you will come, come taste me again," whispered Elliot, and he kissed Adara, his fingers in her hair, her arms going around him.

"No," Luke's voice said. "Nope. No. No. What's happening and why is it happening?"

Adara pulled away. "It's part of the play," she said with a saucy wink. "I can't wait for our kiss scene."

Luke said his new favorite word again. "No. No way. I'm going to see Commander Woodsinger."

"What? Why?" Adara demanded, but Luke was already gone.

Elliot picked up the bucket of paint because he didn't have time to untie the rope from his wrist, and followed.

"Elliot, where are you going with the paint?" Myra asked, sounding distraught, and came after him grabbing at the bucket.

Adara went with them, so Luke arrived at the commander's office and walked in without knocking but with an entourage. Commander Woodsinger looked startled by this entrance.

"I have a complaint," said Luke, throwing himself down in the chair across from the commander's desk.

Elliot and Adara hovered by the chair, not wanting to sit and not wanting to miss anything. Myra confiscated the bucket of paint and carried it to the back of the room, out of range.

"If this is about Serene-Heart-in-the-Chaos-of-Battle again—"

"No," said Luke, flinching. "No, I understand that . . . I have to do my duty." He began to look embarrassed. "It's nothing serious like that. But I'm in Captain Whiteleaf's play."

"My condolences," said Commander Woodsinger.

"There's meant to be kissing," said Luke. The commander dropped her quill with a haunted look. "I don't want to do it."

Adara flushed dull red. "Well, you have to!" she snapped. "It's in the script."

"I won't," said Luke.

Commander Woodsinger looked as if light had broken in on her, shining with the promise of rescue. "This is, I think, a matter to be taken up with Captain Whiteleaf!"

"I can't; she tells him what to do," said Luke. "But I won't. I don't want to let anybody down, but you have to tell the captain I won't."

"I refuse to give the captain any orders about kissing," Commander Woodsinger said with dignity.

Myra clutched her bucket of paint. "Well, the commander has spoken. We'd better go and sort this out amongst ourselves!"

This was not Luke's usual unhappiness about the play.

"Hang on a minute," said Elliot. "Luke doesn't have to do it if he doesn't want to. Nobody has to kiss anybody they don't want to. Plays are supposed to be about fun and enlightening the masses, not forcing people into distasteful acts."

Adara made an explosive noise of outrage. Elliot raised his eyebrows at her and grinned.

"That's true," said Myra reluctantly. "I wouldn't want to kiss someone only for a play."

Luke looked with gratitude at Myra. Commander Woodsinger gazed at her with a clear sense of betrayal.

Elliot swept on. "So you're going to have to talk with Captain Whiteleaf about stage kisses. If they hold their heads at the right angle, it'll look like they're kissing when they're not. You just have to make it clear that's the way it has to be."

"If you leave my office immediately," said the commander, "I will do so."

Adara looked as if she wanted to weep with mortification. "It's in the script! Why didn't you people read the script all the way through?"

"I read the script. And I have no problem with kissing Adara, obviously, she's gorgeous," said Elliot, and then realized what he'd said in front of the girl he was trying to court. "I mean, she could look like a severed thumb and I'd still do it. For my art. I'm an artiste."

Adara tossed her long golden hair over one shoulder. "Well, I don't want to kiss *you*."

"Okay then, you shouldn't," Elliot agreed. "Nobody's kissing anybody. Is everyone happy now?"

Adara did not look happy. Myra looked embarrassed to be there. Commander Woodsinger looked like she wanted to brain him with her paperweight. A certain amount of tension had slid out of Luke's shoulders, though, so Elliot was calling it a win.

"Please leave," said the commander. "If the impulse to come into my office and chatter exclusively about kissing ever comes over any of you again, I urge you to crush that impulse. I will expel you for wasting my time."

Commander Woodsinger was as good as her word, and the play continued smoothly and took up most of their time, and the rest of the time Elliot tried to remember to look out for Luke, not to be mean. He'd promised.

Since he went to Trigon practice, he made Luke go with him one day when the bookstalls were set up outside school. Elliot had a great many credits for academic prowess that could only be redeemed for books. Elliot got a little over-excited, lost Luke and found himself in a literary avalanche before he realized that he was completely hidden from view, and Luke must be wondering where he was. He picked up his booty and emerged.

"Looking for your friend?" he heard the nice bookstall lady ask.

"He's not my friend," Luke's voice answered. "But my friend would want me to watch out for him."

"Hey, loser," said Elliot, coming up to him with his pile of books and a blithe air. "Sorry for keeping you waiting."

"That's all right," said Luke indulgently. "Do you want to go to the last bookstall?"

Don't be mean, Elliot told himself.

"No," Elliot said. "I'm all done."

The kissing matter was not the only complication offered by the play. Nobody liked their costumes.

"No," Luke said, waving the flouncy white shirt as if it were the head of his enemy. "No way. Add buttons."

"How many buttons?" asked Myra.

"How many have you got?"

Luke sat down disconsolately on the edge of the stage, to stare into the distance and dream of buttons. Adara sat down beside him and began to speak of her vision for their love scene. She put a hand on his knee.

Elliot looked at them from behind his curtain. "Would either of you help me with my trousers?"

"No!" snapped Luke, going pink around the ears.

"In your dreams," said Adara, tossing a scornful look over her shoulder. He leaned out from behind the curtain slightly in order to wink at her.

"Maybe. You can never tell what weird things will happen in dreams." He raised his voice. Everything was playing into his hands. He was a genius. "Myra! I need help with my costume, and the mean blonds are bullying me!"

Myra came bustling over, her mouth full of pins, and slid into the changing space behind the curtain with him.

"Luke's not mean."

Elliot smiled down at her adorable naiveté even while she helped him do up his trousers. "Luke's got everyone fooled."

"He's not the only one," said Myra, and gestured at Elliot, who thought this appreciation for his manly charms was a very good sign. "Do you want me to get the paints?"

"Wait, are we actually painting my chest?" Elliot squawked.

He squawked incautiously loud, and Adara and Luke, united for once, burst out laughing. Elliot put his hand outside the curtain to make an obscene gesture.

He studied Myra, whose face was crestfallen. "As long as you're the one doing the painting," he said to her in a low voice, and he thought for a thrilled moment that she blushed.

Later Elliot went out to inspect her handiwork in a mirror and found Adara, whose costume was a more practical version of Luke's, tying up her flouncy shirt to bare her midriff. Elliot glanced at her, appreciative, and Adara was in a good enough mood to catch his eye and wink.

"I'm sure Adara is a very nice person underneath it all and she means well and everything, but I have a few problems with her," said Luke later, when everyone was back in their normal clothes and looking thankful about it. "The first problem is that I don't like her."

"Oh, I don't know. Historically, I have not been opposed to mean blonds," said Elliot.

"Um, mean people are awful?" Luke pointed out.

Elliot rolled his eyes: if Luke was going to be ungrateful whenever Elliot expressed affection, he wasn't going to bother.

The camp was alive with rumors of the Border guard mobilizing to enter elven territory without permission. Elliot knew Luke wanted to go: knew that nobody would listen to Elliot's objections, that they might even think he did not care about Serene. Nothing was decided yet. Elliot was throwing himself into the play and trying not to think about it until the night of the play had passed.

But then the night of the play came, and Elliot saw Luke's parents and Louise in the audience. He was certain that they could not all have come for their posts to watch Luke: he was sure the Sunborns had been summoned.

Elliot did not allow Red Rose to falter. He continued plotting with Radiant's evil stepsister.

The play was received very well. Adara was absolutely magnificent. Luke had hostage eyes throughout and might as well have been carrying a sign that said THIS IS ALL STUPID PRETEND! HELP ME! but he looked the part. Each new scene backdrop got applause, with Myra glowing in the wings. Elliot even thought people liked him.

It was going wonderfully, until the penultimate scene where Red Rose's treachery was exposed and Jewel and Radiant shared their first kiss. When Luke muttered "Radiant, Radiant, wherefore art thou Radiant?" Adara actually kissed Luke on his startled mouth.

Red Rose was meant to turn bitterly on Jewel: Elliot yanked Luke away.

"Lovely child, you think the world is so bright," said Red Rose: they were the only words he ever spoke to Jewel in the play, as if men didn't talk to each other. "You have not learned yet that the light of the world is men burning. The years will pass and you will know what it is to be consumed."

Jewel was meant to look annoyed by Red Rose's spite, and it was the one thing that Luke had ever managed to do believably. Now he couldn't even do that. He looked upset.

Elliot turned, and Red Rose gave Radiant a parting kiss: Elliot made viciously certain that it was a real kiss too.

Red Rose was never seen again in the play, fading out as if his character arc was not as important as any other character's, as if his purpose was more about being alluring than anything else. Elliot had decided to at least make his exit meaningful, so as soon as he had kissed Adara he leaped from the stage and into the audience.

The audience started applauding. Elliot made his way over to the Sunborns, where Rachel was patting the seat behind her and Luke's father was shaking his head slowly and sadly over the whole business.

"Move up one, rearrange yourselves, I want to sit next to Little Red," said Louise, and Rachel and Michael shifted with good-natured grumbles.

Louise sat next to him and kissed him smackingly on the cheek. "You were very sexy," she told him. "Well done. Luke looks like he wants to die, and it is hilarious!"

Elliot cackled with her. After the play was done, a surprising amount of people came over to Elliot and told him he'd been good, though none as memorably as Louise.

Best of all, Elliot seized a moment to ask Myra to meet him on the balcony outside Mr Fleetwood's office. Tonight was the perfect time to ask her to be his girlfriend.

Tonight was the night Elliot would die. It was absolutely freezing on the balcony. He should have stopped to find a shirt, but it had seemed such a good idea to woo Myra with his chest painted in the green and red and blue and gold patterns she had inscribed on them, glancing up at him through her eyelashes as she painted, checking that he was okay.

"Elliot, you are shaking so much it looks like you're about to have a fit," said Myra.

"I am great, never better," said Elliot, when Luke's jacket landed around his shoulders. Elliot clutched it. "Thank you so much," Elliot said, heartfelt. "Now please leave."

"Yeah, okay, sure," said Luke, rolling his eyes and leaning against the stone carapace. "So, the play's over at last."

Myra answered him, but Elliot could not hear over the roar of terrible realization in his mind, like a lion of revelations. He told Luke to go away so often without meaning it that now nobody could recognize when he did mean it.

"Oh my God," Elliot said in a hollow voice. "I did this to myself. I am the boy who cried wolf."

"There's a wolf?" asked Luke, and his hand went to his sword.

Myra clutched his arm. "I can't see a wolf!"

"There is no wolf!" Elliot cried.

Myra squinted. "Then why did you say there was a wolf?"

Here Elliot was, on a balcony under a starry night sky with a beautiful, kind girl who he thought liked him, and thanks to his amazing wooing skills she was poised to flee from the wolves.

"Luke, I need to talk to you inside," he announced. "Myra, I'll be right back, hang out here for a minute."

"With the w—" Myra began, but Elliot had already dragged Luke inside and shut the door on her protest.

Luke looked annoyed. Elliot could hardly blame him. Elliot felt forced to do the one thing he absolutely loathed: be emotionally vulnerable.

"Here's the thing. I like Myra," said Elliot. "Romantically. I want to ask her out. Please go away so I can do that."

"What?" said Luke. "Really?"

"Yes!"

Luke was clearly bewildered, and still upset by the whole play business. "I didn't know. I didn't think—I'll go."

"Please." As Luke went down the corridor, Elliot's heart misgave him. "Hey," he said quietly, and Luke turned. "I wanted to say . . . since it was the first, if you wanted it to mean something, it still can. I don't think a kiss counts, unless you want it."

The light from the torch affixed to the wall was burning low, but it was enough to see Luke blush. "How do you know that it was . . . that I haven't . . . I've kissed loads of people. Loads of times."

"Sure," said Elliot, letting it go.

"There's no need to be sarcastic," said Luke. "Just because you're girl crazy doesn't mean romance is everyone's first priority. There are more important things, to some people."

To better people than you, Luke's tone implied.

"I'm girl crazy?" Elliot repeated. "Oh, okay."

"Yes!" said Luke. "You only started our *truce*, much as you hate it, because you wanted to be with Serene. And now you forced me to be in this humiliating school play because you want to be with Myra. A play, of all the useless, ridiculous things . . ."

There were so many points to argue with in Luke's speech that Elliot hardly knew which one to choose first.

"The play wasn't only about Myra," he snapped. "The play was important to me. I wanted to do something, to find something in this land that wasn't about war. Even the stories about magic land are all about battles, and there has to be something that matters more. If there isn't art and imagination and exploration, what are you fighting for? You must think about that. You can't just be a clockwork soldier, swinging your sword in the direction other people want."

"Just because I don't like plays doesn't mean I'm stupid," said Luke.

"I never said you were stupid!"

"Oh, you have said I was stupid, actually," said Luke. "Many times."

Elliot almost said: *I never meant it* but bit down on the urge. Insults sometimes felt like the only protective armor he had.

"Well," he said, instead. "I didn't mean to force you into doing the play. I'm sorry you hated it, and I'm sorry about what Adara did."

He didn't have much in the way of armor. He was shivering in this stone corridor, despite Luke's jacket. He wondered if he should offer to give it back.

"You thought it was hilarious that I hated it, and you like Adara," Luke snapped.

That was true as well. Sometimes Elliot wished Luke *was* stupid.

"It doesn't mean that I can't be sorry."

"I don't want you to be sorry for me!" said Luke.

"What do you want, then?" Elliot demanded.

Luke's hands were in fists at his sides, his breathing harsh as the crackling of wood consumed by fire. Elliot could hardly make out Luke's face in the low light of the dying torch, but it seemed like Luke wanted something. Elliot took a step forward, and hesitated before taking another.

"I want you to be less horrible," Luke said slowly, and Elliot stopped moving. "If you can manage that."

"I am *trying*," Elliot exclaimed.

"Yeah, well," said Luke. "Thanks for trying. For once." Elliot could have hated Luke for that, for not even noticing how hard Elliot had tried the whole time Serene had been gone, but then Luke took a deep breath and cut Elliot's hatred out from under him with an act of grace. "Good luck with Myra," he said.

Kindness came much more naturally to Luke than it did to Elliot, but Elliot had promised himself he would keep trying.

"Thanks," Elliot said. "And—thanks for being in the play with me."

Luke nodded, a little awkwardly. He retreated down the corridor, and Elliot whirled around and hastily opened the balcony door. "I am so sorry I took such a long time," he said. "I'm sure you must be cold. I swear there are no wolves out here. I am so sorry."

Myra was standing on the balcony where he had left her. "Don't be," she said warmly. "I know what you were doing."

"You do?"

Myra advanced upon him, and slipped her arms around his waist. For a moment it was like being carried away by a warm rush of joy: that something could be so lovely, and so simple. At last, Elliot thought, someone liked him. At last, it could be easy.

"I know you've realized how I feel about Luke," she said.

The warm rush turned to ice. Elliot remembered how Myra had always smiled at Luke, listened to him at the lunch table, how she had looked up at Luke when she fell and he caught her.

"I know you've been making sure I didn't make a fool of myself over a guy who doesn't even like girls. I know you've made sure always to be with me whenever he's around," Myra went on. She sniffed, and burrowed her head further into Luke's jacket, while Elliot stared down at her head in mute horror. "Thanks. You're such a good friend." The play was over, but in reality or fantasy, Elliot was never going to have a leading role.

The only possible response to someone telling you that they wanted to be friends, or that you were a great friend, was gratitude. Elliot had been friendless long enough that he knew friendship was a prize in itself. Myra was lovely, and thought the best of him.

She was lovely, and she didn't love him. She had never even thought of loving him, and though she had never owed him love, though he was grateful for her friendship, Elliot could not help but be disappointed and furious at the whole world, furious at himself for being so stupid and thinking, every time, it would be his turn to be chosen.

It was never going to be his turn. The world didn't work by turns: the sun shone on some people and not on others. It was always going to be Luke's turn, over and over again.

Elliot was aware that what he was doing was wrong, even as he did it, but he still went down to the grounds where the fires for roasting meat were burning down in the mud trampled by all the guests of today. He took off Luke's jacket and dragged it through the dirt and embers.

He might have done it more than once, until he saw golden curls through the last dying flames, and realized Adara Cornripe was sitting on a log by herself.

Elliot went over and sat down beside her.

"Leave me alone," snapped Adara. "I don't want to talk to you."

"Believe me," Elliot said. "I'm not really in the mood to talk myself. But I wanted to say something. I was mad at you, but that doesn't make it right to kiss you when you didn't want me to. I liked playing Red Rose, but I wouldn't want to live that way and I know I don't: I know who does. I'm sorry."

Adara studied him, her own beautiful face unreadable. She did not speak, but she leaned forward, took his face between her hands and kissed his mouth. Sparks flew up skyward from the dying fire, as if hoping they could become stars. The sparks burned behind Elliot's eyelids as he shut his eyes and kissed her back.

Elliot might not have done it, if he had known Serene was coming back the next day.

He didn't know, and so he kissed Adara by the flickering firelight, and the hiss and crackle of the flame echoed the burning in his blood, the hot touch of Adara's hands as they slid up his shirt.

After a long time which seemed burningly short, Adara leaned back but stayed in his lap, stayed kiss-close, and murmured: "I take silphium every day with my breakfast."

"Um," said Elliot. "Is that a contraceptive? Oh God, of course they don't have condoms in magic land!"

It had never been an issue with Serene, as elvish women had to undergo a ritual before they could bear children. Once Elliot had explained how this differed for human women, Serene had felt here at last was the reason human women did not exert their natural female superiority.

Elliot couldn't say she was entirely wrong.

"What's a condom?" asked Adara. Elliot began to tell her, and after a moment Adara lifted her hand. "Stop," she said firmly. "You're putting me off the whole idea. I assume that isn't what you're going for?"

He could not see the fire, only the glow it gave her hair and the sparks that burned in her eyes. He could hear the fire, though: the mutter it made, as if it were impatient with him, too.

He smiled and leaned in, pressed his smile softly against her mouth, felt her begin to smile too.

"No," he murmured. "I think it's a brilliant idea. And I know brilliant. Let's go."

"Come up here," Adara urged him later, in the privacy of her cabin, the lights of candles glowing on wooden walls and rumpled white sheets.

He obeyed her command, moving from the foot of the bed and sliding up along her body to kiss her, then lay back on the pillow and looked at her expectantly. Adara made a noise of exasperation and pulled him back to where he'd been. There was a moment where they were rolling, both with different ideas about what positions to roll into, and almost rolled off the bed.

"Like this?" Elliot asked, looking down at her quizzically. "With a woman? Would that even work? Are you sure?"

It was true he'd seen it in Peter's scandalous literature, but honestly that literature had taken a lot of liberties with the truth, and he'd assumed this was one of them.

"Yes, I'm s—with a woman?" Adara asked, her eyes going wide in her flushed, paint-streaked face. "As opposed to what?"

"As opposed to a man," said Elliot. "What did you think I meant, a mermaid?" He paused. "Though I definitely would give that a shot, if the mermaid was interested and we liked each others' personalities."

"So you like both?" Adara asked, and the way she spoke was very careful indeed, as if each word was a foot placed on a tightrope.

"Why, does that bother you?" Elliot asked, his voice careful in turn.

"No, no," Adara said hastily. "Any guy I know?"

"No," said Elliot. "On account of, you might have noticed we are surrounded by uncouth miscreants."

Adara smiled, her eyes sparkling. He'd kind of thought she would like that: one of the few girls among dozens of boys in warrior training, and smarter than all of them.

"Well," she said. "I am very sure it works this way. The elves have misled you, though they've obviously taught you well in various other matters."

Elliot looked down at Adara, for the sheer pleasure of looking. She was shining by candlelight, her smooth golden skin smudged and streaked with daubs of cerulean blue and forest green and twists of vermilion, her golden curls spread out on the white pillow. She smiled up at him, her face soft and pleased with him, and scratched her nails along his scalp, combing through his hair. He leaned down and kissed her, her beautiful challenging face, as the moment turned slow and shining.

"We'll try it your way. This time," Elliot murmured, and Adara laughed.

Elliot woke with the morning light filtering through the windows, paler than firelight or candlelight but still a bright hopeful gold. He was alone, but he could feel the pillow beside him was warm and could hear the sound of Adara hanging up clothes on the steps outside the cabin: he stretched in the embrace of the bedsheets and thought about Adara. She was smart, she was beautiful, and she hated almost everybody.

He might have stumbled into something wonderful here. Perhaps Myra had done him a favor. Perhaps this time, for the first time, he really was in luck.

"Hey, Adara," came Natalie Lowlands' voice. "Saw you left a guy's jacket on the door, so I slept over in the third cabin last night."

So they had a system for privacy, because they were friends. That was nice. Elliot's own dormitory mates hated him for random silly reasons like "all the ceaseless screaming and drama" or whatever they kept whining about.

Elliot had never liked Natalie Lowlands much: she was from his side of the Border, but she'd instantly adopted a Borderlands surname. She'd become best friends with a Cornripe, learned every weapon, never referred to the world she'd come from and constantly made cutting remarks about elves. Since she was Adara's best friend, Elliot might have to try to like her. He'd never understood the urge to fit in, but perhaps that was because it had never been a possibility for him. Perhaps if he were more socially adept, if he could have remained anything like his real self and had friends, belonged—he would have. Maybe he could understand the temptation.

"Don't tell me you actually bagged Luke Sunborn," Natalie continued.

"I wish," Adara sighed. The pillows and sheets abruptly felt a lot less warm. "No, I had a moment of weakness and settled for the nerdy best friend."

"Eeesh, Schafer. Well, his lucky night."

Elliot got out of bed and found his trousers. He gritted his teeth and committed to the superhuman effort of getting them on by himself.

Adara sounded like she was smiling. "You think so?"

"I know so," said Natalie. "I also know you're going to have trouble with that one. Look how he followed Chaos-of-Battle around for years like a pathetic puppy on an even more pathetic leash."

"You're right, as usual," Adara said, sounding resigned. "My own fault for slumming. I'll have to make it clear to him."

"I'll make it clear to him, if you like."

"Who's making what clear to me?" asked Elliot, emerging from the cabin. He figured he was rumpled enough to do a fairly convincing impression of having just woken up.

Adara and Natalie spun around. Adara was still in her pajamas, but she clutched at her own damp costume as if she were naked. She'd washed off the paint: Elliot wished he'd had the chance to do so.

"How do I put this? Congratulations, you've been dumped by another one," remarked Natalie. "The word that comes to mind is 'loser.'"

"Yes, you got me, how embarrassing, I've slept with two beautiful women," said Elliot. "The words that come to my mind are . . . self high-five." He raised an eyebrow at Natalie, then turned to Adara.

She hadn't said anything she'd meant him to hear, and she wasn't responsible for any hopes he might have had this morning. He thought she might have liked him a little last night.

"Thanks for a funky time," he said, and smiled. "I mean that mostly sincerely."

He plucked Luke's jacket, which was a charred, caked object he would examine more closely later, off the door handle and jumped off the steps of the cabin, taking the winding path through the trees towards his own. With luck, he would make his walk of shame without anyone seeing him.

"Wait!" Adara called out.

Obviously Lady Luck, like everyone else, was not all that fond of Elliot. Elliot turned around, shivering in the early morning air, wishing for a shirt and also dignity. Adara had run after him barefoot in her pajamas: Elliot looked at her dusty feet and her tousled hair, at her still being beautiful. He suspected his own hair required a different description: maybe tornadoed.

"What you heard . . .," said Adara. "It wasn't just about Luke. I was—I like someone else, too. It isn't you," she added quickly. "I know I don't have any hope with either of them, and I was trying to make myself feel better. Can you understand that?"

I'm not a bandage for your wounds, Elliot wanted to snap, but he bit his tongue before he spoke. She had come after him. That was kind of her.

He had kissed her fresh from being rejected by Myra, and before that by Jase, and before that by Serene. Natalie was right: he was a loser, but that was not Adara's fault.

"I can understand," said Elliot.

Adara dropped her gaze toward the forest floor, tangling her hands together as if with his understanding she had lost her confidence.

"Thanks for telling me—what you told me, last night. I won't tell anybody."

"I don't care who you tell," said Elliot, but Adara had spoken as if the promise meant something to her.

That was kind of her, too. Elliot took a step forward and looked at her in the clear cold morning light.

Then he leaned down and gave her a kiss on the cheek. "Thanks again," he murmured, soft as the breeze ruffling her hair, close enough to feel her warmth and feel her tremble, for the last time.

"*Elliot*?" said Luke's voice. "Adara? I don't believe this."

"Awesome," said Elliot, stepping back from Adara. "This is a great day. I cannot wait to see what else happens. I think I might go live in a hole. What do you want?"

Apparently Luke wanted to stand among the trees and gape like an idiot.

Adara glanced at Luke and blushed, looking completely mortified. She was the one with the crush on Luke: Elliot had a moment of pity for her crushing horror.

"Well, it's seven in the morning, so I gotta go practice the javelin!" she said, and ran.

The moment passed. Adara was the one who got to leave, mortified at being seen with Elliot, and Elliot was the one who had to stay.

"I guess I don't need to ask where you've been," said Luke.

"Guess not," said Elliot. "So let's not talk, shall we? That seems best. We have a manly bond, which means not talking . . . very much . . . at all. Ever. And I think that's beautiful!"

"I knew you liked her."

"You're letting me down, loser," said Elliot. "You're letting me down about our bond. That's hurtful."

This was like some terrible emotional game of Clue, he decided. Who is going to most comprehensively ruin Elliot's day? Will it be the school's queen Adara outside the cabin, ashamed to have wasted her time with him? Or will it be everyone's preferred suitor Luke leaning against a tree, being blond and judgmental? Could there possibly be another contender? Will it be secret option everybody?

Elliot glared. Luke glared back.

"I was looking everywhere for you."

"Well, not everywhere," Elliot pointed out. "Obviously."

Elliot did realize his smart mouth was a serious character flaw which would prevent him ever having a mostly silent manly bond with anyone.

"Last night I thought you might be upset about Myra getting with someone else," said Luke, a tinge of spite in his voice. "Obviously not."

Elliot stopped glaring in order to stare incredulously. "Who did Myra get with? You?"

Luke was the one Myra liked, after all. She'd said as much. And Luke had been upset last night.

"Er, no," said Luke, doing some incredulous staring of his own. "Did you hit your head and suffer some kind of memory loss? Do you understand what liking men romantically even means?"

"No, not at all," Elliot said blandly. "You'll have to explain it to me someday. Who did Myra get with?"

Luke looked thoughtful. "Something like Paul. Or maybe John."

"George," Elliot suggested. "Ringo."

"I would obviously have remembered a peculiar name like Ringo," said Luke. "No, I think it was a name starting with P."

"Peter?"

Luke nodded. "Do you know him?"

Elliot had referenced knowing Peter approximately one thousand times, also introduced them many times, and tried to fix them up that one time. It was clear to him that Luke's accusation of other people having memory problems was rich.

It was also clear to him that Peter, who Elliot had cheerfully pitied for having no chance with Myra, was much better at romance than Elliot himself. Myra had said she didn't like Peter that way: how had Peter changed her mind? Could Elliot have got Serene to change her mind?

Elliot looked away from Luke's smug face, down to the tents and the towers. There was a lot of activity going on for this early in the morning. Elliot would have to investigate it, once he got a change of clothes.

Or maybe he would just go live in that hole.

"Good for Peter," said Elliot, and took a deep breath and grimly resumed his walk to the cabin.

He was not enormously surprised when Luke followed and continued to harangue him. "Why do you *do* things like this?"

Elliot rolled his eyes. "Do things like sleep with gorgeous people? I don't know, I would've thought it was fairly self-explanatory."

He stormed on. He heard the crackle and snap of twigs under Luke's feet as Luke stormed after him. Thin sharp spears of sunlight came treacherously through the leaves above, and stabbed at Elliot's eyes.

He could see how this looked to Luke. Adara had been terrible to Luke and then Elliot had immediately slept with her—taken her side, acted as if he didn't think what she'd done was wrong at all.

Except that Elliot had been rejected and Luke chosen twice in the last eight hours. Elliot was in no mood to soothe Luke's hurt feelings when Luke was always going to be the one who was loved best.

There was a brief silence before they reached Elliot's cabin, at which point another question occurred to Luke.

"*Is that my jacket?*" Luke demanded.

Elliot's dormitory mates put their heads under their pillows and sighed in one synchronized movement.

"I have an explanation for what happened to it," said Elliot.

"What is it?"

"I'm coming up with an explanation," Elliot amended. "I haven't thought of one yet, but I'm going to come up with one and it's going to be good."

Luke looked slightly amused, but mostly as if he had added "destruction of my private property" to his long list of Elliot's sins. Elliot rummaged in his bag of illicit goods to fish out one of his T-shirts, since Luke kept looking at all the paint and he'd been scandalized enough for one day. Elliot would plan how to get out of his trousers and into his uniform later, preferably in strict privacy.

"Anyway, why do *you* do things like this?"

Elliot emerged from his T-shirt to find Luke blinking. "Things like what?" Luke asked.

"Uh, coming and interrupting me at highly personal moments in order to make judgements and ruin my day?"

Luke eyed Elliot with the self-satisfied air that Elliot knew from bitter experience indicated Luke was imminently going to be proven right about everything.

"I told you why I was looking for you last night. Didn't you wonder why I was looking for you this early in the morning? Serene's back. I thought you'd want to know. Maybe I was wrong about—"

Elliot never heard the rest of Luke's sentence. He was too busy running.

Behind him he heard one of his dorm mates shrieking something irrelevant about closing the door.

Elliot threw the door of the meeting room open, and scarcely saw the dignitaries around the crowded table, elves and human alike, all solemn and all staring. She was there, at her mother's side: tall, straight-backed, clad in green dark as the woods at evening.

Then she was no longer at her mother's side but in Elliot's arms, his about her shoulders, hers about his waist, his head bowed into the crook of her neck. He held on hard, breathed in hard, and every sense told him that she was back, she was whole, and he did not ever have to let go of her again.

"Ah well, when virtuous young men are unkind, there is much comfort to be found in the arms of floozies," said an elf Elliot didn't recognize, and Serene broke away from Elliot and looked murderous.

"You know that's right," said a guy Elliot didn't know but who was clearly a Sunborn. He was more of a silver lion than a silver fox, and he was speaking in elvish, which was something of a shock. "Gotta love floozies. So which virtuous maidens have been unkind to your young warrior, Sure-Aim-in-the-Chaos-of-Battle? I'd heard she was rather a devil with the gentlemen."

Sure looked amused rather than stern: Elliot supposed it was beautiful that she found unholy joy in tormenting her only daughter. "Oh, a great many silly gentlemen go sighing after my bad girl. But she has her eye on a very sweet young boy—much too good for my girl—called Golden-Hair-Scented-Like-Summer. Now as battle practice, we have tourneys, and Serene asked leave to wear her chosen gentleman's colours tied around her arm. She had asked many times before and always been refused. This time her wish was granted and Golden bestowed the requested mark of favor. What Serene did not know as Golden tied the scarf around her arm was that Golden had apparently rolled the scarf in . . ."

"I'm no good at botany," Elliot said, translating for Louise. "I think the . . . well, from what Sure is saying about the effects, it seems to be a deadlier equivalent of poison ivy. So Serene broke out in a rash and came—last place in the tourney . . ."

"Elliot," said Serene, "shut up!"

Elliot shut up, but Louise was already laughing, and Sure continued: "Golden said he didn't believe she was trying to win the tourney for Golden or for anything but her own vainglory, and he thought Serene needs to stop taking men for granted and be—"

"Something like taken down a peg," Luke whispered in his dad's ear. "I think?"

"Luke!" Serene exclaimed. Luke looked guilty, but then glanced at his father for approval.

"The lad knows elvish," said General Lakelost in the hushed tones of one commiserating with friends on a misfortune: "Does he read a lot?"

"No!" said Michael Sunborn.

"His swordsister is an elf," Elliot pointed out coldly.

"She's not his swordsister, because he cannot have one, because he is only a boy," Sure-Aim-in-the-Chaos-of-Battle hissed.

"And so you consider me unworthy," said Luke in elvish, with a creditable attempt to be formal. "But what if there was a way to prove my worth?"

"Neither he nor my other comrade have the least need to prove their worth," announced Serene. "And how dare you cast aspersions on Elliot's virtue while showing yourself to be overly familiar with a famous trollop, Mother! It would break my gentle father's heart if he knew."

"Oh, you're Gregory Sunborn," Elliot said, gazing at the silver lion in enlightenment.

"The one, the only, the most expensive," said Gregory Sunborn, former courtesan to the elves, and winked. "It was years before your mother ever met your father, who I am sure is a sweet virtuous creature."

"He is," said Serene, boring holes into her mother's skull with her glare.

Sure looked mildly discomfited.

The elderly elf—and elderly for an elf meant a few lightened tresses among the red hair, and a certain stone-like pallor and fixity of expression—coughed pointedly. "I am uncertain why we have been called to this meeting comprised of harlots and children—"

"This is actually partially a theatrical costume," said Elliot.

"Oi, don't call Gregory names just because he spotted a job opening that seemed suited to him due to the long-standing alliance between elves and Sunborns, plus the, well." Luke's mother, Rachel, buffed her nails against her jerkin and looked proud. "The general Sunborn *joie de vivre*. Lust for life, if you will. Passion for . . . passion."

Elliot, who had known Luke literally for years, raised a skeptical eyebrow.

Luke was blushing. None of the other Sunborns were doing anything of the sort. Louise pulled Elliot into the chair next to her and whispered: "Nice shirt. What's a sex pistol?"

"Er," said Elliot.

"Elliot," Serene said in an awful voice. "Do not tell me that you wore that outfit on a public stage!"

"Oh, he wore a lot less than that," said Louise. "Up top, Little Red."

Elliot exchanged a quick high five with her.

"I am uncertain," the older elf said, in a carrying voice, "why we have been forced to attend this absurd meeting, under the threat of your . . . men entering our territory without permission."

"Now, we didn't threaten anyone," said General Lakelost.

Elliot saw how Sure, Serene, and the other elves' eyes all travelled to Commander Woodsinger, as if to see if she agreed. The commander's face was impassive. Then the elves looked toward Rachel Sunborn.

He understood why the Sunborns had been called in, now. Not only did public opinion always tend to go their way, the Sunborns being a law unto themselves meant their women were a law unto themselves, and they could talk to the elves with both sides assuming they were equals.

General Lakelost kept talking. "We simply stated that we, who have a paramount duty to protect the Borderlands, plan to go into a certain territory and bring peace."

"Our territory!" snarled Sure-Aim-in-the-Chaos-of-Battle.

"Currently not your territory," General Lakelost pointed out. "Since it has been overrun by bandits. You should be pleased to have allies who are eager to stamp out the lawlessness in your land."

"And are we meant to believe," Sure said icily, "that you will simply give the land back? It's rich ground. You humans have been wanting to settle there for years."

"We're men of honor," said Lakelost. "We may of course need to establish a garrison there of some selected military men and citizens to grow them food. Obviously the place is too wild and abandoned."

"Did anyone else notice that was not an answer?" Elliot asked.

Humans and elves alike glared at him.

"I agree with General Lakelost," Commander Woodsinger said calmly. "Our mandate is peace in the Borderlands, and our judgement as to what will bring about that peace overrules the wishes of motley groups of citizens."

You can't agree with him, Elliot wanted to yell at her. We supported you, Serene and me. You should agree with us.

"We have already stated that we will treat the Border guard's incursion into our territory as trespass and an act of war," said the older elf. "We have stated that we will fight the guard if they come."

"You have said that," General Lakelost agreed, even though the elf had clearly been addressing the commander. "But will you really commit yourself to fighting a war on two fronts, with the bandits and the Border guard? You elves can say whatever you like. Somehow I doubt you will do it."

"The Border guard could help us, Mother," Serene broke in, to Elliot's astonishment. Elliot made a gesture for her to be quiet that she didn't see, as she was reaching past her mother for Luke's hand. "The bandit threat does have to be extinguished. And my swordsister and I fight much better as a pair."

She and Luke clasped hands and looked defiant.

"Everyone can see what's most important is defeating the bandits," said Commander Woodsinger.

"What's important isn't what everyone sees," Elliot argued.

Rachel Sunborn chipped in with: "We have proven to you that humans can be useful, haven't we? We're the ones who captured Bat Masterson, one of the bandit leaders, out on a raiding party."

"You did?" Elliot demanded. "Well, then someone has to talk to him! If you can make an agreement with the bandits, nobody has to fight anymore!"

Now the elves and the humans were not yelling at each other: everybody was yelling at him.

"A dishonorable bandit—"

"No talks with terror—"

"This is pointless," said Luke.

"I would rather die in my blood—"

"We have nothing to say to him," stated the commander. "He can stay in the pit below my tower where he was thrown, and rot there."

"There's a pit where we keep captives at this center of learning for children?" Elliot threw up his hands. "Oh yes, that's great. That's normal!"

He took a deep breath, and the elves looked scandalized while Luke made a small horrified gesture: Elliot glanced down at the collar of his T-shirt and adjusted it so the scarlet handprint on his collarbone was hidden again, and tried to speak with unimpaired dignity.

"I'll go down to see him. I'll talk to him."

"I will go with you, if you care to have my company," said Serene.

"I'm coming too," said Luke.

"Is it going to be a children's tea party down there?" General Lakelost barked. "This meeting is a mockery—"

Elliot looked around at all of them, at the furious elves and raging humans, at strangers and people he loved all bent on war which could destroy them.

"I'm not mocking anyone," said Elliot. "I want to talk to him. I'll go in on my own."

Commander Woodsinger was the one who showed him the way to the pit, which was under her tower but accessible through a door outside.

"I should tell you that you do not have to do this," she said as they walked through the corridors away from the meeting room. "I fail to see how it could be of any use."

"It might be," said Elliot. "Bat Masterson's not a real name. So this bandit is from the otherlands, and—"

He was about to say: maybe I could talk to him, maybe we might have something in common, but the commander interrupted him.

"So are many people in this camp. Natalie Lowlands, your classmate. Elka Pathwind, the medic. We take Border names and obey Border customs. We do not become bandits."

"Elka?" Elliot repeated, frowning. "Wait—we?"

Elliot studied Commander Woodsinger, who he knew could cross to the other side of the Border, and remembered the graffiti he had noticed on the wall long ago. "Did you leave a name from another land at the Border?"

"If I did, I turned my back on it," said Commander Woodsinger. "You could choose a Border name yourself, you know. Are you very attached to your father's name?"

"I'm attached to my name," said Elliot. "Because it's mine. And I don't know—I don't even know if I want to stay."

"It is rare that anyone with council training is allowed to attend meetings like these," said Commander Woodsinger thoughtfully. "Usually they are summoned to draw up documents afterward. But you have allied yourself with the Sunborns and the House of Chaos, two very influential families, and you see the result. You could have an effect here, if you stayed and were clever about it."

Elliot stared at her, revolted. "I haven't allied myself with anyone. I never wanted—I only wanted to be with Serene."

"Or you could go back to your own world," the commander continued. "It's no concern of mine what you do. Though I admit I am curious to see what you do next."

She gestured him around the back of the tower.

The pit under the commander's tower was dark and deep, a hollow scooped out in the shadows. Elliot came down a narrow flight of steps carved in mud and stone, through a large wooden door opened with a set of jangling keys. When Elliot stepped into the pit he could see the faces of the others high above him, and he felt like a gladiator in the Roman games, being watched by the faraway, indifferent eyes of citizens.

Or maybe he felt like a Christian about to be eaten by a lion. He knew why the general had let him come: Elliot was expendable. If he was killed he would be no further trouble, and they could say they'd tried everything.

He could see the dull glint of a crossbow in Serene's hands. He wasn't expendable to everybody.

They let the bandit Masterson in through a different door, more of a gate that led to the pit from a small dark tunnel. He was tall and thickset, dark stubble on his face and his hands shoved in his pockets.

Elliot knew Serene and Luke. He knew how people stood when they had concealed weapons. He took a step toward Masterson, hands up, showing he was no threat.

"Bat Masterson," said Elliot. "The name of Wyatt Earp's deputy? What was your real name, back in the otherlands?"

Bat Masterson shrugged. "Doesn't matter. I carved it on the wall and left it behind. Can't live there. Don't want to serve the Border guard. So this was my choice, and this is my name."

"Fine, go through life using the name of a winged mouse, I don't care," said Elliot. "But have you considered that the combined might of the Border guard and the elves may crush you? Which leads me to my next question—have you ever thought about a treaty in which the elves concede some territory in return for the surrender of certain seized lands and valuable items such as jewels?"

There had been some attempts at kidnapping people, but the cultural barrier had led to the bandits trying to take the women and being killed in the face, while occasionally a puzzled bandit had been forced to deal with an elvish gentleman screaming he wished for death before dishonor.

"Once you're captured, you're no longer the leader. I'm not in a position to make treaties. And I'm not interested in listening to the chatter of a stupid brat," said Masterson, and hit Elliot.

Elliot had never been hit by a grown-up before, the meaty fist crashing down with all the weight of muscle and bone and discipline behind it. He staggered and felt the inside of his mouth crash and break against his teeth, the warm gush of blood from his lip to his chin. Elliot choked slightly on the blood in his mouth, coughed and grabbed Masterson's arm, moving in between him and the steely glint of Serene's crossbow.

"That may have been the arrangement in your camp, but I bet they would still listen, if you came with terms," Elliot said, speaking rapidly, trying not to let his cut lip blur the words.

He only had an instant: he saw Masterson going for the slight bulge in the shoulder of his jacket. He only had an instant, and he wasted it. Elliot felt a flicker of fear for his life. Elliot looked toward the torch burning in the wall. Elliot thought about a weapon, rather than using his words.

It was only an instant, and then it was too late. There was a knife in Masterson's hand. And there was a bright blur over Masterson's shoulder. Luke had somersaulted from the watchers' balcony above. Luke struck a blow with his sword before his feet ever hit the ground.

Luke's face over Masterson's shoulder was blazingly furious and intent. The blade went clear through Masterson's chest. Elliot caught the man's heavy weight in his arms by reflex, sagged and sank under it so he was kneeling in the dirt with him, trying to staunch the flow of blood with his hands.

"You'll be all right," he murmured as blood leaked out of Masterson's mouth and the light bled out of his eyes. "It's not too late, we can still talk—"

Lies did not stop the man from dying. Elliot looked away from his dead face because he could not keep looking any longer. He looked at Luke, instead.

"You can't just do things like this!" Elliot raged.

Luke's face was not blazing anymore, but shut down as if someone had slammed an iron door on a furnace.

"I can," said Luke. "I did. He hit you. I killed him. That simple."

Elliot bit his lip and was furious with himself for glancing toward that torch, for not having enough faith in himself to keep talking. He felt guilty because he knew Luke had seen him look to the torch, and was sure Luke had known what that look meant. And he felt unexpectedly and wrenchingly sad: for the sunny boy he'd met his first day in a magic land, the boy who'd been sick the first time he'd killed someone. Now Luke wasn't even looking at the dead man. Luke had not even flinched. Elliot wondered what this magic land would make them all into, in the end.

He felt furious and guilty and miserable, and impatient with it all: it was no good to feel that way now the man was dead. He had tried to talk to him, and accomplished nothing.

The others came down afterwards. There was no longer a captive in the pit, or any reason to stay out.

"He was from my world," said Elliot, still sitting in the dirt with the bandit's head in his lap.

"That makes sense," said General Lakelost. "They're a treacherous people there, and strange: metalworkers without morals, not our kind and not to be trusted."

Elliot looked around to see several people, including Luke, nodding. "Hey!"

Luke did not look up from cleaning his sword. "I just meant it's obviously not safe there. You shouldn't go back."

"Do you know how many times I saw people murdered with swords before I came here?" Elliot raged. "Murdered in any way at all? Zero! Zero times! I was not supposed to live like this, and I don't want to."

"It is of no interest to me what you want," said the elder elf. "You wanted peace, and there is no way to get that now, is there? Much good you humans capturing Masterson did us. We decline your help—"

"You are in no position to decline," said General Lakelost. "We are coming into the bandits' territory whether you like that or not."

They were arguing far above his head, like adults with a small child. Elliot felt helpless as if he was one.

"Either way," said Luke. "I'm going back with Serene. I read up on it." Elliot suddenly and forcibly recalled Luke with his book on elvish customs while Elliot was practicing for the play. "Swordsisters are bound to accompany each other anywhere, their loyalty to each other pre-eminent."

"You are not her swordsister!" Sure barked.

"Okay," said Luke. "I also read that if a swordsister's worth is doubted, said swordsister can volunteer to face any challengers, until her—er, or his—worth is proven or she—uh, or he—dies. So. I volunteer. Send challengers. She doesn't ride out without me, unless I'm in the ground."

"That lad reads constantly," General Lakelost muttered.

"He does not!" Michael Sunborn snapped.

"Fine," Sure snarled. Serene grabbed her arm, far too late. "Challenge accepted."

Great, Elliot thought, and shut his eyes, the dead weight of what had been a man cooling in his arms. More killing.

Luke had to go to a disciplinary hearing because of killing a guy. Elliot suspected it was just going to be high fives about being a badass warrior all around, but since Serene had been firmly taken away by her mother, Elliot figured he should wait outside the commander's tower.

He'd forgotten that Luke's family was here, and that for other people, when you were in trouble, family came to help.

He was sitting on the step outside when the sun was blocked out by the massive majesty of Luke's dad's shoulders.

Elliot squinted up at him resentfully. "I hope Luke stops working out," he said. "If he turns into a mountain range like you, I really don't think I'll be able to cope."

"What?" said Michael Sunborn.

"Nothing. Sorry, Luke's dad."

Mr Sunborn sat down on the step beside Elliot. He was way too big for the step. Elliot was shunted off to one corner. Sunborns took up all the room at all times.

"Michael," suggested Luke's dad. "Or Mike."

Elliot considered this. "Nope. Sorry, Luke's dad. I don't think I can do it."

"Alllllll right," said Mr Sunborn, drawing out the words as if he was nobly being patient with Elliot.

"You are just like Luke," Elliot observed. "Must be genetics."

"Well, might be, might not be," said Mr Sunborn. "I don't really know. Rachel's business. But I did have the raising of him, and I think he is like me."

Elliot frowned. "Wait. Explain what you said before."

Mr Sunborn went on because Sunborns took up all the room, were contrary and never listened. "I taught him to play Trigon: first time he caught the ball in his little fat hands I was there to stop him dropping it on his feet."

Elliot had read about fathers playing catch with their kids. "Great," he said. "Congratulations. It's a stupid game, by the way, and he could be spending his time in a far more useful and intelligent manner, but who cares about a tiny thing like that?"

"He likes Trigon," said Luke's dad. Elliot made a small helpless gesture: as if Elliot was not aware that Luke liked Trigon, after spending years in the stupid stands watching the idiot sport. "He likes Trigon, and he likes anything to do with blade or bow, he likes horses and hounds and the hunt. He always liked all the things I liked, and he always trained until he could do them best of all, and he liked that I was proud."

At the foot of the tower, in the clearing circled by cabins, Dale and a few other boys from the warrior-training class were playing ball: not Trigon, not using a glass ball, but something more like catch. Maybe Luke would be playing with them, if Elliot had not failed with Masterson.

Luke's dad did not have to rub it in. Elliot knew it was all his fault.

"He wanted a friend his own age, and I understood that, and I sent him off to the Border camp with my blessing. I understood he'd be set apart from the others a little, because being the best means being on your own sometimes. I understood the elf, because she was set apart in the Border camp too, and she's a lovely girl: can shoot out an eye at five hundred paces. But then the letters started arriving, about books and elvish and plays, and I couldn't put it all together." Michael Sunborn rubbed the back of his neck. "The only thing I don't understand about my son is you."

This was not helping Elliot with the guilt. "I don't really have much to do with anything."

"So what about you?" Luke's dad went on relentlessly. "Do you like him at all?"

"No," said Elliot. "I constantly spend hours at the idiot games of, weeks at the home of, and literally years in the company of people I dislike. Because I am totally off my head."

Luke's dad shrugged. "You're the one who said it, lad, not me."

"Look, I know you think I'm a weirdo, but why the third degree?"

"The third degree of what? You do talk the most awful nonsense," said Michael Sunborn, in that moment supremely Luke's dad. "I'm just concerned about Luke."

"Yes, but why are you concerned about Luke and . . . Wait, I've worked it out," said Elliot. "You are concerned about me and Luke in a romantic context. Ahahaha. No. You are incorrect. I hardly have words to explain to you how incorrect you are. He looks out for me because I'm Serene's friend and he loves Serene. He doesn't even like me in a *non-romantic* context."

Luke's dad frowned. "Doesn't he?"

"Oh wow, oh my God, no, no! Obviously not!" said Elliot. "He likes someone else romantically, by the way. He likes Dale Wavechaser! How could you think that? No. Oh my God."

Elliot could have spent the next several hours alternately saying "No" and "Oh my God" but fortunately Luke's dad cut him off.

"Who's Dale Wavechaser?"

"I can't tell you that! Forget I said anything!" Elliot hissed. "I wasn't meant to tell you about him liking anyone!"

"So I guess you'd be in trouble if I told Luke," Luke's dad said mildly. "Best just to tell me who Dale Wavechaser is, son." He paused. "This is blackmail. It means you should—"

"I know what blackmail is!" Elliot exclaimed. "I'm highly intelligent! I was just taking a small personal moment to feel betrayed by a trusted authority figure!"

"Dreadful," Luke's dad agreed. "So which one is he?"

Elliot looked across the dusty ground and pointed to where Dale was playing, running backlit against the sun, leaping and smiling. It was a flattering angle for Dale.

"Oh," said Luke's dad. "Oh I see. Oh well, I can understand that."

He watched approvingly as Dale horsed around.

"If I preferred men, that's definitely the kind of man I'd prefer," he went on, horrifyingly. "I don't prefer men, mind you."

"I understand," said Elliot.

There was a silence. "Nice-looking lad," said Luke's father.

"Yes," said Elliot, despairing.

"Read much, does he?"

"Nope," said Elliot, even more despairing.

"Plays Trigon, does he?"

"Yes," said Elliot, too weary to despair.

Luke's dad rubbed his hands together. "That'll do very nicely."

"I'm pleased that you're pleased," Elliot informed him. "I'm glad to have cleared up your horrible misapprehension. I hope you will all be very happy together. Now you're here, I assume Luke does not need moral support, and I wish very much to change my trousers."

He got up. The sun was dazzling in his eyes, the carefree sound of Dale and the others playing made his head hurt, and there was still blood on his hands.

"That'd probably be best, lad," said Luke's dad. "The elves were talking."

Elliot walked in through the door of his dormitory, then jumped a foot in the air.

"I couldn't go back to my room," said Serene, lurking behind his bunk bed. "My mother would know to look for me there."

"You might've been safer hiding in Luke's room," said Elliot. "I don't think any of the elves would be remotely surprised to find out that I was scandalously entertaining ladies in my boudoir."

"Ah," said Serene. "But I wanted to talk to you." She did not smile, not even her secret smile most people did not notice was a smile: she did not look anywhere close to smiling. She gazed up at Elliot and though the rest of her was in shadow, her uptilted face and her grey eyes seemed picked out by a spotlight, pearl-pale and imploring.

Elliot came and sat at her feet, taking one of her hands in his: it was strange, because the last time he had touched her like this they'd been going out. It was also the only possible comfort for him. There was nobody else in this or any world who he knew would welcome his touch, would touch him back in reassurance or affection.

Serene linked her fingers with his. "How are you? You look sad, but . . . I have received the distinct impression you have not exactly been pining away for me."

"Who says?" Elliot asked. "But that doesn't mean I haven't been doing other things as well."

"So have I," said Serene. "As you heard."

She looked stony with shame even referring to the incident with Golden. Her pain made Elliot want to be vulnerable.

"I, uh," said Elliot, and bit his lip. "Over the summer, I had a relationship with a man."

Serene's eyes went so wide Elliot was worried they were going to meet over her nose and form one giant elven mono-eye that would stare at him for all time.

"Well," she said at last. "That makes no difference to my enduring affection for you! I thank you for sharing this confidence with me, and I will support you in all your relationships and varied endeavors." She paused triumphantly after reciting that, and added: "I see how that might work better for you."

"Sorry, what?" asked Elliot.

"Well, because you talk so much about the societal prejudices and differing expectations involved in relationships between the sexes. This way both parties can be equal!"

Elliot thought of Jase's face, as he'd talked about his uncle: he thought of the way Jase had gone for someone young and then been upset to find that being young did not mean being malleable. He thought of how Jase had been worried about people seeing them on the street, and about how stricken Elliot had felt when his father had seen them.

"I think that's total rubbish and a bit insulting, actually," he said. "There isn't any kind of relationship that's all problem-free delightful unicorns. You can't have a relationship without issues and prejudices. The way to be equals is if both people agree to be equals, and treat themselves and each other as equals, despite all that."

Serene frowned thoughtfully. "I'm sorry to have insulted you and I will think on what you say. But I don't see how unicorns come into it."

"They were a metaphor," said Elliot. "Which was a mistake, as they are bloodthirsty censorious beasts."

"Have you told Luke?" asked Serene, and when Elliot was silent: "Are you going to?"

Elliot remembered exactly how eager Luke had been to share with him.

"Certainly I am." Elliot smirked without really meaning it. "He'll know just as soon as I feel the need to announce it to our whole class."

"I have not . . . only been making a fool of myself over Golden," said Serene. "My cousin saw that I was somewhat downcast after my—misreading and mistreatment of you, and she took me to a place where she assured me that my suffering would be eased."

Elliot stared. "Serene," he began. "Are you talking about what I think you're talking about? Did you go to an elf brothel?"

"It—it may well have been somewhere that there were, ah, men of a persuadable nature—no, that is to say, men of the evening—"

"ELF BROTHEL," said Elliot.

"Elliot, do not laugh," Serene urged, and Elliot was just about to laugh at her for being a prude when he realized there was a genuine note of pain in her voice. "It was not . . . I did not realize how different the same act could be. I knew that it would be different with true love, but I had never thought that—affection and laughter can transform an act, as well. It came to me once I had left that dark place, and once Golden had scorned me, that I had been a child to devalue your honest affection and constant care for me. That I had been a fool."

He thought he understood now, how Peter might have got Myra: waiting around until someone was at a weak point, low and humbled and hurt, worn down enough by the world to be amenable. And maybe it would turn out to be a good idea.

But Elliot didn't want love to be like that. He loved Serene, and he did not want to catch her in his arms if she stumbled. He wanted to help her to her feet.

And he did not want to be loved as a second choice, as a surrender. He had spent his whole life not being loved at all, and he had thought being loved enough would satisfy him. It would not. He did not want to be loved enough. He wanted to be loved overwhelmingly. He did not wish it had been him who caught Myra, instead of Peter. He did not want to be Serene's fallback, even though it was Serene. He had never been chosen, so he had never had a chance to know this about himself before now: he wanted to be chosen first.

Serene was looking down at him, as if she was thinking about kissing him. Elliot looked back at her, longing and amazed there was something stronger than that longing.

"Serene," he whispered, and she leaned in a little closer at the sound of her name. "It wouldn't be fair to either of us."

Serene looked surprised, but she only had a brief instant to be surprised: the door opened and Luke walked in. He stopped a step within the threshold, taking in their tableau, and Elliot decided that the entire universe had been set up purely to play cosmic jokes on him.

"Are you guys . . ." Luke hesitated and cleared his throat. "Are you getting back together?"

Serene and Elliot looked at each other, and the look meant more to Elliot, felt weightier, than the kiss good-bye he'd given Adara, or how he'd held Myra. This had so much more love in it, and was so much more final.

"No," said Elliot. "No, we're not."

"Well, good," said Luke. "I know how Elliot is, but from what you were saying earlier, you really like Golden, and I still think you have a chance."

Of course Luke and Serene had caught up before Luke had thought to come find him. Elliot didn't even know why he was surprised.

"You think so?" Serene asked shyly. She was smiling. "How goes your courtship?"

"Well," said Luke. "We sat at Dale's table one day while you were gone. I was planning to go over and sit near him, but then Elliot managed to hurt himself with a butter knife. But I think Dale was glad we were there. He was really welcoming. He's so nice."

"He is terribly handsome," Serene said encouragingly.

Luke coughed. "I'm sure Golden is too."

"Oh, he is the most beautiful creature I ever beheld! But Dale is very pretty and very agreeable as well," Serene said consolingly. "Indeed, I am sure more agreeable, because there is no pleasing Golden-Hair-Scented-Like-Summer. Every word he speaks is like being slyly stabbed with a dagger, but everyone thinks he is so virtuous and that it is only right that he should speak harshly to such a rogue as I."

Serene had been with the elves a longer time than usual, Elliot thought, her speech more formal than it had been when she'd left. She'd spent more time with elvish men, because women were less casual in the presence of gentlemen.

"That's so unfair," Luke said sympathetically. "You're not a rogue."

And Serene's speech patterns were completely beside the point, because Elliot was outraged.

"Are you people seriously invading my cabin to drone endlessly at each other about the boys you fancy?" Elliot demanded. "Get out of here, both of you! I cannot believe your tedious faces."

They left him so he could run both hands through his hair, take a deep breath, and think about the repercussions of what he had done and what he had decided. Maybe he would be alone forever.

It would be a long time before anyone chose him first. If anyone ever did.

They turned the Trigon pitch into a field of combat, smoothing the ground as best they could. Elliot joined Rachel on the bleachers rather than going to Serene and Sure: he loved Serene, but he'd had enough of being called a hussy.

"Sit," said Rachel, smiling at him beautifully, and Elliot smiled helplessly back. "Tell me who Dale Wavechaser is."

Elliot's smile froze. He could feel it trying to sidle off his face and hide behind his ear. "What?"

"My husband told me that little Luke has a crush on someone called Dale Wavechaser," said Rachel, nodding to the front of the crowd, where Louise and Michael were standing up to cheer. "But he said he wouldn't point him out because he didn't want Luke to think he was betraying confidences. So. You point out Dale, or I will tell Luke that you told his dad!"

She kept beaming. Elliot gazed upon her sadly.

"That one," he said, sighing and subsiding onto the bench beside her.

Rachel leaned forward in her seat and peered at the crowded benches across the pitch. Dale's bright enthusiastic face was clear, in the very forefront of the audience.

"Whoo, LUKE!" Dale shouted.

"Aw," said Rachel, and her smile spread. "He seems nice. Do you like him?"

"I do," said Elliot, deliberately not referencing any boredom-related stabbings, and Rachel patted his hand. It was nice that she cared what Elliot thought.

Rachel looked pleased. "Then I think that will work out very well."

She seemed perfectly serene on a lovely morning, about to watch her son fight to the death. Elliot leaned into her steady, comforting warmth as they watched: it was Luke up against the elder elf.

"She's called Cold-Steel-to-Vanquish-the-Foe," Rachel said. "Very experienced warrior. This'll be quite a fight."

Rachel sounded approving. Elliot looked at Cold's hair, fluttering like a blood-colored banner in the breeze, and Luke's hair gleaming like a knight's helm, and both of their weapons shining like big pointy metal objects of death. He slid off the bench onto the floor and sat there with his arms around his knees, looking up at Rachel.

"I don't want to watch," he said. "I'm not going to do it."

Rachel glanced down at him. "Is something the matter?"

Elliot gave her a look of disbelief, and put his head down on his knees. He'd already seen someone die yesterday. He'd seen people killed before, and he could bear it. But he did not want to be made into an audience, as if this were a game. He did not approve of anything that was happening, and he would not accept that it was necessary.

He could hear the clash and clang of weapons, a remorseless din in his ears, and Rachel's running commentary on the fight. He wished he could not hear either one.

"Scythed her legs right out from under her, that's my boy! Oooh, nasty. Oh, that's going to sting later. Nice, duck and roll! Funny face, you're missing out."

Elliot resisted the urge to put his hands over his ears like a child. "I don't think so."

Clang, clang, crunch, went the noises, like a giant eating breakfast cereal. Elliot knew the last sound was bone breaking.

"And Cold's down!" Rachel shouted as the crowd roared. "Luke's got his sword to her throat! That's Mommy's little man!"

"Is he going to kill her?" Elliot asked in a small voice, muffled in his own arms.

"No," said Rachel, after a pause. "No, he's letting her up. She's surrendered. You go, champ!"

There was another cheer. Elliot wondered if it was his own terrible personality that made him interpret this cheer as slightly disappointed, as though the crowd had wanted blood.

He did not have long to wonder, because then Luke vaulted over the rail of the pitch—like he had jumped easily down into the deep drop of the pit, and all Elliot had to say was why, gravity, why—and bounded up to his mother.

"Aw, that little feint that broke her arm made me so proud," said Rachel, jumping to her feet and giving Luke a kiss on the side of his face. His cheek and his blond hair were streaked with blood, but she didn't seem to mind.

"Is that your blood?" Elliot demanded, scrambling up.

"No," said Luke. "Don't worr—"

He was cut off by the descent of the elf contingent, either bestowing congratulations and caresses—Serene—or obviously consigning their souls to the uncaring trees—literally everyone else. Serene was alight with her pride and her vindicated faith, shining like a blade in the sun.

"Now," Serene said breathlessly. "My turn to prove myself in combat."

"What?" Sure snapped.

"What?" Elliot echoed, but nobody paid any attention to him.

"Oh, my son can risk his life but your daughter cannot?" Rachel inquired coldly, folding her arms. "Do go on. Someone hand me an axe."

Luke, dusty and tired and smeared with blood, looked over at Serene and smiled. "How about you send whoever you like, as many people as you like, out into the field against both of us? We'll take on anyone you choose. We always do things better together."

Serene looked at him for a long moment and then she smiled, a radiant wash of dawn over a dark land. She reached out and took his hand when he offered it.

They did not fight on the field again that day, but they walked out onto it, hands clasped, bright and dark heads bowed together, exactly in step. They lifted their linked hands high over their heads and the whole crowd cheered, elves and humans alike, louder than they had for the fight.

And Elliot knew that there was one human in the world who Serene loved enough to defy her clan, to break her sacred traditions, to forge an unbreakable bond with against all reason and all law, and force everyone to respect that bond. He knew who Serene loved best.

The world proved to him over and over again what he already knew: that it was always going to be Luke, and never going to be Elliot.

Luke's little display over Serene only added fuel to the fire: now Sure-Aim-in-the-Chaos-of-Battle had admitted Luke Sunborn was going to the wars, of course the rest of the humans from the Border guard were going too.

It was simply a case of arranging matters to best suit everyone. Elliot brought up the fact they could draw up a few unofficial agreements.

Elliot tried not to forget what Commander Woodsinger had told him—that it was a privilege to be in here, that he could change something, maybe, even if he could not change enough.

Even though he could see what was going to happen, with a terrible inevitability he did not know how to stop: that the Border guard were going to creep into the elves' land, and then in five years . . . maybe ten . . . the elves would try to take it back. War coming out of war, over and over, and all Elliot could do was put it off, as if he were bailing out a sinking boat with a leaky bucket. He tried to put in things that would please the elves without hurting the humans, and vice versa. He argued with people who believed nothing should ever change, as if fixing something broken was sacrilege. Surely there was a better way to do things, out in his world, in the civilized world.

Except there were still wars in his world. It was only in stories that there was one clear evil to be defeated, and peace forever after. That was the dream of magic land: that was what could never have been real.

Everyone imagined a battle that would bring peace, and the only thing that had ever worked, ever brought peace for even a heartbreakingly short time, in any world, were words.

Every time he wanted to snap someone's head off and storm out of the council room Elliot excused himself, found a cool stone wall to lean against, and told himself: Go back and be sweet, be nice, nod and smile, get those clauses in there. He smiled until his face hurt, until his teeth hurt, smiled so much that Cold-Steel-to-Vanquish-the-Foe unbent enough to escort him to the lunchroom after another session with Elliot trying to argue very politely for codicils that everyone else very calmly didn't care about. He left Cold at the door with a smile.

"You're in a good mood," Luke remarked, offering a smile in return.

"No I'm not. I hate you guys," snapped Elliot. He collapsed on the bench with his head in Serene's lap, and then peered under his lashes at them.

Luke rolled his eyes and continued to eat peas. Serene patted Elliot's head and continued to read. Neither of them showed any signs of leaving.

Elliot was walking back to the commander's tower and the meeting room and the piles of paper he was trying to use to make peace, as if peace were a house of cards everyone else was intent on upsetting but him, when he saw the cranky medic making for the tent.

"Hey," said Elliot.

The late afternoon was warm and glowing. It lent her face something that was almost like softness, but not quite. Her long copper-red braid glowed in the bright light. There were plenty of redheads in the Borderlands: half the elves were redheads. Elliot had never thought twice about her hair. Not before.

"I don't have time to talk to you," said the medic, walking faster. "Or rather I suppose I do, but I don't want to."

It was the kind of thing she said which usually made Elliot smile, but he did not smile this time.

"I think you probably have time for me to ask a quick question," said Elliot. He felt ill, sweat under his collar and his knees trembling, but he could not be a coward this time. "I know who you are," he continued. "Do you know who I am?"

The medic Elka Pathwind, who had once been Elka Schafer and his mother, looked at him for a long moment. She had brown eyes, dark as pansies: they were nothing like his.

"I know who you are," she said slowly. "I guess you want to talk to me more than ever. I can spare a while. I suppose I owe you that."

They could not just stay here, where anyone could walk by and interrupt them. Elliot began to walk toward the edge of the camp, where the fence ran. He leaned against the fence, his boots in the dirt: leaning, he was closer to her height. She was tall for a woman, but shorter than him, shorter than Serene. Her passionless pale face was level with his now.

"Are you angry with me?" she asked. She sounded almost curious.

"No," Elliot blurted out.

"Good," she said. "I did the best thing for you, I think, leaving you with your father. He was always—very devoted."

"He was very devoted to you," Elliot snapped. "It doesn't transfer."

He meant love: that love could not be given from hand to hand like a parcel, that what had been gold from his father in her hand had turned to ashes in his. He could not say the word love, though, not with her looking at him.

She surveyed him. "Was he cruel to you, then? You look perfectly all right."

"I am all right," Elliot muttered.

"Just having a tantrum, then?"

Elliot lifted his chin, so he could look down on her. "Was he cruel to you?" he asked in return. "There are a lot of reasons for a woman to leave. I read about them. You were—you were pretty young."

He'd prepared a lot of things to say to her: that he didn't blame her, that he forgave her. None of them seemed right, now.

"There were a lot of reasons to stay," she said. "Have you ever thought, when you're done here, that you will have no qualifications in the other world? The world did not stop turning when you turned thirteen. It will have left you far behind."

"I've thought about it," said Elliot.

"Hmm," said this strange woman. "In the other world, there were two choices for me: I could be his wife. Or I could live in penury and, if I tried to tell the world the truth about where I'd been, be called mad. So I was his wife. He always tried to be good to me, I think. But in this world, I don't need him. I don't need anybody. So I came back. The wall we come over, I cut my old name on it with all the other names from the otherlands, and I walked away."

I carved it on the wall and left it behind, Bat Masterson had said. His mother had left behind more than her name.

"You became a medic," Elliot said slowly. "You don't become a medic if you don't—care about people."

She shot him an annoyed look. Elliot almost found it comforting, the sign of the cranky medic he'd liked, rather than the distant stranger he'd been speaking to here at the edge of the world.

Then she sighed, and the crease between her eyebrows smoothed as if the sigh had unfolded the skin.

"Do you want me to talk about why I became a medic?" she asked eventually. "I will. Do you want me to talk about why I left your father, whether I considered taking you with me? Ask me what you want to know, and I'll tell you. Like I said . . . I suppose I owe you."

Elliot had thought out different reasons she might have had for leaving. He would not hate her, even if she said that she had not considered taking him with her. She hadn't had a job then, or any money: she might have thought leaving him would comfort his father. She might have been depressed after having him, confused at her lack of maternal feeling. The way his father had loved her was not the way people should be loved. Usually women didn't have a whole other world to run to, but she had.

He had thought out so many reasons.

"Do you have anything," Elliot said, very slowly, "to ask me?"

"What, ask for your forgiveness?" she demanded, crossing her arms over her chest. "No."

"I am not the one who brought up owing, or forgiveness," said Elliot, his voice very smooth. "Is it on your mind?"

She looked like she wanted to slap him. He wished she would.

"I meant," Elliot said, after a moment. "Do you want to know how I am? Or how my father is? Do you want to know what I like? What I want to do when I grow up? Do you want to know who I am or who I love?"

"I know who your friends are, remember?" the medic retorted. "Everybody knows that. The elf girl and the gay Sunborn kid."

Elliot's eyes narrowed. "There is a lot more to Serene than just being an elf. And there's a *hell* of a lot more to Luke than being gay, like that's what makes him remarkable among the Sunborns. He happens to be their champion. Though," he added quickly, "value systems based on physical strength and martial prowess are meaningless!"

Elka Pathwind looked at him, her head tilted but her eyes still wide, her expression neutral. "The commander sometimes talks about you. She said you were crazy."

Elliot hesitated. "Well . . . do you want to know if I am?"

His mother shook her head. "Why are you so eager for me to ask you questions?"

Because in every scenario he'd ever thought through, every time he had waited on the stairs of his house in the terrible silence, she had come back. She had taken steps toward him, every step from wherever she'd been to where he was. He hadn't stumbled painfully over her. He had known, in his imagination, whatever she did or whatever she said to him, whatever her reasons for going, that she had come back.

This was different. She had not come to him. He had no reason to think she had any interest in him. She had to give him a reason.

"Because I want to know . . . if you care to know anything about me."

"Not really," said the medic at last, with a shrug. "You're no concern of mine."

It was almost evening, the sun drowning in the clouds. It was later than he had thought.

"Okay," said Elliot, after a pause. It was a longer pause than he would have liked. He wished he'd been able to speak sooner. "Then I think we're done here. I just—I wanted to be sure of where we both stood. Now I am."

She gave him one last look, assessing and coming to a decision. There was a certain easing of her expression that Elliot thought might be relief. She nodded.

"I guess this could have gone worse," she told him, and walked away.

Elliot supposed she was right. It could have gone worse. He could have tried to have a relationship with her, ignored all the signs and blundered stupidly and hopefully on. He could have forced her to spell out her indifference even more clearly.

Elliot stood leaning against the fence for some time: the first place he had learned about magic, met Serene and Luke, chosen to stay. He had believed in a lot of stories, back then, including the ones he told himself.

He was sure his mother had a story: that there was more to why she had left, why she had come back here, why she had chosen the job she had, why she thought the way she did about the world. He was not going to hear it, though. They were not going to have the bond of shared stories and joined lives. She did not care to listen.

"Hey," said Luke after some dark indeterminate length of time, wandering up to him.

"I can't do this right now," Elliot snarled at him.

Luke stared. "Well, nice to see you too."

Elliot didn't want to be cruel, he thought suddenly. This was the moment to tell everything, if there had ever been such a moment, when all his defences were burned down. He had to say it: *I just found my mother, and it turns out that what I always feared is absolutely true. Neither of them ever wanted me at all. I have been unwanted for my whole life. By the way, I like guys as well as girls, and I'd appreciate it if you'd quit implying I hit on everyone. You are one of only two people I love, and I have to know if I have any real value to you.*

It would be a miracle if he could get all that out, but after that he thought he could manage to say: *Take me to Serene*, and maybe: *I think I'm going to cry.*

"I didn't mean that the way it sounded," he said, and tried to work out how to say everything else.

"It's hard sometimes, with my family," said Luke into the silence.

"Oh," Elliot said, his voice brittle. "Is it?"

"Being just ordinary, I mean, when they're all . . . you know."

That was literally the most ridiculous thing Elliot had ever heard. He did not know what had possessed Luke to come over and start talking random absurdities at one of the most horrible times of Elliot's life, but apparently Elliot had to cope with this. He felt like a burn victim, having someone come at him with a grater.

Elliot badly wanted to snap at Luke, but he did not dare. If he let himself lose his temper, it was going to be ugly: he was going to do or say something terrible. He did not even know what poison he might spill, but he knew that Luke did not know anything. Luke did not deserve it.

"You're ordinary? I seem to recall some sort of championship," said Elliot, his voice astonishingly calm in his own ears. "That is what not being hit in the head multiple times does for me. I have this astonishing recall of past events."

"Yeah, but that was a misunderstanding."

"A misunderstanding of what? By whom?"

"Doesn't matter. Look, my mother is being tiresome and she wanted me to ask you if you wanted to have din—"

And the easy, casual way Luke could say "my mother," the way he could complain about her, left Elliot suddenly with no reserves of patience in him.

"I don't need any more Sunborn time, no," he told Luke. "I want to go to the library, where perhaps I will finally be left in peace."

"Suit yourself, then," said Luke. "You always do."

"Oh, you know me," Elliot said savagely. "Constantly getting what I want."

Elliot did not go to the library or his room, since Serene might be in either place, and Serene would take Luke's side. He went to the commander's tower, right up to the very top.

He could see the Borderlands laid out from here, blue and green that went blurred in his vision suddenly, like a turquoise gemstone, like something he wanted to hurl away. He didn't want magic any more, he didn't want any of it.

Elliot sat down on the stone floor, put his forehead on his drawn-up knees, cradled his head in his arms, and tried to breathe in wet angry gulps.

"Are you . . . quite all right, Cadet Schafer?"

It was Commander Woodsinger's voice, Elliot realized after a moment. Though he should have guessed it immediately from the fact there were no soothing back-pats or offers to fetch help. He looked up, blinking, and she was looking down at him. Her face was grave as it always was.

"No," said Elliot. "I'm not. That medic, Elka Pathwind? She's my mother. She left me when I was a baby, and she doesn't want me now. She looked at me as if I was some years-old mess that she'd thought was behind her, something rotting and useless and—and hateful, and I do not know what to do except maybe prove her right. I'm not—I don't know how to be—I'm planning on being emotional and too much trouble and everything you hate, so why don't you just go? Go! Get out!"

He put his head back down on his arms. He wondered if he would be expelled for telling the commander to get out of her own tower, and sort of hoped he would be. He kept trying to breathe, to breathe, until it finally seemed like breathing might be possible.

It occurred to him that he had heard himself gasping and heard the thunder of his own useless furious heart in his ears, but he had not heard her leave.

Then the commander spoke. "Do you want me to send her away?"

Elliot twisted around and stared at the commander. She was standing straight as a spear, staring out at the Borderlands: her profile was set as something carved on a coin.

"What?" Elliot asked blankly.

"Do you—"

"I haven't been stricken deaf so I can't hear stuff said to me by someone standing next to me on top of a tower with nobody else around," said Elliot. "I was just expressing disbelief. Why would you send her away?"

Commander Woodsinger cleared her throat. "Well—"

Elliot stared up at her. It was easier to breathe, the more uneasy the commander was.

"I mean she's a perfectly competent medic. Useful to have around the place. Isn't that what you care about? Your job and the camp?"

"Obviously," said Commander Woodsinger.

"After all, you don't want to have a personal relationship with any of your cadets," Elliot pointed out. "You told me that."

"It is possible that I believe you might—might—have the potential to be even more useful than a capable medic," said Commander

Woodsinger. "In time. If you listen to your tutors and especially your commanding officer. Now vacate the tower: you do not have my permission to be here."

Elliot scrambled up, rolled his eyes at her, and made for the door.

"Wait, Cadet Schafer!" Elliot turned and waited: Commander Woodsinger looked him over, then looked as if she wanted to say something. Her mouth formed a few different, undecided shapes. Eventually, she said: "You always forget to salute."

Elliot hesitated. Then he walked quickly back to her, leaned down, and kissed her on the cheek.

"CADET SCHAFER!"

"It's okay," said Elliot. "You don't have to tell me that you like me."

He took a step back, saluted, and left, taking the tower steps two at a time.

She didn't have to tell him, because he could tell. That was what it meant, when people came to find you, when they cared enough to sacrifice for you, when they supported you, when they came back.

He could tell when someone cared. And he could tell when someone didn't.

The next night there was a celebration for the agreement between the Border camp and the elves, and their current ride to war.

Elliot was not in a party mood, but fortunately his friends were basically terrible at parties. Serene preferred to brood handsomely in a corner, impressing many gentlemen but not really speaking to anyone, and Luke sat being pleasant but twitchy, like an unhappy rabbit, until he could make his escape.

Unfortunately, the place was full of Sunborns. They were all treated to the sight of Rachel Sunborn grinding up on a distant cousin called, Elliot thought, Ursula Sunborn. It cheered him up a little, as did Luke's expression, which said, in letters of fire: O Welcome Death.

"Where are your delightful relatives, Serene?" Elliot asked.

"They decided not to come because they were certain they would be exposed to the sight of gentlemen behaving in a licentious and ungentlemanly fashion," said Serene, with deep thankfulness.

Elliot looked around where many gentlemen were indeed behaving in a licentious and ungentlemanly fashion, getting super drunk and in the case of five members of the Trigon team standing around cheering as Adara Cornripe and Natalie Lowlands made out for their benefit.

Elliot let his lip curl. "Charming. They certainly are missing out," he said dryly.

Said dryness was spoiled when Louise Sunborn spilled half her mead on his head. Elliot sputtered and stared up at her.

"Sorry, Little Red!" she said, and burst out laughing. "You are hilarious when you make faces! Come and show me some of the moves from your play."

Elliot got up. He did it for Louise, who was drunk and wanted to have fun, but having her arms around his neck, looking at her simply beautiful and simply happy face, actually made him feel a little better. He made the stage dance easier so she could follow a few of the more showy moves, and Louise clapped as he shimmied up her body and laughed delightedly when she dipped him. He was concerned he was going to be dropped, but the Sunborn musculature saved him and she didn't.

"Ha, you are such a cutie," she said, flinging her arms back around his neck and whispering in a very loud voice. "Hey, Mum said something interesting to me. So I hear little Luke has a crussssssh! At last. He's a late bloomer, I'm not meant to tease him. So point out this Dale Wavechaser to me, or I'll ask Dad to do it! Oh no wait, Dad said I should say I'd ask Luke . . . and I wasn't supposed to say Dad told as well. . . . This is just a terrible mess, Little Red. Show me my baby brother's crush or I'll beat you up. But gently." She patted his head.

"You have to promise not to tell Luke," said Elliot.

"I will be the soul of discussion," Louise promised, her finger to her lips. "Or maybe I mean a different word!"

Elliot sighed and jerked his head in Dale's direction. He was actually standing near Luke, which Elliot thought was progress, even though Luke was studiously avoiding his eye and talking to Serene.

"Oh, hello, not bad." Louise whistled. "Thanks for pointing him out. This way I won't try to sleep with him."

"He prefers men," said Elliot.

"Sure," Louise said patiently. "But he hasn't met me yet. Anyway, doesn't matter, because I was hoping to make like Cousin Gregory and bag an elf tonight. Someone told me that Cold brought his beautiful young sons and is keeping 'em cloistered! What can I say, I like a challenge."

"Do you speak elvish?" Elliot inquired.

"Um . . . no," Louise said. "I don't like books and learning, and I don't need to bother with them, because: look at all this." Louise gestured haphazardly to herself, all gleaming curls and generous curves, her scar stretching as she smiled. "Men look at it, and then they find a way to talk to me. You doubt it?"

"Um . . .," said Elliot, and spun her and caught her, and they both laughed. "No."

"Please don't sleep with my sister," Luke blurted out when he returned.

"Wow, do you think she'd go for it?" asked Elliot, winking at Serene, who shook her head at him in a severe fashion. "I mean, no way I could ever get that lucky, am I right? But if you really think I have a shot, I guess I could make a pass. . . ."

Louise was ten thousand miles out of Elliot's league, and even if she would ever be willing to consider it, it would probably be too weird, but it was hilarious that Luke had managed to come up with this one. Elliot was trying to think of a way to milk it further when he followed the new direction of Luke's scowl to Adara.

"Hey, Elliot," she said, pushing her bright locks off her forehead, where they stuck as if she had been sweating. "Do you want to dance?"

"Sure," said Elliot, and took her outstretched hand so he could spin her out onto the dance floor. He could not resist saying, with just a touch of malice: "I thought you were having fun where you were."

Adara did not look him in the eyes, which was impressive considering they were dancing close and she was a tall girl.

"Mission accomplished," she said, jerking her chin in the direction of the corner of the tent, where Natalie was making out with a Trigon player who had an overbite. "She's having fun with him now," said Adara breathlessly. "And I'm—I'm having fun with you. Aren't I? And we could have more fun later."

Elliot was about to snap at her when he noticed the slightly choked way Adara was speaking, as if she had misery stuck in her throat. He thought of the way Adara had reacted when he'd told her about Jase, the way she'd spoken to Natalie, and the fact Adara had told him she liked someone else. He felt lousy, suddenly, for being angry at her, for thinking she was performing when she was just like him.

"We're having fun," Elliot said gently. "But we're not doing anything later."

"Why not? Isn't it enough to just have fun?" Adara asked.

She had to swallow a few times before she got the words out. She was even more upset than Elliot had thought. Elliot gathered her closer into his arms, made sure her face was hidden against his collar.

"Not when the person I'm with isn't having fun. Not when it's not clean—for fun, or for love, or because there is potential there for one thing to move to the other. And not when the person I'm with wants to be with somebody else more," said Elliot, into her hair. "Never again."

They danced, turning in slow circles. Elliot could see Serene turning her head to talk to Luke, the curve of her neck and the curve of her smile. Elliot could see Myra and Peter dancing together. Peter's face was alight and Myra's was not.

He danced with Adara until the song was over, at which point he left her: another boy was very willing to scoop her up in his arms.

"Didn't expect to see you back," said Luke.

"I must say considering what Luke has told me that I am surprised as well," said Serene.

"Thought she was going to make a spectacle of herself again," said Luke. "Some more."

The slightly snide tone of voice he was using reminded Elliot of the way he himself had been thinking about Adara, before he'd danced with her. He felt the back of his neck prickle with a combination of annoyance and guilt.

"I don't think anything she or I do is any of your business," said Elliot. "Nobody is interested in your opinion. So keep it to yourself."

He got up and made his way across the dance floor, to the other side of the tent, where Gregory Sunborn was sitting. He was quite alone but looked entirely satisfied with his situation, as he did at all times, and Elliot recalled the saying "the cat that got the cream" and also how he'd thought of Gregory as a silver lion.

"Hi," said Elliot, and went over to sit by him.

"Oh, hello," said Gregory. "Luke's friend. Young Louise calls you . . . Little Red, doesn't she?"

"I'm Elliot, but whatever. You know a lot about people, don't you?"

Elliot was not making random judgements based on Gregory's former profession as a famed courtesan for the elves. He had noticed that Gregory was among the few humans who could calm both angry elves and rampaging Sunborns and the general, and that Gregory himself seldom, if ever, lost his temper. If Gregory had actually seemed to care about treaties at all, he would have been an ideal ally.

Gregory smiled. "They're my specialty."

"Terrific," said Elliot. "So if someone gave every sign of not wanting anything to do with you—if they left you, and didn't approach you again, and said they weren't interested in you—then they don't care about you, right? And you should leave them alone."

Gregory blinked. "I was hoping for something a little more challenging. Yes, you should leave them alone."

"Okay," said Elliot. "That's what I thought."

There was quiet between them that the music flowed through, like a river. Gregory tilted his head, as if appreciating the song.

"It doesn't necessarily mean they do not care about you," said Gregory. "But it might. Eventually, you have to stop waiting for people. If they care about you, they'll find you when they can: they will show you. And if they don't . . . after a certain amount of time and effort, isn't it wasted energy? All light burns out. Best put yours where people will appreciate it and be helped by it, and make it last longer." He paused. "Caring about people who don't care about you is a very unprofitable use of your time, and I mean that both figuratively and absolutely literally."

"Yes, all right," said Elliot. "I understand. Thank you for your wisdom. Please, please do not get any more literal."

"You're welcome for my wisdom. Which reminds me of a small favour I'd like you to do me. We're all very concerned about young

Luke," said Gregory. "And a little birdie might have told me something about someone called Dale Wavechaser. Could you be a darling and point him out for me, or should I ask Luke which one he is?"

Elliot groaned and hid his face in his hands. "You Sunborns are not subtle. And if you go on being unsubtle, Luke is going to find out, and he is going to kill me!"

"Interesting, Little Red," said Gregory Sunborn. "So which one is—"

"That one," said Elliot, gesturing dramatically.

Dale waved innocently back as he danced past.

"Oh, quite pretty," said Gregory, eyeing Dale with the air of a connoisseur.

Elliot put his head back in his hands and thumped his forehead against his palm. "I'm so dead."

The party was not cheering, in the end, but good news came in the morning. Apparently the small slice of bandit territory they had managed to reclaim—and Elliot noticed, immediately resettle with humans—was being assailed by murderous mermaids.

Elliot was overjoyed.

"I promised I would never come on a military foray without your express permission," Elliot said virtuously. "And I never will. Can I have your permission to go see the mermaids, please and thank you?"

"I don't think you understand what the words 'direct order' or 'ask permission' mean," said Commander Woodsinger as she readied her own pack for the expedition. "Or 'military protocol' or 'chain of command.' Some of your tutors say you're rather bright, so I'm not sure what the problem is."

"You're so right," said Elliot, sidling into the commander's tent. "I have to give you a reason why I would be a valuable asset on the mission! I think I can speak to mermaids."

Commander Woodsinger looked around her bare room for patience. "And if you thought you could speak to the little bluebells by the side of the road, should I take you on every forest mission?"

"I mean I've been researching mermaids in depth, and due to that research, I am sixty-eight percent certain I can converse with mermaids, and thus perhaps resolve this matter without bloodshed!" Elliot looked at the commander's expression. "Seventy-two percent certain."

"Cadet Schafer, how would you describe your conversational style?"

"Er . . .," said Elliot, and grinned. "Drive it like I stole it."

"I am simply wondering where your misplaced confidence in your own ability to have charming and all-resolving discussions comes from."

"Fair point," said Elliot. "But is there anyone else with an even forty percent certainty they can talk with mermaids in the Border camp?"

Commander Woodsinger paused. Elliot was ninety-five percent certain she was counting in her head, or possibly praying.

"Fine," the commander said at length. "But this is going to be under controlled circumstances, with an entire array of armed forces at your back."

"Thank you so much for your permission, Commander, you know I would never leave camp without it," said Elliot.

All that other stuff seemed like more of a suggestion to him. He was sure the mermaids would not feel like chatting when faced by hostile forces.

He kept that to himself until they sailed—the first time Elliot had ever been on the sea—to the village in the nearby bay. They were welcomed by the villagers, who seemed settled into their new home already and who seemed to be under the impression they had come to slaughter all the mermaids.

The villagers held a mermaid-slaughtering party, of which Elliot approved very much. It gave him the chance to work under the cover of darkness and noise.

He made his way over to Luke, who was explaining to several raptly disappointed young ladies that he did not not dance.

"Hi, loser, I want you," said Elliot.

"Oh no, what now?" said Luke, and Elliot beamed.

"I'm going to do something very dangerous," said Elliot. "And I need you to hold the rope."

The lake by the village was vast, so big Elliot wondered if he should think of it as a lagoon. There were three large named rivers that fed into it: Scimiar, the largest, the one that ran out to sea, was so wide and calm it looked like a road. Elliot could see the shine of tiny rivers running beneath the undergrowth all around, like the faintest threads of silver embroidery running through swathes of dark fabric, all of them feeding it. There were woods all around, trees so thick and tall that harpies could have nested in their boughs, and yet the trees only seemed like a midnight-black fringe on the edge of all that water. The moon was full, shining so bright it seemed to have suffused the whole sky with a faint silver glow.

Under the full moon, between silver and dark, the mermaids' lagoon waited. The water was shockingly cold as Elliot waded in, so cold that the first touch of lake water around his ankles made his teeth clench. He kept walking, and ripples chased each other before and after him, one ripple silver and one dark.

Silver and dark, silver and dark, moon bright and night black, the rings in the water formed around him. He felt stones and earth and slime beneath his feet, weeds tangling around his legs, as he walked. He was up past his chest and standing in a dark ring when the soft brush of another weed, gently unfurling against his leg, clutched instead and formed a grip cold and hard as steel.

Elliot was only able to get out one shout before he disappeared beneath the surface, and he knew the mermaid did not intend for him to break the surface and give another.

The scream had lost him his air: he felt another gasp escape him and saw it rise, a bright silver bubble among green weeds. Below the surface the water still looked silver, but it was a shadowed silver, almost pewter, and in the dull silver world Elliot glimpsed among the weeds a white face and sharp teeth.

Then she was on him, fast as a shark, terrible and defying all stories like the unicorn. She had him pinned to the stones at the bottom of the lake, her hands stone-cold and twining-strong. Elliot fought the urge to struggle and lash out: he used his last moments of strength and air to gesture to her. He made the gesture so many of the mermaids were making in so many of Maximilian Wavechaser's sketches.

The mermaid hesitated. He thought, he was almost sure she did, and then the rope around his waist tautened and dragged him inexorably across the stones and out of her reach.

Elliot broke the surface of the water gasping and choking, but he called out in a breaking water-logged voice to both Luke and the mermaid: "Stop. Wait."

"Are you kidding me?" Luke snapped, his voice traveling across the water from the trees with great clarity and greater annoyance. "I did what you wanted. We came out, you got half drowned. Now you want to stay here and get all the way drowned? The mermaids don't want to talk! The mermaids want to *drown you*!"

Elliot waved him off and, disinclined though he felt to do it, ducked his head beneath the water again. The mermaid had not gone. She was under the water, lurking, her pale weed-green eyes watchful. Her eyes widened at being watched back. Elliot made the gesture again, then had to break the surface of the water and breathe.

He was drawing another gulp of air into his smarting throat and burning lungs when he saw something else break the surface of the water. At first it only looked like a nest of debris, a tangle of weeds, but then it rose, and he saw bared to the open air her bone-pale face, her water-cool eyes, her rows of glittering sharp teeth. The mermaid.

Elliot smiled.

In a voice that was soft but sounded jagged, like something broken and made into a new shape it was never meant to form, she spoke. "Human," she said. "Do you know what you were saying?"

"This?" Elliot made the gesture again. "Mermaids were—doing that, with their hands, in a lot of the sketches with mermaids that I could find. I figured it was something that people say to each other all the time—like hello or good-bye or how are you."

"It means," she said, and her voice was almost dry, "'Do you want to drown him or shall I?' Except less polite than that."

"Oh," said Elliot, and laughed. "Of course. It's something that you say to each other all the time, when in the presence of humans. Oh my God. A million scholarly works on mermaids are full of pictures of mermaids giving humans the finger. Well. The finger of death."

"Your friend on the shore is right," the mermaid whispered, then she was on him again. He was flat on his back in the water, her cold merciless weight on top of him, and her strangling-tight fingers were in his hair, pulling him down under the surface as she murmured in his ear: "Your kind can drown in an inch of water. You think I can't kill you because of a rope?"

The harpoon landed in the water, inches away from them. The mermaid stiffened: Elliot put a hand on her arm.

"Wait," he said. "I don't want to hurt you. I only want to talk."

"But harm him and *I* will hurt you," Serene's voice called from the trees.

The mermaid's head turned, the moon picking out silver in the dark drowned green of her hair. "Elf!"

"Yes, elf," said Serene. "Serene-Heart-in-the-Chaos-of-Battle. And that should tell you that I missed you on purpose. Try to harm my friend again, and I will not miss."

The mermaid's head swung from side to side. She was poised to run or to attack. Elliot did not think she could see very well, outside the water.

"Don't go," Elliot said urgently. "She won't hurt you unless you drown me."

"You think I can't? You're in my element. You think you're safe?"

"Not completely," said Elliot. "But I thought it was worth a little risk. Don't go and don't drown me. Aren't you the least bit curious about what I have to say? I'm curious about you."

The mermaid shrugged. "We had to do it," she said. "We had to get those people away from our lake. We have eggs to be raised here, and they have been fouling it for the space of fifteen moons."

Fifteen moons.

"But . . . then those people who were fouling your lake, they were bandits," said Elliot rapidly. "Not villagers interested in farming and trade. The bandits weren't planning to stay, so they could leave as much of a mess as they wanted, but these people won't. Didn't you notice they were different?"

"You all look the same to me."

Elliot smiled and said, "That's because you're not looking closely enough."

They looked, and spoke, all night long. She seemed interested in looking closer, Elliot thought, as she held her hand up against his. Her fingers were cool against his, and webbed at the bases.

"I haven't seen a human before," the mermaid confided to him. "Not for long. Once they are drowned, your kind's skin turns to—I think your word is—soap in the water."

She laughed and Elliot laughed back, marveling, though he could hear Luke on the bank muttering that he did not think it was funny.

"That's so true," he told the mermaid.

He only wanted to look at her, and see her looking at him. Her skin felt different than human skin, looked different: her very eyes looked different, lucent in her skull. Those are pearls that were her eyes, Elliot thought, but her eyes had been pearls all along. She was a story made flesh.

"You keep turning up your mouth at the corners."

"That's a smile," said Elliot. "My kind do it before laughing, sometimes. Do your kind not do it?"

"No. My kind just laugh, and sing, and . . ." The mermaid looked at him, wondrous and wondering, and then leaned forward. Elliot experienced a thrilling shock like a cold ripple in the water, as he felt her cool mouth on his, felt the press of her sharp teeth beneath her flesh. She leaned away. "Do your kind do that?"

Elliot could not help laughing. "Yes. My kind do."

"I don't believe this!" Luke yelled.

"I can't believe you're so annoying! Sorry about him," Elliot told the mermaid. "So, can I tell the villagers we have a deal?"

"Are you sorry to be parted from the mermaid?" Serene asked sympathetically. "I know you listen to my and Luke's romantic troubles, and I would be hap—"

"About that, I don't want to listen to those, please stop."

Since she returned, Serene had been talking endlessly about Golden not refusing her permission to write to him while she was at the wars. Which meant that Serene had permission. Except that Golden never wrote back, unless you counted the letter of Serene's Golden had returned with DRIVEL written over it in violet ink.

Elliot had been forced to read one of Serene's epistles, which were 100% about her valor. He had dictated a letter asking Golden about his hobbies and interests: so far no luck, but it had to be less boring for the poor boy.

Elliot sighed and stared out at the sea. "Not exactly sorry. A bird might love a fish, but where would they live? Not to mention the other anatomical difficulties . . ."

Serene looked sad about having a gentleman discussing intimate details and wandered off to persuade the captain to let her steer.

Luke jumped out of the rigging and landed on the deck near Elliot.

"Nobody should've been able to make that jump without breaking a leg," said a sailor. "That's absurd."

"I know!" said Elliot. "I know, right? I've been saying it for years. Be my best friend."

The sailor's eyes glowed. "He's amazing."

"Get away from me, never speak to me again," said Elliot, and moved to what he thought was starboard.

"I'm sorry about him," said Luke behind him. "He's always been like this. It's terrible."

Elliot wondered if he felt ill because of this, or the way the boat was lurching in the rising wind. The boat actually seemed to be skipping like an expertly thrown stone from one crest of a wave to the other, and as it lurched again Elliot made a grab for the rail, and missed.

Everything fell away. Someone shouted out his name, and that was the last thing he heard over the roar of waves and wind, like gods having a shouting match.

Then he was in the dark, dark water, choking, flailing, as if he could fight the waves, and in the darkness there were pearls. Mermaids' faces, Elliot thought, and felt their strong cold hands fasten onto him. *Till human voices wake us*, Elliot remembered, *and we drown . . .*

"Elliot?" Luke asked, and Elliot found himself not drowning with two very worried faces hovering over him.

"Speak to us!" Serene commanded.

Elliot coughed and said: "I told you so."

Luke laughed a little wildly and looked up into the black sky, hands spread palms up, as if asking the stormclouds why they had visited this horror upon him.

Elliot lay on the deck and said: "I told you that mermaid liked me."

Meeting mermaids was the one thing about a magical land, in three years, that had finally gone right. Elliot had hoped meeting a mermaid would feel like the end of the story, feel like he could close the book.

Instead, he found himself laughing along with Luke, and wishing he could meet harpies.

Almost as soon as they were back from seeing the mermaids, Luke and Serene were sent off to war with the bandits. Only the best war-training students were chosen, which was always going to mean Luke and Serene.

Elliot thought about that: about being left behind all his life. He knew he should be. He knew he'd be useless in a battle, but he hated sitting here and thinking about it. And he knew that even if this war was won, another war would start between the humans and the elves. Maybe not this year, not with the treaty in place, but in five years, or ten years.

Life was not like this in the other world, he thought. And he had seen mermaids now.

"Hey," said Dale, passing by. "Want to go for a swim in the lake?"

Elliot had not been to the lake since he was fourteen, with Serene, but Serene wasn't here any more. "Why not?"

He was right to do it, he thought as he plunged into the clear spring water. He felt it envelop him, a shivering delightful rush over his bare chest and through his hair. He opened his eyes and the world was pale and shining, and he walked out of the water grinning and met a kiss.

Dale's body was lithe and slippery against his, his kiss cool and sweet, and Elliot cupped Dale's face in his hands and pressed him up against a tree. Then a flash of memory and horror burned through Elliot and he jumped back as if Dale was the one burning.

"I should not have done that! I am the worst person in the world!"

"Um," Dale said. "Why?"

"Because of Luke!"

"What?" Dale asked. "Oh my God. You *are* the worst person in the world! When did you guys get together?"

"What—no. He likes you," said Elliot, and ran his fingers through his wet hair. "And now I've officially told everybody."

He'd told, and he'd kissed Dale, and he'd let Luke down, and he was letting Luke down again because the sneaking thought crept in: if Dale really did like Elliot better . . .

Elliot lifted his head, but Dale was glowing.

"Wow," he said. "Luke Sunborn." He caught himself, politely. "I mean, I think you're great, and I like all the flirting—"

"I have not—" Elliot began furiously, and stopped to consider all of his own previous actions in light of Dale's remark. "Actually, I see why you might think that."

"But wow. Luke Sunborn. You know?"

The question was unexpected as a blow that came when Elliot was absorbed by reading, and hurt in the same way. He remembered Luke with his arms around a little kid, Luke pulling off his shirt on the Trigon pitch, Luke in the corridor after the school play. It was, perhaps, time to admit Elliot did know.

"I guess," Elliot conceded ungraciously. "I mostly sublimate it."

He swallowed after this admission and looked away from Dale's face, so surprised to hear Luke liked him and so happy to hear it.

Elliot might have thought: *Wow, Luke Sunborn*, occasionally, but most of the time he knew he did not want his heart crushed by his other best friend, and even if Luke had some sort of break with reality and wanted it, Elliot did not want a partner who thought everything Elliot cared about was unimportant.

Dale apparently had no doubts.

"Oh," said Dale. "But he likes me, so I don't have to sublinear it."

Elliot opened his mouth and then shut it, in mercy.

"Just play it cool. He's going to ask you out eventually. And don't worry about this. I think water might be my lucky element." Elliot grinned. "The last person I kissed was a mermaid."

"Really?" Dale's face screwed up. "Gross."

Elliot drew in a deep breath to yell at him, then let it out. Dale and Luke were going to be together, and Elliot wanted to remain on good terms. He put it down to yet another reason why Elliot and Dale would not work together, including "sublinear."

Then the sound of an elvish horn sang through the trees.

Elliot froze. "Get back to camp, I'll stall them," he said, and ran for the road that wound through the trees and into a melee of horses.

Apparently tired warhorses reacted badly to people stumbling into their midst and flailing wildly.

"Nice horsie," Elliot called, and when the horse reared: "Well, that's not very nice."

Luke jumped off the rearing horse with his usual attention to gravity and calmed it with a pat to its straining neck. More equine favoritism.

"I didn't mean for that to happen," said Elliot, giving Serene a quick wave. "I just wanted—um, a word with you?"

"You can speak when we get back to camp," Commander Woodsinger said from high atop a glossy, sidling beast.

"Can't we have one now? Please," said Luke, and the commander shrugged, still looking loftily down.

"Congratulate us, Cadet," said Commander Woodsinger. "War's over."

Elliot frowned. "For now."

"If it starts again, I know that you will be certain you can talk your way out of it," the commander told him.

"He will not be the only one confident in his abilities," said Serene, and Elliot beamed at her, even as the commander motioned the troop forward and home.

"So what did you want to ask me about?" Luke said.

Elliot stared. "Um . . . I forget."

"You're impossible," said Luke, storming off with his horse in tow.

For once, Elliot was glad Luke was angry with him. He deserved it. But Elliot could not help thinking of how many secrets he was keeping from Luke right now, in an attempt to make things easier between them. It was not working. Everything between them had just become more difficult, and more distant, and it was not like anything between them had ever been easy.

~

They were all in Elliot's cabin for the ten thousandth time talking about their love lives. Serene and Luke were, that was. Elliot was reading a book.

"I cannot quite describe the lucent quality of his golden hair," said Serene. "But I did write a poem about it. It's not very good."

"I like, uh, his muscles," said Luke, blushing. "And his tan. He's getting a lot better at Trigon, too."

"If only his heart was not as cold as he is fair," said Serene, waving her letter. "He returned my own letter to me again, I can feel it rustling in the envelope! I don't want to know what he's written on it."

She was apparently lying, because she immediately opened it, and then stared.

"Elliot," she whispered, and Elliot looked up from his troll history. "That letter you told me to write—Golden, he wrote back! He wrote me a letter!"

Elliot glanced at the page. "I'm not sure 'That's more like it' counts as a letter."

Serene and Luke high-fived.

"Um," said Luke. "I mean, if your advice for Serene worked—do you have any good advice for me?"

"I do. I'm glad you asked," Elliot said seriously. "Let me tell you a secret that gets people to go out with you. Lean in. A little closer."

Luke leaned in, his face anxious, and hopeful, and limned with gold. Elliot looked deep into his eyes.

"Ask him out," said Elliot, and slapped Luke upside the head.

"Hey!" said Luke, not quite grinning. "Hey! You're supposed to be a pacifist!"

"I am a stone-cold pacifist," Elliot claimed. "That was a verbal reprimand . . . that got out of hand."

"Do not have a catfight, boys, even if it is that time of the month," said Serene, and when she saw them staring at her, she explained: "You know—women shed their dark feelings with their menses every month? But men, robbed of that outlet, have strange moodswings and become hysterical at a certain phase of the moon?"

There was the familiar pause of Luke and Elliot deciding to let that one go and change the subject.

"You don't understand," Luke told Elliot. "You don't know what it's like to feel about someone the way Serene and I do."

"Does feeling have any correlation with how you're acting?" Elliot snapped. "Because you're both acting like idiots, and I don't want to be an idiot like you."

Elliot left his own damn cabin and went to the library instead of saying he knew what first love felt like. Because Luke was right: his hadn't been fairy-tale love, storybook love. Unlike him, Serene and Luke were going to be loved back.

On the last Trigon game of the year, Elliot watched more of it than usual, because it might be his last time. It did not justify his attention, since Luke tediously won and Serene tediously cheered as usual.

Then Luke pulled his shirt off before going into the changing rooms, and Elliot jumped up and ran in after him. He found Luke already changed back into his cadet uniform.

"Take off your shirt," Elliot ordered, clicking his fingers.

"Uh," Luke said. "No!"

"There's something wrong with your shoulders!"

Elliot had only seen them for a moment—he had not been looking all that much—but he knew what shoulders were supposed to look like, and it was not like that. Elliot had felt jarred seeing the shape of Luke's shoulders change somehow, as if heat was blurring his vision, but what was blurring was not vision but flesh.

"I just strained them or something!" Luke shouted back. "They'll stop hurting in a few days. It's nothing to make a fuss about."

The rest of the dressing room was staring at them. Dale had his shirt off, which was nice but not helpful. Elliot tried to think of a way to drag Luke down to the infirmary which did not involve Elliot himself going to the infirmary, where the medics were.

He couldn't do it. Luke was probably right: Luke was probably fine. Luke was always fine.

"Luke," said Elliot. "If they don't. Promise me you'll go to the infirmary over the summer."

Luke looked convinced this was all some plot to humiliate him, but he muttered: "I promise."

It was the best Elliot could do, when he could not ask Luke or Serene to take care of themselves in future. They had never made a fuss saying good-bye to each other: Luke and Serene were going home to their families and were always sure they would see each other again soon, and Elliot always wanted to pretend he was as secure as they were.

Elliot knew he could count on Luke to keep his word, so that was that: Luke would be taken care of, Luke and Serene were both on the path to finding love, and there was peace in the Borderlands, at least for now. Everything was settled, as much as it could be.

Time to go home.

Maybe time to stay. If he was ever going to stay, it had to be now.

His dad had always hired someone to come in and cook and clean. They never stayed long. Elliot had learned to stay out of their way, after he heard one on the phone, complaining about needy brats who gave her the creeps.

When he got home for the last summer, though, Elliot found a woman called Gemma who seemed pleased to have company. He supposed he wasn't a potential burden anymore.

"Are you going inter-railing round Europe with those kids down the road?" she asked. "Wait, no, silly me, of course not. They're going today, aren't they?"

"Is it that time already?" Elliot asked, and checked his watch. "Would you excuse me for one moment?"

He dashed up the steps from the kitchen into the hall, where he found his father walking in the door, briefcase in hand.

"Would you like to get rid of me all summer?" Elliot demanded. "Then give me some money now."

His father looked at him, then fished inside his suit jacket for his wallet.

So it was that when Tom and Susan Whatevertheirsurnamewas, who had occasionally been set up on awkward you-live-on-the-same-road playdates with Elliot between the ages of five and twelve, arrived at the platform for the train for London, Elliot was waiting for them.

"Great news!" Elliot declared. He looked them over: Tom's glasses didn't suit him, Susan's hairband matched her shirt, and he felt he was caught up on them. "My dad says I can come inter-railing with you."

"But we didn't—" began Tom.

"But we haven't seen you in y—" began Susan.

Elliot fixed them with a brilliant expectant gaze. He'd found that usually burned away all but the words people were absolutely certain they wanted to say.

Tom and Susan sagged, clearly not having enough conviction to follow through.

Elliot beamed. "We're going to have so much fun, guys."

V

ELLIOT, AGE SEVENTEEN

Inter-railing *was* fun: they soon formed a group of people the same age as they were, the group losing and finding new members at every train station but with a few people there for the long haul. Tom and Susan were still wary of Elliot on account of thinking he was pure mental, but herd mentality kicked in: they did not want to be left out. Elliot's favorite member of the group, though, was a Greek girl called Pinelopi who was traveling on her own because she loved adventure.

In a nightclub they found in one of the back alleys in Prague, with a sword stuck in the stone floor of the lowest level, Elliot tried to kiss her.

She leaned away and laughed. "I thought you were gay."

Something about her easy casual laugh made Elliot laugh too. "And what gave you that idea?"

"Well, the way you were looking at the half-naked guy juggling fire upstairs was one clue."

Prague did have quality entertainment.

"I'm bisexual," Elliot told her, and leaned in again slightly: not touching her, but silently asking her permission to do so.

"Well, the thing is . . .," said Pinelopi, and Elliot's heart sank as he saw her searching for words, waiting for something like '" don't think I could ever really trust a guy who" or "too weird for me, thanks" and felt his heart sink because more than hoping for anything else, he'd *liked* her. "I have a boyfriend," Pinelopi finished.

"Oh," said Elliot. "You never said."

Pinelopi shook her head. "No. This trip for me is about deciding a lot of things—whether I want to go or stay somewhere, who I want to be. I didn't want to close any doors on myself. But I—love him, and more than anything else, I don't want to close the door on that."

"Oh," said Elliot, in a different tone, and smiled. "Understood."

They walked out to see the sights, the next day: the spun-glass frosted fairytale that was the old city in Prague, as if you could cross the fragile arch of a bridge and enter into a world that was all fretwork and ice. From then on, they usually went out together during the day, and met up with the others in the evening and for train rides. There was the stop in Luxembourg and its shimmering gray caves, and the restaurant where nobody could read the menu. There was Florence and the Duomo, a shell-pink building that rose unexpectedly before them out of the night and a shower of summer rain, as if it had risen from the sea.

Elliot went out on his own in Paris, though. He bought gingerbread ice-cream in the early morning and ate it standing on one of the many bridges spanning the Seine. He went from one side to the other, looked at the wiry spike of the Eiffel Tower and the gold-inscribed dome lurking behind it, then from the other side the closer gilt-and-glass bulk of the Louvre. Paris as the morning light washed over it, in glowing pearl and gray.

This was a whole world, the world he'd been born into, and there was so much of it he had not seen. Instead he was going to see seas with mermaids, harpies in the trees, trolls in the mountains. In five years or even ten, when the wars came, he would be there. He could have done something in this world, and he was not going to do it. He was going to do something else, and in choosing one path, another was lost. He spared a moment to feel something almost like grief.

He thought of Pinelopi, and what she had said about not wanting to close the door on love. He thought: as his mother had, as his father had, in their different ways.

If he'd really meant to stay, he would have told Luke and Serene. He would have worked out a way to say good-bye properly. He would have made and kept promises to return another time.

Elliot had thought about staying, but he'd never meant to. And he wasn't going to.

Elliot threw what remained of his cone off the bridge and walked away. The dark rippling river flowed on, without him watching.

When Tom and Susan got off in London, Elliot kissed Pinelopi good-bye and went too. They took the train down together, and early onset nostalgia made Tom and Susan share all their pictures with Elliot and urge him to come by in a couple of days.

"Keep in touch this time, right, mate," said Tom, punching him in the shoulder.

"Light blows as a male substitute for physical affection is a remnant from a brutal warrior culture, trust me on this," Elliot told him, and left the platform.

Gemma was in the kitchen, making dinner before she went home. The house was otherwise gray and still, utterly unchanged. Elliot sat at the kitchen counter and talked to her lightly about his summer, showed her a picture of Pinelopi and a picture of the castle complex in Prague.

"I expect you'll be back to school soon," said Gemma.

"I expect I will."

She hesitated, wiping her hands off on her apron. "I'm not sure if I'll be here when you get back. This place is a little—it's a little much for me."

She didn't have to tell him how it was. He had lived here for years, in a house that wanted to be silent until the silence was broken by a certain step and a certain voice, in a house holding its breath for someone's return. If anyone held their breath long enough, they were dead.

"Who says I'm coming back?" asked Elliot.

He helped her get some glasses down from the top shelf: he was tall enough to reach it, now.

Then he had dinner with his father. It was quiet as usual, but not quiet like usual: this was a watchful quiet. Elliot waited, throughout the whole meal, and watched his father for even a glimmer of desire to speak.

He was not terribly surprised when it did not come.

He followed his father into the other room, and waited again in the quiet, in their last silence, broken only by the clink of his father pouring himself his first drink of the evening.

Then his father sat down, and Elliot spoke.

"You know what day it is. You know what's coming."

"I know that you're going," said his father, his voice tired, as if Elliot had been annoying him for years, as if he was incredibly difficult to bear with.

Elliot stood at the window with the light coming in and tried not to let the heaviness of that look weigh him down.

"Do you know something else? If you'd loved me, I would've stayed," said Elliot. "If you loved me, I would never have gone."

"What do you want me to say?" his father asked. "I never felt it. I don't have it in me."

"I don't want you to say anything. Not anymore. I wanted to say something."

Elliot got up and opened the door, stepped outside the room and looked back, at his father waiting in his chair, drink in his hand, even the light coming in the windows full of dust. Even if his mother came back, Elliot thought, his father wouldn't know what to do or how to feel. What is not used becomes atrophied. He didn't have it in him. And if she returned, Elliot would not be here.

"Your loss," Elliot said to both of them, and shut the door.

That was love: Elliot couldn't command it, couldn't demand it. He could only leave the chill echoing place where it was not.

There was one more thing that Elliot had to do before he left. Carving his name onto a wall that most people would not see, symbolically leaving his name behind, was not really his style. So he bought some spray paint and a ladder.

All over the gray façade of his father's house in scarlet letters he wrote: ELLIOT SCHAFER. He almost added: "was here" but did not, partly because it was a little too clichéd vandal for him, and partly because it did not encompass all he wanted to say: was here, is no longer here, is somewhere almost unimaginably different, is all right.

He washed the red off his hands, whistling, and went to check on his pack. He'd packed everything he could think of, including an iPod loaded up with every favorite song old Joe had ever played for him. It would probably all go up in flames, but he was taking a chance.

He climbed the steps up to the clouds. He walked down to the Borderlands. He did not leave his name behind him, but carried it with him, along with his bag.

"Give it to me," said Luke, sounding weary but also determined to stop Elliot hurting himself. "Whatever contraband you have, hand it over right now."

Elliot did not, of course, but he appreciated the concern.

"WHOO! Go Luke!" Rachel and Serene stood up and yelled, their voices rising over the chaos of the year's first Trigon match.

Under his breath and the sound of cheering, Elliot muttered: "Whoo."

Once the excitement had settled slightly, Rachel lowered herself back down to the bench with a jingle of gold necklaces and reached out for one of Serene's hands and one of Elliot's.

"Luke asked me not to tell you guys," said Rachel. "Well, he asked me not to tell Elliot. I think he thought you would tease him, because this is a little embarrassing."

"High five because the teasing continues to get to him," said Elliot. "You'd think he'd have built up an immunity over the years. Our sensitive flower."

Serene gave him the dead-eyed stare that he loved.

"Self high five," Elliot decided. "Nice to know he still cares."

"But the secret isn't just embarrassing," said Rachel. "It's—it has the potential to be dangerous for him, and scary. He's going to need his friends. And I know you two love him and will support him."

If he hadn't come back, Elliot thought, he wouldn't have been there to support Luke, and he was glad all over again, even if he was a little worried. But Rachel looked calm, and she loved Luke: she would not have been calm if she did not think Luke was going to be okay.

"Though I am honored by your confidence, I am unsure about learning something about my swordsister which he would rather I not know." Serene bit her lip. "On the other hand, if you truly believe my knowing would be to his benefit . . ."

Serene's decision made, Rachel looked to Elliot, and the soft rays of sunlight caught the glitter of her chains and rings, the gleam of her hair, but above all the glow in her eyes, loving Luke and asking for help. It was a look that expected to be answered, a loving, demanding look confident there would be a similar look returned. The turn of summer into autumn would be easy this year, golden and sweet, and Elliot could not help believing they were all going to be all right.

"Sure," said Elliot, laughing. "Please tell me an embarrassing secret about Luke. I would love that."

The news that Luke's biological father was not Michael Sunborn but, in fact, a harpy, was received with stunned silence.

For about ten seconds.

"A harpy?" Elliot asked, staring at Rachel. "So you know all about harpy customs, and their language, and how their matriarchy differs from that of the elves—though I suspect most of the differences arise because in the case of the harpies there are many more women than men, whereas in the case of the elves the numbers are far more equitable—"

"Elliot," Serene interrupted. "Your thirst for knowledge and interest in other species is both praiseworthy and endearing, but—not right now."

Elliot looked at her. Then he looked at the Trigon pitch.

"Oh, right," he said. "Of course."

He squinted over at Luke's golden head, shining amid the dusty hollows of the pitch. He remembered Luke jumping from impossible heights, seeing impossibly distant things. Everything made sense now. They had not been the superlative attributes given to a fairytale hero, after all.

"And he's really going to grow wings?"

Rachel frowned. "They think so. He came in with shoulder pains and the medics said they were quite advanced. That he should have manifested them before now, actually, but he was probably trying to will them away. One medic remarked that he must be very stubborn, but I explained that my Luke has a beautiful nature."

Beautifully pig-headed, Elliot thought as he nodded and smiled and carefully did not agree or disagree.

"Wings," he said easily. "So cool."

They were. Luke did not know it yet, but he would be forced to submit to measurements.

Rachel frowned some more. "He didn't seem—happy. He said that he didn't want you to know. Especially, Elliot, and I know you boys are always joking around like this, but especially not you. I'd appreciate it if you could support him, but let him take his own time to tell you about this."

Especially not you. Elliot tried to keep his face bland and pleasant. It made perfect sense to him, if not to Luke's mother. Rachel didn't know that Luke was not actually Elliot's friend.

"If he doesn't want us to know," Serene said, "it could be a long time before he tells us about it."

"Could be days," Elliot agreed.

Luke was one of the world's worst secret keepers, and painfully sincere. Elliot gave it a week, tops.

"I have given my word that I will keep this secret, and my sword-sister will not be desolate or unsupported while I live," Serene said. "You can rely on both of us."

Rachel tucked her chin into her mass of glittering necklaces, not quite hiding a smile. "Do you know," she said, "I suspected I could."

Elliot returned his focus to the Trigon pitch, where Delia Winterchild had just thrown the glass ball too short. Luke flung himself off one of the crags to catch it, and a murmur ran through the crowd, as if the whole audience were a beast about to rouse.

It had almost looked like Luke was flying.

Luke's face was extremely guilty when he came over to his mother after the game so she could pet and praise him. She gave him a lightning-fast cossetting before saying she had to leave.

"You were wonderful!" Rachel said, kissing Luke all over his face. "And I have to run now, darling. See you at Christmas!"

Her love was like sunlight, delivered in a box and wrapped with a ribbon for Luke alone, but Elliot watched Luke watch her go, and thought of how it might feel, to have sunshine put in your arms and then abruptly taken away: maybe, since Rachel was a soldier, never to return.

Especially at a time like this, when Rachel's exuberantly loving nature had put Luke in a situation he had never anticipated.

Elliot and Serene both made sure to act entirely normal, which meant Serene expressing admiration and Elliot extreme indifference.

"Good form," said Serene.

"Did you win?" Elliot inquired. "I may have dozed off in the stands for a minute there."

Luke snorted in his direction, then went off to get changed. Elliot saw people watching Luke, saw the dark look Delia Winterchild had bent on him, and realized one of the medics must have talked. It was always news that was going to get out, and fast, but Elliot had been hoping for not quite this fast.

He scanned the crowd, looking for people who were whispering delicious new gossip or wearing the expressions of those who had just seen a rumor confirmed before their eyes.

Then he became distracted by another thought.

"Serene! Serene, do you realize what this news means?" Elliot demanded. Serene raised her eyebrows interrogatively. "The worst threat to peace in the Borderlands is the alliance between the trolls and the harpies, which so far has precluded any alliances between them and any other groups. Which means we're always interacting with them as if they're the enemy. But now we have Luke. Harpies tend to nurture and protect the males, because there are so few of them."

"Very natural," Serene murmured. "If you are truly dedicated to a man, you protect him from even the harsh breath of the wind and the cruel eye of the sun."

"Nobody's interested in being protected from air and light, but okay!" said Elliot. "My point is, culturally children, especially male children, are welcomed back to the nest and treated well. This is our chance to form an alliance, and that means that the Borderlands will become a chain of linked alliances, and not enemies. This is fantastic!" He rubbed his hands together. "Two harpies, one stone," he added, and then saw the way Serene was looking at him. "A diplomatic stone! A diplomatic stone."

"I do not think that we should focus on treaties at this time," said Serene. "I think we should focus on being emotionally supportive of Luke. And you should take the lead on it, because your sweet masculine nature predisposes you to understanding and empathy."

Elliot gazed upon Serene. She gazed back at him, her beautiful face full of faith in him and his innate manly tenderness.

"I'm being emotionally supportive the best way I know how," Elliot said eventually. "By which I mean, I'm leaving, and I'm going to the library."

He left, and checked out every book about harpies in the library.

Bright-Eyes the librarian gave Elliot his familiar disapproving look, because Elliot was a wanton floozy with many late fines. "You realize there is a limit on how many books you can take out of the library."

Elliot looked around and saw his former student Cyril Leigh hiding from him behind a bookcase. "Come over here," he commanded. "Take out half these books."

Cyril obeyed. Elliot thought that this terrified obedience, even years later, showed that he had not been a bad teacher after all.

He stowed away the books in his own private cabin—final year was amazing—and then took one up to the top of the commander's tower.

The sun was setting on his first day back in the Border camp, and he was never going back to his father's house.

The sinking sun threw orange and yellow ribbons over the whole land. Elliot looked out over unexplored oceans touched by fire, the shimmer of lakes already in shadow, the fields humans had made and the stretches of deep forest, treetops haloed with sunset, where the elves and dryads lived. Above which the harpies flew.

If they made a solid treaty with the harpies, that would give the Border guard breathing room to work out last year's lousy arrangements between elves and humans. They were at peace with the dryads and the mermaids, and the elves and dwarves' alliance was working better than any alliance with any people ever before. A solid treaty with the harpies, and it would be possible to approach the trolls.

Peace was possible, across the whole of the Borderlands, not peace everlasting but peace for years, peace enough so that all of the groups in this land past the Border would know what it was like to live with and work with each other. They could all learn about each other, and every piece of knowledge about each other gained would take them a step further away from being enemies. Elliot had said he wanted peace before he finished school.

He sat in the stone towertop, book in his lap, making notes while the light lasted.

Woodland and farmland, sky and sea, and peace for years. That was what this news about Luke could bring. Elliot had come back for his friends, and now almost at once this had happened. It seemed meant.

If only he could pull it off.

Later Elliot brought his harpy book and his notes to Serene's cabin, where they sat around her fire and reveled in finally having privacy and no annoying dorm mates.

Or they should have, if the atmosphere had not been so strained. Usually Luke was the good-tempered one, who would respond to anything either of them said and would not take offence even when Elliot was being—he was man enough to admit it—extremely offensive. Now Luke was very quiet, staring into the fire, and Elliot did not know exactly how to carry a whole conversation and at the same time make urgent notes about harpies.

Serene decided that she would cheer everyone up by talking about how amazing her love life was. Apparently she and Golden had pledged their troth, and also made out.

It did not seem to occur to Serene that it might be insulting for her ex to see how much more excited she was about kissing Golden than she ever had been about anything with Elliot. Nor did it seem to occur to Serene that hearing about her amazing new love life might be slightly upsetting for Luke, when he could not seem to get it together with Dale.

"I was sure he would find it cheering!" hissed Serene, as soon as Luke had left. "Everybody revels in the bards' tales of love."

"Well, yes and no," said Elliot. "Everybody revels in the bards' tales of love, but at the same time, everybody is bored and annoyed when forced to hear about their actual friends and their irritating love lives. It's just one of those things."

Serene looked crestfallen.

"Kidding," said Elliot hastily. "I'm kidding. I'm happy for you."

He kissed Serene on the cheek and made his way out into the night. He truly *was* happy for Serene, even if it stung a little. And he thought back fondly to his occasional glances up from his book at

Luke, to see Luke golden by firelight and Luke's eyes already on Elliot, mutely beseeching him for help. That had been hilarious.

It was possible that Elliot should not have found it hilarious.

It was possibly time to accept that Luke had terrible friends and would require support from another quarter.

Elliot wandered around in the dark knocking on cabin doors and receiving responses like "Schafer, I thought I was finally free of you! Go away!" until he knocked on the right door and heard Dale Wavechaser's voice, raised in a welcome to the world, saying: "Come in!"

Elliot pushed the door open and said: "It's Elliot."

He felt fair warning had to be given.

"Cool," said Dale, and did not look dismayed by this information at all. "I was hoping you'd stop by."

Elliot did not see why that would be. He considered the matter, and considered Dale, sitting on his bed and looking rumpled, happy, and extremely handsome. He decided it did not matter.

"Dale," Elliot said winningly. "Dale Wavechaser. Like I know another Dale."

Dale did what Dale usually did around Elliot: smile, but look puzzled. It was a lot more goodwill than Elliot was used to.

"I wanted to talk to you," Elliot added, coaxingly. "Considering this new information about Luke. You have heard the news about Luke?"

"Yeah." There was a sudden flash in Dale's eyes, like light striking a mirror. "I was thinking you might come by."

"Oh?" said Elliot, lost again.

"I mean, I was hoping you'd—want to talk to me about this," said Dale. "This—news about Luke changes things."

"Yes!" said Elliot. "Yes, it does!"

Dale hesitated. "Of course I still really like Luke. But you and I have so much in common."

"Sure, if you say so," said Elliot. "Now, here's the plan. Luke is a romantic, and I had several intricate schemes worked out in which you two seemed to gradually and naturally come together." He made a gesture indicating how Luke and Dale would have slowly mutually discovered the treasure of love. Dale stared in what appeared to be horrified fascination. "However, Luke is in need of immediate cheering up and an ego boost, so I think you should get together right away. I'm going to arrange it. Follow my lead."

He became enthused as he talked, and paced around Dale's little cabin. There were no books in it at all, which he found unsettling, but such things did not matter to Luke.

"What?" said Dale.

"I'd really like to get this done quickly, so I may not be as subtle as I usually am."

"Oh my God," said Dale.

Elliot beamed, nodded, and clasped Dale's shoulder in what he hoped was a gesture of manly agreement.

"*And* if you woo Luke fast, you can definitely come on our trip to make an alliance with the harpies," he promised. "You should try to come. It will be a historic occasion."

"That's true," Dale said. "It would look pretty impressive to commanders, to have been on the harpies expedition."

Dale had no appreciation for history in the making, but Elliot decided to forgive him for that.

"Absolutely,"

"Oh, but, Elliot, I don't know about this—you being unsubtle business, or—"

"You wound me with your lack of faith. Trust me! Trust me. Good night. Good talk," Elliot said. "I'm so pleased you're seeing things my way, Dale."

Elliot did not confine himself to bothering Dale. He also dedicated himself to bothering Commander Woodsinger, who had written to Celaeno, the leader of the nest that Rachel said Luke's biological father had belonged to.

"Good morning, good to see you, just here to show normal military-style respect for you as a cadet to his commander," said Elliot every morning, poking his head around the door. "Did you hear back yet? I like your haircut, by the way."

Commander Woodsinger had cropped her wiry black curls very close. It was extremely military, but it suited her.

"Please do not comment on my appearance or inquire as to my private correspondence, Cadet."

"You're right," Elliot said. "I shouldn't. Only it was reported to me—"

"By one of your spies?" the commander asked.

"No, no," said Elliot. "Not spies. People I have terrorized into doing my bidding and watching other people and places for me. You pay spies. Anyway, a little bird told me—"

Commander Woodsinger sighed. "Celaeno has professed herself eager to meet Luke, and willing to allow a troop from the Border guard to accompany him, and discuss the possibility of an alliance that might be drawn up between our people."

"Ohhhh," said Elliot, deeply pleased. "Sounds like you could use someone from the council course along."

"That would not be standard."

"But you don't live by the man's rules!"

"I live by the law of the land," said Commander Woodsinger.

"Well, this wouldn't be against the law," said Elliot. "Obviously. I have the greatest respect for the law, or whatever. This would just be you, in the wisdom of your command, making an exception to standard practises. For the good of the treaty and your cadets."

Commander Woodsinger sighed again, this time more pointedly. Elliot could almost feel his curls blow back. "I do realize how vital this treaty could be, Cadet," she said. "I intend to lead this mission myself."

"I wouldn't want anyone else to lead our mission, Commander."

"And I have not said you are permitted to come!"

"I understand that, you're thinking about it," said Elliot. "I have faith you will consider the matter from every angle and arrive to the right decision. Which is, to be clear, that you should let me go with you."

He looked around the tower room. It had not changed much since he was thirteen. Commander Woodsinger did not have an eye for home decoration. There were the same stone walls, and the same large desk, only with less paper on it, and no candle too close to the parchment.

And there was a commander behind the desk he respected. He had not really understood what command meant, four years ago.

"Cadet Schafer, since you mentioned my personal appearance, do you know why I got this haircut?" Commander Woodsinger inquired. "It was so that, when faced with your rank insubordination, I would be able to resist the urge to tear my hair out in handfuls."

"Aw, Commander!" said Elliot. "You were thinking of me over the summer. I'm touched."

"Get out of my office," the commander told him. "Get out."

"So you're saying you'll think about letting me come along?" Elliot inquired. "So I'll leave you to think about it."

"Out!"

Elliot paused, trying to find the absolute right thing to say to her. This was so difficult, because it was not just about peace treaties. Because it was about Luke. Elliot could not say *I have to come because he needs me*, because that would be absurd. It was obvious to anyone that Luke did not.

"Even if the treaty was not vital," he said at last. "I have to go."

The commander was silent. He saluted her and went out the door and down the steps of the tower to collect his latest harpy book. He was learning a lot about harpies, but he wished he had started years earlier. Now he only had days, and he had to make a perfect compendium on harpy culture for Luke, so that Luke would understand, and he would not mess the treaty up, and he would not be angry and afraid anymore.

The Border camp was not taking the news about Luke all that well. It might almost have been better if it had been someone who was not Luke, their chosen hero: the cadets acted almost as if they had been betrayed, as if they had been lied to, when Luke had not known himself.

There were too many off-color jokes, remarks in class and whispering outside of class. It reminded Elliot of the way people had acted when he and Serene were going out: little pushes, to make what they did not want to see go away. Except Luke could not make what he was go away.

It was terrible, but these people were terrible and their opinions were terrible. Luke should not let it get to him so much.

This was, obviously, the first time public opinion had not been entirely in Luke's favor. Elliot felt sympathetic about that sometimes, and other times he thought to himself: Wasn't Luke lucky to have lived a charmed life for so long? This little taste of what everybody else got might be good for him.

Elliot tried not to think like that. Sadly, he was most inclined to think like that in Luke's presence, and be sympathetic when Luke was far away. Luke had no idea how concerned Elliot was about him, in classes they did not share or during Trigon games or last thing at night.

And then there was the irritation that came with looking at Luke's stupid sulky face.

Luke confessed three days in, after a particularly bad class and during dinner, which now they were in final year they could eat together rather than in their allotted groups. It was so strange how you got close to being an adult, and suddenly you were a person with a right to privacy and the ability to pick your friends.

Luke had been very quiet throughout dinner, his expression like that of the sun in shock after being subjected to his first cloud. Then his face screwed up in sudden resolution, and he announced: "I'm half harpy."

"Yes, we know," said Serene. "Your mother told us at the Trigon game. But she said not to tell you."

Luke looked betrayed. This seemed unfair to Elliot, since demonstrably they were excellent friends who were prepared to receive Luke's confidences.

"Yes, we know," Elliot chimed in, supporting her statement. "I have not been compiling a comprehensive and yet comprehensible to even the slowest—that's you—record on harpies for my health."

Luke's face was shocked. "What? Give me that!"

Elliot held it out of his reach, smiling. "What will you give me for it?"

"What do you want?" Luke asked, and the way he spoke made Elliot feel very uncomfortable. He sounded like Elliot had sounded when he was younger, negotiating through clenched teeth for the return of his schoolbag.

Except Luke couldn't feel that way. Elliot had done all this research for him: it must be obvious how Elliot felt.

Elliot tried to play it off with a joke. "Let me hide my contraband in your place. I think the commander's planning a raid on mine."

It actually would be very handy to have somewhere else to stow his stuff. Elliot had tried to bring a lifetime's supply of Sharpies. If the commander looked in, it was going to seem as though Elliot had a problem.

"All right," Luke said after a pause. His eyes remained fixed on Elliot. Elliot wondered why, until Luke asked: "How much contraband do you *have*?"

"That isn't important at this time," said Elliot.

Then he hastily turned the conversation to the far more important matter of the treaty, but Luke kept regarding him suspiciously.

Later Elliot carried some of his bags into Luke's cabin, and began to hide bags of Sharpies and calculators in corners, under the floorboards, and behind every book he could find. He was relieved that there were some books in Luke's room.

"Elliot," Luke said, sounding almost awed. "This is *so much contraband*."

"I do like to think of myself as something of a dashing pen pirate," Elliot told him. "The pen is mightier than the sword, you know."

Luke frowned. "Do you, um, want to have a duel?"

"Violence proves nothing," Elliot said.

"Might prove some things," said Luke.

"The fact that we're even arguing about this proverb only proves the enormous power and importance of words," Elliot said triumphantly.

"So that's a no on the duel, then," said Luke. "I guess we disagree on the importance and also the meaning of words like 'proof.'"

Elliot laughed. "I can't believe nobody else knows you're a jerk."

He hid a pencil case filled with ballpoint pens behind a stuffed owl, and then glanced at Luke. That had been Luke's cue to protest, with what seemed to be genuine indignaton, that he was *not* a jerk.

Instead, Luke was staring out the window of his cabin, arms folded, jaw tight.

"You should go canvass the Border camp," he said. "I bet plenty of people share your low opinion of me now."

"My what?" said Elliot. "Why are you being ridiculous? I told you, you being half harpy makes no difference to me at all."

Saying the word might have been a mistake. There was a tic in Luke's jaw suddenly, and he set his shoulders.

"Set" was not really the word for what Luke's shoulders did at this point. There was a suggestion of something uncoiling, or unfurling. There was clearly something remarkable going on under the leather.

Elliot wanted to ask if he could see, but he had the feeling Luke would take that very, very badly.

"Well," Luke said grimly. "I guess you're the only person in the Border camp whose opinion of me hasn't changed. That's great."

Luke *wanted* to make what he was go away. That was what Elliot had not counted on.

Luke could not make what he was go away, though. That was a lesson Elliot and Serene had both learned a long time ago, Elliot thought. None of them could make what they were go away: you had to accept it. Maybe it would be a good lesson for Luke to learn, in the end.

Luke did not seem happy, but he was dealing with it. Commander Woodsinger informed Luke that his presence would be required on the mission to the harpies, and Luke agreed.

"That's great," Elliot said when Luke told them.

"Is it great?" Luke asked. "What exactly do you think is so great about it?"

"I mean . . .," Elliot said. "Aren't you a little curious about the harpies? I know you're doing your soldierly duty and all, but don't you think it might be an adventure?"

Like sailing the seas to find mermaids, or wandering the woods to find dryads, only better: this made finding a part of your self in the sky possible, for Luke.

"No," said Luke flatly. "Stop treating my life as if it was a *game*."

They were so entirely out of sympathy on this. Elliot supposed it did not matter: they hardly ever agreed on anything. It was only that Luke was more irritable, this time around, because he was off balance, because he was unhappy.

Getting together with Dale would make things better for Luke. And gaining an alliance with the harpies would make things better for everybody. Elliot had the situation well in hand.

~

The day of the mission to the harpies was one of those dawns that appeared to have been dropped on the floor and retrieved covered in dust. It was a gray dispirited thing, the day looming ahead dark as the forest.

"I never said you could come with us," said Commander Woodsinger. "I said I would consider it, and you simply assumed that you could. Why is that, Cadet?"

"Well, be fair," said Elliot. "You never said that I couldn't."

"The Border camp is full of people who I did not expressly forbid to come on this mission. Those people are sleeping in their beds, because it was not necessary for me to specifically inform them they were not welcome on a mission I did not invite them to."

"But Commander," said Elliot. "We're special to each other."

Commander Woodsinger gave him a look that was even more forbidding than usual. It was not that she was ever soft or gentle with him, but Elliot thought she might prefer him to speak to her differently when there was a troop of warrior-training cadets who could hear her. He glanced toward their politely listening faces, beyond Serene and Dale. He was grateful Luke was not here yet.

He thought about the fact Luke was not here yet for a moment, and then started to smile.

"The truth is, Commander Woodsinger," Elliot said. "Luke needs me."

The commander raised her eyebrows.

"This is a time of extreme emotional turmoil for him, when it is necessary that he be calm, accepting, and understanding of another culture," Elliot went on. "As one of the people who has been, over the years"—geographically—"closest to him, I feel I would be an asset."

"You with your intensely soothing personality, Cadet," remarked Commander Woodsinger, and a cadet standing behind Serene yelped with laughter.

Elliot thought this was going well. The commander looked less forbidding: if this was the way she saved face and Elliot was allowed to come along, Elliot would take it.

He decided to risk a little actual truth.

"And I want to be with him," said Elliot. "In this time of emotional turmoil, that is."

"It does make sense that Cadet Sunborn might require a certain amount of extra support during this mission," said Commander Woodsinger. "I will permit you to accompany us. You must make sure to be accompanied by a cadet from warrior training at all times, to scrupulously obey every order you are given, and to pull your weight when we are setting up camp."

Elliot saluted. He was very glad the matter was settled, because at that point Luke, who might be gloomy enough not to be early but who was too much of a soldier to ever actually be late, turned up. He looked bowed down, as if he were carrying the whole gray heavy morning on his shoulders.

He gave Elliot a suspicious look. "Why are you here?"

"I'm coming with you!" Elliot informed him.

"You are not coming with us," said Luke. "You were not on the list of cadets assigned to this mission. Because you are not in the warrior training course!"

Luke was so cranky. Elliot beamed. "Ah, but you see, I explained to Commander Woodsinger that this was a time of emotional turmoil and you needed me."

Luke's face was indescribable. Elliot deeply regretted not bringing another camera to the otherlands.

"You what?" said Luke. "I what?"

Elliot made a heroic effort not to laugh, and gave Luke a soulful look. "Don't worry about my schoolwork, buddy. I'm just glad to be here for you."

"I suppose the three of you are inseparable," said Commander Woodsinger. "But you could have asked earlier, Sunborn."

Elliot had not realized that the commander also wished to be hilarious. He shot her a delighted smile. She stared impassively through him.

"He was shy, ma'am," Elliot said. "He's so bashful and modest."

Luke seemed to be struggling to find words: Elliot was familiar with the small hoarse sound he made when too outraged to speak. He had never thought of it as birdlike before.

Then the commander stopped being hilarious and started being unreasonably cruel. She said that Elliot and Luke had to share a tent, just because Serene and Elliot had done a few—well, more than a few—scandalous things in a tent in the past.

"But ma'am!" Luke protested. "I was going to go in with Serene."

"If I wanted to be taking shameless advantage of Cadet Schafer," Serene observed. "No slur intended to his virtue, but . . . I would be."

Elliot would have preferred Serene not announce that in front of the troop, but he could not say she was lying. He also felt it was clear he should have a tent of his own, and he had an excellent scheme to make that happen.

He looked again at the faces of the troop. Oh well. Luke probably suspected already, and Elliot had always said he would make the announcement in front of a class. Close enough.

"It's true," Elliot said, nodding vigorously. "But I need a tent of my own, please. I require extra blankets because it is very easy for me to take a chill, and there are space issues! Besides, I go both ways and I have wandering hands. Nobody is safe with me!"

Nobody looked even faintly surprised, including Luke, who just looked cross.

"You're not going in with Serene, because I am!" Luke snapped.

"This is why we don't take cadets from the council course on missions!" said Commander Woodsinger. "No experience roughing it. No more arguments, Schafer, for once in your life. You go in with Sunborn. Chaos-of-Battle can go in with Wavechaser, since he doesn't fancy women. Schafer, you'll just have to restrain your wandering hands."

Elliot rolled his eyes in her direction. He was clearly going to be an invaluable asset to the mission, and a key part of drafting the treaty between harpies and humans. It was only reasonable to give him his own tent. In a world where diplomats were truly respected, he would have a tent, and people to fan him and hand him ballpoint pens.

Instead, he was forced to trudge through the woods with a heavy bag on his shoulders. Treacherous tree roots kept trying to trip him up, and the uneven ground kept getting away from him.

"I am trying my best," said Elliot, making sure to project an air of noble suffering. "But I am not a sporty type."

Commander Woodsinger gave him a wry look. "You're doing fine. And you can run a four-minute mile."

"So what?" said Elliot. "Wait, is that good?"

Serene and Luke both looked unimpressed, but he became aware that Dale and several other people were nodding with some conviction.

"Wait, have I been *tricked* into being athletic?" Elliot demanded. "Have I been *bamboozled* by people who turned out to *both* be inhumanly sporty?"

He realized what a tactless thing that was to say when Luke's half smile tore off his face like a bandage ripped off too early. Luke put his head down and charged ahead, regardless of tree roots and slopes. Serene kept pace with him easily, and Elliot used some of his apparent-athleticism (he had been tricked!) to do the same.

"I can't believe you," Luke said after a moment. "I cannot believe what you told Commander Woodsinger. I cannot believe the things you think it's all right to say and do, just so you can get your way!"

Elliot had no idea what Luke was talking about. Elliot had not been getting his own way when he was forced to run all those miles. Elliot might have got his own way about this mission, but it wasn't like Elliot had never done anything like this before.

He had not expected, he realized, that Luke would truly not want him there.

The realization kept him silent for a while. There was nothing Elliot could do to make Luke want him. And Elliot still had to be there, for the treaty, despite what Luke wanted.

He hadn't intended to make anything worse for Luke, though. He had no idea how he managed to mess things up, every time. Surely it was some sort of reverse special talent.

They were all quiet, for a long time, Elliot because he did not want to make things worse and Serene in a strong, womanly, supportive way. Elliot did not know why Luke was being so entirely silent, with that absorbed, desolate look on his face. It couldn't be only because of Elliot. He had to be nervous about meeting the harpies. He must want to talk about it.

"Why are you being so quiet, loser?" Elliot asked at last.

"I'm not being quiet," Luke said. "I'm not talking to you. Because you used my actual feelings to get yourself on this trip, and you made it so I'm not sharing with Serene, and you lied to our commander. I didn't ask you, I don't need you, and we're *not* friends."

That made everything very clear.

Elliot had, in fact, made what was already a difficult time much worse for Luke. He absorbed that, took a deep breath, and apologized extensively and at length. He explained that any sort of a treaty with the trolls was proving impossible, and the harpies were the only alternative. He wanted to make sure Luke knew that tormenting Luke had not actually been Elliot's plan. He promised to make it up to Luke.

After Elliot was done talking, Luke looked a little less angry.

Elliot told himself things were all right, or would be all right. Elliot would make Dale and Luke happen. Luke would be in a much better mood then.

"I read some of your notes," Luke offered, after a moment. Elliot wondered how far Luke had read. "About Caroline the Fair."

Not very far, then. Elliot nobly refrained from pointing this out.

"Who was Caroline the Fair?" asked Serene.

"She was a half harpy famous for her beauty," said Elliot. "She had wings the color of pearl and gold. She couldn't fly, so they ended up being decorative, but obviously they really worked for some people. Forty rich men battled for her hand, and each promised Caroline a milk-white steed if they could have a walk with her down by the seashore and a chance to win her heart. Several of the men were drowned by mermaids, with whom Caroline may have had an agreement. She died single with forty milk-white horses. What I'm saying is, she was a fox. A fox with wings. What I'm saying is, as half harpies go, we could do way better."

He was worried a minute later that this would only upset a newly touchy Luke further, but Luke just rolled his eyes and almost grinned, so that was all right.

"I'm not making any agreement with mermaids," Luke said. "I'm tired of mermaids."

"He who is tired of mermaids," Elliot said, "is tired of life."

"He who is tired of mermaids has been hearing about them every day for almost four years," said Luke. "No arrangement with mermaids. Forget it, mermaids."

Elliot and Serene laughed. Luke looked pleased. Sometimes Elliot thought that Luke believed he wasn't funny.

Of course, sometimes Elliot told Luke he wasn't funny.

Elliot remembered sitting in the shadowy privacy of his cabin, writing notes about harpies as exhaustion made the candlelight blur in his vision. He'd liked the stories about Caroline the Fair: he'd chosen someone who had been happy, and whom he thought Luke would find interesting.

There were other stories of half harpies who had lived sad short lives, or wicked lives. Elliot had not written about them.

The books had agreed on one subject. Half harpies tended to be very good-looking. There was much discussion of fine bones, high cheekbones, and aquiline noses. Elliot remembered meeting horrible Neal and Adam, and thinking of how they looked like Luke, but lacking something.

Elliot felt this was a real bright side to harpy heritage.

Though it was not always the case. Some half harpies, like some harpies, had beaks. Not everyone was into beaks.

He thought Luke might be comforted by the idea that his wings might not work: that he might carve out a normal life among humans who would not avoid him as the Border camp's cadets had been.

Of course he could, Elliot wanted to tell him. All of the cadets would get used to it. It was only now that things were new, and strange.

The forest they were walking through was new and strange, too. Elliot had never walked this deep into the woods before. He was used to trees which were not very much bigger than people, but now there were trees so tall that Elliot thought their tops were wreathed in cloud, like the tops of mountains. Elliot could not imagine how the dryad of one of these trees would be, how tower-tall and removed from any semblance of humanity. These were the kinds of woods stories warned you not to get lost in, not to venture off the path into.

Elliot found them a little thrilling.

Then they reached the old battlefield where harpies and trolls had once tried to reclaim territory from humans—though human records said the battle had been a treacherous attack. Elliot was not sure whose records to believe, since nobody could be trusted when they wanted something.

The ground that humans, trolls, and harpies had all wanted stretched gray and bleak and uninviting before them. Elliot heard

Luke make a low, disgusted sound in the back of his throat. He had stepped on a human skull, half embedded in the earth.

Elliot's notes had not focused too much on the harpies' relationship with the dead. Harpies' lives were intertwined with the dead as mermaids' lives intertwined with water: they tore apart the corpses of their enemies, carried off their enemies' bones to decorate their own bodies and their own nests. They cast the remnants of their loved ones into the air, and kept mementoes of them: the hair of the loved and lost braided into their own hair. Love and hatred endured long past death, for harpies: death changed nothing.

Elliot had thought Luke might be disturbed.

And so much of what Elliot had read came from outside sources and not the harpies themselves. He wanted to talk to them, to hear them tell their own stories, to find out the truth.

Past the battlefield was a new forest which humans called the Forest of the Suicides, to mark how many had died on its borders. Elliot wondered what the harpies called it.

There were harpies soaring above the trees, like vast birds or strange clouds. They were waiting for them, Elliot thought. They were waiting for Luke.

When they entered the Forest of the Suicides, the leader came.

She came flying, in a rush of wind and wings, and for a moment Elliot thought Luke might run. Elliot went around Serene, so that Serene and he were flanking Luke, so they were on either side, ready to support him. Elliot saw the flash of Luke's blue eyes, registering his presence, and then saw him look at Serene. Luke lifted his chin.

The leader of the harpies was beautiful and bizarre, her clothes bones, her body a lion's, an eagle's, a woman's, and yet wholly her own. She had braids and an air of natural authority that reminded Elliot of his commander, and she had eyes only for Luke. Her eyes were blue, as well.

"I am Celaeno, the leader of this flock," she said.

Luke said, his voice polite but challenging, hesitant but unafraid, and sure of who he was in the face of any claims otherwise: "I'm . . . I'm Luke Sunborn."

Sunborn must be a name she knew: a name the humans must have shouted on that long-ago battlefield beyond the trees. Maybe they should have advised Luke not to say his surname. Maybe he would not have listened, if they had.

Celaeno hesitated. Then she bid Luke, and all who had come with Luke, welcome.

It should have been easy. After a round of introductions the harpies had made them welcome and left them to eat and rest, the tents had been set up, and all that was left to do that evening was make Luke happy.

Elliot went to the cooking fires and fetched Dale over to Luke's side. Then Elliot made a massive, heroic sacrifice and initiated a conversation about Trigon. Luke was glowing. Dale looked so happy, it was almost sad.

Elliot concentrated on not bleeding out of the ears with boredom. He waited, like a matchmaking panther, to pounce on the precise right moment, and then excused himself. He invited Serene to excuse herself, too.

"I'm comfortable here," said Serene.

It was possible Elliot should have explained his scheme to Serene before now. Still, Serene loved Luke and was occasionally capable of tact: surely she would be driven off by Dale and Luke's undeniable chemistry.

Elliot had been gone for approximately two minutes, lurking by the cooking fires and making conversation with Delia Winterchild, when Dale fled.

"Excuse me," Elliot said. "I see an emotional situation going wildly awry."

"Yeah," said Delia. "That's life."

She looked amused. She had never liked Luke, Elliot knew, not since the wars that had killed her twin and made Luke a hero. Elliot had always understood that, but Darius's death had not been Luke's fault. He didn't want her kicking Luke when he was down.

He did not have time to argue with her right now, because he had to go back and scold Luke for letting Dale get away. Elliot could not, he felt strongly, help those who would not help themselves to some sweet sweet loving.

Telling Luke off did not go well.

"Excuse me if I'm a little hesitant when I know I can't even take off my shirt in front of somebody," Luke snarled. "Because I'm turning into a monster!"

Elliot was so shocked by this view of what was going on that he went silent. There was nothing he could say to Luke to make this better, he thought. Luke did not care what Elliot's opinion of him was. Elliot had to insure that Dale proved to Luke that *Dale* did not think of him that way: that Dale still wanted Luke, more than anyone else.

That night, in their tent, Elliot said anxiously: "But you did have fun, talking to Dale?"

If Luke had not had fun, Elliot was out of ideas. Luke had seemed so pleased, just to be having the conversation. Elliot did not know where it had all gone wrong.

"Yeah, it was nice when we were all talking. But then you left for no reason," Luke said accusingly. "And Dale ran away."

"Okay, I get it," said Elliot. "It's all my fault."

The next day, Luke had a private meeting with Celaeno, and that meant Elliot had free time to make friends with several very nice harpies, then cut Dale off from the rest of the troops and tell him what he thought about that running-away business.

He was very unhappy that he had to leave the harpies, since several of them seemed startled and delighted by his inquiries about their customs. He might have been slightly sharp with Dale.

"It got very awkward after you left," Dale mumbled.

"I'm going to have to leave at some point when you get together," Elliot said. "Unless you and Luke have some very specific exhibitionist fetishes, which I would not judge you for, but I have known Luke a long time and I find the idea vanishingly unlikely. You have to pull yourself together. You can't go running off like that again. You have to think of other topics which will engage Luke," Elliot instructed. "I think it would be nice if you played a pick-up game of some sort. Also maybe a romantic picnic in the Forest of the Suicides. I don't think the name should put you off. Besides, the harpies have a different name for it. I don't know what it means yet, but the sound is very pretty. You should ask one of them how to say it. And you should try to strike up a conversation with Celaeno. You do realize she is related to Luke, right?"

Dale looked badly startled.

Elliot nodded. "She's one of his biological father's nestmates. Though harpies don't have words like 'aunt.' That does mean, however, that Luke is technically of high rank among the harpies, which is cool, don't you think?" He gave Dale an expectant look. "What a catch."

"Elliot!" Dale screamed. "Stop!"

"What?" Elliot asked defensively. "I'm just making a scheme for your future happiness. You don't want to be happy in the future? What's your objection to the future? What's your objection to happiness?"

"I don't have an objection to happiness," Dale said. "It's just—Luke."

"You have an objection to Luke?" Elliot snapped. "What possible objection could there be to Luke? He's smart—and he's champion—and he's radiantly good-looking—"

"He's great," said Dale.

Elliot frowned. "Well, I don't know if I'd go that far."

Dale gave Elliot a look that said he was surrendering when Elliot was not aware they were fighting a battle. Many people seemed to approach conversations with Elliot this way, so he shrugged it off and gestured for Dale to speak.

"He's just a little—"

"Constantly eternally insistently in your face twenty-four seven?" Elliot cut in sympathetically.

"Distant?" said Dale.

"Well, obviously we're having a slightly different Luke experience," said Elliot. He folded his arms and regarded Dale, who seemed dispirited. It could simply be an effect of prolonged conversation with Elliot, but in case it was not, Elliot added encouragingly: "Luke is shy! That's the problem. He's shy because he likes you so much. It's beautiful if you think about it. Don't you think it's beautiful?"

He regarded Dale sternly. Dale nodded.

"Good," said Elliot. "Good."

"It's really nice of you to go to all this trouble," Dale offered, after a moment. "I mean . . . you're really nice. Knowing you care that much . . . about me . . . is nice."

"Ahahaha," said Elliot. "Sure. And if you follow all the details of my plot carefully, everybody will be happy forever. Won't that be nice? Now, remember we don't know each other."

"Luke knows that we know each other—"

"But we can't know each other too well!" Elliot warned.

Dale did not look ready for this level of subterfuge.

Elliot gave up on a soothing tone and patted Dale's (second-most muscular in the Border camp, hello) arm instead. "Everything is going to go great, provided you do exactly what I want."

He sensed a presence at his side, glanced in that direction, and found himself staring at a dead rabbit.

"Aaaaagh!" said Elliot.

"I'm gonna go," said Dale, and ran.

The dead rabbit, hanging at eye level, stared at Elliot with a glazed regard. Elliot eventually pulled his gaze away from the creature and looked to the harpy who had alit on the grassy bank beside Elliot and was holding her prey aloft with what seemed to be pride.

"This is for you," she told him.

"Oh," said Elliot. "How kind. How did you guess that I love . . . dead things?"

She inclined her head. He could make out the actual pattern of feathers in her hair: it was so fascinating. He found himself smiling with reflexive admiration, even in the presence of dead rabbits. Then he wondered what smiles meant to harpies, when some had human-looking mouths and some had beaks. Surely the greater variety made for a greater range of expression. He wondered if he could ask.

"I caught it myself," the harpy told him.

Elliot appreciated the harpies' efforts to bond across the species divide and make this treaty work. He wished she had approached someone else, as even after years on this side of the Border he felt queasy around dead uncooked animals. The rabbit dangled, swaying slightly from side to side. Elliot averted his eyes from its hypnotic swing.

"I am one million percent genuinely impressed," he said firmly. "You're Podarge, aren't you? Celaeno mentioned that you were an expert gardener. I would be so interested to learn the differences and similarities between human and harpy methods. You seem like the ideal person to talk to. If you would care to share your expertise."

Podarge ducked her head and blushed, color rising around her beak. "If you really want me to."

Oh. Oh, Elliot understood why he had been brought a dead animal. He brightened up.

"I do," he said. "Would it be forward of me to add that I really like your hair?"

"I like *your* hair!" said Podarge. "I can see it from leagues up in the sky."

"You sure can," said Elliot. "Like a small localized forest fire, and up until this moment I thought of it as just about as disastrous."

Luke's heritage was great, he thought, and forays to make treaties were great, and he, Elliot, might be about to get a girlfriend who could fly! A flying girlfriend! He could not wait to tell Serene.

Then he saw Celaeno and Luke approach. Normally, he would have been pleased to see Luke and his aunt (his flying aunt!), but at this precise moment he felt he could have done without them. He tried to make a subtle gesture to Luke to go away. Luke squinted and frowned at him.

"You have feathers in your hair."

"Yeah, they get all over, I've just learned to accept it," said Elliot as Luke came over, pulled the feathers out, and threw them on the ground. "Or not."

Celaeno looked at Elliot, Podarge, and the rabbit. She had a somewhat severe air about her at all times, but it was increased enormously now. She looked at the dead rabbit as if it had wronged her family.

"Podarge, a word in the air, if you would."

Podarge jumped at the tone of command—literally jumped into the air, so she and the bunny swiftly became nothing more than a speck against the clouds.

Elliot could not work out where it had all gone wrong.

"That was my dead creature," he said forlornly. "It was for me."

"Yeah, you're hilarious and what you told Commander Woodsinger was *so* believable," Luke muttered.

Luke had now referred to something that Elliot had told Commander Woodsinger about fourteen times. Elliot could not imagine what he meant, and Elliot was really starting to worry he'd told the commander something ludicrous, like that he wouldn't cause any trouble. He also didn't know why Luke thought he was currently making a joke.

Things did not look good in the awesome flying girlfriend department. Possibly Celaeno thought that human and harpy mingling would be detrimental to the treaty. Elliot sighed wistfully. He did not want to do anything that would damage the treaty.

"Did you get on well with Celaeno," he asked, poking Luke. "Tell me you didn't say anything stupid. No, wait, it's you: tell me you didn't say anything *too* stupid."

Luke did not look mildly irritated, as he usually would have. He looked tired, and he still had that certain air of low-lying anger which had hung around him like a shadow since his mother had told him the truth, and which Elliot had never seen on him before.

"I don't know," he said, his voice heavy. "She said stuff about . . . my wings. I don't think she knew what she was talking about."

"She does have a pair of her own, though," Elliot pointed out.

Luke gave him a dark look. "She gave me a skull to drink out of."

"Oh, loser, tell me you respected her traditions and drank out of her skull!"

Luke sat down on the bank and ran his hand through his hair, then stayed with his head bowed and his hand in his hair, as if he'd wanted to put his head in his hands but did not want to betray that level of vulnerability.

"I drank out of her skull," he said. "I tried to be polite. I wish all of this was over and we were going home."

"I think Dale went that way," Elliot tempted him.

Luke did not respond to this offered treat.

Elliot offered a different treat. "I think Serene is practising with a couple of other cadets and a longbow in the woods!"

Luke did not go off to excel at physical activities. Luke chose to sit in the dirt, because that was a super fun time.

"Do you want to hear about the significance of the dead and the attitude to mortality in harpy culture?"

Luke lifted his head for just long enough to give Elliot a baleful stare, then dropped it. "Of course I don't."

The autumn sun streamed down on the grassy bank, on Luke's bent golden head and hunched broad shoulders. The stream of sunlight was broken by the moving dark, the fluttering shadows cast by the leaves, and the wheeling, moving shadows cast by the harpies high above, their presence disrupting the whole sky.

"So leave," Elliot suggested, settling himself on the bank. "Go find something more fun to do, because I'm going to talk about it."

"Can I stop you," Luke muttered.

He could, actually: he could have belted Elliot across the mouth to shut him up, which had been done before, though the idea of Luke doing it was so ridiculous Elliot found it actually funny. Luke could have surrendered like Dale or just given up and walked away. But it had been four years now, and he hadn't: so Elliot's priorities were first Luke, then the treaty, and a long, tragic way back, flying girlfriends.

This was not the hilarious situation Elliot had originally believed it was. Luke was upset, in a new and disturbing way. If it meant delivering Dale on a plate, carrying through peace with the harpies single-handed, or just filling in the time until Serene returned and was able to comfort him in ways Elliot had never learned, they were going to get through this.

"Listen up, moron," Elliot said tenderly. "There are some things you should know."

Word seemed to have got out that the humans were friendly.

That evening around their cooking fires, more than a dozen harpies approached Elliot specifically, to tell him details about harpies' domestic lives and religious beliefs. Nobody made any advances of a sexual nature to Elliot, though.

Not that Elliot expected people to constantly make advances of a sexual nature to him. Podarge's move had got his hopes up that harpies were into redheads, however, and it was a disappointment when even very attractive harpies his own age treated Elliot in a strangely aunt-or-cousin-like fashion. As if he were one of the family.

"I'm so interested in harpy marriage customs!" Elliot said brightly.

"How lovely," one harpy with beautiful blond braids told Elliot. "You should wed in high summer and wear one of our oak-leaf coronets in your hair. Celaeno would make you a coronet with her own hands."

"I'd be delighted," said Elliot. "Hypothetically. If I get . . . hypothetically married."

The harpies were weird, but they were nice. They were welcoming, even though too many of the troop remained wary of them. Elliot cast dark glances at Dale and Delia, who both lurked in a terrified clump outside the light of the cooking fires and away from the harpies.

Commander Woodsinger was stiff but perfectly civil, and Serene, naturally, was being an avatar of elven perfection, discussing weaponry and different battle techniques and hot gentlemen. Elliot heard her shyly confiding about her sweetheart back in the elven woods to a few harpy warriors.

Luke was also very good, somewhat to Elliot's surprise. He stayed close by Elliot, which was absolutely correct behavior because Elliot knew the most about harpy customs, and he drank out of several skull cups and even, at Elliot's not-really-but-trying-to-be-gentle-nudging, talked about archery and other forms of hunting. Elliot knew enough about archery, to his eternal shame, that he could tell they were talking about it from the perspective of having better eyesight than humans. He wondered if Luke knew that.

The harpies were making a real effort. The harpies wanted Luke. Elliot could not even imagine how it would be, to have two families who wanted you.

He tried not to be angry with Luke, who had always belonged to a family who wanted him, and had not wanted another.

He was angry with the rest of the troop, and expressed this at length later in his and Luke's tent.

"Elliot," said Luke. "I know you're not in warrior training, so you are not as familiar with missions or battles that require sleeping outside. Maybe you're not familiar with tents. But the thing is, tents are made out of material. Material is not like walls. People can hear you through tents."

"Oh, really?" said Elliot. "Thank you for that information about tents. Very useful." He raised his voice. "And another thing about how unacceptably rude the company is being . . ."

Luke gave Elliot a look that suggested he thought *Elliot* was being unacceptably rude, so Elliot was forced to explain to him at length why the treaty was necessary. He even brought up something that had been worrying him for some time, but which he had never mentioned before.

There were humans living on the other side of the wall who could climb over. There was every chance somebody from Elliot's world would see something to exploit on the other side of the Border, and come for it. If that day came, the people of the Borderlands had to be ready, and they had to be united.

Luke did not look convinced about any of this, but he listened.

"We'll have the alliance," he said, at last, and Elliot thought it was meant to be comforting. "You're very good at being friendly with the harpies. Maybe too good."

And what was that supposed to mean? Elliot frowned. Luke grinned.

"Celaeno called you a pretty thing," he said, and Elliot was flattered for an instant before Luke set fire to the moment by adding, in an unacceptably casual voice: "But don't worry: I told her you were my boyfriend."

What? said Elliot, from the depths of his soul. What? What? What?

"You did what?" he asked. He was proud of himself for not shrieking.

Luke frowned, as if he found Elliot's calm, measured response to insanity unsatisfactory in some way. "You're welcome."

Elliot realized, with a sudden burning sense of indignation, why Celaeno had taken Podarge and Elliot's dead bunny of love away, and why all the harpies had treated him like a member of the family. Because Luke thought this was an appropriate time to torment Elliot with practical jokes.

"Why are you out to ruin my life? Is it your idea of fun? Oh no, no awesome autumn flings for Elliot, his life has to be a never-rounding end of misery because Sunborn says, is why, because that's hilari—"

"Oh my God," Luke exploded. "Don't tell me you would let one of those creatures touch you!"

There was a sudden silence. Luke looked upset, but he did not look as if he realized the depths of disgust and self-hatred he had just revealed. Elliot had no idea how to respond to any of it: to how Luke felt, or what Luke had said, to the argument Luke thought they were having, or the argument they were actually having.

He felt like a child who had wandered off the path into the dark woods. He was not remotely thrilled any more. This was not an adventure. This was just being lost in the dark.

Elliot did not work out a way to respond. He wasn't the one who could convince Luke he was wrong. He changed the subject awkwardly to the horrific privations of camping, and pretended to go to sleep soon after.

Luke scoffed at his complaints about being cold, uncomfortable, and far from civilization, but once he thought Elliot was asleep, he covered Elliot carefully with his own blanket. Elliot had his eyes closed, but he felt Luke's breath against his cheek, and Luke's hand drawing the blanket over Elliot's shoulder.

Once Luke was asleep, Elliot sat up in the tent and his new nest of blankets, and looked down at Luke. He was sleeping curled up around his pillow, gold hair in his face, and even his sleeping face looked troubled and puzzled, the face of someone for whom trouble was new.

For a moment, Elliot thought that he would throw away the treaty and everything the treaty meant, if only he could make Luke feel better.

It was a ridiculous thing to think. Elliot was worried he was coming down with something.

When Elliot woke up that morning, he was comfortably warm, which was excellent. Luke was bothering him about something, which was not.

Luke kept yammering at him to wake up right now, but there didn't seem to be a battle or a literary dispute or anything too urgent going on, so Elliot continued snoozing. He was really warm, for the one of the first times in the Borderlands, where the weather was worse than England and the heating situation was medieval. The blankets felt heavy and warm as down, and when Elliot cracked an eye open he saw the tent arched above him, gold and shining.

Except the tent was not gold.

Elliot opened his eyes.

There was no need for alarm. The tent had not magically transformed into a golden dome overnight. The tent was simply filled with wings. The idea sounded scary, as if Elliot had been enveloped in a storm of birds, but the reality was anything but. The moment was quiet, the wings motionless and serene, even the sounds of the outside world muffled. The wings, gold-touched pearl like those of Caroline the Fair from long ago, caught the light filtering in through the fabric of the tent. They turned into bright gilt arches which were, somehow, soft and warm and alive.

Elliot reached up a hand and ran his fingers lightly, very lightly, down the radiant row of feathers.

"Elliot," Luke said, sounding as if he were holding onto the fraying edge of the robe of Patience. "Do not touch them!"

Which was when Elliot was forcibly reminded that these living wings belonged to a living person, and his behavior was completely terrible. He snatched his hand back and, in a move that would have surprised absolutely no one who had ever met him, began to babble.

He heard his own voice, bringing up Jase and the fact Jase'd had ginger in his goatee. He was stunned and dismayed by his own lack of subtlety. Really, he was bringing up his ex-boyfriend? Really? Elliot despaired of himself. He might as well have said 'Whoa, Luke, buddy, enough of your personal feelings of self-doubt and trauma over body horror, because those wings are really working for me.'

Fortunately, Elliot babbling was normal enough behavior that it actually seemed to calm Luke down. Luke worked out how to fold his wings back up, and Elliot only made one joke containing the words "morning wing" which was restraint, because he'd thought of forty-seven.

"Shut up forever," said Luke, trying to pull his shirt on. He had chosen a linen shirt rather than his usual leather, but the shirt still presented him with a certain amount of difficulty. For obvious reasons.

Moment with the wings aside, Elliot was a bigger person than to stand around checking out his friends when they were in trouble. It didn't matter how shirtless they happened to be. Such things were totally irrelevant to him.

"Okay," he said. "Let me help you."

"No!" Luke snapped.

"Okay," Elliot soothed. "Only someone has to. Do you want me to get Serene, or Da—"

"*No,*" said Luke, and his voice was terrible, cracking or turning into a croak like a raven's, Elliot could not tell and it did not make any difference, because either way it meant Luke was totally freaked out.

"Okay," Elliot said for a third time, voice as soft and consoling as he could make it. "Give me a knife."

"What?" Luke asked. "Oh no. What are you planning to do with a knife?"

This was familiar alarm, alarm Elliot knew perfectly well how to deal with: alarm at what terrible thing Elliot might do next.

"Trust me," Elliot said, almost laughing.

"Oh no," Luke muttered again, and handed him the knife.

It was one of the knives Luke habitually carried, familiar enough to Elliot that it was not disturbing to handle. The bone handle was worn smooth in Elliot's hand, and since the knife was owned by Luke, who took conscientious care of all his things, the blade was sharp enough to cut fabric with ease.

Elliot pulled the shirt out at the back so it billowed, slicing the material at the points where the shirt folded, so the material would still conceal the wings but there would be room for them to unfold.

Luke was obviously a long way from relaxed, the muscles of his shoulders knotted and the feathers in his wings trembling as if caught in an upward draft of wind. Elliot put a hand on the back of Luke's neck absentmindedly as he did his extremely rough version of tailoring for wings.

"Shhh," he said.

"You shouldn't," Luke said. "You shouldn't have to touch—"

"I don't mind," Elliot said, calm and factual.

He stepped back and examined his handi-or-knifiwork critically. It really was not so bad.

And this was a good development, Elliot thought. Rachel Sunborn had said so, and the medics back at home and the harpies here had all agreed: it was time, and past time, for the wings to come out. This was always going to happen, and not the disaster Luke imagined.

Also wings were cool.

He did not express these feelings to Luke. It was not Elliot's body. If it had been, Elliot might be considerably more disturbed. Luke did not have to agree that wings were cool, Elliot reminded himself. He just had to cope.

He was coping all right, Elliot thought. He was recovered enough to be cranky about Elliot's clothing.

"What is that on your shirt?"

"It's a rock band," Elliot answered.

Luke gave him a look that clearly conveyed Luke's disdain for the idea that stones could form a group.

"And what are those?"

"They're jeans. Remember?"

"Oh, I remember. And they're as awful as I remember," Luke scolded. "And they're contraband! You can't wear contraband. The commander will be furious."

Elliot was amused. "We're on holiday. Besides, what's she going to do about my contraband clothes? Execute me?" He fished one of his pens and a notebook out of the pocket of those jeans things, glanced up and saw Luke still looking disapproving. He stepped in and drew the pen over Luke's throat, pretending to be the commander cutting it. "Confiscate them?" he said, and grinned. "Hardly. I have to go meet Podarge, she's a very nice lady, she promised to show me how harpies garden."

He left Luke alone to go do what Luke was obviously dying to do, which was walk into the veiling trees of the forest and remove all the feathers from his hair. Elliot himself was not on any search-and-rescue feather mission. His hair was a trap made of ginger snakes, and he was living in proximity to a hundred harpies. It was time to embrace the unintentional feather headdress.

Podarge gave Elliot a wistful look as he met her near her nesting tree.

"I do apologise for yesterday's misunderstanding," she said.

"Heh," said Elliot. "About that . . ."

He tried to work out a way to explain Luke's joke that did not make Luke sound prejudiced against harpies. He gave up.

"No worries," he said finally. "You know, when I go home I would love to keep in touch with you through letters. Would you be willing to write to me?"

Podarge looked worried.

"I really want to learn about aerial gardening through the seasons," Elliot said, truthfully.

"I suppose it couldn't hurt," Podarge decided.

Elliot glowed. "Wonderful!"

Surely in one of those letters, he could manage to casually mention that he was single and fancy-free. And the letters meant they could get to know each other better. Project flying girlfriend might still be on.

"Now," said Elliot. "Tell me—"

That was when a shadow blotted out the sun. Elliot realized, in a dark moment of revelation, that harpies did that on purpose: that they knew where to fly so they would cast a shadow over the camp and send a silent alarm.

Podarge was already in the air when the second, unnecessary alarm sounded. The harpy shouted: "Troll force in the woods!"

Elliot was aware of exactly how badly this could go, when the trolls saw the humans in the harpies' territory and understood that an alliance was being drawn up. A troll sentry must have seen one of the troop, and if the harpies had not informed them the humans were coming, the trolls might be very angry indeed.

One of the spears landed in the ground beside Elliot, thick as a young tree with a pointy end. Elliot regarded it thoughtfully.

Then he ran to find Serene.

There were a lot of trolls, far more than would have been in even a group of sentries. This was planned. And, Elliot thought, weaving through the trees and out of sight: this was vicious. He could see the trolls, so much larger and stronger than humans, flinging members of his troop around like dolls. He thought the trolls were out to prove to the harpies how useless human allies would be.

The harpies were amazing, swooping down and plucking humans off the ground and out of the trolls' reach. The humans, in turn, were adapting to being picked up and carried off fast. Elliot saw Natalie Lowlands grasped in a harpy's talons and using her bow. With the harpies' help, it was easier for humans to keep their distance from the trolls, so the trolls' greater strength and reach mattered less.

Elliot was still keenly aware that he could be crushed at any moment. He was relieved and delighted to find Serene.

He was less relieved and delighted that she was out of arrows, whirling around and trying to stab three trolls at once.

"Elliot!" she called out. "Fear nothing! I will save you!"

"Um, is your hair actually soaked with blood?" Elliot asked, delicately.

Serene gave him a blank look, then stabbed a troll in the foot with a sharp tooth on the forest floor. Elliot suspected the tooth actually belonged to the poor troll in question. She danced backward as the troll bellowed in rage. "Not my blood."

"Oh," Elliot said doubtfully. "That's cool, then."

Another troll came at Serene, and Serene laughed a high, pure, joyous laugh. Elliot flattened himself against a tree. Serene looked so small, valiant and daring and utterly outmatched, blades flashing and hair swinging as she turned in the circle of trolls. The trolls were closing in, and Elliot did not know how to help her.

Then came a descent of gold from the trees. Elliot caught his breath.

It was Luke, and he was flying. He was a gilded waterfall of flash and feathers, and he carried Serene away.

This became a less spectacular moment when the trolls, robbed of their prey, turned their heads and noticed Elliot.

"Hi," said Elliot, seeing one troll's eyes narrow. "Hey? No?"

No sign of comprehension on any of the trolls' faces.

"You know," Elliot continued, edging around the tree. "I understand your point of view. I should have learned trollish sooner. I should not expect people to comprehend my language. This is all happening because of my poor judgement."

The trolls advanced.

"*Parlez-vous francais*?" Elliot asked, and bit his lip. "I didn't think so."

He heard the scream of someone, a human badly hurt or dying, in the distance. Then he heard a far more welcome sound: the sound, above Elliot and descending, of wings.

Luke had barely landed before Elliot flung his arms around Luke's neck. He held on while Luke ascended, which was a strange unsteady and wonderful feeling, mindful of the fact Luke had only started flying today.

"Don't let me die. I'm brilliant and worth at least four soldiers, and you'll need me when the battle's over."

"I won't let you die," Luke promised.

Elliot could feel Luke's heart hammering, closer than the beat of wings in the wind. His own heart was going pretty fast. No more excuses: he was going to learn how to speak to trolls this year.

Luke dropped him, with care, at a point among the trees where Elliot could still hear the sounds of battle but could not see any of the combatants.

"Stay here where I can see you," Luke said, absently palming the back of Elliot's head. "I'll be in the air. I'll see if anyone approaches and I'll deal with them. Don't go anywhere."

"I'm not an idiot," said Elliot.

Luke's eyes narrowed down to sapphire chips.

Elliot saluted and smirked at him. "I'll do exactly what you say. I swear. Sir."

Instead of ripping all his hair out, Luke flew away. Elliot mentally congratulated Luke on this choice.

Elliot waited outside the trees, listening to the sounds of battle, until they faded away. He had his usual special time of wondering whether everyone he cared about was dead, but he listened even harder and made out the sound of human voices, laughing and shouting with triumph, and the shriek of harpies dominating a victorious battlefield. Elliot made his way back to the campfire, where he was met by an anxious Serene.

"There you are," she said, patting him down, searching for any sign of injury, as he cradled her blood-streaked face in his hands and studied her for any sign of the same. "You're safe! And Luke's safe. And we won!"

"Where's Luke?"

"With the other harpies," said Serene casually.

Elliot frowned. "I doubt he's—er, doing what harpies usually do to the bodies of their enemies."

Maybe he was, though. Maybe it was like flight: maybe it was instinct. Whatever the case, Elliot hoped that Luke was at least being polite to the harpies, because as long as Luke could keep it together, this treaty was made. The trolls had made a fatal mistake. There was nothing like a common enemy to unite people.

Serene felt this was the case, too.

"Commander Woodsinger, can Cadet Chaos-of-Battle and I have a teeny, weeny look at the current draft of the treaty?" Elliot asked.

Commander Woodsinger, flushed with triumph and the exertion of battle, paused and finally nodded. "Try to keep your edits teeny weeny, all right, Cadet Schafer?"

Elliot did not make any promises. Serene sat beside him, leaning her chin on his shoulder, and they looked at the parchment.

"Oh, now that won't do," said Serene, pointing.

Elliot uncapped his ballpoint pen and opened his notebook.

A very happy time followed, in which he changed every word of the projected treaty. Several of the troop stopped by as they worked. Delia Winterchild delivered, with obvious reluctance and a troubled face, the news that Luke had saved her life during the battle.

"Of course he would do as much for any comrade," Serene said innocently.

"So true," said Elliot. "What a guy."

Delia went off to think it over by herself. She had not been particularly kind to Luke since the harpy reveal. Elliot figured this would do her nothing but good.

Dale dropped by purely to check on Elliot's well-being, because he was a sweetheart.

"I was looking for you all over," he said, crouching down. "I know you can't fight. I was really worried."

"That's so nice," said Elliot, scribbling. "So unnecessary, but so nice."

"Couldn't you promise," Dale said, and hesitated. "To stick by me, if you're ever caught up in another battle? I wouldn't ever let you be hurt."

Elliot glanced up from the page, and into Dale's kind eyes. He felt a pang of anxiety, as if something was badly awry, but Dale was only showing concern. It was good of him. It wasn't anything to be worried about.

"Don't worry about it," Elliot said at last. "Luke and Serene take care of me."

"Of course we do," said Serene, smacking a kiss on Elliot's cheek. "And we always will."

Elliot wondered if he was imagining it that Dale went away looking slightly crestfallen.

"Despite the fact he is a warrior, he has a beautiful warm nature," Serene remarked. "Manly and nurturing. I think that he is such an excellent choice for Luke's sweetheart. I could wish he had a slightly more broadminded attitude to elves, but I think he is improving, and besides, men can be rather prejudiced sometimes, bless them."

"Am I?" Elliot asked. "I mean—more so than women you know?"

"You are exceptional, and exceptionally dear to me," said Serene, and Elliot could not help smiling. "I do not mean to insult Dale," Serene went on. "I am ready to love him."

So was Elliot. He had been trying for years, partly for Luke's sake and partly for Dale's own. It made Elliot feel guilty that he still found Dale painfully boring at times, especially when Dale was so good to him.

At times like these, warm with Dale's regard and Serene's, Elliot was prepared to admit the fault was his. If he was a better person, he would appreciate Dale more, and he would never dream that Dale's kindness meant anything more than it did.

The mere idea was laughable. Elliot remembered how the kiss with Dale by the lake had ended, how Dale had been suffused with incredulous radiance to hear Luke Sunborn liked him. He had not given Elliot another thought. Serene had witnessed Dale expressing concern for Elliot tonight, and seen nothing amiss with it. Even Serene, who loved Elliot better than anyone in any world, knew that nobody would choose Elliot when they could have Luke.

And if that hurt sometimes, it was nothing Elliot had not known for years, and nothing he could not deal with.

Elliot finished drawing up the treaty. Serene was leaning companionably against him and reading when Luke came up to them. His wings were folded and he looked a little pale and tired, but he was entirely whole and unhurt. Elliot lifted a hand in greeting and, since Luke was being quiet, informed him of all the things that were going right in the world. Serene and Luke had rescued Elliot from being squashed by trolls, and peace seemed assured.

"We're going to have a treaty, as soon as the harpies are done," Elliot continued blithely. "I bothered Commander Woodsinger and she let me see a copy of the treaty and it was a mess, but I have some notes here and I think we'll all be secure and the harpies will find it satisfactory—I asked Podarge—"

"Oh yes," said Luke. "As soon as the harpies are done doing what, exactly?"

There was a silence, broken only by the distant shriek of harpies, and if you listened closely, the sound of tearing flesh.

Luke was standing over Elliot and Serene. There was a strange light in his eyes.

"I guess you're not thinking about that," he said softly. "All you're thinking about is all you ever think about . . . how clever Elliot Schafer is, and how stupid the rest of the world is. Because you're a snotty little brat."

Elliot abruptly stopped trying to think about anything from Luke's point of view. "I'm sorry," he bit out. "Are you—*Luke Sunborn*—actually telling me that I think too much of myself?"

"I just want to know why, exactly, you think you're so superior. You can't fight, you don't have any friends—"

Elliot had one friend. He had Serene. The truce between them had never been anything else, to Luke, and maybe nobody but Serene at the Border camp really cared about Elliot at all.

It was nothing Elliot did not know, and nothing he had ever thought Luke would rub in. Luke had everything. He could at least have the decency not to sneer at Elliot for having so little, even if it was Elliot's own fault.

"I can't fight?" Elliot snapped, because that was the only thing he could bear to address. "Who cares? Who wants to? But I forgot: that's what you base your life on. Being one of the Sunborns, being warriors as if war is ever anything but a terrible failure of peace. Oh, I'm Luke Sunborn, nothing matters but what a good little soldier I am and how excellent I am at games and how I look and how everybody worships at my feet, and you'll never realize how little any of that matters—how could you? You're too stupid and narrow-minded: too wrapped up in strutting around convinced of how fantastic you are, being handed every break in the world."

"It's not easy!" Luke roared back. "Being a Sunborn, having everyone expect you to do it right and be the best, it's not—"

If Luke thought having a family who loved him was so difficult, he should try the alternative.

"Oh, poor baby," Elliot sneered. "Being Luke Sunborn is so hard! Even when I get wings they look perfect! I take every benefit of being a Sunborn and act like I don't even notice them! My loving family have expectations of me!"

He did not expect his voice to sound as savage and resentful as it did, as if he hated Luke, as if he always had.

"So that's it? My family." Luke nodded, calmly, as if he was simply confirming what he had long suspected. "You've always been jealous of them. And you've always thought I was stupid, but I'm not: I know what's going on. It wasn't about us being Sunborns, was it, Elliot? It was for the same reason you keep coming back to the Border, year after year, despite us not having any fancy eye pods. Nobody wants you in the human world, do they? Nobody ever did. I don't blame them."

Elliot should have laughed at Luke saying dumb stuff like "eye pods," should have been able to brush this off and say that Luke did not understand anything.

Only Luke did understand what mattered. What Elliot had never spoken of, what he had tried to hide and flattered himself his friends did not know . . . it had been obvious all along. And Luke had revealed it, so simply, tearing away all the color and imagination of this world as if it were nothing but painted backdrops for the school play, leaving Elliot with nothing but the gray façade of his father's house.

Nobody wants you in the human world, do they? Nobody ever did.

He was not able to laugh.

Elliot got up, and Luke watched him with wide wary eyes. Even looking at Luke was unbearable. Elliot's blood felt as if it were on fire, burning and racing, as if it would char away his skin from the inside out and expose his bones. He'd tried as hard as he could, he thought, pretended as hard as he could, and it had not been enough. This was over. He was done.

There was nothing left but the urge to make Luke sorry.

Elliot went searching among the cluster of troops standing away from the harpies, at the edge of the woods. He found Dale among them, talking, and he walked over, and silenced Dale with a kiss.

To his distant surprise, Dale responded. Dale kissed him back, kissed him beside the roaring campfire, and went with him into the wild dark of the woods.

The moonlight-cast shadows of branches painted black traceries on Dale's skin. Dale's mouth was eager and welcoming against Elliot's, a little warmth in a long cold night.

Take that, Luke Sunborn, Elliot thought. *I can take something from you, after all.*

He was ashamed of himself, but that came later.

Elliot woke in the woods, to find dawn caught in the trees. He clambered up, adding clothes and subtracting leaves and dirt from his person. He left Dale as he made his way, not back toward the camp, but to the other side of the woods. He couldn't stay where he was, and he did not know how to go back. The only place to go was farther away.

That was how he stumbled on the battlefield at the edge of the Forest of the Suicides.

Elliot knew intellectually what harpies did to the bodies of the fallen, at the end of a battle. He'd read about it. Reading was not the same as seeing it.

Elliot stared around at the torn flesh, dried blood, and settling flies. He tried to imagine how this scene must have looked when the blood was fresh and the sun was setting last night, when Luke must have seen it. He remembered how he had editorialized the accounts of harpies on the battlefield for Luke. Luke had not known what to expect at all. Luke must have seen this, and seen desecration, and monstrousness, and believed it was in his blood.

Then Luke had come back to them, and snapped at them, and Elliot had not given him any leeway. There had been a lot of times where Luke, the one who was usually less hurt and more secure, the happier one, had let Elliot get away with snapping at him, had defused situations Elliot was trying to escalate by just accepting whatever Elliot dished out, had not taken what Elliot said in the wrong way or assumed the worst of him. He'd been able to afford generosity. He'd also chosen to be generous.

Elliot had, he realized, been waiting for Luke to hurt him for years. Since the first day, he'd thought it was only a matter of time until Luke punched him. The more Luke mattered to him, the more Elliot expected to be hurt. When the blow had finally arrived last night, he had not thought about anything but the pain.

Except that Elliot should have known better: four years of friendship should have told him more than his childhood fears. Luke would never hit somebody who could not defend themselves. Luke would not taunt somebody about their broken home for fun. Luke had been wounded and lashing out.

Unlike Luke, when Elliot had been the one who was less hurt, he had not chosen to be kind.

Elliot understood, now, why Luke had been so edgy around Elliot since they all learned about Luke's heritage. Luke had been really vulnerable, for the first time, and he had not trusted Elliot not to hurt him.

He'd been right not to trust Elliot. Look at what Elliot had done.

Elliot put his face in his hands. When he looked up, it was to find Serene standing beside him at the edge of the woods, gazing out on the battlefield. A shadow crossed her pearl-pale, tranquil face: it was the only sign she gave that the sight before her disturbed her at all.

"I was wondering where you were," said Serene.

"Were you?" asked Elliot.

"Well, no," said Serene. "Not really."

"Right," said Elliot. He looked out at the battlefield, rather than keep looking at her. That scared him less.

"I told Luke that the way he spoke to you was excessive, and that he owed you an apology," Serene stated.

"You—you did?"

Elliot had not thought Serene or anyone else would care what Luke had said, after what Elliot had done.

"Then you made your startling appearance at the campfire with Dale," Serene continued. "I have never seen gentlemen conduct themselves in such a fashion before. Except in certain woodcuts that my cousin showed me when we were young, but that is not important. I noticed that you then went off into the woods."

Elliot winced. "About that . . ."

"Do not explain matters to me. I did not come down with the last fall of leaves at the season's turning," said Serene. "There is no need to carve me an explicit woodcut."

"Not sure how to carve explicit woodcuts anyway," Elliot murmured. "Though I might be willing to give it a hilarious try."

"After this incident between you and Dale Wavechaser, Luke's paramor . . ." Serene said slowly. "I still feel that the way Luke spoke to you was excessive, and he owes you an apology. Just because he is finding adjusting to a harpy lifestyle difficult does not mean he is allowed to mistreat his friends."

"You don't understand," Elliot said. "We never told you. We're not friends."

He told Serene all about the truce he and Luke had agreed on in the library so long ago. Serene listened.

When Elliot was finished, Serene said: "May I ask a few questions?"

"Yes," said Elliot.

"So this truce was all your idea," said Serene.

"Yes," said Elliot.

"And you kept bringing it up," said Serene.

"Yeeees," said Elliot.

He felt like this was coming out wrong, somehow.

"And you think Luke's the one who's not really friends with you," said Serene.

"Yes!" said Elliot, and Serene continued to look at him. "May . . . be."

He was reminded, suddenly, of how Luke turned up all the time: at lunch tables where Elliot was, at the play Elliot had insisted on joining. Serene would have wanted Luke to look out for Elliot when she wasn't there, but it was ridiculous to imagine she would have cared if Luke ate lunch with Dale. Elliot thought about following someone around for years while they made clear they wanted nothing to do with you.

That could not be what was going on. Luke had no reason to do that. This was something Elliot would do, Elliot would suffer. Never Luke.

"Yes," Elliot said again.

Elliot was right about this. He had to be.

If he was not, then he had not just been cruel to Luke last night. He had been cruel to Luke for years.

"No," said Serene. "This is stupid. Why do men always overthink—no, I beg your pardon, Elliot, I did not mean that."

The Serene of years ago would not have cut herself off and begged his pardon for what she had not quite said. Elliot would really like to meet Golden one day, though he flattered himself he'd had a hand in changing her as well.

She took a deep breath. "I confess I do not know why you thought any of this, or understand why you have been acting in this fashion."

Elliot looked out at the still, terrible battlefield, at the bodies and the flies. He wanted to say, *because I'm terrible*, but Serene knew him, knew about Dale, and had still come after him. She wouldn't agree with him.

Maybe it wasn't true.

"What Luke said about the human world . . .," Elliot began carefully. "It was true. Did you—know that?"

Serene was quiet for a moment. "I hadn't thought it out like Luke must have," she said. "But I did suspect something was wrong. You never talked about your home."

"My mother left when I was a baby," said Elliot.

Serene sniffed. "*Lahrame*. Only dishonorable women abandon men and children who they should be responsible for. But I know it happens, too often, and I am so sorry."

Elliot parsed out the elvish word she had used, colloquial and unfamiliar to him. He thought it meant something like "deadbeat."

"It's actually more common for men to abandon than women in my world," he said. "I guess that's because society trains your men, and our women, to feel they are ultimately responsible for the children. But of course both genders . . . I'm sorry. I'm getting sidetracked. Home wasn't good. I don't make friends easily. Not just because of home, but because of me. I might have got some things wrong and done some things wrong. Last night, for instance. Among many other times."

Elliot shrugged and turned away from the battlefield. He had to go back to the camp sooner or later. There was a treaty and its final details to be worked out.

Serene's quiet voice held him still.

"I have often wondered. . . ." Serene began, and then corrected herself. "I have often worried that . . . being a woman, I can be oblivious to other people's feelings, and I am less able to talk about and deal with emotional situations. I have sometimes thought that if I were a man, or—or perhaps a human woman, I would have been able to treat you with more tact and sensitivity when we were younger. Or that I might have observed the trouble between you and Luke sooner, and known how to mend it. If I were different, perhaps everything would have been better between us three."

"I can only speak for myself," said Elliot, and took her arm as she held it out, in courtly fashion. "But I have always felt that it was a privilege to be your friend, and I have never wanted you to change in any way at all."

"How strange," said Serene, and he was caught off guard by her rare smile. "I always thought exactly the same thing about you."

Elliot knew he did not deserve it, but he could accept this grace from Serene. It was Luke who Elliot would have to apologize to, knowing that an apology would never mean anything: it was Luke who was never going to forgive him.

"I'm never going to forgive him," Luke snapped at Serene.

Elliot had waited until the treaty was completed and they were marching home to approach Luke, hoping that Luke might have cooled down a little.

Apparently not.

In retrospect, while Luke might be pleased he was going home, he was probably not as delighted as Elliot by the treaty, which had agreed trade and *rendezvous* points for human and harpy sentries. Celaeno had deliberately put a feather from her wings into Elliot's hair afterward, which Elliot was certain was a mark of affection. Of course, Celaeno was still under the massively mistaken impression that Elliot was dating Luke.

Actually Luke was probably mad at Elliot about that too.

And he might have noticed the fact that Elliot had been forced to dodge Dale all day.

Waiting had obviously been a terrible idea.

"Hi, Serene," Elliot said, announcing his presence, and sneaked a guilty glance at Luke. "Er, hi, Luke."

Luke did not respond, and he did not look at Elliot. He would usually do that, no matter how mad he was.

This was hopeless. Elliot should just be tactful for once, comply with Luke's clear wishes, and go. Only Serene had seemed certain they were actually friends, that it went both ways, and if they were, then Elliot owed him an apology before he left.

There was no way to do it right, so he was just going to do it.

"Okay," Elliot said, and took a deep breath. "I'm really sorry. I went too far and it was spiteful and wrong and I'm very, very sorry. You were right about stuff back in the human world and I wanted to hurt you, but it was a low blow and I'm ashamed of myself. I honestly feel terrible, Luke. I can't apologize enough."

"Oh—no. It's all right," said Luke.

Elliot stared, and Serene snorted.

Luke went on, his brow furrowed. He was having difficulty getting the words out, but he was looking at Elliot again. "Look, he's not—he's not my boyfriend or anything. And I'm sorry, too. I shouldn't have said any of that. It was dishonorable and you didn't deserve it. I'd just seen the harpies on the battlefield, and I was—I was upset. I think the human world sounds stupid anyway. You should stay here with me and Serene."

He had done something wrong, and said he was sorry and meant it, and been forgiven. It was as simple as that, and Elliot could not believe it.

You should stay here with me and Serene, Luke had said, as if what Elliot wanted was what Luke wanted as well.

Elliot could not help but think of how often he had struck out wildly to defend himself, when just saying what he felt would have worked.

Except it would not have worked, not on his father, or his mother, or on Jase or Adara. It only worked when someone cared how you felt.

He did not know how to act, if Luke cared what he felt.

"If anybody's going to cry," Serene offered after a pause, "I don't have a handkerchief."

Serene thought she was a laugh riot. Elliot made a face at her, and saw Luke make a face himself: a little grimace which Luke often made at parties, hoping someone would say something to smooth over the moment.

Elliot did in fact have another minor concern to raise.

"Okay, now that that's settled, you two have to help me. Hide me! I don't want to talk to Dale."

"Elliot Jerome Schafer!" Serene sounded scandalized. "You cannot play fast and loose with a man's affections. Are you some sort of rogue?"

Elliot thought being a rogue sounded very dashing, but clearly Serene did not.

"Serene!" Elliot protested. "It's so awkward. And he is so boring! He can barely string two words together. Can't you guys just stay with me at all times and don't let him talk to me until he gets the message?"

Luke cleared his throat, and offered: "Maybe we could."

"*Thank you,*" said Elliot.

He thought that was extremely nice and very understanding of Luke. In fact it was becoming suddenly clear to Elliot that he had been consistently wrong about which of his friends was the kind-hearted one. Luke Sunborn! Elliot saw what all the fuss was about now.

"Certainly not. Men! Have you no idea of honor?" Serene asked, which was rich since Luke had mentioned honor earlier and Serene had obviously rubbed off on him to an almost alarming degree. "You cannot dally with a man and then abandon him without a word. A man's heart is like a flower: beautiful but delicate, easily crushed by a careless hand."

Elliot looked back at the troop, catching sight of Dale, whose face brightened when he saw Elliot looking. He returned his gaze to Serene's implacable expression and regarded her with narrowed eyes.

"Fine. But for the record, my heart is NOT like a FLOWER."

He trudged grimly back to meet his doom. Dale perked up even more as he approached.

"Hey, Elliot. I was wondering—"

"Hey," Elliot interrupted. "So I think we can both agree our night together was a tragic mistake. Let us also agree to forget it completely, and never speak of it again!"

Iyara Treadbrink, one of Dale's friends and the cadet currently marching beside him, gave Elliot an appalled look and then determinedly fell back so she would no longer be part of the conversation. Elliot wished he could do the same. Life seemed great for Iyara.

"Oh," said Dale, his face falling. "Um. I have to admit I'm disappointed."

That was very flattering, but also made Elliot feel wretched. He bit his lip. "I'm sorry," he said, trying out the genuine apology thing again. "I behaved badly. But there is Luke to think of. You mustn't give up! You really like him. And I think despite this setback, which I take full responsibility for, that your pursuit of him will be successful."

He nodded encouragingly at Dale and wondered if this was enough to get him off the hook and back to Luke and Serene.

Dale began to smile again. Oddly, Dale's warm smile sent a terrible creeping chill down Elliot's back.

"You think I'm still interested in Luke?" he asked.

Horror hit Elliot, like a bus might an unwary pedestrian. "Yes?" he responded tentatively. "Obviously? Why would you—not be?"

Dale made a little face. "Well, that's what I've been trying to tell you. I mean, I like Luke, of course, but obviously things have changed."

"Changed?" Elliot asked politely.

"Well, the harpy thing," said Dale. "I mean, I know he's not like the others, the actual beasts, and I thought it was something I could get past . . ."

"How kind," said Elliot.

"But it was impossible to feel quite the same way after finding out something like that." Dale's smile broke into a grin. "And you and I have always got on really well, so . . ."

Several of Elliot's past conversations with Dale replayed themselves in Elliot's head, looking quite different this time around. It was obvious, now he thought about it. He'd assumed he knew Dale, and given him the benefit of the doubt.

He'd thought Dale was good. He'd thought Dale was kind. He'd thought Dale was like Luke.

Elliot was not good or kind himself.

"So," Elliot said, clear and cold. "You wanted Luke more than me, until you found out Luke was half harpy, which meant he was stained, flawed, and beneath your notice. Then I became preferable to Luke, for the sexy reason that I am entirely human. Lucky me."

Dale's grin faded a little. "I wouldn't put it like that."

He began to talk, as if he could still persuade Elliot, about being dazzled by Luke but having had more conversations with Elliot or something. Elliot was not exactly listening. There was a twist in his chest, of pain and outrage both. He was thinking about Luke giving Elliot his blanket at night, and Luke's shy glance at him, amazed that Elliot had actually apologized, ready to forgive him at once.

"Do you know the first time I saw you," he said to Dale, his voice rising. "I thought you were stupid?"

Dale stopped talking. His mouth fell open.

"I haven't changed my mind about that," Elliot proceeded. "The only reason I ever talked to you was because Luke liked you, so I knew I'd have to deal with you. The only reason I asked to be friends was because Luke wanted you. And the only reason the other night happened was because I had a fight with Luke."

Dale's face was pale. Elliot felt a different twist, this time one of satisfaction, and vengeance accomplished.

"Personally," he said, "I'd rather stab myself in the arm than spend an hour talking to you." He saw Dale's eyes widen, and nodded. "I guess you thought I was nice," Elliot said. "Wrong! But then, I didn't know you were a self-centred, egotistical, prejudiced jackass, and I should have been able to work that one out, shouldn't I?"

"You're insulting me?" Dale snapped. "You drop a boulder on me from nowhere and then you insult me?"

"You're right!" Elliot raged. "What am I doing? You don't think Luke is worthy of your time? Without Luke, I never would have wasted a second of my time on you. As of now, I'm done wasting my time with you. You're not worth it."

He stormed back to Luke and Serene. There were a lot of people looking at him. It might have been a good idea to keep his voice down.

"Keeping everything very cool and professional, I see, Cadet," remarked Commander Woodsinger as he went by.

Elliot did not know why the two most important women in his life had to be deadpan snarkers.

Rain began to fall, reminding him that he had chosen to come live in a world where there was no central heating or truly waterproof fabrics. He drew level with Luke and Serene and asked, in dejected and martyred tones, to be sheltered by Luke's wing before he died of a chill.

Somewhat to Elliot's surprise, Luke did let his wings unfurl and protect Elliot and Serene both. Neither Luke nor Serene told Elliot off for yelling at Dale, and Elliot was pretty sure that Luke had not heard what Elliot was yelling about, and everything was all right.

After Elliot had spent a while being smug about escaping the rain, Delia Winterchild ran in under Luke's wing too, and said something awkwardly positive about them. She looked guilty and grateful, both at the same time.

Elliot had known it was only a matter of time before the prejudice of the cadets crumbled in the face of all they knew of Luke, and all Luke had done and would do for the Border. Elliot believed that even Dale was going to overcome his distaste of harpies, and Serene agreed with him.

"Elliot must have put Wavechaser off by screeching at him," was the way Serene put it, since she was the cruel one of the friends group, but she was right. Dale and Luke were definitely going to get together.

Elliot was certain everything was going to work out, once again, for Luke Sunborn.

For a change, Elliot found, he did not mind at all.

"So your middle name is Jerome?" asked Luke as they made their way home. "Ha!"

Actually Elliot was mistaken. Both his friends were cruel and terrible people. He felt quite cheerful about it, though.

Things were better for Luke when they returned home from the Forest of the Suicides. Elliot wished this was because peace had been achieved between humans and harpies, and people recognized what a milestone that was, but he suspected it was actually because there were fresh tales of Luke being heroic and the Border camp were all battle groupies.

Also, a lot of people were into the wings.

"Can I touch them," said Adara Cornripe one day, after Trigon practise.

There had been talk of cutting Luke from Trigon, but then everyone on Luke's team had wept and had nervous breakdowns at the idea of cutting Luke from Trigon, so nobody talked about it anymore. Luke preferred to wait until everyone else had changed, though, so he came and sat with Elliot in the stands until everyone else was gone.

Elliot faithfully went to Trigon practise, even though Serene had stopped going. She insisted that she had to pen long letters to her elven betrothed, even though Elliot had told her that her behavior was disgraceful and she should put swordsisters before misters. It was humiliating. People were going to think Elliot had a real interest in sport. Elliot felt the very least Luke could do was bring out the wings and shelter him when it was drizzling.

He had not bargained for Adara.

"I'd rather if you . . .," Luke began as Adara tweaked some feathers.

"Why did you bother to ask when you were already doing it?" Elliot snapped, irritable because he shared her impulse.

Adara sent him an unrepentant wink, but removed her hand. "All right, I'm not touching the wings."

"Luke," said Elliot. Adara looked interrogative. "They're his wings, like they're his arms. You're not touching Luke."

"You're no fun," said Adara. "Well. Hardly ever."

"Thanks," said Luke after Adara was gone. "I don't like it when people I don't know that well get too close."

Since Elliot had seen Luke sidling away from people and refusing to dance at parties for years now, this was not news. What was new was Luke telling Elliot something like that: trusting that he would not use the information against Elliot.

What was new was that they were both trying not to hurt each other, and trusting that neither of them wanted to hurt the other.

"I was being a huge hypocrite," Elliot pointed out. "I grabbed the wings first thing."

It was a little embarrassing to admit, but Luke had known Elliot for years and must have noticed him wandering around going "oooh elves dwarves mermaids ooh."

"That's different," said Luke. "That's okay."

Elliot glanced over at him, but Luke was looking at something in the distance, profile and wings touched with the gold of the setting sun.

"It had better be, because unless you study for your military history exam I'm going to pull out all your feathers and stuff a pillow with them," Elliot threatened. "I will tell everyone you have harpy pattern baldness. Don't test me. Do not test me!"

Luke laughed.

Elliot was not as good at this new "being nice to each other" thing as Luke, but it was a great relief to Elliot that, now Luke knew Elliot liked him, he was no longer taking Elliot's horrible personality personally.

Dale, emerging from the changing rooms, said: "Great game, Luke," and pointedly did not look at Elliot.

Luke smiled, then glanced at Elliot and stopped smiling.

"It's fine, Luke," said Elliot. "You like each other, he's mad at me for insulting him, he will get over it. Trust me, I am an expert. I insult people all the time."

Luke raised his eyebrows. "This is shocking new information."

Elliot laughed. "You're such a jerk," he noted approvingly.

A silence followed his statement that went on too long. Elliot glanced over at Luke with sudden apprehension that he'd gone too far. Luke did not look angry or hurt, though. He was staring at the horizon with a concentration that Elliot did not think belonged to the sunset.

"Is that why you didn't tell me?" Luke asked. "What you told Commander Woodsinger? Because I'm a jerk?"

"You're not a jerk," Elliot snapped.

He understood when Luke gave him a look that accused Elliot of being contradictory and unreasonable. He felt it was fair.

"You're not usually a jerk," he explained. "And when you are a jerk, I usually like it."

He looked at Luke, who was clearly torn between embarrassed pleasure and hot defence of himself as not a jerk at all. Elliot, who was totally a jerk, found it extremely amusing.

"Anyway, why do you keep talking about what I told Commander Woodsinger?"

"I don't," said Luke. "I never think about it."

"Cool," said Elliot. "What did I tell her, though? Did I tell her about the jellybeans?"

"No, you . . . What happened with the jellybeans?"

"Best you don't know," Elliot decided. "Did I tell her about the ill-fated attempts at sorcery?"

"No," said Luke. "Please don't. I remember those. We would all get expelled."

It had been a great sadness to Elliot, that even in a magic land, humans could not do magic: that in no world could you solve any of your problems by lifting your hands and wishing. Apparently, it was always harder than that.

"Oh no," said Elliot, genuinely stricken. "Did I tell her about the food processor?"

"No," said Luke, sounding vexed.

Elliot barely heard him. "I'd have to be drunk," he said. "I swore to myself I would never tell anyone. I didn't know what was going to happen to it when I brought it over the Border. There are some things the commander should never know. There are some things nobody should ever know."

Luke snapped. "I was not talking about food processors. I never talk about food processors. I don't even know what a food processor is. I was talking about the fact that you date people called *Jason* as well as people called Serene and Myra and Adara!"

Frankly Elliot thought the most surprising thing about this was that Luke managed to remember all those names.

"Oh." Elliot squinted over at him. He thought about moving away from Luke, but that meant coming out from under the wing, and it was still raining. "I don't think I mentioned Jase."

"I may have asked Serene," Luke muttered. "I wasn't sure if you were—telling the truth or not." Off Elliot's unimpressed glare, he said: "You never told me!"

"Sure I did. I told you the same way you told me, by announcing the fact in front of a group of our peers." Elliot would have left it at that, a week ago, but he was trying to make things better between them now. "It's true that perhaps repeating the exact same thing you did was maybe not the most mature moment of my life."

He thought this was a truly magnanimous and mature gesture, but Luke appeared to be lost in thought and to have missed it completely.

"About the class announcement. I wanted you to know, but I didn't want to tell you. You always made fun of me," said Luke. "I didn't want you to make fun then."

"I wouldn't have!"

"I didn't *know* that, Elliot," said Luke. "Harpies can't read minds."

It was the first time Luke had referred to himself as a harpy, which Elliot thought was promising.

"Yeah, all right," Elliot grumbled.

"I'm not like you," said Luke.

"Obviously," said Elliot. "No need to rub it in."

Luke shook his head, puzzled but plunging ahead, the way Luke did, with fear pushed to one side in a way Elliot had never quite been able to master. "I mean, I don't always know what to say to everyone, and I can't go get anyone—apparently *anyone*—that I want, and I can't—"

"Oh, right," said Elliot. "Because Serene didn't dump me and break my heart."

There was a long pause.

Eventually, Luke asked: "She did?" in a tone that expressed not just disbelief that Serene would do that, but disbelief that Elliot's heart did that.

"She did," Elliot confirmed. He did not look at Luke, but at his own hands, knotted in fists as if he could defend himself, or keep hold of something. That had never worked. He let his hands open, and let go. "I wanted to stay friends with both of you, and I pretended it hurt less than it did. I wanted to be with her, and I couldn't manage to make her want the same thing. I couldn't manage it with Jase or Myra either. Look, I don't think about bisexuality—"

"What's bisexuality?" asked Luke.

"Dating people called Jason as well as people called Myra," Elliot said. He thought of several other terms: he should probably write Luke a list. "Why is language in the Borderlands so weird? Some of it's modern, and some of it's medieval, and I guess that makes sense with the influx of a certain amount of new blood to the training camp every year, but how do some words and phrases transfer, while others don't? Why do you know the word 'jerk' and not the word 'bisexual'?"

"I guess people say the first word more," said Luke.

Sometimes Luke said things as if they were very simple and obvious, and it adjusted Elliot's worldview a crucial fraction. Elliot sat absorbing this latest.

"I think you were going to talk about your feelings," Luke continued, stumbling over the word "feelings." They had both been talking more slowly than usual, as if negotiating a forest full of traps. "Could you do that before you give me the lecture on linguistics?"

Elliot was proud that Luke accepted the lecture was coming.

"I don't think about who I go out with in terms of persuading as many people as possible to have fun with me," Elliot said. "It's that way for some people, and that's fine, but it's not for me. I think about it in terms of—infinite possibilities. I think it's beautiful the possibilities are infinite, but it also means you make a choice. Like choosing how to spend your life, where you're going to live, what your life's work is going to be. Except in this case, the possibilities are people, and they have to choose you back."

"Oh," said Luke. "I didn't—know you thought about it that way."

Elliot rolled his eyes. "Well, that much was obvious, Sunborn. I may also have made my announcement when I did because you are always insinuating that I throw myself at everyone within range, and I didn't particularly want to tell you and hear that."

"I wouldn't have!" Luke exclaimed.

"I didn't *know* that, Luke," said Elliot. "Nobody can read minds."

Because Elliot was a jerk, all the time and mostly on purpose, he mimicked the way Luke had said it. He was sorry the next instant, because of how sorry Luke looked.

"Yeah, well," Elliot said. "We both know now." He found all this sitting close sharing sunset confidences unsettling, so he got up and added, in a loudly reassuring voice: "Don't worry about Dale. He'll get over me being a jerk. You always did."

"You're not a jerk," said Luke, and smiled up at him. "I mean, you're not always a jerk." He hesitated, then added: "And when you are a jerk, I usually like it."

Ever since the march home, Dale had been complimenting Luke, and taking care to spend time with Luke, and ignoring Elliot with extreme prejudice. Elliot understood perfectly. It was going to be very awkward when Dale and Luke actually got together, but Elliot felt he was prepared.

The Borderlands were at peace, and the Border camp felt at peace, for a change. Peter and Myra seemed happy together, against all odds. Adara was in many ways terrible, but she was openly cutting a swathe through many gentlemen and several ladies in the Border camp, and Elliot was pleased for her. Podarge the harpy turned out to be an even better correspondent than Serene's cousin Swift, and wrote Elliot regular interesting letters. Serene was happy with her missives from her beloved Golden, which sometimes contained pressed flowers and embroidery and sometimes contained very polite and gentlemanlike criticisms of Serene's moral character. Luke was being treated well by the Border camp, he and Elliot were getting along, and he was going to be happy with Dale.

It was an enormous shock when Luke asked Elliot out on a date.

Elliot was trying to teach himself trollish via a two-hundred-year-old book by a man who'd had a traumatic break-up with a troll. This meant a lot of commentary along the lines of "This is how trolls say I love you. FOOTNOTE: BUT THEY DON'T MEAN IT!"

"You realize you can't have a quarrel with a book," Myra observed. "Quarrels have to go two ways."

Elliot stopped clutching his hair with despair and smiled at her across the library table. "I've always been able to hold up both ends of an argument all by myself."

"I shouldn't doubt you," said Myra. "Nobody else has ever managed to fight with Dale Wavechaser."

"What can I say," said Elliot. "I have a talent."

Myra was quiet for a moment. "He's really going after Luke." She paused. "I mean, I always figured they might end up together, but if he starts dating Luke and keeps hating you, won't that be—an uncomfortable situation?"

"That's my middle name," said Elliot. "Did I never tell you? Elliot 'Uncomfortable Situations' Schafer. I make situations uncomfortable, then I deal with them. It's a really bad superpower."

"We're in our last year at Border camp," said Myra, and she sounded a little sad. "We're going to be sent to our new postings, and we have to decide where to apply. We won't all see each other every day, not the people we love or the people we hate. Everything's going to change." She took a deep breath. "Peter and I are going to break up. I want to go live among the dwarves, and he would never want anything like that. I think we can stay friends, but just in case we can't, I worried about which one of us you would choose."

Elliot winked at her. "You shouldn't worry."

Myra tried not to smile, but did not entirely succeed. "Don't you worry? If Serene goes back to the elven woods to be with her sweetheart, and if Luke goes with Dale wherever he's posted, that you might lose touch and drift away from each other?"

Elliot worried. He just tried not to. He'd come back to the Border camp to be with them, the two people he loved, and he knew they both had obligations to family, to each other, to their duties, to their loved ones, which meant they might both leave him.

Drift away, Myra had said casually, as if it was not a terrifying phrase. Elliot could imagine being a boat, untied and unanchored, floating out to sea, with nobody looking for him.

He had only just worked out how to be with Luke, when they were both friends and knew it. He was afraid to think about losing it all.

"Serene's Golden writes great letters. Maybe Golden will be another of my penpals."

His attempt to sound light and laugh it off failed. Myra looked at him with her grave dark eyes.

"I'll be one of your penpals," she told him.

"You'd better," said Elliot. "Dale Wavechaser, I suspect, will not."

"No," said Myra, and hesitated. "I was—surprised to see Dale running after Luke like he is. I would've thought Dale would be bothered by the harpy thing."

Elliot opened his mouth, anger already sparking, but fury was quenched in the dark pools of her eyes.

"Dale hardly ever speaks to me," Myra said gently, reminding him why she might know better than Elliot what someone's attitude to nonhumans was. Elliot bowed his head, and Myra added: "He barely looks at me."

"Dale is an idiot," Elliot bit out. "And I told him so."

"Did you?" said Myra. "I wondered what the fight was about."

"I wasn't nice to him," Elliot admitted. "I was horrible to him, actually. But he said stuff about Luke I wouldn't listen to from anyone. I'm not sorry."

Myra made a face. "Did you tell Luke? I'd want to know something like that."

"I didn't," said Elliot. "Luke has liked Dale for years. I wouldn't know how to say it. And I've . . . in the past, I've been known to be . . . my interactions with Luke and my whole personality is . . ."

"Abrasive," Myra suggested. "Deliberately off-putting but also accidentally off-putting."

"Thanks, Myra," said Elliot. "You get me."

"I've been around you when Serene and Luke were sent off to war," Myra said. "I remember. Also Peter sometimes wakes up crying from the traumatic dreams."

Elliot shook his head. "Peter's the weak link. But you see why I can't be the one to ruin Luke's life. He'd assume I wanted to, or that I thought it was funny, or I was exaggerating. I can't do it."

"No, I see what you mean," said Myra. "Still, what if Dale can't go through with it?"

"Go through with what, exactly?" Elliot asked, and paused. "I mean, no need to be explicit, I've seen many pictures in Peter's private pornographic materials."

"His what?"

"Never mind," Elliot said firmly. "Forget I said anything about that."

Myra regarded him suspiciously, then gave up. "I just mean, if the harpy thing bothers Dale that much, Luke's going to see it sooner or later. I'm worried Luke's going to get hurt."

"Well since you put it that way, that's a very reasonable concern," said Elliot. "And I am also deeply worried! All right. Do you think we could sell Dale to pirates?"

Myra stared. "No, Elliot."

"We have to do something!"

"No, Elliot," said Myra. "We don't. I was just talking. I was simply discussing our classmates and their relationships like a normal person. We do not have to *sell* anybody to *pirates*."

"I'm a problem solver," said Elliot. "I want to solve a problem."

"I think I'm getting a migraine," said Myra, gathering up her books.

"Hey, where are you going?"

"I really like you, Elliot," Myra said. "But I can only take so much. You understand?"

He understood. There were many people who could not take as much as Myra: at least with Myra, he was pretty confident she would come back. He waved to her, a little disconsolately, as she went.

He could not concentrate on his trollish now. He read the line "Troll flesh has the appearance and texture of stone, but is not actually stone (FOOTNOTE: But their hearts are truly made of stone!)" four times. He pictured Dale breaking Luke's heart in six different ways before he registered Luke coming up to his table in the library.

He felt a little better, then. Dale could not break Luke's heart while Luke was in the library.

Elliot could not keep Luke under his eye at all times, though. He could barely keep an eye on Luke now, when he was trying to work out how trolls used tenses.

Luke actually looked pretty tense himself.

Maybe the heartbreak had already happened.

"Do you want to come to the Elven Tavern with me?" asked Luke, which was not a heartbroken thing to say.

He did not look heartbroken, exactly, Elliot decided, though he had never seen Luke heartbroken, so he could not know for sure. His shoulders were held stiff, wings clearly straining under the leather, and he was both staring at Elliot and trying to avoid Elliot's eyes. Maybe he had news. Maybe he had terrible news. Elliot scanned Luke's face. Elliot was not certain that he was great at analyzing people.

"Well, sure," Elliot answered, when Luke started looking freaked out about the silence. "Let me finish up here. You go get Serene."

"No," Luke said. "I mean, do you want to go—with me. Just us. So we can—talk."

It was terrible news, then.

"Oh my God," said Elliot. "Are you sick? Is it harpy cancer?"

Luke started to laugh. Elliot started to talk about the statistics for harpy cancer. Luke would have known about the statistics if he had read the papers Elliot had written out for him. Luke was making his own life difficult, and he only had himself to blame.

"I don't have harpy cancer," Luke said, once he was done laughing. "Do you want to go out on a date with me?"

Oh, that was nice. Very nice. Very hilarious. Elliot had really thought they were learning to treat each other better.

Elliot regarded Luke with loathing. "Ha. Very funny. I don't have time for this, and this book is not properly citing its sources."

He got up and hit Luke over the head with the book by the troll's ex, perhaps hitting him harder than a truly committed pacifist would have. He went and found some different and with any luck more helpful books on trollish, and came back to find Luke waiting for him, book pushed aside, leaning back in his chair. He looked down at Luke, feeling lost.

"Seriously," said Luke, face tilted up to Elliot's, and he did seem serious. He seemed almost vulnerable.

Elliot understood then. Something had happened with Dale, and it had not gone well.

He remembered Dale saying there wasn't a lot of choice at the Border camp if you liked guys, and his discussion with Luke, so Luke knew for the first time that Elliot was a possible option. He could understand Luke, even: understand feeling bruised, and looking to someone you trusted not to hurt you. He could even understand it if Luke wanted to spite Dale, show him that he could take what Dale had wanted. Elliot himself had used Dale to get revenge on Luke.

When you cared too much about one person, other people seemed to matter less, and sometimes you treated them as if they did not matter at all.

Elliot thought of his father, who had wanted his mother or no one, Serene, who had wanted Golden, Adara and Myra, who had wanted Luke, and Jase, who had wanted a compliant figment of his own imagination. He thought of Serene last year, almost-offering to be with him again because she thought she could not be with the one she really wanted. He had not taken her offer then, and he would not take Luke's now. Everyone Elliot had ever wanted to love him had loved someone else better: had wanted someone else more.

"Seriously," Elliot responded. "That's not a good idea."

"What happened between Luke and Dale?" Elliot asked Adara Cornripe the next day at lunch.

"Please don't sit down," said Adara. "I can't be seen associating with you sober, in daylight, in lunch-table intimacy. My social standing would not recover."

Elliot hovered his lunch tray over the table, as if he were going to put it down. "Talk fast."

"The word is that they were in a clinch and Luke's wings came out and Dale freaked," Adara told him, eyeing the tray as if it were a grenade. "But it was Luke who called the whole thing off."

"What else could he do?" Elliot asked.

"I don't know, Dale might have come around," Adara said. "I mean, would Dale be the first person in the world to react to a sexy situation with 'What is that and oh no, what is it doing?' Clearly not."

"If you're the one who introduces body negativity into the sexy equation, you're the one who should do the groveling, and the weeping, and the 'baby, please take me back' talking," said Elliot. "That's mathematics. Sexy mathematics."

Adara's gorgeous face turned thoughtful. "Does Luke want Dale to come crawling back, then?"

"I assume."

"Then I won't make a plan to ruin Dale's life," said Adara. She saw Elliot's startled look, and shrugged. "I owe Luke. Besides, if he was into it, I'd fly him all around the Border camp like a bad bad flying pony."

"Aw, I'm so touched, I feel like putting down my tray."

"Do not do that," said Adara.

"What would you think about selling Dale to pirates?"

"I think you're ridiculous and not amusing, Schafer," said Adara. "Don't you dare put down that tray."

"What are you doing, Elliot?" Luke asked. "Come on."

He put a hand between Elliot's shoulderblades and pushed Elliot, gently, in the direction of their usual lunch table. Elliot stepped away from him hastily, and went.

Elliot knew then what had happened, that it had been just as he suspected, and he was sorry for Luke and angry with Dale in equal measure.

He tried to forget what Luke had suggested, and when he could not forget he tried to remember it wasn't serious. Not that Luke would make a joke of such a thing, but that Luke had been hurt and searching for a solution. Luke was new to romance.

As the days passed and Luke carefully avoided Dale and took to following Elliot to the library, he tried to remember that Luke had not meant it.

"Luke asked me out," he told Serene one evening when he dragged her protesting out to Luke's Trigon practise. Oh, the tables, how they had turned.

"He told me he was going to," said Serene.

"I said no."

"That's probably for the best," Serene remarked.

That confirmed everything Elliot had suspected. Serene was Luke's swordsister. She knew Luke better than anyone, and she would not want Elliot to be hurt again.

This knowledge helped during Elliot's occasional moments of weakness.

Luke's cadet uniform got redesigned to incorporate the wings, a sword belt added. During archery practise he couldn't carry a traditional quiver, but had a whole new shirt that was basically a row of arrow pockets and straps to hold it together.

Everything seemed back to normal when girls started showing up in groups again to watch Luke at archery practise.

Elliot, of course, did not care about archery practise and was waiting for Luke to be done already so they could get some dinner. He was leaning against the fence and reading. He hardly looked up from his book at all.

Maybe he did once or twice. Serene and Luke were having a contest, and Serene was trash-talking Luke in a very polite elvish way, which made Luke throw back his head and laugh. There was a stir and a sigh from the assembled viewers.

That was Luke, the Sunborn champion, the prince from illustrations in a book of fairy tales come to life. That much did not change. Elliot found himself having a number of non-fairy tale-approved thoughts, moving from the rare sweetness of Luke's laugh to the lean muscles that slid under his skin as he drew his bow, the glitter of sunlight outlining his upper lip. But Elliot remembered watching Luke pull off his shirt on the Trigon pitch. That hadn't changed either.

The only thing that was slightly different was that Elliot could transform his thoughts into reality. He had turned Luke down, but he was fairly certain that he could take it back. All he would have to do was walk over and lean close, touch Luke, curl his fingers around the swell of his bicep or run a nail down the brown arch of Luke's neck.

Except that this change was not permanent. Luke was stung by rejection and looking for a safe bet. How Luke looked for him in a room now, how his whole face changed when he caught sight of him, that would all go away soon.

"Are you two done?" Elliot asked, strolling over. "Whichever one of you wins has to bring me dinner, so I guess whatever happens . . . I win! I just made up that rule."

"It was a draw," Serene admitted grudgingly, and stomped off to retrieve her arrows.

"Do you remember when you cut up my shirt to allow for the wings?" Luke asked in a low voice.

Elliot studied the archery targets as if he had actual interest in them. "Can't say I do, buddy."

He saw Dale Wavechaser often lurking around Luke and looking sad rather than glaring as he did whenever he saw Elliot. Whenever he saw Dale, Elliot had perhaps an unreasonable number of visions of what "in a clinch" might have meant. He also perhaps thought about this too often when thinking about it only made him angry. Elliot told himself that he was just concerned for his friend. He knew that had been Luke's first kiss, and Dale had ruined it for him with his prejudice and insensitivity, and Dale was probably going to get another chance despite being an idiot who did not deserve one.

When these justifications broke down, Elliot reminded himself that being angry didn't help. Luke and Dale were going to work this out. Elliot had to protect himself and stay out of their way.

So Elliot continued on as if Luke had never asked him, and focused on work. He heard rumors of trolls and humans seen together. Nobody seemed to know if the humans were from the villages, or bandits again, or if they might possibly be humans from over the Border. He threw himself into researching that, and learning trollish, and wrote to Serene's cousin Swift, Luke's cousin Gregory, and Podarge the harpy. He even sent a message in a bottle to his mermaid. He concentrated on being strong and independent and career focused, damn it, and he was not swayed by Luke saying he might ask to be posted to an elven fortress, so he and Serene and Elliot could all be together.

Then Podarge's letter came, saying that armed troll and human forces had been sighted too close to the Forest of the Suicides, and the harpies requested their new allies' aid. Elliot started yelling for the commander, Luke and Serene started planning to call in elven reinforcements, and Bright-Eyes the librarian started yelling about the library being a place of quiet and learning.

Elliot realized that this was a call to arms, and they would not be taking a councilor, least of all one who was still in training.

Except that he had to come.

"You have to offer the trolls peace," he argued. "You have to offer an agreement that looks good. I have to be there to negotiate it!"

Luke shouted back at him. Faintly, as if in the distance, he could hear Bright-Eyes begging for silence, but Elliot did not look at him, or anywhere but at Luke, as if he could make Luke get it through sheer force of will.

"No other councilor was brought to see the harpies. They don't know anyone else, they just know me! Luke, come on, you have to understand. You'd do anything if you thought it was your duty."

"I understand," Luke snapped.

He did not say anything else. Elliot stared at him for a fraught moment, not sure what Luke's understanding meant. In the end, all he felt he could do was make his own position clear.

"I'm going, with or without your help."

Luke took a deep breath and said: "I'm helping."

Whether it was due to the word of a Sunborn or the previous treaty with the harpies, Commander Woodsinger let Elliot come.

"You do get along with the elves," she remarked.

That was true. Swift was coming, and Elliot would be happy to see her. He was also prepared to make eyes at any valiant elf maiden who might tell him more about elven diplomacy.

They marched through the night, packs on their shoulders, dryads whispering love songs to the crescent moon.

"I wonder if one of the girls will bring me word from Golden," said Serene. "Not that any of those rough soldier girls would be allowed a moment alone with my treasure."

"That would be awful," said Luke.

"A scandal!" Elliot agreed, and they exchanged a grin over Serene's head.

Later, when morning had turned the sky into hammered gray pearl, Luke's step slowed and Elliot unconsciously matched it, so they were walking slightly behind Serene.

"I wanted a chance to talk to you before the battle," Luke murmured.

Panic rose in Elliot, like a bird from a shaken tree. He was relieved to be interrupted by the arrival of the elven army.

The elves moved in a column, hair like silk under helmets of steel, a shining line of defence between them and the Forest of the Suicides. Luke squinted in at one elf in particular, and Elliot's eyes followed his gaze to a tall blond guy on a horse. Luke was right, he thought for a minute, the guy was super hot.

Then he realized something was very wrong with this picture.

An elven guy, *fighting*? Elliot looked closer, and noticed that the guy had done something to suggest a lopsided bosom lurking beneath his breastplate, and done his hair as the women wore theirs. This culture of tunics and braids was not Elliot's culture, so he could not tell how convincing the guy actually was as a woman.

Ahead of them, Serene exclaimed: "*Golden*?"

Not that convincing to someone who knew him, Elliot reflected, and then he realized the full splendor of what had just taken place before his eyes.

"Serene!" cried Golden, Serene's sweetest treasure and one true love. "I've come to fight by your side! Don't worry, I can take care of myself! I've been practicing with the sword while Mother and Father thought I was doing embroidery."

Serene made a creaking sound, as if the hinge on her jaw had rusted. That might explain why she could not seem to close her mouth.

Glee filled Elliot, like champagne poured bubbling into a glass. He clutched Luke's sleeve as if to show him this amazing scene, even though he knew Luke could see perfectly well. He wanted to show the world. He wanted a tapestry made to commemorate this moment.

"Luke," he whispered. "This is the happiest day of my life."

"I knew you would understand," Golden told Serene, with the confidence of a sweet blond bulldozer. "I knew you were open-minded, and caring, and not a rogue who consorts with loose human men like Father said!"

Elliot had no idea his fame had spread to the delicate ears of elven gentlemen.

"You truly respect men! You call them comrades. You fight with them! And now I'm going to fight with all of you!"

"Your—how did you—" Serene croaked, and gestured to her own bosom, which was splendid and not lopsided at all.

"Ah." Golden looked smug. "I made some pudding and sneaked the extra into bags I sewed up and popped them right in my shirt. They're very realistic, don't you think?"

If Serene didn't marry him, Elliot would.

"Serene. You understand, don't you? You always told me you believed men were equal to women!"

A sea change, obviously terrifying to Serene as it was delightful to Elliot, swept over Golden's face. His brown eyes filled with tears, like a velvety pansy filling with dew. His lower lip quivered, proud but overset with emotion.

"Golden, I assure you—" Serene fumbled for words. "Your courage does you much credit and I—"

"Yes?" Golden asked, with menace.

Serene gulped and offered: "I like a man with spirit?"

Golden hesitated, then allowed himself a small smile, and allowed Serene to approach and touch the fingertips of his gloved hand.

"Come away," Luke murmured.

"Nooooo," Elliot wailed. "I won't. I won't. You'll have to kill me. This is better than a play."

"It's not a play," Luke said quietly. "She's our friend, and she loves him, and they could die. Let them have a moment."

He hooked his arm around Elliot's neck and dragged him away. Elliot did not fight, because stupid Luke had a point, as he so often did, and he had ruined the entertainment by pointing out it was reality.

The trolls and the enemy humans were waiting in the woods. The harpies were above, wheeling in the sky, and Luke was close to him, close and warm, but he was going into battle as surely as Serene and Golden were. He might not be close or warm for long.

Elliot had wanted magic to be real, he thought, as he had thought a thousand times. Maybe just a little less real than this.

The lurching, dismayed sensation in the pit of his stomach was not at the thought of reality or mortality, but because Luke had grabbed Elliot and flown up into a hut in a tree.

Elliot gave a manly yell of terror, and then stumbled back across an earthen floor. It was the first time he had been inside a harpy's home, he thought, and it was fascinating in the ways it was like a nest and in the ways it was like a house, woven twigs but with a roof, packed earth at the bottom of the nest. For some reason, it was not quite as fascinating as Luke's blue eyes in the shadowy hut, or the rapid rise and fall of his chest.

"I'm sorry. You're right, we do need you for the treaty, and I don't mean to disrespect that or you, but you'll be in danger down there and you can't help until the fighting is done. I'll tell Celaeno you're here—"

"Good idea," said Elliot, who had no aspirations toward being savaged for trespass by enraged harpies, and who also had to concede he was not much use in an actual battle.

"—I'll tell any harpy I see so they can consult with you and you won't be stuck here if I get killed—"

"Luke!" Elliot cut in. "I already said good idea! Please don't talk about getting killed!"

"What? Oh."

Luke looked truly surprised that Elliot might be concerned about Luke's potential impending demise. Then he smiled, a small smile, as if the most important thing about Luke's potential impending demise was that Elliot might be concerned.

Luke was so terrible and impossible. Elliot had no idea how to deal with him. He rumpled his hair and tried to explain why being put in a safe treehouse was all right by him.

"I don't actually want to be on the field of battle. I wouldn't be any help, and fields of battle are horrible places. That's why they're called fields of battle instead of fields of licorice, or . . ." Elliot could hear himself babbling, much worse than usual, and gave up. "Try not to die, Luke. Okay?"

"I always do," murmured Luke, which was a blatant lie. "I'm sorry," he added, and Elliot did not think he was sorry about lying. "This isn't meant to be disrespect either, it's just that I am—and you're so—"

Despair went through Elliot, like a cold wind through winter-bare branches. He'd been trying, so hard, and now he'd said something wrong, right before Luke might die, and he had literally no idea what it was.

"I'm so *what*? Are you actually about to insult me right before you go off to war? Oh I don't believe this, you *loser*—"

He did not get out another word past "loser," because Luke crossed the floor, took Elliot's face in his hands, and kissed him.

Wow, Elliot thought. Wow, Sunborns are *very grabby*.

Men of action and not words, Elliot supposed. Well, it wasn't like that was a huge surprise.

Elliot was really trying to keep thinking, though he might have lost the ability to do so coherently. He reminded himself forcefully that Luke was not very experienced, and he should be careful, or gentle, or pull away, or something. Except he didn't do anything of the kind, and Luke was, no surprise, a quick study.

He kissed Luke back, hands sliding through Luke's soft hair, Luke's wings draped warm around his shoulders. He felt tense and scared and safe all at once, in the calm place in the middle of a lightning storm.

He was full-on making out with Luke Sunborn, in a house in the sky over a battlefield.

Oh, God damn it, the battle, Elliot realized, and felt honor bound to step back and remind Luke there was a war on.

"Oh," said Luke, sounding dazed, and then: "*Oh*. I have to go."

"No, really?" Elliot asked, trying to be normal and sounding cranky, which was close enough. "Do tell."

It was a good effort, Elliot told himself. He should be very proud of himself for restoring the *status quo*.

"Wait," Elliot called out, as Luke was turning to go.

Actually Elliot was an idiot who ruined everything, always. He ducked past one of Luke's wings and took hold of his leather shirt in one fist, held him pressed against the wooden frame of the doorway and kissed Luke hard on his startled mouth, with despair and fear and tenderness. Luke kissed him back, as if he had an answer for all Elliot's questions. His hands would have shaken, if he was not holding on so hard.

Then he let go. He pushed Luke right out of the harpy's nest and sent him wheeling down to the battle below.

It was nothing, Elliot told himself. Battle ardor. Battle fever. Battle emotional stuff! People did things in battles they wouldn't necessarily do otherwise, on account of the adrenalin and fear of death. It didn't have to mean anything.

Elliot sat up in his eyrie, listening to the sounds of battle below, then stood up quickly at the sound of wings.

It was Celaeno, not Luke. Elliot felt betrayed by the universe.

"Luke left me here so I would be safe during the battle," he explained. "Are Luke and Serene all right? Did we win? Do you need me for peace talks?"

"We are victorious, but I have not seen Luke or his comrade," said Celaeno. "And you are welcome in my nest at any time, as you are the chosen partner of my nestmate's son."

Ah, yes. Elliot had forgotten about that particular demented lie of Luke's.

"Partner, sure," Elliot said. "Totally. So, peace talks?"

"The trolls have agreed to talk with us," said Celaeno. "They trusted in a group of humans who are strange to us, and who carried strange weapons that did not work. If they had worked, I fear today might have had a different outcome."

"Could you take me down?" Elliot asked. "Could you take me down right away?"

Celaeno clasped him in her arms and brought him down on a gentle drift of air to land light as a leaf beside the harpies' captives. There was a man with his hands tied, sitting propped up against a tree. There was a gun on the ground by his feet.

"I don't care," the man said sullenly, as soon as he saw Elliot. "I don't care what the monsters do to me. I was . . . I was taken to this horrible place when I was a kid, and I told them I wouldn't be part of their awful camp, and I managed to get away from them. But I always remembered this place. Remembering got worse and worse, every year. So when some guys came and said, do you want to go back and get rid of them all, wash this filthy nightmarish place clean . . . I said yes. I don't care. I'm not sorry. The things I've seen, that creature and dozens like it, a man with wings, awful women pale as ghosts with pointed ears, even the stone animals they said were on our side: it isn't right." He squinted up at Elliot, half-resentful, half-afraid. "Are you even human? What are you?" he asked.

Elliot bent and picked up the small, gleaming gun. He saw himself for a moment, reflected in the man's terrified eyes: someone tall and strong and strange, with wild hair and a cold face.

"Me? I'm just like you. I'm one of the kids they brought over the wall," Elliot said. "Only I stayed."

He'd known this would happen. He'd been sure some of those kids would remember, and come back. On both sides of the wall were strangers and weird sights, terrible until you loved them. Our lands were always otherlands, to someone else.

He held the gun, which was heavy for something so small. Celaeno had said they did not work, which was lucky. Elliot would have thought a gun would work, if a music box did. He wondered: If someone tried more old-fashioned guns, might they work? He could suggest some of the Border guard who could cross take different weapons over, and try them.

Or he could not suggest that. He was the only one he knew of doing experiments with technology past the Border. He could let the instruments of death alone, for a while, until he was absolutely sure they were needed.

He handed the gun to Celaeno.

"Get every one of these to a forge," he said. "Melt them down."

"Hey!" said the man, desperate not to be left with winged horrors. "Hey, where are you going?"

Elliot turned around, boots crunching on the fallen leaves, and looked down at him.

"I have to talk to some people," Elliot replied, "who are more important than you."

Celaeno took him to the trolls, who seemed startled but pleased that the Border guard still sought an alliance with them rather than continuing the hostilities the trolls had begun. Their captain spoke human, but seemed amused by Elliot's clumsy trollish.

They set up tables and wrote out two new treaties, one between the harpies and the trolls, and one between the humans and the trolls, right away. Commander Woodsinger came up to them at some point, standing at Elliot's shoulder and reading over the parchments spread across the table. She did not comment on the treaties, but she had her seal out, ready to sign.

"I feel the tension between our peoples is simply due to a lack of communication. I'm so glad our two species will be learning more about each other and reaching a beautiful understanding together," said Elliot, looking up at the troll captain through his eyelashes.

"You're not really my type," said the troll. "No offence."

There was an awkward pause. Then Commander Woodsinger burst out laughing, in the middle of negotiations, with people who had been a hostile force less than an hour before.

"I'm glad my humiliation brings you so much joy," Elliot hissed.

Commander Woodsinger rested a hand on his shoulder. "So am I, Cadet."

Trolls tended to be more literal than humans, and less deceptive, or at least not deceptive in the ways Elliot was used to. Flirting was definitely out, especially the kind of flirting Elliot employed with the elves. All the trolls thought it was weird.

They liked Commander Woodsinger, though. Elliot was going to have to learn to be more stoic.

The peace talks went on, through the tattered remnants of the day and throughout the night. At one point Elliot looked up, startled, to see they were affixing torches into wrought-iron holders on the nearby trees. Under the warm light he saw, different from all the shadows and branches and bones, a curve of wings and a glint of rich gold.

It was Luke. He was sitting on a tree stump, and had made no effort to attract Elliot's attention. He showed no sign of restlessness. He was just waiting.

Elliot did not feel in any way prepared for Luke Sunborn, exhausted after another triumphant battle, waiting patiently until Elliot was done with peace talks.

So when Elliot was done, Elliot went to him and illicitly commandeered the commander's tent for a nap. His judgement might have been impaired by exhaustion.

In the commander's tent Luke asked him, after a blatant rejection, two kisses, and less than one day, if Elliot was serious about them. And instead of pointing and laughing, Elliot said that he was.

Elliot agreed to be in a *committed relationship.*

It was very possible that Elliot should be committed.

The trolls were staying awhile with the harpies, to re-confirm their centuries-old alliance. The elves agreed to accompany the humans back to the Border camp, guarding the human hostages. There was some debate about what to do with them.

"Do not execute them," Elliot said urgently over breakfast. "Do not execute anyone. Please induce magic amnesia so they can only recall this land as a dream."

"For the last time, nobody can do that," Commander Woodsinger told him.

The captain of the trolls, whose name was Wfscv'dshfcdz, which translated to "Majestic Eagles Circle the Luminescent Quarry," raised his or her craggy eyebrows. "That boy seems sweet, but a little simple," he or she remarked in trollish to his or her second-in-command.

Elliot diplomatically pretended not to understand.

"We could sell them as slaves to the dwarves," suggested Celaeno, and everybody glared at her. She lifted her wings in surrender. "I was just trying to help."

Nobody wanted to hear about the Geneva Conventions. While Elliot was trying to explain them, Serene strolled over with Golden on her arm. Elliot was deeply relieved to see them, but distressed by the fresh wound on Golden's face. That looked like it would scar.

Golden's head was held high. He seemed to care as little about scars as Louise Sunborn did.

"Before we do anything with the humans from across the Border, we need to find out more from them," Serene said. "With luck, this expedition was all the humans who might prove a threat to us, but if they have confederates over the wall, we should know about it."

Even if this particular group had been stopped, there would always be humans who had access to the Borderlands and there would always be children who knew the truth, and would remember.

The Borderlands had to be ready for them.

"I suggest we take them back to the prisons in the Border camp, and send daily reports on the information we gather," Serene continued.

Golden regarded her proudly. "Some of the boys in my finishing school say that all that matters about a woman is that she be a doughty warrior," he observed. "Not me. A woman of little intelligence would be no challenge at all."

"Hi, I'm Elliot," said Elliot, reaching across the table to take his hand. "I'm very intelligent, and I'm very pleased to meet you."

"I am Golden. I've heard a great deal about you from my betrothed," Golden told him, with perfect finishing-school politeness and an unreadable expression on his face.

Elliot was not sure if Golden was judging the floozy, or jealous of Serene's former paramour, or simply reserved. Golden was the one Serene had wanted, always, and was much better-looking than Elliot.

If Golden needed reassurance, Elliot did not know how to provide it.

"Um," Luke said, suddenly hovering. "Hi."

Elliot had not seen him since the early morning, when the commander had kicked them out of her tent and carried Luke off to archery practise. The lives of those in warrior training were not their own.

He glanced up at Luke, then back at the breakfast table. "Hi."

There was an air of nervous tension about Luke. Elliot wondered if Luke had already realized what a mistake he had made.

"So . . . hi," said Luke.

"Hi," Elliot repeated, with maybe a tiny edge of laughter.

Luke bowed his head hastily down to Elliot's and kissed him. The only warning was a bright flicker in Elliot's vision, and then Luke's mouth on his, a warm dry press of lips. Elliot was caught off guard, but he fastened his fingers in the shoulder of Luke's shirt and kissed him properly, the way Luke should be kissed in the golden early morning: slow, almost lazy and yet not lazy at all, with the radiance of the sun filtering through Elliot's half-closed eyelids, spreading lines of light against the dark.

"Cadet Sunborn," said Commander Woodsinger. "Have the other cadets dismantled their tents? I left you supervising, you may recall."

Luke straightened up. The rest of the morning flooded back.

"Of course, Commander," he said, and Elliot narrowed his eyes in the commader's direction. As if Luke were going to forget his responsibilities. "The cadets are ready to march at your word."

"See to it that they are in formation, then return to bid farewell to your aunt," said Commander Woodsinger.

Luke saluted and left. Elliot looked after him as he went: even the tips of Luke's ears were red.

He looked back at the people assembled around the breakfast table. The commander's expression was amused. Celaeno seemed moved by young love. The troll captain and his or her second were eating plum stones and appeared entirely uninterested in Elliot's love life, which was how things should be.

Serene's mouth had fallen open, for the second time in two days. Elliot made a face at her.

"This must be very startling to you, my dove," said Serene, clearing her throat and turning to her betrothed.

"Not really," said Golden. "Do you think all the boys do in finishing school is embroidery? La, the very idea!" He patted Serene's hand. "Women are such blockheads."

He favored Elliot with a bright smile.

Elliot smiled back.

"I thought you said no when Luke asked you out," Serene hissed.

"Well," Elliot said uncomfortably. "I mean, I did. I mean, I knew he didn't really mean it, so we agreed it was best. Didn't we?"

"Didn't really mean it? I thought we were agreeing it was best that you let him down easy!"

"Me?" said Elliot. "Let Luke down easy? I'm sorry. I just need to confirm the people we're discussing, here."

"Didn't really mean it," Serene said again. "What about Luke strikes you as insincere exactly?"

"I wasn't insulting Luke."

"That's not the point. The point was that I thought you didn't like him that way."

Serene stared at him, her eyes agate and accusing, and Elliot realized she was worried he would break Luke's heart. He did not know what he had done to make Serene, of all people, think he was a heartless playboy.

Elliot scowled at her. "Why would you think that?"

"You refer to him as 'loser' more often than you call him by his given name," Serene said. "You regularly criticize his intelligence and his mode of behavior. You told me you thought you were allergic to his face. You asked if there were any herbal remedies!"

"So?" said Elliot. "So what? I don't get what you're trying to say."

He got up abruptly from the table, almost pushing it away from him, and walked away into the trees. He did not go into the battle-field, but he walked until he found a bank where he could sit and put his face in his hands.

He was terrible at feelings. He had never practised them, for long years in his father's house, and he was like one of the kids in warrior training who hit themselves over the head with their own bows. He'd got it wrong. He'd got it all wrong this time, and he was sure he would get it all wrong again in the future.

Of course Luke, who thought of the world in terms of codes of honor and lived life like he was in a story, had not thought about spiting Dale. Of course he had at least not consciously thought about how little choice there was, for someone who exclusively liked boys, at the Border camp. Of course he did not have a casual crush.

Of course instead Luke would romanticize an attachment he had to someone he knew and trusted.

Of course, Luke thought he was in love.

Elliot was going to mess this up so intensely and comprehensively.

None of this was Luke's fault, not his mistake or Elliot's own remorseless hunger for love. Elliot could not fit into some story-book idea of love, could not be an agreeable partner slotting into someone's life like Dale would have been. Elliot should try not to hurt Luke, even though he did not see any way around it, any way to escape from the disaster Elliot could see coming: how he would ask too much from Luke, shatter all his illusions, ruin everything.

Elliot lifted his head. The sun shone through the tree branches and cast patterns of light and shade on his palms. He forced his fingers to uncurl, as they had curled on Luke's shirt, and let shadows slide through his empty hands.

Maybe if he broke it to Luke gently. Maybe if Luke lost his romantic illusions soon.

~

On the march home, Elliot paired off with Luke, the same way Serene was pairing off with Golden.

"I've been wanting a chance to talk to you."

"Yeah?" Luke asked. "I, um, I wanted to—talk to you too."

Elliot's heart sank. He did not know if he could do this.

"Well met, Elliot of the riverstone eyes," said a voice behind them. "Give you good morrow, Luke of the golden locks."

Swift-Arrows-in-the-Chaos-of-Battle, Serene's cousin. Normally Elliot would have been delighted to behold her auburn beauty.

"Hi, Swift," he said, and kissed her cheek. Luke muttered something incomprehensible.

"I heard you fought as bravely as any woman in the battle last eve," Swift told Luke generously.

"Oh, thanks," said Luke.

Hardly anyone noticed Luke's sarcastic voice, and Swift was immune to any sarcasm at all. She beamed at him.

"You deserve praise, my dear boy. Now, forgive me for my forwardness, I have heard the happy news that you two are involved in—some sort of liasion."

"Oh my God," said Luke.

Elliot, who was slightly more used to Swift, grasped Luke's wrist in a gesture of silent support.

"Many congratulations, or whatever it is you say when that sort of irregular thing occurs," Swift continued. "Some women say that the idea of two men together, while appealing, is a little ludicrous. I mean, really, what is the point? Some say."

"Are we there yet?" said Elliot in a hollow voice.

"Foolish boy, we only left the Forest moments ago." Swift chuckled indulgently. "Of course, though I am but a rough soldier, I do not espouse such narrow-minded ideas. However, if you ever *did* feel inclined to invite a woman to your bed-sports, I would be honored to be the woman selected."

Elliot removed his hand from Luke's arm as if it had become a column of living flame. He did not dare look at Luke, and could not exactly explain to Swift that Luke was what Swift would probably call a maiden.

"Thanks for the offer," he said. "Very kind. I'm thinking maybe no."

"You can go to hell," said Luke.

"I'm thinking a firm no," said Elliot.

Swift did not take offence. She smiled, eyebrows raised. Elliot imagined she thought Luke was being feisty. "I should perhaps not have mentioned this matter in the springtime of your boyish dreams," she admitted. "But I am usually posted far from the Border camp, and if the wish came upon one of you for a strong woman, I desired you to know my feelings."

"And now we know," said Elliot. "And alas we cannot unknow."

"You are a saucy, redheaded creature," said Swift, which horrific statement Elliot absorbed in silence. "And well, we all know what they say about the Sunborns."

"Really," said Luke in a tight voice.

Elliot watched them, staring over the gulf that was their cultural divide—Luke not wanting to hit a girl, and Swift obviously not considering being hit by a boy was an option.

"Oh yes," Swift chuckled. "Gregory Sunborn lived with the elves for many years, and there were rumors of wealthy men as well as women warriors rich with the spoils of battle. Gregory had visits from kinsmen and kinswomen, too. Not that the Sunborns need to prove their fame. The whole Borderlands speak of the Sunborns, the laughing warriors, singing through battle and dancing through fire, the lovers who ride away. Why, your own mother, rogue that she was, dallied with a harpy."

"Don't talk about my mother," said Luke in a low and menacing voice.

Elliot coughed. "We're coming up against a cultural difference here! Swift, imagine if someone implied your father was free with his favors—which I am sure he is not."

"Of course he is not!" Swift snapped. "I am not saying anything the whole world does not know. The Sunborns—"

"I don't want to hear any more of what you think about the Sunborns." Luke did something close to snarling, a predatory bird's cry and a hiss tangled together in his voice. "I don't sing. And I don't dance. And I don't want anyone else."

Elliot felt a lot of things in that moment, but fiercest of all was the pity he felt for Luke, at how much Elliot was going to let him down.

"What, not ever?" asked Swift. "That's going to get boring."

She sounded, in that moment, like Rachel or Louise Sunborn. Or Michael, or Gregory. Swift had not been wrong about the Sunborns. They were all going to be baffled, and when it did not work out, none of them would be surprised.

Elliot could not correct her. She was right.

They were plunged into an awkward silence, when fortunately Serene and Golden joined them and Swift could no longer talk about such matters in front of a chaste young gentleman.

Golden surveyed the group and began to talk to Elliot about what he might do to control his hair situation. Elliot was aware he was "making conversation," and he thought that elven finishing schools were marvelous. Also he appreciated the tips. He was always searching for some way to control the hair situation.

As their little troop drew near the camp, Elliot saw there were people waiting for them, and if Elliot was any judge, they were ready to hear about Luke Sunborn's latest victory and cheer.

"I like it," Luke said in an abrupt whisper.

"The camp?" Elliot asked. "I have a certain sentimental attachment by this time, too."

Luke's expression of discomfort was replaced by a different expression and one with which Elliot was more familiar. He looked annoyed. "Your *hair*. Don't do anything to it. I like your hair." Luke paused. "Though I'm not sure why, because it is a situation that has got entirely out of control."

Elliot grinned.

At the gates of the camp, Elliot said, in a low voice: "Can I come to your cabin later?"

"Um," Luke said. "Yes. Yes!"

"Just to talk," said Elliot.

"Obviously," said Luke. "What else would we—what? Talking. Of course."

"Cool," said Elliot as Luke was engulfed by the crowd.

Luke was always being engulfed by crowds. He might be insecure enough now to look for affection from a reliable source, but Luke did not realize how many fish, or indeed potential mermen, there were in the sea.

Elliot had evolved a master scheme: transform himself into more of a trusted friend than a boyfriend, a confidant, to become a pathway to different and better things. They could come to a mature and mutual realization that their romantic relationship would not work out.

"If you're happy to be with Luke," Serene said, under the noise of the crowd, "I'm happy."

Elliot nodded. "Great, thanks."

"You don't look very happy," Serene continued.

Elliot bared his teeth at her. "I'm ecstatic."

Behind them, Swift-Arrows-in-the-Chaos-of-Battle said in an awestruck voice: "Who is *that*?"

Elliot looked where Swift was looking. Bright-Eyes the librarian was standing at the gates of the Border camp, scolding the returning cadets about their late fines.

"Come on," he said. "I'll introduce you."

Luke's cabin was one of those built farther out from the camp, among the trees. The Border guard had strung lanterns in the trees overhead, so cadets could follow the path of light to their rest. The lanterns glowed like cat's eyes in the dark, bright and watchful in a coil of branches, like a cat's limbs and tail. Elliot recalled one book about magical lands in which there had been a disappearing cat who mocked people. The leering lanterns and the waiting trees seemed to be mocking Elliot: perhaps the whole night was mocking him.

Elliot walked under the trees to Luke's cabin, knocked on the rough wood of the door, and went in without waiting for an answer. This was part of his new campaign of casual friendship.

"Hey," he said casually.

Luke's room was neat with the terrifying neatness of someone raised to military discipline, but Elliot suspected he had still been cleaning up in some fashion. Luke was holding a knife, but dropped it when Elliot came in. Elliot stared at the blade skidding toward his feet, and then at Luke's open, dismayed face.

"Sorry!" Luke said.

"Sad to say, I think I'm used to hurtling weaponry by now." Elliot picked up the knife and tossed it back at Luke. Luke caught it with no fuss, as Elliot had expected.

A slight pang of unease went through Elliot as he strolled into the cabin. He was used to someone having easy expertise with murder weapons, handling blades with careless confidence. That was who Luke was: that was who Elliot was, now.

He thought of the way the man from the humans' side of the Border had looked at him. He had not known, before, how much he had changed. He had not fully realized how the people of the Borderlands looked to people from across the Border.

He thought again: they had to be ready.

And he was not distracting himself with thoughts of diplomatic crises from his personal crisis at all.

Elliot paid a fond visit to several items of contraband he had hidden in Luke's room, including an old radio that occasionally crackled and never went on fire. He had high hopes for the radio. He talked about classes, and Golden, and the disturbing fact that Bright-Eyes the librarian had worn scarlet flowers in his hair that evening.

"So," he said, once Luke was sitting on his bed, looking relaxed, and Elliot felt that an air of undemanding camaraderie had been established. "Uh. Wanna talk about boys?"

"Um," Luke said. "What do you mean?"

They were both amazingly eloquent. Elliot was amazed by them.

"It's just I thought we could talk about them," said Elliot. "Given that you didn't know that I could"—he searched for friendly and not sexy words—"sympathize and empathize with you!" he said triumphantly. "I'm sure you've had a lot of crushes on guys, right?"

"What?" said Luke.

"Adam or Neal?" Elliot asked. "Gregory Sunborn? I always thought he was kind of a silver fox. In a leonine way. A silver lion."

"*I* think they're all related to me," said Luke.

Luke's parents were both Sunborns, so they were related to each other. Elliot did not point this out. He was amazed to discover that he had a line he was not willing to cross. Parents were one unsexy step too far.

"Do you want to hear about Jase?" Elliot asked. "He was"—an asshole—"kind of good-looking."

Luke made a face. "I don't."

"Golden?" Elliot hazarded.

"*Serene's Golden*?" Luke demanded, sounding scandalized. He stared at Elliot. "Do you think Golden—do you—"

"Not really," said Elliot.

Luke did not look any less upset. He got off the bed, standing and then pacing, scrubbing a hand absently over his face. Word was that Luke and Dale had got pretty hot and heavy in Dale's cabin, before it all ended in tears and interspecies prejudice. Elliot was doing terribly, in comparison.

Elliot was not supposed to be trying. He was supposed to end this before he let Luke down and so they could stay friends.

"When was the first time you realized you had a crush on Dale?" he asked, forcing himself to sound relaxed and friendly, prepared to hear a long story about some good-looking boy on a Trigon pitch.

"What are you *doing*?" Luke demanded.

"I don't *know*!" Elliot snapped. "I don't know what I'm doing. I'm sorry."

That had not sounded very casual at all. Elliot stared into Luke's blazing eyes. He had wanted to be taller than Luke for years, and now he was, and it did not matter.

"You want to talk about boys, and crushes, you want to laugh about it the way my family does," Luke said. "Fine. Let's talk about when I tried to be with Dale, and I couldn't stop thinking about you."

Elliot opened his mouth to say "What?" and found he was incapable of saying any words at all. This was absurd. Elliot had great mastery of many words, and "what" was not a difficult word. Luke had ruined everything he knew about himself.

"Let's talk about how I came to the Border camp to make friends, and I met you, and you didn't like me at all. Everybody always liked me before. I couldn't figure out how to get you to like me. At first you didn't even remember my name."

Elliot wondered if it would make things worse or better for him to tell Luke that he had only pretended to forget Luke's name in order to torment him. Apparently he had succeeded beyond his wildest dreams and maybe actually driven Luke out of his mind.

"Let's talk," Luke continued in a savage voice, having seemingly not noticed that he was the only one talking, "about the fact you kept reminding me that you thought I was a waste of space and we weren't friends. Eventually I had to tell myself fine. We weren't friends. I told myself I didn't care about what you thought of me or how you behaved or whatever stupid way your mind worked. I didn't want to deal with you. I'd spend my time with people who didn't hate me and everything about me. I told myself there were a lot of people in the Border camp I could get along with just fine."

Elliot nodded with conviction. That made sense.

"But I didn't go *away*, did I?" Luke demanded. Elliot shook his head, bewildered all over again. "If I didn't want to deal with you, why was I always pathetically hanging around? You made it clear you didn't want me there. *I* wanted to be there. It was me."

Luke was applying the word *pathetic* to himself. It was possible nothing would ever make sense again.

"Let's talk about when you kept asking me who I had a crush on, and you wouldn't *drop* it, because you're relentless, and so—I said Dale. It wasn't a lie. He said he liked guys too, and I thought it made sense. He was good-looking and he liked Trigon and he liked me. There was no point in thinking about anything else, and I didn't. You didn't even want to be my friend."

Let's *not* talk, Elliot wanted to suggest for the first time in his life, because he could not quite process all these revelations and thought he might be in shock, but Luke appeared to be on a roll.

"*Then* let's talk about when we were doing the school play, and you were playing that stupid character, and you were wearing that stupid costume, and you were being nice, and it was all for Myra but I didn't know that at the time, I didn't know—"

"*What*?" said Elliot, finally able to say the word.

He had thought he could deal with anything Luke threw at him: anger or disappointment or scorn. He had not expected to feel utterly wrong-footed, as if he had stumbled into a reality that was different than the one he had always perceived and had no idea how to react.

He also had not expected to be at a loss for words when Luke could find so many. Even the most basic facts of his life had utterly betrayed him.

"Do you want to talk about the night of the play, when you talked to me about Adara kissing me and how it didn't have to count, and I thought—I thought—"

"What?" Elliot asked for the third time. "What did you think?"

Luke glared at him, then stalked over to sit on the bed again. He covered his face with his hands.

"And I never thought about it again, until I tried with Dale and I couldn't not," he said, his voice savage but muffled. He tore his hands away, held them in fists at his sides, and turned his face from Elliot's sight. "I didn't think about it because it was useless and I don't think about useless things," Luke continued furiously. "What good would it do? I couldn't have you."

Elliot came and sat on the bed beside Luke. He did not remember deciding to do that, he thought as soon as he had done it. Nothing was going according to plan, along the lines of the story he had laid out in his head. He reached out a hand and turned Luke's face back to him.

"Hey," Elliot murmured, cupping his face in his hands, kissing him, trying to make the kiss say *I did not mean to hurt you* and *I won't do it again.* He covered Luke's face in kisses and felt Luke draw a breath in against Elliot's mouth, trembling and close. "You have me."

Luke kissed him back, and the long kiss that followed meant something else, meant a thousand wild things at once. The kiss seemed to electrify and magnetize their bodies, sealing them tight together even though every inch of Elliot's skin was crackling. Luke touched Elliot's face and his hair, his expression wondering. Elliot slid a hand up under Luke's shirt, stroking lightly and feeling the contrast of sleek skin and tucked-away feathers under his fingertips, held on to Luke's shoulder with his free hand.

Then the wings burst through the thin material of Luke's shirt, arching over his shoulders and blocking out the light. Elliot started back. A wing hit him in the face and he tipped off balance, off the bed and hit his head against the wall.

"Oh my God," said Luke. "Are you all right?"

Elliot sat up on the stone floor, feeling a little dazed but not entirely from the blow, and burst out laughing. "Fine," he said. "I think all the hair protected my skull."

He was still blinking, when Luke told him: "You can go, if you want."

"What?" said Elliot.

Oh, great. They were back to that. If Elliot found himself frequently reduced to this level of verbal inadequacy, he was disowning himself.

"I know you think I'm stupid," Luke began.

"I don't think you're stupid," said Elliot. "I feel I have to make that clear. But I do want to reserve the right to call you stupid in future just the same."

"Look, I get it. You came in here talking about how hot your ex was, and then how hot Dale was, and none of that was a good sign, then I panicked and started ranting at you, and now I've knocked you into a wall. You've been with so many other people, and I got everything wrong. You don't have to stay because you feel sorry for me. I know I messed this up."

"Four people is not that many!" Elliot protested vehemently.

He stood up so he could see Luke's face without the curtain of a wing between them, and saw that Luke looked unhappy, again, so soon after Elliot had promised himself he wouldn't hurt him. Seeing Luke look like that cut through defensive feelings tangling and trying to form a thorny protective shield in Elliot's chest. He felt defeated in a strange warm way, almost as he had when his defences were worn away by exhaustion in the commander's tent, except this time he knew more and had chosen to let the defences fall. He heard his voice come out gentle.

"But maybe it's enough to know that everyone messes this up," he said. "Let's review everything you just said. Basically, I'm a terrible person who is always cruel to you—"

"No," said Luke. "No, I wasn't trying to insult—"

"And you are *totally into it*," Elliot said. "That's weird. Like you might want to talk to somebody about that."

"I just talked to you about it!"

"Someone who's not me," said Elliot. "I'll only mock you. Because I'm going to mess this up. I came here panicking to talk you out of this via a cool casual segue into friendship where we talked about other guys. Do you remember teaching me how to run and how I kept stumbling and wheezing and falling on my face?"

An amused smile crept its way onto the bleakly humiliated plain of Luke's face. "Yes."

"And you thought it was super funny, even though I was a bookish child totally unaccustomed to extreme physical exertion and as it turned out I was being held to supernatural standards by wicked bullies. Nobody's good at something when they start out."

"You're not the one who's starting out," Luke said. "You're not the one who is going to mess up."

"I am starting out," said Elliot, and took a deep breath. "You know the stuff you said about my home life is true."

"Elliot, I am *sorry* about that."

"Yeah, I'm sorry about it too, but it's true," said Elliot. "I didn't have any friends in the human world. I didn't have anyone." He smiled. "You of all people know I did not display any expertise in having friends in this world. I had a few disastrous romances. Serene and Adara didn't take me seriously, and I shouldn't have taken Jase seriously. I didn't learn how to . . . run when I was a kid, and I still don't know how to do it without falling down on my face."

Elliot was still standing a foot away from Luke, pulling at his own hair. Luke was sitting on the bed, his wings glowing ivory arches above him, his face still unhappy though it had softened when Elliot talked about running, and Elliot saw him understand what Elliot meant.

This was enough distance and unhappiness. Elliot walked toward Luke, and saw Luke barely breathed as he watched him coming, as if he was afraid he might scare Elliot off. Instead of being scared off, Elliot eased gradually into Luke's lap. The wings could not get him there. Instead, there was Luke's face, very close, still hardly breathing.

"I'm going to make you a promise. I swear to you, Luke," Elliot murmured in his ear. "I'm going to mess this up."

"Yeah?" Luke asked, his voice rough. "How are you going to mess it up?"

"I've messed up in the past, but since this is you"—Elliot laid a kiss beside Luke's ear and when Luke shivered he followed the trail of shivers with kisses along the line of Luke's jaw, where faint golden stubble scraped against his mouth—"and I have a history of getting things wrong with you—" Elliot reached Luke's mouth, and paused there. Luke's shirt was basically in shreds from the sudden wings. Elliot peeled the torn remnants away from Luke's chest and shoulders, slid his hands down Luke's skin and murmured, "I have a feeling it could be pretty spectacular."

"Yeah?" Luke whispered. "What are you going to do?"

"Well, I've already spoken extensively about the hotness of my former lovers," Elliot pointed out.

The muscles in Luke's shoulders and jaw both locked at once, tense, and not in a good way.

"I don't like that," he said flatly.

"I know, forget that, it was terrible," Elliot said hastily.

Some people liked it, he knew, but he could see Luke hated it. He imagined Luke telling him about how hot Dale was, and he did not think he would like it himself. He felt a little light-headed with his own daring, as if he were edging out on a thin rope over a cliff or facing the challenge of a treaty he did not know how to draft. He had always tried to show everyone before that he would not mess up, tried to win affection while feeling the weight of a hard lump of despair telling him it would not be possible. There was tension and terror in this, but Elliot laid his face against the side of Luke's face and did not feel that despair.

"Since it's you, and I'm unused to complimenting you, I am also going to offer very bad compliments."

Luke laughed, and Elliot felt his muscles relax slightly. He turned his face into Elliot's, something very natural about the movement as if Luke had been turning to kiss Elliot for far longer than two days. He kissed Elliot, a little clumsily at first but almost immediately turning it into something devastating, all-consuming and all-conquering. As was the Sunborn way. He kissed Elliot as if he really wanted to: as if he wanted nothing else.

Then he said: "I don't think I've ever heard a compliment from you. Like what?"

"Picture this: the should-be tender morning after the night before, and I turn to you and say, 'Congratulations on being athletic and well-meaning, Luke!'"

Luke laughed. "That would be bad."

"I honestly wouldn't mean it badly," said Elliot, and helped Luke take off Elliot's shirt. For a moment they were in a tangle of shirt and sheets that was complicated by the addition of wings. Elliot laughed, kissed Luke and tasted his laughter, stopped laughing, and held on.

"What else?" Luke asked, voice scraping in his throat. He bowed his bright head and kissed Elliot's chest, and Elliot's heart pounded.

"I am also just going to constantly insult you," Elliot announced. His lightly stroking fingertips touched the place where golden skin was cut off by leather. He could undo tangled leather ties with one hand, with the incentive of Luke's breathing, changing rapid and desperate, in his ear.

"Don't insult me," breathed Luke.

"Oh," said Elliot. "I'm going to. There will be the more elaborate insults, but also just the casual everyday insults and insulting nicknames, like . . ."

"Like what?" Luke whispered.

Elliot looked down at Luke, gold and pearl and flesh and blood, storybook strange and known by heart. Luke was looking back at him and really seeing him, and he could see the brilliant blue of Luke's eyes turning almost black. He felt the strain of Luke's body, arching up to be as close to him as he could.

"Hey loser," Elliot murmured, "I want you."

As a graceful segue back into platonic friendship went, Elliot had to admit it had not gone well.

If he wanted to be brave and tell the truth, as Luke had, maybe he had not wanted it to.

It was difficult to get to know Golden, but Elliot was trying. One advantage was that he was as intelligent as he was good-looking, and he spent a lot of time in the library with Elliot, Myra, and Serene.

"They restricted our books in the finishing school," Golden confided in a rare moment of openness. "It was very annoying to work out ways to get forbidden books. I did manage."

Golden wore a reminiscent smile, as if thinking fondly of past lawlessness. Elliot did not know him very well yet, but he liked him a lot.

"Will you miss the library then, my sweet?" Serene asked tenderly. "Will you miss me, too?"

"I suppose I would miss . . . the library," said Golden. "If I were leaving with the rest of the elven contingent. Except I am not. I explained to Commander Woodsinger that, as your future spouse, I wished to learn more about your military duties, and that moreover since I had run away with the soldiers I could not go back to the elven woods unmarried. Papa would have hysterics. The commander has kindly permitted me to attend certain select classes during your final year. I think I will learn human military history, and how to throw javelins."

"You'll like military history," Elliot approved. "Can't speak to the javelins."

Serene sat stunned.

"We are not to be parted?"

Golden sneaked a pleased glance at Serene's expression, half adoring and half amazed. "No."

Serene kissed Golden. It was an intense kiss, until Golden drew away with a horrified look at the witnesses to his immodest behavior. He looked toward the librarian, obviously expecting a scolding, but Bright-Eyes-Gladden-the-Hearts-of-Women beamed benevolently down at this display of young love.

Elliot felt deeply wronged.

"Why did you not ask me to come with you to the commander's office?" Serene asked after a pause.

Golden looked mildly surprised. "For moral support, do you mean? I suppose I could have, but I'm the independent type."

Elliot smiled to himself, remembering standing in the commander's office with Serene and Luke years ago. Going to support Serene then had been, he reflected, one of the best decisions of his life. He was ready to support her through anything. Including the crisis of realizing that she might be more emotional and needy than that tender flower, her betrothed.

The door of the library opened, and Luke came in. He was in the library more often these days, which Elliot thought was an excellent life choice. Elliot was about to gesture to the chair beside him, when Luke spoke.

"Just came to say good-bye," he said awkwardly. "I have to ride out with the elven troops, so the Border guard can give their thanks for the elves' support in person."

"Farewell, Luke," Serene told him. "Good fortune ride with you. My apologies that I cannot accompany you as I would wish."

"It is ridiculous that I am going, and it's all your fault," Luke told Elliot. "Serene and Golden can't come, because elven society is rocked by their scandalous elopement, and so I have to go, because I'm the only warrior cadet in the Border camp who can speak fluent elvish."

"Ha ha," said Elliot. "Enjoy."

"Right." Luke hesitated, rapping his knuckles against the table. Elliot turned a page of his book. "Okay. So I'm going."

"Okay, bye," said Elliot.

He heard the door swing shut, turned another page of his book, and looked up to find everyone staring at him.

"Boys!" said Myra, at the same time as Golden said: "I fear human men are not given the chance to develop their natural masculine intuition."

"What?" Elliot demanded.

"Are you stupid?" asked Myra. "Are you going out with Luke or not?"

Elliot hesitated. "Yes."

"He came specially to say good-bye to you," Golden said, more politely, but his tone also questioned Elliot's intelligence. "I do not know if you are not interested, or protecting yourself, but you cannot guard yourself against the whole world. You only succeed in placing a barrier between yourself and the world." He hesitated. "I know that from personal experience."

It was the first crack Golden had let himself show Elliot, in his ivory-and-gold façade: it was the first time Golden had shown Elliot that Golden wished to be known. Elliot appreciated that Golden wanted to be friends. He wondered what hurts Golden's world had inflicted on him, and how they were different from the wounds the world had inflicted on Elliot, and Serene, and even Luke.

Elliot hoped he would get to know Golden better. But he had something to do first.

He shut up his book and pushed it away.

"I think I'll go say a proper good-bye to Luke."

The patient silence of his library mates indicated they thought that would be for the best.

They were right, Elliot thought. If he was not inherently unlovable, if he had not chosen someone who would never want him as much as he wanted them, then he had to take the risk and try. He had to trust that they would both try.

It was terrifying. It was what people did, all the time, on both sides of the Border.

Elliot lingered a little longer, out of panic, and addressed Serene. "I'll give Luke your love, shall I?"

"He knows he always has my love," said Serene. "So should you, by now. Go tell him something he does not know."

She gave Elliot her small, almost imperceptible smile. It felt like a blessing.

"All right," said Elliot, and ran out of the library.

There was frost on the ground, but Elliot felt the ice breaking under his feet as he dashed around the towers and cabins, down the dirt path to the gates where elves and humans were mounting up in preparation to go. Luke was already on his horse, scanning the horizon. There was a knot of people between them, checking saddlebags and saying good-byes, defying Elliot's attempts to weave through them.

"Excuse me, sweetheart," said Elliot. "Darling? A moment of your time? Sugarplum? Sugargrape? Sugarassortedfruitsandvegetables?"

Luke did not even turn his head.

"HEY, LOSER!" said Elliot.

"Elliot," Luke said at once, looking around and then jumping easily off his horse. "What are you doing here?"

Just the truth, Elliot reminded himself. Not what he thought someone else wanted to hear, or what he thought would protect himself. Just the truth, and trusting that someone else would care to hear it.

He took a deep breath. "Just came to say good-bye," he said. "And… I'll miss you."

It was absurd to feel like this, both embarrassed and too vulnerable. Luke was his boyfriend.

"Yeah?"

Luke's voice scratched on the word. Elliot wondered what Luke would say if Elliot told him that Elliot thought Luke was extremely good-looking and that Elliot was terrified of losing him. He feared Luke would assume Elliot had head trauma.

Elliot probably would have to have head trauma to get that out. Luke was able to pay Elliot compliments, even though they came out with the clumsy force of insults or missiles. Luke was, Elliot thought, better at this than he was. Which made perfect sense: Elliot might have had a boyfriend and a girlfriend before, but Luke had been loved his whole life.

Elliot wanted to get better at this than he was. He wanted to learn how.

There were people all around: supercilious elven warriors, the commander watching with an expression both wry and judgemental.

"Yeah," Elliot said, stepping up to Luke. "Take care of yourself. Don't get hurt. Seriously, I know better than to ask for no heroics, but if it comes down to it, consider leaving someone else to die. For me."

Luke pretended to consider it, for a minute. "Nah."

"Well, okay," said Elliot. "Just be careful, then."

He took hold of Luke's upper arms, pulled him towards Elliot and kissed him good-bye, the way he should have kissed him in the library. Luke relaxed against him, soldier's muscles loose under Elliot's hands, soldier's discipline gone for a long thoughtless thrilling moment. It took Elliot another moment to open his eyes and realize the sudden shade and warmth came from Luke's wings, which had not been out before.

"Um," Luke said. "I'm very embarrassed. Please go."

Elliot patted him on the shoulder. "Terribly sorry about all of this. Everybody is looking at you. Have fun with the elves."

He pushed a wing affectionately aside and headed back toward the camp. Elliot looked over his shoulder and saw Luke already looking after him, Luke's expression still startled but undeniably, transparently pleased by this turn of events.

Elliot enjoyed the warm glow for about half a second when he saw the other cadets who had come to say good-bye following him.

In the lead was Dale Wavechaser. His face was set in stony lines, hard in a way Elliot had never seen him look before.

Dale caught up to Elliot. Elliot let him. They walked alongside each other in silence for a while.

The other cadets were hanging back, as if kept off by a forcefield of awkwardness.

"You and Luke," Dale said at last.

"Ah," Elliot responded, brilliantly. "Yeah."

"So I guess you really liked him, all along," Dale said. "I mean . . . you said as much."

Elliot caught himself looking around, paranoid, as if he had committed a crime and he was scared someone would see. He crushed the guilty impulse, and nodded.

"And I guess . . ." Dale's voice was heavy now, like footsteps dragging to an unwanted destination, "he always liked you."

Elliot opened his mouth to deny this vehemently and completely, to say that he had never been wanted or wished-for, but he remembered Luke last night, telling him about the play, and shut his mouth again.

"And where does all this leave me?" Dale asked. His voice was bitter. "Aside from feeling like a complete idiot."

Elliot kept walking silently beside Dale and tried to sort it out, the conflicted mess of not caring about someone else enough. He was not used to being the one who cared less, and having to admit all this to himself: that he had hurt Dale, both intentionally and unintentionally, that Dale had genuinely cared about him and been kind to him, that he still did not find Dale interesting to talk to, that he still did not want to associate with Dale or anyone else who thought about Luke or Myra the way Dale did.

"I don't know," he said at last. "I'm sorry. I really am."

"Doesn't change much, does it?"

It didn't.

Dale sighed, and was kind for the last time. "Don't worry about it, Schafer. I'll be fine."

Elliot gave him a small smile before he walked away. "I'm glad."

Elliot went home alone, by the river that fed into the lake where Dale had kissed him and Serene had caused a scandal by doing only what the boys did. He was thinking about Dale and about trolls and about peace, and most of all about Luke. He was so deep in thought he almost walked into the river, but then he heard a ring like a bell and felt his shoe knock against something hard. He looked down and saw a glass bottle, half embedded in the mud of the riverbank.

It was the same bottle he had sent down the river with a message for the mermaids, but it did not have the piece of parchment he had put inside. Instead, as Elliot pulled out the cork, he found a round flat stone, and inscribed on it were symbols he had never seen before, in a language he did not know.

He did not know if it could possibly be a message from the mermaid he had met, or whether it was a different mermaid, curious and reaching out. He did not know what the message said.

But he could learn what the words meant, learn to speak the language of strangers. He could find out, and reach out.

It was one of the first days of blue skies and sunlight, though the air still had a bite to it, reminding them all the year had not quite turned tame. Elliot was extremely pleased to welcome the spring, as for a few weeks there, especially those camping in the frosty woods with harpies, he had felt as if it would be always winter. Always winter, and never central heating.

Serene, Golden, Elliot, and Luke were all due to meet out in the fields where Serene, Elliot, and Luke had gathered years ago, after Serene had been banished from the lake. They wanted to discuss where to go next year, without teachers eavesdropping on them or Commander Woodsinger offering any more unsubtle hints.

Serene and Luke's parents had all written four very different letters of very urgent advice. Rachel had even written to Elliot. The Sunborns had been collectively surprised and, reading between the lines, mystified when Luke let them know that he had a sweetheart whom they might have met before, someone who preferred books to athletics and whose conversational stylings Adam Sunborn had once described as "You know when a nest of hornets goes mad." Elliot knew the Sunborns had been expecting something entirely different. He could not blame them if they were disappointed in their hopes for their much-loved Luke, or if they grew cold to Elliot, or if they found themselves unable to take the situation very seriously.

He had opened the letter from Luke's mother with a certain amount of trepidation, but Rachel's letter to Elliot had been sweet to him as she ever was, and finished with the hope that he would come and stay with them on the break before they began their posting, that he should think of the Sunborns' place as home, that he was always welcome. Elliot believed her. He kept her letter, folded up carefully between the pages of one of his favorite books. He still thought Rachel Sunborn would be a very nice mother to have. Luke's father had not sent a letter. He had sent Elliot a jumper he had knitted himself, the warmest thing in the Borderlands next to the shelter of Luke's wings.

Much though Elliot appreciated Rachel's writing, he would not do what Rachel wanted. They had all agreed not to let anybody else influence them.

They wanted to decide on their own.

Luke arrived first, because Elliot had told him to come early. Elliot saw him coming, a dark shape against the sun, but he came to Elliot swiftly and landed lightly, folding his wings back as they sat cross-legged and knee to knee in the green grass.

"I have something to tell you," said Elliot. "I haven't told Serene. I want to tell *you*."

He was used to having Luke's attention, but perhaps he would never be used to having focus like this, so absolute, as if for a little while Elliot could be all that mattered in the world.

Elliot drew in a deep breath and said, before he could lose his nerve: "My mother," and then he was able to take a breath, knowing he had committed himself. "She left when I was a baby. My father never forgave me for it. She's in the Border camp now. She's one of the medics—the one with red hair like mine. She doesn't want anything to do with me. You can't do anything about it. I can't do anything about it. I'm going to leave the Border camp at the end of our last year, and I don't imagine I will see her again. I wanted you to know, because—I want you to know me. That's all."

"Thanks for telling me," Luke said, soft.

They sat there for a little while. Elliot slumped backward, almost overcome with the relief of having told, having it no longer be the secret that he was unwanted and always would be, having it be a smaller secret because it was shared. He could tell Luke was trying to think of the right thing to say.

"Medics," Luke said at last. "Who needs them?"

"Every stupid warrior in this camp, or else your wounds would become infected and all your limbs would become gangrenous and drop off." Elliot rested his cheek against Luke's shoulder. "But I appreciate the sentiment."

They sat like that for a while longer, until they saw Serene and Golden coming in the distance. Serene was ruffled, as Luke was, from a long day of warrior training, though Luke was more ruffled, on account of the flying. Golden was not ruffled at all. He had apparently spent the day in the library, making pro and con lists for the fortresses they could ask to be assigned to. Elliot leaned his head against Golden's elaborately coiffed one as he admired the lists.

There was peace in the Borderlands for a time, peace in the freshly turned blue skies where harpies flew, peace over the fields where humans and trolls dug, peace in the forest where dryads sang, and peace in the lakes and rivers where mermaids swam. There had been no sign of unrest and no sign of humans coming across the Border again. Not yet.

They had to take advantage of this opportunity. They could go wherever they wanted, if they could only decide where that was.

"I would suggest not the elves," said Serene, always the most decisive of the group. "My mother is not pleased with me seducing an innocent and highly born young boy. I think Golden and I should be married several years before we venture back into elven realms." She hesitated. Over the years her rare faint smile had grown, Elliot realized, far less rare. "Besides," she added. "I would welcome a new challenge, so long as I have old comrades with me as I face them."

That left the dwarves, the trolls, the human fortresses, the dryads, and the possibility that the mermaids might permit the stationing of Border guards near their waters for the first time.

"We could always flip a coin," Elliot suggested.

"All right," Luke said, coming through like he always did. He produced a coin from the pouch at his belt: the circle of gold shone, bright as a promise, in his palm. Luke looked up into Elliot's eyes. "Where are we going? Call it."

You leave your father's house, Elliot thought. And then you work out where to go next.

"You have to ask?" Elliot smiled. "Tails for mermaids."

ACKNOWLEDGMENTS

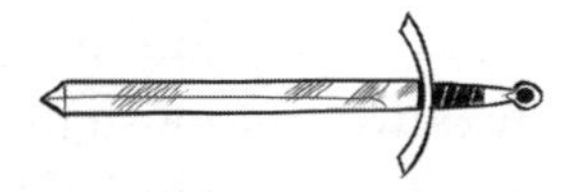

I'd like to start these acknowledgements in a perhaps startling fashion: with deep gratitude for the internet and people who write comments on it. *In Other Lands* began as a "short story" (haha! Hahahahaha . . .) I decided to write on my blog, as a present for my readers . . . at a time when I badly needed to rediscover the joy of writing. Obviously, I went completely out of control, and yet so many people said they liked it, came specially to book signings to tell me about their love for a story they could not get signed (now you can, my sweets!), offered praise and insights, and asked me for more. Stories do not often get written serially, but this one was, and it would be a completely different story without those initial readers who accepted a gift graciously and gave me many gifts in return.

The only way I know to prevail in difficult times is through the support of my family, my Irish friends, my English friends, my American friends, my Australian friends. The world is vast, and full of grace. (Sometimes the internet reminds us of both these things. Sometimes the internet reminds us of other things, but the internet does not get as much credit for sharing love and goodness as it should.)

A special thanks to Holly Black, Courtney Milan, Seanan McGuire and Jennifer Lynn Barnes, all writers I admire and friends I cherish, who let me know they were reading the story as it was posted online ("oh my god how can this be!" I screamed. "You put it on the world wide web, dummo," they kindly did not reply) and encouraged me by saying they liked it, saying not to stop, and taking it seriously when I did not: taking me seriously when I did not.

Holly really was with me every step of the way: she was the first person to ask "Why are you writing a book on your blog?" ("It's a short story," I said. "It's over a hundred thousand words long" she said. "Imbecile" she did not say) and years later she and Kelly Link provided final edits, including Kelly giving the book its name and the sentence "That sex scene needs to be way longer and way better" being uttered as I screamed and tried to drown myself. Sorry. Sorry about everything, Holly and Kelly. Thanks to Carolyn Nowak for the most unsurpassable unicorns and excellent elves in town, and Paul Witcover for catching so many of my fool mistakes. (Any fool mistakes remaining are entirely down to foolish me.

My publisher Small Beer Press, Gavin J. Grant and Kelly Link. I still remember the email Kelly sent me offering to publish the book. I read it in Savannah airport, and sat in a chair in Starbucks deeply touched but also trying to think of a way to dissuade her from this kind but obviously doomed course. (Later everyone told me I acted like Spider-man, trying to break up with his true love for her own good. Watch out for supervillains just the same, guys. Surely they will be gunning for those as virtuous as thee.)

ABOUT THE AUTHOR

Sarah Rees Brennan (sarahreesbrennan.com) was born and raised in Ireland and now lives in New York City. She is the *New York Times* bestselling author of *Tell the Wind and Fire* and the Lynburn Legacy series among others.